A SHOPKEEPER'S Daughter

Rachel Wisdom

Dec. 2014

RACHEL WISDOM

WESTBOW
PRESS

A DIVISION OF THOMAS NELSON

WestBow Press books may be ordered through booksellers or by contacting:

WestBow Press
A Division of Thomas Nelson
1663 Liberty Drive
Bloomington, IN 47403
www.westbowpress.com
1 (866) 928-1240

Because of the dynamic nature of the Internet, any web addresses or links contained in this book may have changed since publication and may no longer be valid. The views expressed in this work are solely those of the author and do not necessarily reflect the views of the publisher, and the publisher hereby disclaims any responsibility for them.

Any people depicted in stock imagery provided by Thinkstock are models, and such images are being used for illustrative purposes only.
Certain stock imagery © Thinkstock.

ISBN: 978-1-4908-1542-8 (sc)
ISBN: 978-1-4908-1543-5 (hc)
ISBN: 978-1-4908-1541-1 (e)

Library of Congress Control Number: 2013921024

Printed in the United States of America.

WestBow Press rev. date: 12/10/2013

For Grandma,
who loved sewing, art, and royalty,
and who most certainly would have loved Sonja

Acknowledgments

When I first began writing this book during the spring of my freshman year of college, I could not have imagined how long it would take (three years instead of the three months I had in mind), nor did I imagine how many people it would involve. I would like to thank all those friends, relatives, colleagues, professors, and institutions that helped along the way as *A Shopkeeper's Daughter* went from distracted scribbles in the midst of my lecture notes to a full-fledged novel.

First, thank you to the long list of people who read various drafts of the manuscript and provided feedback. You were all an invaluable source of encouragement and revisions. Thank you to Cari Belmar, Jessica Belmar, Ryan Belmar, Becky Bryant, Mark Cote, Rebekah Gantner, Betty Geno, Cynthia Georges, Stephanie Hammond, Natalie Kutat, Florence Lewis, Sara Marks, Ann Nicholson, Amy Pawl, Britt Royal, and Jessica Stamps. I would especially like to thank my high school teacher Larry Hughes, who read this in an early form that did not even deserve to be called a "draft" and who had the courage to gently tell me what a complete disaster it was; my friend and former colleague Shirley Ikemeier, who has been one of this book's biggest cheerleaders (and who was so excited about the draft that she took a day off work to finish reading it); my late grandfather, Matt Gambill, who was nearly blind but who had the patience to listen attentively as I read the entire novel aloud to him; my former English teacher Pam Bye and my aunt Vicki Stamps, who not only read earlier drafts but who also did the painstaking work of later proofreadings; and most of all my parents, Rod and Gail Wisdom, who read these pages until their eyes bled.

I also want to thank all those people and institutions who assisted with various parts of my research, answered questions, helped with translation, or provided information: Guinn Batten, Sherry Blough, Stanton Braude, Mary Elizabeth Hall, Michael Kahn, Tove Klovning, Petar Milic, Charles and Dorothy Norland, Alex Norton, Neil Richards, Chancellor Mark S. Wrighton, Assumption Greek Orthodox Church of St. Louis, the Norwegian Society of St. Louis, the Oslo Public Library *(Deichmanske Bibliotek)*, the Royal Library

Copenhagen *(Det Kongelige Bibliotek)*, the Washington University Medical Library, and Washington University Olin Library. I would also like to thank Lexa Martinez De La Cueva, the talented photographer who provided the back cover photo, and Stan Hammond, who was a huge help with building my website.

Special thanks go to two Norwegians who exemplify the love of Norway and the genuine kindness that I found everywhere in the country. Thank you to Reverend Kjell Jordheim of Columbia, Missouri, who welcomed me into his home multiple times to translate research materials; and to Bjørg Bjøberg of Balestrand, Norway, who was so excited about my novel that she took apart a display in her antique museum in order to let me look at an old magazine.

Of course, these acknowledgments would not be complete without a shout-out to the Danish side of the Gambill family, who made my 2010 Scandinavian research tour ten times more awesome—Lilian, Nathalie, Kaj, Maja, and Thea, I could not be more eager to see you again this summer. I extend my most very special thanks and sincere gratitude to my great-aunt Lilian Gambill, who very hospitably provided me with a place to stay at her home in Copenhagen, accompanied me to Norway, collected every royal biography she could find, and was always ready to answer all my harebrained questions.

Rachel Wisdom
November 2013

Royal House of Glücksburg - 1959

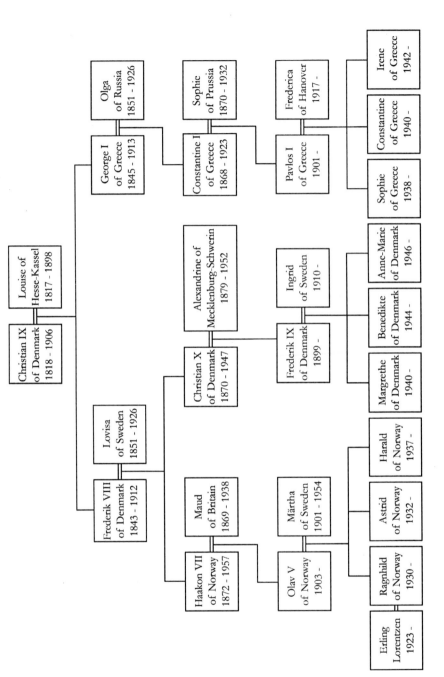

This is the prettiest lowborn lass that ever
Ran on the greensward. Nothing she does or seems
But smacks of something greater than herself,
Too noble for this place.

William Shakespeare
The Winter's Tale
Act IV, Scene IV

Chapter One

"Oh, excuse me!"

Paying far more attention to the music than the direction she was moving, Sonja Haraldsen had just gone twirling through a doorway and crashed into a tall, solid young man.

"Are you all right?" she heard him say as he grabbed her arm to steady her. "Oh—your dress—I'm so sorry—"

She glanced down, suddenly realizing that the contents of the wine glass in his hand had splattered all over her pale pink dress. Was every other party guest watching this?

"It's fine," she murmured hurriedly to his chest, too embarrassed to glance up at the man's face. "Please excuse me." She darted back into the kitchen, desperately hoping she could somehow lessen the dark stain.

She had not wanted to come tonight, she thought as she wetted a towel and began scrubbing the soft chiffon. It was the first time she had been out at all since her father's death three months ago, and she was only attending Karl Stenersen's birthday party at her mother's insistence. Now here she was, preparing to spend the evening fighting a losing battle against the stain she'd clumsily created.

She had been trying, as always, to look perfect tonight and had worried all day about whether she was wearing the right thing. It was a spaghetti-strap, tea-length dress she had made last spring with long-stemmed appliqué roses on the full skirt, and after much deliberation she had deemed it suitable. A great difference it made now, she thought. Suddenly, the whole situation struck her as ridiculous, and she laughed.

"Miss? Have you had any luck with that dress? I'm terribly sorry."

The man she'd twirled into, she supposed, still scrubbing her skirt. He sounded truly regretful. "No, it wasn't your fault. I should have been watching where I was—" she looked up at him "—going," she finished in a mortified whisper. She was looking into the face of the Crown Prince of Norway.

For a moment, she merely stared. Was it really…? Yes, this was the striking young man she'd seen on countless magazine covers and in hundreds of newspapers. But what on earth was he…she hadn't seen him earlier…but then, she'd only been at the party ten minutes or so…

"Your Royal Highness," she gasped, sinking into a deep curtsy. "Sir, I had no idea…my apologies…" She felt her face redden, and she silently prayed for the hardwood floor to swallow her whole.

"No, it was entirely my fault." It wasn't, and the laughter she could hear hidden in his words indicated that he knew it. He reached out a hand and lifted her out of her curtsy. Towering over her—she guessed him to be a few inches over six feet—he was even more attractive in person than in all the photos she had seen. His eyes shone brilliantly blue, and his build suggested he had the strength of an Arctic moose, but his smile held her attention the most. It was small and hesitant and barely showed his teeth, as though he were so shy that he hoped neither his smile nor himself would be noticed. *Charming,* she thought.

"I'd be happy to pay for that dress if it's ruined," he went on.

Of course it was, but she was too stunned by his presence to care any more. "I'm fine. It's fine. It doesn't matter. I'll go home tonight and see what I can do. I'm quite good with fabrics. I'm a seamstress." She closed her eyes momentarily in embarrassment. She was babbling, and she knew it. This was likely the only time she'd ever meet royalty, and she was not achieving anything near the perfect impression she would have desired to make.

"Oh, do you sew?" He sounded interested, but she did not believe it to be any more than years of practice at surviving dull conversation.

"Yes," she said, then shut her mouth. Mindless chatter would not help.

Suddenly the Crown Prince blushed. "I'm sorry—forgive me—I ought to have asked your name." He paused. When she said nothing, he continued. "Well, what is it?"

"What is what?"

"Your name!"

"Oh!" Her cheeks were surely a deeper shade of pink than his now. "I didn't know—that is, you *didn't* ask, you only said you should have asked, so I didn't know that you really wanted to know. I'm sorry. Sir." Perfect. Now he thought she had the intelligence of a strawberry.

He laughed, his small smile erupting into a grin. "I do want to know. In fact, I *still* want to know. What is your name?"

"Sonja Haraldsen," she said, realizing she still had not given it to him and laughing herself. She was surprised to find herself slowly relaxing in his presence.

"I'm Harald of Norway." He offered her his hand, and she shook it, then giggled again at the absurdity of the moment.

"I know *your* name!"

He nodded. Then suddenly he asked, "Would you like to dance, Miss Haraldsen?"

"Excuse me?" Surely the Crown Prince hadn't just asked her to dance. Surely not, not after such an embarrassing performance on her part.

"Would you like to dance?" he repeated with a small smile.

Panic seized her. Dance with the heir to the throne? *What do I do now?* "I—why, yes, yes, I think I would," she answered.

"I think I'd like to dance with you, too," he said in a tone of the utmost seriousness. "However, you'll have to guarantee me that you won't go twirling into anything and taking me with you."

She laughed, and he took her hand. There was something very strange in having her hand in the Crown Prince's, and she forced herself to swallow her nerves as he led her back into the party and onto the dance floor. The music was American rock and roll—Bobby Darin's "Dream Lover"—and she was spinning and twirling, leading most of the dance, but if his easy laughter were any indication, he didn't mind. He was having fun with her, she realized, and, much to her surprise, she was having fun as well. She could not recall any such sensation in the three months since her father had passed away and she had been called home from England.

He asked her where in Oslo she lived, where she'd gone to school, how she knew the host—she was far more interested in *his* answer to the latter and discovered that, having attended elementary schools a few blocks apart, she and the Crown Prince had so many mutual friends that she was almost surprised she had not seen him at other social occasions.

"Do you have any siblings?" he asked.

"Yes, but they're much older. My brother was sixteen when I was born, and my sister was thirteen. I'm my mother's little afterthought," she said good-naturedly. It had always made her feel special to think of herself as such. "I grew up more as an only child than anything else—I think I was absolutely spoiled rotten." She laughed and returned the question without thinking, searching for something to say to him. "Do you have any siblings?"

"Yes—" he began as embarrassment swept over her again.

"Oh, yes, of course you do, it's the Royal Family; I *know* you've got two sisters." She ought to have just stopped there, she realized a second later, but, in a panic over the fool she was making of herself, she kept talking. "Princess Ragnhild is the oldest child, she's seven years older than you; Princess Astrid is the second, she's two years younger than Ragnhild; then there's you." Why on earth did she feel the need to recite his family to him? He must think she was crazy.

He merely laughed. "Well done, Miss Haraldsen."

"Are you close to your sisters?" It was a question she would have asked anyone else, but its impropriety and personal nature hit her as soon as it had left her lips. "Oh, I'm so sorry, sir, that's none of my business." She was losing track of how many stupid things she had done and said in his presence.

He laughed again. "Don't apologize; it's nice to have a normal conversation with someone—"

"Really, sir, you don't have to answer that—" She bit the rest of her sentence off, chastising herself for both interrupting him and telling him what he didn't have to do.

"No, I'm not offended at all; I don't mind answering it. I don't see Ragnhild very often since she isn't living in Norway, but Astrid and I are very close."

She nodded, thankful for his graciousness. She was surprised to hear the song soon drawing to its close—she had held his attention for an entire dance.

They wandered out onto the lawn together where many of the other guests had already gathered. At nine o'clock it was nowhere near sunset yet, and all of Oslo was eager to enjoy the brief warmth of the long summer days.

"Did you say you were a seamstress?" he asked.

"Yes, that is, I'd like to be. I've been working in my family's clothing store for now—it's mostly bookkeeping, but I do alterations, too. Someday I'd like to do some kind of fashion design or have a shop of my own. I went to dressmaking school here in Oslo." She grinned. "I might have gotten a job after that, but I was only seventeen and certainly had no notions of *working* yet, so I went on to another fashion school in Lausanne. After that I *still* didn't want to come home and get a job, so I spent some time in Cambridge—"

"Oh, did you study in England? I was at Oxford—Balliol College."

She laughed, imagining herself as a Cambridge student. "No, I didn't study; I was working in a pub and just enjoying England, although I did take a few English classes at a little school for Scandinavians. I think it was just good I only spent a year in Lausanne; I don't think my waistline could have stood it any longer."

"Your waistline?"

"Yes, I don't like Swiss food, and do you have any idea how much weight a person gains if she tries to survive on chocolate for twelve months?" Forty pounds, in her case, which had taken *months* to lose.

He seemed to struggle to hide a laugh and then asked her more about her sewing, taking a great interest in what she did. They danced again and again, each song passing in a mix of small talk and laughter as she ignored the strangeness of slow-dancing to "I Only Have Eyes for You" with the Crown Prince. They were still deep in conversation as the lingering rays of sun were replaced by moonlight around eleven. He liked her, she realized, and seemed eager to spend the evening in her company. She liked him, too. She was flattered to receive the attention of the Crown Prince, and she knew she hadn't felt this happy about anything all spring, but she gave it all very little thought. She would never see Prince Harald again, and the night would amount to nothing more than a magical story to tell her grandchildren.

Monday morning had nothing of a fairy tale about it as Sonja woke at six, dressed, and took the bus from the suburb of Vinderen into downtown Oslo. She had work to do before the store opened at nine and was soon bent over an evening dress draped in layer after layer of tulle, an alteration due to be picked up that day. She had reworked the train twice already and knew her work had been completely acceptable. Yet she had taken the stitches out both times and started over, dissatisfied with the slightest imperfection, even those that were invisible from the outside and irrelevant to the rest of the dress. Sonja did not mind—she liked having the power to make something exactly the way someone wanted it, and she was enjoying the exquisiteness of the dress.

Her sewing equipment was set up in the office suite at the back of the store, from which she could soon hear the opening employees trickling in. Her mother—who had been asleep when Sonja had returned late last night and just getting up when she'd left that morning—arrived an hour later.

Dagny Haraldsen was a slip of a woman in her early sixties whose daughter had inherited her striking features and big brown eyes. She was one of the old-fashioned sort of Norwegian women who had been born one of seven children in a small town before the twentieth century dawned, who had survived many a Scandinavian winter with only the warmth of a kitchen stove, and who had been raised with the old *I Jesu Navn* prayer on her lips from the time she could walk. Her upbringing had instilled an independence that had led her to leave home at age eighteen for distant Oslo and a strength that had pushed her to continue the family business after her husband's death.

Another woman of her generation and experiences might have been known as formidable.

Sonja only knew her as warmth itself.

"And how was the party last night?" Dagny said as she unlocked the door to her own office.

Sonja had not wanted to go to Karl's last night and had refused all social invitations since her father's death in March but had been shoved out the door by her mother. "You must not just *sit here*!" Dagny had exclaimed.

Sonja shrugged. "It was all right, I suppose." She was bursting with the news of having met the Crown Prince but would not let it out just yet.

"Tell me about it," Dagny instructed.

Sonja launched into a lengthy description of the music, the food, the other girls' dresses, and so on, intending to slip His Royal Highness in later. "...but I ruined my dress ten minutes after I got there...that is, Crown Prince Harald ruined it."

"Whatever did Crown Prince Harald have to do with it?" Dagny said absently as she flipped through some papers on her desk.

"I bumped into the Crown Prince, and he spilled a glass of wine on my dress."

"You bumped into—" Her mother froze. "Sonja, are you saying you met the Crown Prince last night?"

She let the grin she had been holding back spread across her face. "Yes, and he's wonderful. He danced with me all evening..."

There was an excited squeal from Dagny, followed by a lengthy discussion of "what the Crown Prince was *really* like."

"Of course he wanted to spend the rest of the party with you," her mother said with pride. "Of *course*. It isn't surprising at all."

"I'll probably never see him again," Sonja interrupted.

Dagny waved this away. "Yes, but it speaks volumes of you that he was so interested in you. And more importantly, I haven't seen you smile like that since you came home from England."

She hadn't, Sonja knew—she had not felt like doing anything more than sitting at home. Getting up had been a struggle some days as her grief had slowly turned into a dull feeling of emptiness.

"Haakon!" Dagny exclaimed as Sonja's older brother stepped in the store's back door. "Your little sister has been dancing with the Crown Prince!"

Chapter Two

"I WANTED TO MAKE SURE YOU WERE AWARE OF THE IMPORTANCE OF SOPHIE'S visit next week," King Olav said over dinner, Harald's first meal at home after his semester at the Military Academy had ended.

As far as Harald was concerned, the visit's chief importance was his own hope that seeing the Greek Princess again would permanently remove Sonja Haraldsen from his head, where she had replaced any coherent thoughts for the last three days. It was her big brown eyes that had first drawn him in, but there was also something at once delicate and adorable about her whole face, with her high cheekbones and round nose. She was small—no more than five feet tall—and she somehow seemed more like a tiny pixie than a human girl. The beauty of her features was exaggerated by their animation—she seemed incapable of speaking or listening without her face displaying every bit of what she thought or felt. Even if she hadn't been so exceptionally pretty, he doubted he could have taken his eyes off her, so captivated had he been by her expressions.

Aside from her appearance, Harald simply found her fascinating. He had thought she'd darted into the kitchen after the wine spill because she'd been so upset, but he'd arrived only to find her laughing about it. He thought she was slightly mad, but wonderfully so. He had never spoken so easily to anyone he'd just met, or found anyone so easy with him.

"I'm sure you've noticed that I have been…*encouraging* you to spend time with Sophie whenever possible," the King continued.

Harald thought it was likely that the Palace walls had noticed this. "Yes, sir."

"My eventual intention in all this is a match between you and Sophie of Greece at some point in the future. What would you think of marrying her?"

This was not a shock. As a child he had believed that his own marriage would be built on love as his parents' was, but he had grown up to understand that such love matches were rare in the royal houses of Europe. He had accepted that he would marry for dynastic convenience, whether he loved the girl or not.

But Sonja Haraldsen's laughter was still playing over and over in his head…

He forced himself to ignore it. He *liked* Sophie, and he was well aware that this was not always the case in royal marriages. "I think it's an excellent idea, sir," he said, willing himself to mean it.

"I'm glad we're in agreement," said the King, calmly taking another bite of his moose as though he and Harald had just selected the menu for an upcoming state dinner rather than a potential bride. "Naturally, of course, it's far too early for any mention of an engagement, but we do need to demonstrate an increased interest in Sophie in order to gradually convey our intentions. Depending on how next week goes, I'm hoping to hint to her mother that a future match might be a possibility. You, in turn, might hint to Sophie that your feelings for her are not merely platonic."

His feelings, of course, were exactly that, and he found it difficult to imagine himself conveying the opposite. How exactly did one show a vague acquaintance and distant cousin that one was interested in marriage?

"And how would you like me to do that, sir?" He was not entirely sure he wanted to hear the answer, not while his mind was still focused on Sonja.

The King, a man who, since his wife's death five years ago, had been far more occupied with matters of state than with the minute details of female psychology, shrugged. "I don't know that sort of thing. Ask your sister."

"How is Astrid? Is she still recovering?" Harald had intended to ask this when they sat down for dinner and he had noticed that she was apparently not yet well enough to join them. However, he had been bombarded as soon as the first course had begun with the agenda for Sophie and her mother, Queen Frederica's, visit.

"She had a slight relapse last weekend, but she's doing quite well. When I went to see her this afternoon, she said she'd been sitting up most of the day but didn't think she ought to try to come upstairs for dinner."

"I'll go see her this evening."

"She'll be happy to see you. The one thing I did hope for next week," the King continued, "was that you would invite Sophie to accompany you to the Academy's graduation ball at the end of the summer."

The graduation ball. The perfect occasion, he realized suddenly, to invite Sonja Haraldsen to...

"It would be absolutely *ideal*, Harald. Both she and Frederica would see the invitation as highly significant, and there would certainly be some publicity for the two of you as a couple, which could lead to an engagement as soon as Christmas and a wedding by this time next year."

Engaged to Sophie by Christmas…married to Sophie next June… Harald simply could not imagine it. He had seen her two or three times in the last year at various family weddings, funerals, and the like, each time pushed to go and speak to her by his father. He liked her well enough, but in truth he barely knew her. Now he might be *married* to her in a mere 365 days. Not exactly the love match he had once hoped for.

And Sonja Haraldsen…

This was not about him spending a carefree evening with some girl he'd met at a party. He was supposed to be focused on courting Norway's next Crown Princess and future Queen.

Harald nodded. "I'll speak with Sophie about the ball."

He joined his sister in her apartments later that evening, finding Astrid with one of her young ladies-in-waiting, Kirstine. They were seated by the open window, a light shawl wrapped around Astrid's shoulders despite the warmth of the day. Kirstine excused herself at his entrance, and Astrid reached for the cane leaning against her chair, moving to stand.

He shook his head, telling her to stay seated, and then leaned down to kiss her cheek in greeting. "How are you feeling?"

"Better today." She smiled.

As he sat down across from her he studied her face, noting the paleness that suggested she was not yet entirely well. At twenty-seven, she was five years his senior and effortlessly pretty, with short dark curls and an elegant bone structure that suggested a flawless pedigree. She was dressed simply but very well for a day spent at home, in a skirt and silk blouse with her trademark triple-strand pearls.

Astrid had first fallen ill with rheumatic fever a year ago in the midst of their father's consecration tour.[1] In addition to the damage it had done to her heart, the disease had left her weakened, struggling with near-constant pain in her legs, and prone to recurrent attacks, the most recent of which she was just getting over.

"Father said you got worse again last weekend."

---

1   A Norwegian monarch is not crowned and has no coronation; instead, a consecration service is traditionally held at Nidaros Cathedral in Trondheim, asking God's blessing on the new reign. The consecration is usually followed by a lengthy tour around the country for the new King and Queen, or the new King and whoever the First Lady may be—in this case, the King's daughter.

She waved the statement away—she did not, Harald knew, like to dwell on her illness, preferring, when possible, to pretend there was nothing wrong. "It wasn't too serious. Congratulations on the end of the semester—it will be nice to have you home again, *lillebror*."[2]

"Thank you." Astrid had long had a tendency to continue addressing her brother by his childhood nicknames. He found this both endearing and irritating.

"When is graduation this year?" she asked.

"August twenty-ninth."

Her eyes sparkled. "There's a ball, too, isn't there, Hajan?" The childish form of Harald that she still used often.

"Yes."

"And you're taking…?"

"Sophie of Greece."

"Father's told you he intends for you to marry her, then." Her tone changed slightly, and she sank back in the chair, an odd look crossing her face. He took it as a sign of a sudden pain or fatigue but did not mention it, taking his cue from her. "Do you want to?" she asked abruptly.

He was no stranger to Astrid's directness, but the subject itself still seemed so unreal that he could not find an answer. "I…it's certainly…I'm not…she…" He looked away and out the window, but not before he saw Astrid raise her eyebrows, two distinct arches that tacitly suggested she thought his answer was *no*.

"…she's a nice girl," he finished lamely.

"But you don't particularly want to marry her, and there's someone you would rather take to the ball."

Yes. There's this seamstress… "No, there isn't." How did she *know* these things?

"Well, that works out perfectly. I think people should be with whomever they *want* to be with, so if Sophie's the one, I think that's wonderful."

He looked back at Astrid, who was now smiling innocently at him. Surely Astrid—*Astrid*, of all people, the responsible young woman who had, at the age of twenty-two, taken on the role of Norway's First Lady after their mother's death, fulfilling the duties that would have been a Queen's without complaint—surely *Astrid* was not encouraging him to do anything other than marry Sophie, as was expected of him.

They were silent for a few minutes. He knew he was going to tell her about Sonja, and what irritated him most was that he also knew that she *knew* he was going to tell her and had likely known this all along.

---

2   Little brother

"Her name is Sonja Haraldsen, I met her last weekend at a party at Karl Stenersen's house, she's a seamstress, she's from Vinderen, she's beautiful, and I find her absolutely fascinating. Is that everything you wanted to know?"

"That will do for now, thank you." She smiled sweetly. Had she not been so sick so recently he would've kicked her. "Do you want to take Sonja to the ball?"

"Yes, but I'm not going to." He paused. "Are you saying you think I *should* take her?"

She was silent for a moment. "No...not necessarily. If you do want to see her again, and if you think there could ever be something between you and this girl, then I think...you should at least consider asking her to go." The bright blue of her eyes clouded over. "But I still don't know if you really ought to do so. Suppose you *did* fall in love with her. Everything is so...*complicated* when you're in love with a commoner, Hajan. Keep that in mind."

He took note of the implicit reference to their sister, Ragnhild, a subject that was rarely discussed in the Palace. King Olav's eldest child, she was two years older than Astrid and had always been regarded as the rebellious one in the family. As a teenager, she had fallen for one of the royal bodyguards and had eventually announced that she wanted to marry him. After several months' worth of arguments within the royal family, Ragnhild and Erling Lorentzen had been granted permission to marry in May 1953, provided they left the country and she renounced her status and the title of Her Royal Highness. All duties as First Lady of Norway had thus fallen to the second daughter, Astrid, at their mother's death in 1954. Ragnhild and her husband had spent the last six years in Brazil where Erling had been able to expand his family's business, and Harald had last seen her a year ago when she attended their father's consecration. They had not been close in the years before her marriage, and the gulf between them had only widened.

Ragnhild's history was a sharp warning to any other members of the royal house—namely Harald—who might wish to marry a commoner. She had managed it, but only at the price of exile halfway around the world and the loss of an official status as a member of the Norwegian Royal Family. Clearly, it was not a possibility for the Crown Prince, the only heir to the throne.

"Do you want to play chess?" Astrid asked, breaking into his thoughts. "Come on, it'll give me something to do, and I'll even let you move your own pieces this time," she added with a grin, referencing the many times two decades ago she had, in search of a playmate, plopped her infant brother down across from her and played both sides of a game herself.

Chapter Three

PRINCESS SOPHIE OF GREECE ARRIVED IN OSLO, ACCOMPANIED BY HER mother, Queen Frederica, on a sunny Wednesday afternoon. Harald, of course, had gone with his father to receive them at the airport and was now standing on the tarmac at the foot of the stairs, watching as his third cousin stepped out of the plane behind her mother.

He would not have required any convincing to admit that she was beautiful—a living picture of what every little girl imagines when she hears a story about a beautiful princess. Her round face and soft eyes suggested the sweetness of her character, her short, dark brown hair was curled in pretty waves with a delicate hat perched on top, her eyelashes were long and graceful, and the shy smile she offered him from the top of the steps was a sparkling flash of white set against the bronze skin acquired over twenty years spent in the Mediterranean sun.

Harald did not have much time to contemplate any of this, however, because Frederica was charging down the stairs, her thin high heels clicking quickly against each one. Sophie followed behind her, albeit with much more hesitant steps.

"Olav!" Frederica called out. "How wonderful to see you again!" They kissed, and when she stepped back the King opened his mouth to speak, but Frederica had already turned to Harald. "And Harald! I can't *begin* to tell you how *thrilled* Sophie and I are to be here; we've been *so* looking forward to this visit and I *must* say I think the two of you will have a simply *wonderful* time together!" She gave him a knowing wink and kissed his cheek. He forced himself to reciprocate. *Pushy. Overbearing. Interfering.* Or so Frederica was often described by the Greek papers. Harald had little grounds for disagreement.

"But I won't keep you from Sophie any longer! Sophie, come and greet your cousin!" Sophie had been hanging back next to the King, whom she had presumably greeted while Harald had been accosted by her mother, and was now glancing demurely at Harald from beneath her long eyelashes. Although she had inherited Frederica's looks—the two women might have been mistaken for twins were it not for the twenty years between them—Harald reminded himself thankfully that she had not inherited her mother's personality. There was a distinct reserve to Sophie that was completely alien to Frederica.

"Hello, Harald," Sophie said softly in English, the common language of royal Europe, as she stepped forward, offering him a white-gloved hand.

"Good morning, Sophie."

"Good morning."

Now what was he supposed to say? Neither being overly talkative by nature, conversation had never flowed easily between them. Silence had never troubled him, but it had acquired a distinct awkwardness now that he knew he was surely *expected* to be conversing with her.

"How was your flight?" he asked after a moment.

"Quite pleasant." She kept her eyes lowered demurely and said nothing further.

Another silence. "How is the weather in Greece? It must be very hot this time of year…" He winced inwardly at the forced conversation.

"It's been rather hot. Nothing like here."

Silence. She was certainly *not* Sonja Haraldsen. The memory of the evening spent with her at Karl Stenersen's party, of her lighthearted chatter and their easy manner together, crossed his mind before he could prevent it.

No, he told himself. He was going to forget Sonja Haraldsen, forget the party, forget everything. He would be marrying Sophie of Greece, and surely—*surely*—things would become more natural between the two of them at some point.

As Queen Frederica and King Olav herded the couple toward the waiting car, Sophie slipped her arm into Harald's.

He felt nothing at all, a sharp contrast, he had to admit, to his response the first time he had touched Sonja Haraldsen's hand as he had raised her from her curtsy in Karl's kitchen.

"She's just finished school, you know," Sophie was saying in response to his question about her younger sister, Irene. They were attending the party the King had arranged in her honor that evening at Skaugum, the royal residence just outside Oslo. Reserved for the Crown Prince's family, the mansion had been unoccupied since Olav had become King and had moved into the Palace with Harald and Astrid.

"I can't begin to tell you how strange it seems that she's old enough for that now," Sophie went on. "Seventeen. I don't think of her that way at all, but—"

Harald could not have repeated the end of Sophie's sentence and the words that followed it for anything—her voice suddenly seemed so distant that she might as well have still been in Greece, because across the hall, he had spotted a small young woman with a glass of champagne in her hand, her short, full-skirted party dress a brilliant blue that made her stand out against the red walls…

But surely it couldn't be. He could only see her from the side, and she was quite a distance away. Harald tried to turn his attention back to Sophie.

"When did you last see her?" she was asking.

"I don't think I've seen Irene since your mother's fortieth birthday two years ago."

A slight blush came into Sophie's cheeks, and he realized she knew he hadn't been listening. "Benedikte, Harald. Not Irene."

Benedikte? A Danish princess, his second cousin and her third. How on earth had she ended up talking about Benedikte? "Benedikte. Sorry. I—we were in Denmark last winter," he said, attempting to cover their mutual embarrassment.

Was that girl Sonja Haraldsen? He glanced that way again…surely it was Sonja. Why on earth would she be here? She was standing at the edge of the dance floor next to Sverre Pettersen, a friend of his who was graduating with him from the Military Academy…did Sverre know her? Was he the one who had brought her?

It didn't matter. He forced his attention back to Sophie, guilty at his repeated rudeness.

"…but I'm sure you already knew they were discussing that," she was saying.

"I hadn't heard," he said, hoping it wasn't something obvious and that he could induce her to repeat herself.

"What do you think of it?"

He paused. "Sophie, I…"

She smiled, her eyes dancing. "You're awfully distracted this evening, Harald."

He could hardly tell her that he was attempting to sneak glances at another girl. The proper answer that would be expected of a suitor came to his mind easily: "I was only thinking that you look very beautiful tonight."

She blushed again and lowered her eyes demurely. "Thank you."

It was not a lie. She *was* very beautiful, possibly even more so than Sonja Haraldsen, and most men—those who weren't smitten with a girl on the other side of the room—would have considered themselves lucky to spend an evening with her.

He ought to be dancing with her, an activity that would hopefully create less need for awkward conversation. "Would you like to dance?"

Another smile that warmed the crystal blue of her eyes. "Of course."

He swept her off onto the dance floor, into a waltz that, for the first time in his life, seemed incredibly stilted compared to what he had enjoyed with Sonja Haraldsen. He could see Sonja out of the corner of his eye, in the arms of Sverre Pettersen, and at such a close distance there was no mistaking her.

He drew near enough to hear her laugh, to catch bits and pieces of her conversation in the midst of the music, to notice again how expressive her face was, especially those brown eyes… Of course, it all only served to make everything worse. After two more dances—as soon as he felt he decently could—he suggested they rest, allowing him to leave the floor and put as much distance between himself and Sonja Haraldsen as possible. Sophie, apparently finding his company as awkward as he found hers, murmured something about wanting to speak to Astrid and disappeared into a group of young women that included his sister.

He could speak to Sonja. He turned to look for her, scanning the crowd of dark suits and short evening dresses twirling about the grand room. He *needed* to see her again… There was Sverre, but Sonja was no longer with him. He was talking with another friend of theirs, Anders Larsen. Harald made his way to him, searching for a casual way to inquire about Sonja.

"The girl you were dancing with earlier—I think we've met…" He paused as though he had forgotten the name. "Sonja, isn't it?

"Sonja Haraldsen," Sverre offered. "Do you know her?"

"I think we met a couple weekends ago. At Karl Stenersen's home, I think it was… Anyway, she only looked familiar to me. Did she come with you?"

Sverre nodded. "Our fathers used to work together, and when you invited me this evening, I thought she might enjoy coming with me. So," he continued, "Sophie of Greece…you certainly have the press excited about her. Any chance there's a good reason for them to be so excited?"

"Maybe," Harald replied with a small smile, determined to play the role of the royal suitor.

"She's certainly very pretty; I can see that much from here."

"Oh, absolutely."

"Do you know her brother?"

"Constantine? Not well—I've met him a few times." Sophie's younger brother was the Greek Crown Prince.

"Have you heard the stories about him?" Sverre asked.

"All those girls he's slept with?" Anders interjected

"It's some Greek actress at the moment, I heard," Sverre said.

"And the kid's only, what, nineteen, twenty?" Anders's tone suggested he was impressed.

"You heard any of that, Harald?"

He was aware of some of the rumors surrounding Constantine, and, while he had no way of being certain, his experience was that such stories usually had at least some basis in fact.

"I don't know—I don't really know him," he said, unwilling to comment.

The keeping of mistresses was by no means unheard of in royal circles, but Harald had always found it an abhorrent practice. It debased the monarchy and the Prince in question, and he had to imagine men had little regard for their mistresses—they were willing to disgrace these women in front of the whole country, setting them aside when they were tired of them. In rare cases, he knew, men did eventually marry their mistresses, but this never removed the stain in the public's eye. He thought of Wallis Simpson, who was now the respectably-married Duchess of Windsor, but who would only be remembered as the King of England's mistress.

"Here's Sophie now, Harald," said Sverre, and Harald looked back to see Sophie edging her way through the crowd toward them.

He introduced her to Sverre and Anders, who made the necessary bows, and then agreed to her suggestion to dance again. As they stepped back out onto the dance floor, Harald glanced back to see Sonja entering the hall again and making her way toward Sverre. If only Sophie had stayed with Astrid and her friends a few minutes longer... No, he told himself, Sophie was the one with whom he was supposed to be spending the evening. Sophie, the future Queen of Norway. Sophie, his intended bride.

"What are you thinking about?" she whispered.

"You." He leaned down and kissed her softly. She blushed and lowered her eyes but seemed quite pleased.

It had been meant sincerely—that is, he had *tried* to mean it sincerely—but it led him back to Sonja, the thought hitting him with the sudden intensity of a summer thunderstorm. *He would never have the chance to kiss Sonja Haraldsen.* Would he regret it the rest of his life? No, he thought hastily, it doesn't matter. Sophie—*the girl he was going to marry*—was what mattered.

Yet he would have to speak to Sonja before the evening was out.

It was another two hours before Sophie slipped off to the restroom and Harald had another chance to search the room for Sonja. There was a small group of others from the Military Academy and their dates, but Sonja and Sverre were nowhere to be found. Had they left already?

Feeling increasingly hopeless, he was standing on the edge of the room, scanning the crowd and half-listening to the conversations around him. Next to him were Johan Ferner and Kirstine, Astrid's lady-in-waiting and nurse. Johan had formerly been the two princesses' sailing instructor and had won a silver medal for Norway at the '52 Olympics. Over the past ten years, he had become Astrid's frequent sailing companion and a friend of the whole Royal Family. A divorced man whose family owned a small men's clothing store, he had always seemed a quiet, decent sort.

Johan and Kirstine were speaking quite intently. "I'm not really worried about tonight—of course, actually dancing would be out of the question," Harald heard her say.

Johan responded inaudibly, his back to Harald, and then Kirstine spoke several more times—all simple "yeses," "noes," or "quite wells." Then Johan said something that made her pull away and exclaim, "For heaven's sake, be careful! You know it's got to be a secret."

But Johan was ignoring her, staring across the room. Harald followed his gaze to see Astrid smiling knowingly at the two.

Johan whispered something to Kirstine, guiding her out the nearby door into the next room.

Curious now, Harald stepped closer to the door in hopes of hearing more. What had to be a secret? He had not even known Johan and Kirstine knew each other well, assuming that their only encounters were Johan's visits during Astrid's illnesses.

He strained to hear Johan's words, but caught only the beginning of the sentence: "If I were to…"

Whatever he said, it caused Kirstine's face to brighten with absolute delight. "Oh, Johan, I—wonderful, how wonderful!" She laughed. "Oh, I'm so glad! I…the best ring would be something simple and traditional, I think… oh, but this is so wonderful!"

He did not hear Johan's next question, but Kirstine's response was quite clear. "Oh, most certainly yes!" she exclaimed. "Surely you weren't in doubt?"

Had Johan just proposed? The whole conversation seemed to point in that direction, and the fact that there should be some sort of secret relationship between the two made a certain amount of sense. Johan was present quite often whenever Astrid was ill, something which Harald had attributed to the closeness of their friendship. But Kirstine herself was nearly always present at such times, and, if their relationship had to be hidden for whatever reason, it was perhaps one of the few occasions when they could see each other.

"Harald?" He whirled around to see Sophie had joined him. "Shall we dance again?"

Chapter Four

SONJA WAS PREPARING LAMB FOR A FAMILY DINNER ON SUNDAY AFTERNOON, her mother involved upstairs in the panicked, last-minute cleaning she engaged in whenever they were to have guests. Sonja's much-older siblings, Haakon and Gry, were both coming, as well as Haakon's wife and baby and Gry's husband and her teenage children. Sonja had not found the weekly dinner easy in her father's absence, but she did look forward to holding her three-month-old nephew and seeing Gry's children, who seemed to have spent more time growing up with her and Dagny than with their own mother.

There had never been much affection between Sonja and her sister, but it was a different matter with Haakon. She had always been his pet, his little princess, and her admiration for him was boundless.

The phone rang, and she dried her hands, going to answer it in the front room.

"Hello?"

"Miss Haraldsen?" Not a voice she could place.

"Yes?"

"This is Harald." Harald? Who did she know named Harald?

"I'm sorry—could you give me your last name?"

"Um, Schleswig-Holstein-Sonderburg-Glücksburg." *The Crown Prince.* She felt her face turn bright red.

"Oh, Your Royal Highness! I'm so sorry, sir, I didn't think—"

"Never mind." He paused. Why on earth was he calling her? The entire situation of stepping away from preparing dinner to take a phone call from the Crown Prince was inconceivably foreign to her, and she wondered if she hadn't misunderstood something.

"I'm glad I had the chance to meet you at Karl's," he said.

"Thank you, sir, but I'm sure the pleasure was all mine."

"I was hoping to be able to speak to you Wednesday evening, but I never had the opportunity."

He had wanted to talk to her? It was shocking enough to imagine that he had even noticed her at Wednesday's party. Other than observing that there seemed to be very little chemistry between him and Princess Sophie, she had barely given the Crown Prince a thought.

"I didn't realize, sir."

"You don't need to call me that. Harald is fine." He paused. "I was hoping it would be possible to see you again."

See her again? Surely he couldn't mean that the way it sounded. He said nothing more, and she realized he was waiting for her to speak. "What do you mean?" Nervously, she twisted the phone cord around the fingers of her left hand.

"I'm graduating from the Military Academy at the end of the summer, and…" He paused again, and it occurred to her that he was nervous—far more so than she was, and his shyness somehow calmed her. "Miss Haraldsen, I was wondering if you would be able to accompany me to the graduation ball on August twenty-ninth."

"I…Your Royal Highness, that is, Harald, I…" She sank down onto the couch. Had the Crown Prince just asked *her* to a *ball*?

"I know that's quite a few weeks away, but I thought you might want the time to make a dress…"

"I don't know what to say…I…"

"Say yes, Sonja, say yes—you don't mind my calling you Sonja, do you?"

"I…no, no, of course I don't mind. And yes. Yes, I would love to go with you."

"I'll pick you up around seven, then, on the twenty-ninth?"

"That would be lovely, thank you."

They said goodbye, and she set the phone down, staring at it for a moment. Had she really just…? Slowly, the situation sank in…and she was nearly giddy with excitement.

Sheer happiness had become such an unfamiliar feeling over the last few months that she could not quite recognize it at once. She only knew that she felt something…*wonderful*…inside her, some sense of exultation that had made her suddenly, brilliantly alive again.

"Mamma!" she called out, dashing into the hall and running up the stairs two at a time. "Mamma! I'm going to a ball with Crown Prince Harald!"

The doorbell rang just as Sonja was rolling on a final coat of lipstick. She felt a small quiver of excitement run through her. *It's just a graduation party,* she reminded herself. *Be natural.*

But on the other hand she expected it to be perfectly wonderful. Beautiful dresses in the medieval banquet halls of old Akershus Castle, with dancing till midnight, and all with a Prince...

She allowed herself a dreamy smile in the vanity mirror, then firmly reminded herself of the reality of the situation. He was His Royal Highness Crown Prince Harald, Heir Apparent to the Norwegian throne, and she was Sonja Haraldsen, a seamstress and a shopkeeper's daughter. The idea that there would be anything more between them than one perfect evening was laughable, and she knew it.

One perfect evening. She meant it to be perfect and intended to make it so.

She heard her mother speaking to Harald at the door. Mrs. Haraldsen's deference and what seemed like a combination of shyness and nerves on Harald's part made them both sound equally hesitant and awkward. Sonja forced herself to swallow her own nerves.

She touched her short brown hair, curled in loose waves around her face—did she need more spray? Did she need more make-up? Less? She considered adding more eye-liner, but no, her eyes were already large and didn't need anything more—but was that brown shade right for her eye shadow? Should she have matched her eye color like that? She so wanted everything perfect for tonight...

Breathe, she told herself. *The first time the Crown Prince saw you, you had that ridiculous wine stain. Anything's an improvement.*

With a final glance in the mirror, Sonja stood up from the vanity and let herself twirl around once, watching her full skirt spin out. She had, of course, made her own dress, rejoicing at the excitement of making an evening gown for herself for once. The soft silk was pale pink with a soft floral pattern, and she had sewed yards and yards of lace and tulle into the skirt.

Part of what Sonja loved about sewing was the *potential* she always felt she sewed into clothing, the hope for something wonderful to happen in it. It was a feeling she had not experienced during any of her sewing since her father's death in March, at least until she had started on this ball gown. This fabric had been the first to feel alive to her again, the needle once more an extension of her finger, in the way it had been not so long ago.

As she started down the stairs that led into the front hall, she was at first occupied with her dress. It was, as she had suspected, unmanageably massive, and she had to arrange it carefully to fit onto the staircase. The back of the skirt was dragging along the steps behind her, she realized, but she was focused on those in front. It was most disconcerting not to be able to see her feet.

"Sonja." She looked up at the sound of Harald's voice. He was standing at the foot of the steps, and she blushed at the thought that he had been watching her struggles with the gown. "It's nice to see you again," he said.

For a moment she was too overwhelmed to respond as her gaze met his. His blue eyes had a startling warmth and intensity, and she found she couldn't look away.

"You look lovely."

"Thank you." Ordinarily she would have said more, but she was distracted by an odd sense of breathlessness and excitement of a sort she hadn't been able to feel in months. *Get it together,* she told herself firmly.

She stepped off the final stair, and his white-gloved hand overwhelmed her own. She almost laughed as she glanced down—her hand suddenly looked like a small child's in his. She studied his uniform, the crisp pleats in the stiff black fabric, the silver buttons, the gold stars at the collar…

"My car's out front," he said. She nodded, finding herself, for the first time she could remember, at a loss for words. "Mrs. Haraldsen—thank you," he added, turning to Dagny, who curtsied gracefully. Sonja had the distinct sense that her mother might have been practicing for this.

The spell was broken and everything seemed natural again when he opened the passenger door of his car for her. Getting in with such a full skirt, she realized, was a much more difficult prospect than she'd imagined. As she attempted to gather it elegantly into the car with her, there seemed to be a great deal more material involved than she had *any* memory of sewing into the dress. She looked up at Harald and saw that he was struggling to hide a grin.

"Help me, would you?" she said, starting to laugh as it continued to spill out of the car. "I've never *worn* anything like this before…"

He laughed with her as he helped her shove the rest of the pink silk and the stiff layers underneath inside. Their eyes met again, and for a long moment neither of them spoke. Then she looked away, embarrassed as she remembered that there could never be anything between them.

She made conversation easily during the drive. He was no more talkative than he had been the evening they had met, but she had never had any problem filling silences, and he seemed content, even quite pleased, to listen to her chatter.

And then the old, fourteenth-century fortress of Akershus was in sight. It was not, from a distance, an imposing building—it was a medieval castle, not a modern palace, and it was not an unusually large or tall one. It was, however, easily seen from its position perched on a rocky ridge over Oslo harbor. The twin spires of its courtyard were visible from the road, and as they drove closer Sonja could see the brown stone walls.

A sudden wave of panic broke over her. There were a million ways that anyone, particularly a seamstress with no experience in such a setting, could commit some gigantic faux pas on such an occasion. She felt as though she'd been asked to copy an elaborate designer dress without any sort of pattern. And surely they were the couple at whom everyone else would be staring. Had she been crazy to accept his invitation?

She looked down at her lap and nervously smoothed the silk piled on top of her. Pink. What on earth had she been thinking when she'd picked this fabric? It was fun and youthful and completely appropriate for her, but who had ever heard of *pink* at a military ball? Surely all the others would look far more sophisticated. What would they think of her? What would *Harald* think of her? Perhaps he was already regretting asking her to accompany him.

And then there were her pearls, a single, tiny strand. She was otherwise bare of all jewels. Amidst the wealthy of Oslo, she would stand out like a patch of mud on an otherwise-pristine field of snow. She had so desperately wanted to get everything *right* tonight, and she suspected that she was already failing miserably. She took a deep breath.

"Are you all right?" he asked.

No. She suddenly wasn't even sure she wanted to go at all. She ought to have just refused him last month when he had invited her.

"I'm fine," she lied. "I suppose I'm a bit…nervous."

"You don't need to be. It's only my classmates."

"Don't you think I'm going to stand out terribly?"

"No, not at all." Then he blushed and added rather quietly, "Although you might stand out as the prettiest one there."

She smiled, continuing to fiddle with her necklace but finding herself enchanted once again. It was his shyness that had first left an impression on her—a charming quality, she had thought, in the heir to the throne.

Harald parked at the edge of the complex outside the old fortress wall. The area was filled with other uniformed graduates and their dates, and any further unease melted when she stepped out of the car and her arm slipped into his. They walked silently through the entrance gate, the thickness of the wall—she guessed it to be seven or eight feet—reminding her of its role in the defense of medieval Norway.

The atmosphere inside the complex, however, was that of a fairy tale, not a medieval war. It was a pleasant green park sloping uphill, and it was filled tonight with girls in ball gowns and young men in dress uniforms. There was a scattering of red-roofed buildings still in use by the military, but these were dwarfed by the old castle rising up over the harbor.

Sonja, however, was far more occupied with the cobblestones at her feet than with the old buildings or the warm summer air or the muffled squawking of gulls on the other side of the wall. She had last visited Akershus on an elementary school trip and had, in the intervening fifteen years, forgotten how far of a walk it was to the castle and how uneven the stone paths were.

"Are you all right?" Harald asked as she surveyed the ground warily. It would not have been an easy walk in flats, and she—along with all the other girls who were slowly and carefully making their way up the hill—was in three-inch heels and a dress that greatly restricted her view of the path.

"Yes," she said, giggling at the situation. "It's only—this won't be easy in these shoes." She lifted her skirt to show him.

"Oh! Of course not…" He glanced down at the little pink heels dyed to match her dress. "Well, hold on to me." His grip on her arm tightened. "I won't let you fall."

And he wouldn't, she realized as they continued to walk over the large, jagged rocks. He was something of a rock himself, and the few times she began to trip she barely had time to stumble at all before he was steadying her again. He held her quite firmly, and they were both laughing, the sudden klutziness of her and every other girl in the crowd breaking any ice still left between them.

"I can tell," she said, still laughing, "that this is the Military Academy's event—no school with any women in its leadership would have attempted to hold a ball here!"

"You're probably right. It would never have occurred to me that all the dates would be walking around on stilts."

"I have to." She grinned. "Think how short I'd be if I weren't wearing these shoes!"

"That's a rather sobering thought." He smiled back down at her.

At last they were crossing the stone bridge into the castle's courtyard, stepping inside through a rounded wooden door, and climbing a winding staircase—there was more laughter between them as she negotiated this in her dress—to the second level. The ball would be held in four connecting rooms, and the stairs opened into the first of these. The ancient stone walls, antique chandeliers, faded tapestries, and old royal oil paintings created a medieval scene that seemed to have leapt off the pages of a book. The soft notes of a waltz drifted through the air.

She floated happily through the first three halls on Harald's arm as he introduced her to friends of his, who in turn introduced her to their dates. She received raised eyebrow after raised eyebrow when he gave them her name, and she could barely keep from laughing at the absurdity of it all when some of them spoke to her quite deferentially. *Sonja Haraldsen?* she could almost hear them thinking. *Should we know that name? The family* must *be terribly important.*

Yes, she thought, *it's a long line of tailors, farmers, and fishermen—*

Then he swept her off onto the dance floor, where she was conscious of hundreds of eyes on the both of them. Laying his right hand on her waist and taking her right hand in his left, he held her as though she were made of the most fragile and delicate glass. The floor slowly cleared, leaving them alone in the center. She felt no need to speak, finding that it was enough to look up into his warm blue eyes. Soon, she was unaware of all the stares, the old castle, and the strangeness of the moment, thinking of nothing other than Harald.

She spent the next few songs in his arms as well, and they were joined by more and more other couples until the floor was full again. She thought she might float away on happiness as she spun in and out of his arms, her skirts twirling around her. The sun was sinking lower outside as the night wore on, and the rooms were bathed in the soft glow of candles and chandeliers.

It was like waking up in a dream that had taken her back several hundred years.

She might have remained in her blissful state for the rest of the evening had she not stepped into the restroom to fix her hair after dancing. Gazing into the mirror, she tucked a few curls back into place.

The girl standing at the next sink had been eyeing her curiously since she had come in. "Who *are* you, exactly?" she asked.

Sonja glanced at her for the first time. "Sonja Haraldsen. Why?"

"You're the girl with the Prince. I've been wondering all evening if you were foreign royalty, but you're clearly Norwegian, which means you must come from one of the old noble families. But Haraldsen doesn't sound familiar..."

No, of course it didn't. Her nerves were suddenly on edge again. "I'm not anyone important. I'm a seamstress. I just—I just happen to know Prince Harald."

"Oh, I see." The girl smirked. "A *seamstress.* Don't you think you're a little lowborn, then, to be out with the Crown Prince?"

Sonja said nothing. She did think exactly that—it had been easy enough to forget who she was on the dance floor, but the impossibility of her situation returned to her easily. The sudden awakening was like having ice cold water splashed in her face.

"Don't lose your glass slipper on the way out, Cinderella," the girl said in a tone of mocking sweetness as she flounced away.

Sonja stood still for a moment, examining her reflection. She had no business being here, and she knew it. Surely that was what the whole party would think if they knew who she was, what the whole *country* would say if they knew whom the Crown Prince had chosen as his date for the evening. This was why anything further between the two of them would be hopeless. She ought not to have been thinking of anything further, anyway. She had always known this would last for tonight alone.

But she would at least have one evening with him, she told herself, pushing her worries away, one unforgettable night that she was determined to enjoy. All the more reason for it to be so perfect.

And it was exactly that, in spite of the small notes of doubt that sounded in the back of her mind as she waltzed across the hall with him.

They went upstairs into the last of the four halls, a dark, Gothic room with a stained glass window which required little imagination to believe that the calendar read 1459 instead of 1959. Buffet tables had been laid out, and somehow—she was not sure how—she made him laugh over the mushroom sauce. It was not the first time she had made him laugh that evening, and it was an experience she had not had with anyone in months. She was slowly realizing he was making her laugh as well—it was something of a surprise, but beneath his shyness and behind his status as the Crown Prince, he was remarkably *fun*.

Returning downstairs with glasses of wine, they sat down across from each other, their knees touching, in one of the window alcoves with stone benches set into the wall and covered by plush green cushions. She gazed thoughtfully down into the floodlit courtyard, deeply regretting that he was the Crown Prince and therefore someone she would likely never see again. He was speaking far more freely by this point and was quietly telling her about the previous day's graduation ceremony.

"You know," he said as they finished the wine, "the view of the harbor from outside's wonderful at night like this." And it was, she realized as soon as they stepped outside onto the stone pathways surrounding the old fortress. It was one of those late summer nights where there was no breeze or chill at all, nothing but cool, still air and no reminder of the cold fall and freezing winter that would soon follow. The lights on the walls of the castle cast a dim, golden glow over them both, the stars had come out overhead, and there were hundreds of twinkling lights on boats and in buildings in the harbor below.

She smiled. "Thank you for the invitation tonight. It's been wonderful."

"I'm glad you came...I'm glad I met you at Karl's."

"I hadn't wanted to go to that party," she admitted. "My father died last winter, and I...I hadn't wanted to do anything since then. I only went because my mother insisted. And I'm glad she did. This—tonight—has really been the only good thing since March." She blushed, suddenly awkward at revealing all this to him. "But never mind. I just wanted to...thank you."

"No," he said softly. "I understand."

In the comfortable silence that followed she recalled that his mother had died five years earlier.

They lingered outside in easy conversation for awhile, gazing out at the lights of Oslo, and then returned to the ball for more dancing, the magic of the evening only growing. She discovered again and again that she could make him laugh, and he barely took his eyes off her.

When it all ended at midnight he drove her home, neither breaking the companionable silence until he had parked outside her house and walked her to the front door.

"Thank you," she said. "It was all lovely."

"May I see you again?" he asked, his voice rising with hope.

She wanted to see him again, desperately, and the enchantment of the ball was still swirling around her, but she knew that any romance between the two of them had been doomed from the moment of their births. *Don't you think you're a little lowborn to be out with the Crown Prince?* Wouldn't that be everyone's attitude?

"Harald," she began, "this has all been wonderful, and I *do* want to see you again, but...don't you think people would find us terribly unacceptable as a couple?"

They would, and both of them knew it. But as they gazed at each other in the soft light of her front porch, the opinion of the rest of the world seemed extraordinarily insignificant. "What does it matter what people think?" Harald said after a moment. "What difference should it make between the two of us?"

Sonja looked into his eyes and found that she had no answer. She also found that she didn't need one. A second later she was in his arms, and he was kissing her.

Chapter Five

THE GRADUATION BALL, HARALD REALIZED A WEEK LATER, WAS THE NIGHT he had fallen—or, perhaps more accurately, realized he had fallen—for Sonja Haraldsen. He could not have named what it was in her that so captivated him. She was beautiful, of course, but so was Princess Sophie of Greece, and he had most definitely *not* fallen for *her*. There was something in Sonja's laughter—and in its frequent occurrence—that captured his attention, and there was something in the animation of her face and her whole figure. There was something in the natural easiness he felt in her company. And there was certainly something in the slight spaciness she could project on occasion, the aspect of her personality that had sent her twirling into him at Karl's party and that left her, on occasion, without the social propriety everyone else had always displayed in his presence. It suggested a warm energy for fun and for life, and he imagined that it had been behind one of his favorite moments of the evening after they had each filled a plate from the light buffet.

"Didn't you take any mushroom sauce?" she had said, glancing down at his plate.

"I don't—" he began, in a futile attempt to tell her that he had never much liked it on fish.

"Here." She smeared a decent amount of the stuff onto his fish. "Try it, you'll like it," she announced authoritatively.

Harald had never been given an order by anyone other than his parents or a commanding officer, and he certainly had never been interrupted or had his wishes ignored. He thought she was a bit crazy, or at least odd, but he decided he liked that.

He had laughed and eaten his fish with the sauce on it.

Over the next couple months, they shared nights out in groups, dinners alone in the private rooms of restaurants, and days spent hiking the hilly countryside. It became a game to them to slip quietly into a movie theatre once the lights had dimmed and the credits begun and sneak out again just before the end, unnoticed by anyone. Quiet evenings were spent together at the unoccupied royal residence Skaugum or at Sonja's home, where they spent many hours talking with her mother. Dagny had welcomed Harald as though he were one of the family, and there was a warmth in the Haraldsen house that he had not felt since his own mother died.

In no time at all, he had fallen very easily in love with Sonja. It was naturally no more difficult for Sonja, in turn, to fall in love with him. She did not *want* to fall in love with him, suspecting that she could be nothing more than a brief fling for the Crown Prince and fearing that the relationship would only end in heartbreak for her if she let herself grow too attached. Yet she could not help but love the way he made her laugh, his complete lack of pretension, that shyness she found so charmingly humble in a man who knew he would one day be King, the deference with which he treated someone as far beneath him as herself, the gentleness in his caresses that seemed so at odds with his size, or the protective manner that left her feeling so secure in his arms. She could relax with him, she discovered—an odd enough feeling for anyone with the Crown Prince, she realized, but stranger for her. A slightly obsessive perfectionist, she had never been able to date anyone without feeling some sort of elaborate performance was required of her. Yet she had not felt any such compulsion with Harald, from the night at Karl's party where she had so completely failed at the perfect impression she would have preferred to make. He seemed to enjoy her missteps more than anything else she did, and she was able to let herself have fun with him.

They both knew, of course, that any future between them simply could not be. They understood, although it was rarely spoken aloud, that this could not last, but somehow that only served to make it that much sweeter. And so they lived only for the moment that fall, taking care to hide their romance from all but the closest of friends. It would be over, they realized, the moment the public—and King Olav—heard the slightest hint of it.

And perhaps the public and the King never would have had Harald not been sure he and Sonja were alone one November evening. They had slipped out of a party at a friend's home and gone walking through the neighborhood, braving the twenty-degree temperatures, made worse by a strong wind, in hopes of privacy. Surely no one else would be out here in such cold weather at such a late hour, and, as Harald's eyes swept over the scene, there truly did not seem to be. And surely, even if there were, he could not be recognized in the dim glow of the streetlights.

"Sonja." He turned to her.

"We're alone then, are we?" She often had an odd mannerism when she spoke, lowering her chin slightly as though to look down and then raising her eyes upward, making them seem even rounder and bigger. She did this now, and the combination of her eyes and the soft laugh in her voice…he knew he ought not to assume such a thing on a public street, knew they could be discovered at any moment…but he found himself reaching out for her, drawing her close to him… their arms slipped around each other…he breathed in the scent of her hair as his fingers ran through its softness, felt the slight shiver in her body as another gust of wind blew…and then his lips found hers…

Their kiss required no thought, and it would never have occurred to them in that moment that he was the Heir Apparent and she was a common-born shopkeeper's daughter. It seemed instead to be the most natural thing in the world.

Neither of them heard the pop of the flash or saw the photographer in the distance—a young man who had been a discreet distance behind Harald since he had left the Palace that evening and who now believed he had something that would interest the morning papers.

Olav and Astrid were seated together at one end of the long table when Harald entered the dining room the next morning, a steaming mug of coffee in front of the King and the day's newspapers piled next to his plate.

"Sit down," Olav said, a dangerous edge to his voice and his face a mask of hardened stone. Harald slowly took a seat. "What were you *thinking*?" Olav snatched up the paper on top of the pile and thrust it in front of his son.

"Crown Prince Harald Involved in Passionate Romance with Commoner," the headline proclaimed. Beneath it was a sizable photo of Harald and Sonja locked in each other's embrace, apparently taken the night before. Somehow, Sonja had been identified as well—the caption read, "Crown Prince Harald, 22, was spotted last night in the company of Sonja Haraldsen of Vinderen. Miss Haraldsen, also 22, is an aspiring seamstress and the common-born daughter of an Oslo shopkeeper." Harald numbly skimmed the rest of the article, which reiterated Sonja's commoner status, questioned his judgment, mentioned rumors of a courtship with Princess Sophie of Greece, and drew an unflattering and thinly veiled parallel to Edward VIII of England and Mrs. Simpson.

Slowly, Harald laid the paper down and looked back at his father. Olav's face had only grown whiter, his lips thinner, and his eyes narrower.

"*So,*" the King said. "*So…*"

"I don't…I don't know how that picture was taken," Harald managed to gasp. "I…I know it will be horrible for Sonja when she finds this…"

"That's all you can say? You're worried about *this—this girl's reaction?*" Olav seemed to levitate a few inches off his chair. Harald was far too involved in the situation to find any of this at all funny, but Astrid, who could take the role of the disinterested observer, snorted in an attempt to hide her laughter.

"Something amuses you?" Olav snapped, turning to his daughter.

She shrugged.

"I'm glad at least one of us is entertained by this," Olav muttered.

"I realize, sir," Harald attempted, "that this is an embarrassing situation for the Royal House as well. I had no idea there were any photographers around when that photo was taken, and I did make an effort to ensure that we were alone."

"An effort? *An effort?*" the King sputtered. "You were in public, Harald! Outside! On a street! Yes, there was a photographer around! There has been a photographer around since before you could walk! *You're the Crown Prince!*"

"I know, sir. I wasn't thinking."

"Clearly. Not that it would matter, Harald, had you been alone. This—this shouldn't even be happening in private! A shopkeeper's daughter, Harald! *A shopkeeper's daughter!*" Olav's eyes bulged, and his face turned from white to red. Astrid glanced up at the chandeliers as though wondering if their father's shouts might bring them down. "How long has this been *going on?*"

Surely nothing good could come of telling his father that he had fallen for Sonja Haraldsen as long ago as August. "I'm not sure, sir," he lied. "Awhile."

This seemed to take the fire out of Olav's argument, and the King could suddenly manage nothing more than the small whimper of a wounded mouse. Astrid took her father's silence as an opportunity to inject herself into the conversation.

"Father," she began, toying with her necklace, "I think if Harald truly does love this girl, then he ought to be allowed to see her. There's just—there's no reason they should be kept apart."

The King stared at his daughter as though she had sprouted a second head. "Of course there's a reason! Are you both *insane?* Harald has a *duty* to marry a suitable consort! What you seem completely unable to understand, Harald, is how damaging this behavior is to your ability to eventually make a suitable match! That is, Sophie—*Sophie*—" His eyes bulged again, and he seemed to be absolutely overcome at the mention of her name.

"Maybe Harald and Sophie aren't quite meant for each other," Astrid offered—hoping, Harald suspected, to distract Olav before he either dropped dead of a heart attack or leapt across the table and strangled Harald. "If I might say so, sir, I think this match has even less to recommend it than—"

Having recovered enough to speak again, Olav cut off his daughter's ineffective attempt to change the subject. "Harald, must I remind you how hard I've been trying to bring about a match between you and Sophie? And what are Pavlos and Frederica going to think when they catch sight of this photo? A fine chance you'll have of marrying their daughter when they discover your recent activities *in the midst of a courtship with Sophie—*"

A courtship with Sophie? He'd sent her a few letters and entertained her during her weekend visit last June. "I haven't been courting Sophie—"

"The two of you agreed to correspond with each other when she left Norway this summer. What else does that amount to?"

Very little, as far as he had understood. "I was only—"

"But regardless of your letters, this sort of thing is a mistake you cannot afford when the pretender to the Spanish throne has shown such interest in her!"

"Juan Carlos is interested in Sophie?" A rumor he hadn't heard.

"Yes, and he's far more aggressive about it than you are. If you aren't careful, she'll be married off to him, while you throw away your future—and the future of *this house*—for a few brief kisses from some—from some *common little shopkeeper's daughter!*"

⸺

"You haven't seen the paper yet, have you?" said Alice, one of the cashiers, in response to Sonja's greeting when she entered the store.

"No…what paper?" There was something in Alice's expression she couldn't quite read.

"*Verdens Gang.* Is it true, Sonja? Was that really you? Are you really dating the Crown Prince? There's this photo of you together…"

The odd sensation of freefalling gripped her, and she grabbed hold of the counter.

"It *is* true, isn't it?"

"I'm going to get a paper," Sonja answered weakly.

The world seemed to blur around her as she hurried out of the store. The sun had only just risen, and the wintry morning air was a sharp shock to her lungs as she breathed in. But it did not occur to her to turn back for a coat, and she half-ran through the rush hour crowds down to the street corner where she knew she could find a newspaper stand. Surely this wasn't what it sounded like…how could there possibly be a photo…she slowed her pace, dreading what she would find. She and Harald…they couldn't possibly continue if news of their relationship was out in the press…she might never see him again… Trying to ignore the panic sweeping over her, she forced herself to look at the front page of the copy she bought. No…it simply wasn't possible. Frantically, her eyes skimmed over the article: *Sonja Haraldsen, age 22…common-born daughter of an Oslo shopkeeper…certainly brings the Crown Prince's judgment into question…a constitutional impossibility for anything to ever come of the romance…* She felt hundreds of eyes up and down the street staring at her, and she realized she was shivering from more than the freezing temperatures. *No one recognizes you,* she told herself. *The picture isn't clear enough.* All the same, she wanted nothing more than to be back inside the store, and she hurried back to it as quickly as she could without attracting attention.

Chapter Six

"Sir, Her Majesty the Queen of Greece is on the line for you."

Frederica? Olav could not think of anyone he wanted to speak to less, but it had to be done. Against his better judgment, he picked up the phone.

"Olav?"

"Yes?"

"One of the Norwegian papers was brought to my attention this morning. I assume you know which one."

"Yes."

"The photograph was terrible enough, Olav, and then, of course, I proceeded to read the translation of the article. '*The young commoner who accompanied Crown Prince Harald to his graduation ball from the Military Academy last summer appears to be more than a friend, as was stated at the time. Late yesterday evening, the couple was found in each other's arms—*'"

Surely she wasn't going to read him the whole article. "Frederica, I'm aware of what it says—"

She ploughed ahead. "Of course, I was even *more* displeased—and I wasn't *at all* amused in the first place—when my daughter's name cropped up: '*Although rumored to be courting Princess Sophie of Greece, it would seem that the Crown Prince's attention has drifted to Miss Haraldsen.*' Olav, I can't even *begin* to tell you how damaging it is to Sophie's interests to have her future subjects reading that Harald prefers a common bride to her." She sniffed. "It would appear that Harald is *somewhat* less interested in Sophie than you've led us to believe."

"Freddy, let me assure you that Harald is legitimately interested." It was a lie, and he knew it. "He thinks Sophie's beautiful, talented, graceful, well-prepared for the throne…"

"Yes, well, I certainly hope that's the case. Harald has thus far demonstrated very little *personal* interest in my daughter. One could get the impression that you're the only one with any real interest here."

"No, no, not at all—"

"I must say the contrast between Sophie's two most prominent suitors is *stunning*. Juan Carlos of Spain has displayed a *clear* interest in my daughter—the boy is falling all over himself. Harald we haven't heard from in *weeks*. Now I at least know *why*, he's evidently been very *busy*—"

"Yes, well, I would hope that you..." Where on earth was he going with this? "...can be understanding of Harald," he finished. "That is, you must understand that Harald is a passionate young man, but he will prove a dedicated suitor for Sophie in time."

She paused. "Naturally, you will understand, I have not shared this incident with my daughter. Sophie thinks the *world* of Harald and would be absolutely *devastated*."

"Of course," said Olav quickly. Unless he was very much mistaken, this meant Frederica was still decidedly interested in Harald.

"Let me be frank with you, Olav. You may be aware that Pavlos and I prefer Harald over Juan Carlos?"

"I had thought perhaps—"

She ignored him. "Naturally, I have my doubts about the Spanish throne, and it remains uncertain whether or not Juan Carlos and his future bride will ever reign, although it *is* a distinct possibility, which is frankly the only reason I'm considering his suit at all. Thus I would prefer Sophie to marry Harald. However, any more of this behavior and I may reconsider and decide that we'll take our chances with the Spaniards."

"I understand, and I will certainly convey this message to Harald."

"That would be wise. I'm sure there's no need for me to remind you how desperately you need a bride—"

There wasn't.

"—but, given Harald's status as the only heir to the Norwegian throne, unless he finds a suitable girl to be his Queen and bear *his* heirs, it will mean the eventual end of monarchy in Norway. Not that I believe there's any serious danger here—surely we can expect Harald to see his foolishness soon."

He was not oblivious to the threat in her voice. "Certainly, Freddy. I'm sure that there will be no further incidents."

⌘

"I think the central problem here, Harald, is that you simply don't understand how serious this is." Having left instructions with his aides not to interrupt them, King Olav was prepared for a rational discussion with his son.

"I want to be understanding, Harald, and I realize that you like this girl, and I want to respect your judgment in that, but in this situation, Harald…this just can't go on. I'm going to expect that you will break off this relationship."

"I'm not going to do that, sir."

"Harald, I spoke with Frederica of Greece earlier today, and she's willing to forgive this incident. However, she made it clear that if she hears of any more of this sort of behavior, everything is in serious jeopardy."

He paused, used to having his instructions obeyed, but Harald said nothing.

"This simply cannot continue, Harald. I *insist* that you stop seeing this girl."

"I'm not going to do that, sir."

"*Harald*—" The boy's calm defiance was infuriating.

"I'm not breaking up with Sonja, sir. There's nothing in my obligations as Crown Prince of Norway that requires I not see Sonja Haraldsen. I'm not refusing to keep the option of a match with Sophie of Greece open—Sonja and I understand we can't marry, but we want to be together as long as we can. Frederica won't hear anything further about it. I have every intention of being more discreet and much more careful in the future to spare Sonja the media attention; I'm sure it's horrible for her."

The King was not used to compromises, but he *was* used to knowing and getting exactly what he wanted, and what he wanted was for the relationship to be kept out of the press. He didn't much care who Harald spent time with so long as Frederica didn't know anything about it, and Harald was apparently still at least *open* to Sophie of Greece, and young men at this age might fall for a new girl every weekend. *He* certainly hadn't; he had fallen hard at eighteen for the Swedish Princess Märtha and never thought of anyone else, but that would surely not be the case for Harald. Harald could not possibly have such strong feelings for a shopkeeper's daughter.

"Harald," Olav began.

"I'm not breaking up with her, sir."

"I'm not telling you to. However, it seems we have a shared interest in keeping this—issue—out of the press. Considering how discreet you've been for—how long, Harald?"

"Three months, sir."

"—for three months, surely you can manage to stay out of the limelight in the future. And since you've indicated you intend to keep an open mind about Sophie, I'm going to allow you to continue seeing the other girl as long as you continue to agree to the meetings set up between you and Sophie, and as long as you continue your correspondence with her—"

"That would be fine, sir," said Harald, a small smile of victory on his face.

"I am not finished, Harald. I was also hoping, since you would prefer the girl were kept out of the spotlight, and because I would very much like to report this to Frederica, I was hoping that we could agree to something of a fake separation… No, hear me out on this, Harald. We can announce to the media that the two of you have separated, they'll lose interest in her, Frederica will be happy, *I'll* be happy, and you can continue as you were."

"I think that would work, sir," Harald said slowly. "I'll want to discuss it with Sonja first—"

"Your Majesty? And Your Royal Highness." A young secretary opened the office door and nodded to both Olav and Harald. The King turned to him with annoyance. He had been quite specific with the staff that he had a very important matter to discuss with the Crown Prince and wanted no interruptions, but before he could speak, the young man did. "Sir, Her Royal Highness is ill. She's asking to see you, sir."

"Ill?" The floor seemed to be dissolving beneath him. This was not, Olav knew instinctively, a headache or a mild cold. "What's wrong with her?"

"Rheumatic fever again, sir. She fell ill around ten this morning, sir."

Olav nodded. "Thank you." He left immediately for Astrid's apartments.

He had become intimately familiar with the symptoms of rheumatic fever over the past year and a half since Astrid had first contracted the disease. It occurred when the immune system responded to an initial infection of strep throat by attacking the heart and various joints, and recurrences were common. There would be swelling in the heart which brought stabbing pains in her chest, difficulty breathing, and the ever-present risk of cardiac failure. This always resulted in further scarring of her heart, leaving Astrid weak and delicate even after the illness had run its course. Inflammation would move every several hours between the larger joints, causing her intense pain, and her temperature would rarely drop below one hundred, often climbing several degrees higher. She was usually ill for weeks at a time, suffering for days on end before there was even the slightest sign of a gradual recovery.

And, much to Olav's frustration, there was little that could be done for her.

He walked quickly down the stairs to Astrid's ground-floor apartments, meeting Johan Ferner in the hall outside. Johan's eyes were to the floor, and he took no notice of the King.

"Johan?"

He looked up at Olav's voice, his face lined with worry. "Your Majesty." He bowed.

"Were you here to—did you know Astrid was ill?" Olav asked, ignoring the unsettling feeling that he seemed to have been among the last to know.

"Yes, sir, and I stopped briefly to see how she was. I'm on my way out—I didn't go in; I only knocked and spoke to the lady-in-waiting."

"How is she?"

Johan paused. "I think she's really awfully sick, sir. She's in terrible pain—it's her knee right now—and she's...it's hard for her to breathe."

Olav's hope that she would not be stricken so badly this time sank. Wordlessly, he shook Johan's hand.

Astrid's darkened bedroom was bathed in the dim light given off by a single lamp on her dressing table, and everything was cast in shadows. One of her young ladies-in-waiting was seated in a chair next to the bed where Astrid was lying, shivering in spite of the heavy blankets. She was propped up against several pillows and laboring for each breath. Kirstine stood, dropped a discreet curtsy, and backed away as Astrid stretched a hand out toward him.

"Pappa," she whispered.

He moved to sit on the edge of her bed.

<hr />

The flashes of a few cameras had gone off on Sonja's way home, and the store had been besieged by phone calls all day, but her main concern was her grief over Harald. She had known this day would come, but she had not expected it so soon, and she had come to like him far more than she had ever intended.

She was immensely grateful for a peaceful dinner with her mother, but she jumped when the phone rang. Did the press have her home number? Dagny raised her eyebrows and went to answer it. "Oh, Harald!" Sonja heard her say after a moment. "Yes, she'd love to talk to you!"

She was at her mother's side instantly, taking the phone from her.

"Sonja?"

"Harald?" The sound of his voice on the phone was an immense relief after the stress of the day, but she was reminded of her dread that this was to be the end of any sort of relationship.

"Are you all right? How are you?"

Frazzled. Dazed. Upset. "I'm...a bit overwhelmed."

"I'm sure," he said sympathetically. "There have probably been photographers and reporters swarming all over today."

"It's completely out of control."

"Which I'm sure you're not happy about. And my father—he isn't happy about the press attention you're getting either."

The King. She swallowed.

"I know we've been proceeding with the understanding that we couldn't—continue—in the public eye. But Sonja, I *like* you very much, and I think it would be possible for us to continue seeing each other, provided we're discreet."

Continue seeing each other? Her heart leapt at the phrase, but reality halted her excitement. "But everyone already knows—"

"The Palace is going to leak the news in the next few days that we've broken up…if that's all right with you."

"Yes! Of course it's all right." Happiness spread through her for the first time that day. "May I ask you something, Harald? Is the King…what does he think of this? Does he mind that you're seeing me?"

"He's furious. He demanded that I break things off with you, and I refused. There was a certain amount of shouting involved—he's very much used to having his way," he said calmly.

"You fought with the King? For me?" She knew she cared deeply for him, far more deeply than she had ever meant to, but the thought that the Crown Prince had equally strong feelings for a seamstress was a surprise. The realist inside of her had often suspected that he was merely marking time with her. Perhaps there *was* something more there…

"Of course." He sounded somewhat taken aback, as though it would not have occurred to him to do otherwise.

"Thank you," she said softly.

Harald stepped quietly into Astrid's bedroom that evening, hoping to find her asleep. She was nothing near it and was lying curled up on her side, her face drawn and her eyes glassy with fever.

The lady-in-waiting and nurse seated next to her bed rose when he entered and came over to him, dropping a quick curtsy. "Your Royal Highness."

"How is she?" he whispered.

"Not very well, sir," Kirstine said. "The inflammation's in her right wrist, and she says her legs feel like they're breaking."

Harald sighed. "And her heart?"

"Less chest pain than there was earlier today, and she's breathing a bit easier. We gave her the shots earlier this afternoon."

He glanced at Astrid, noting the bruises already growing on her uncovered arms from the penicillin injections. They would do nothing for her symptoms but would kill the bacteria, allowing for her eventual recovery.

"She's slept off and on," Kirstine continued. "His Majesty was up here for a couple hours, and Mr. Ferner stopped by and spoke to her for awhile."

"I thought the King said Johan Ferner had come but hadn't actually seen Astrid?" he asked, catching Kirstine's slip.

"Yes, well…" She trailed off, her manner uncharacteristically flustered.

"Hajan?" he heard Astrid call, her voice thin, and his thoughts returned to his sister.

"Thank you, Kirstine." He nodded to her, and she curtsied again as he went to take a seat in the chair. "How are you feeling?" he asked Astrid, brushing his hand through her hair.

She sighed. "Everything hurts." She was holding her right arm stiffly against her body, her wrist red and swollen to twice its normal size.

He held back, wanting to lay a hand on her shoulder but afraid of causing her further pain with his touch. "Can I get you anything?"

She shook her head. "How did things…" she paused for breath "…end up with Father?"

"Everything's fine—Sonja and I can keep seeing each other as long as we keep out of the papers."

"So Father's all…right with it?"

"That's a strong word." He smiled and went on to tell her his agreement with the King, falling silent as her eyes closed for longer and longer intervals until she was asleep.

Harald would spend many hours sitting with Astrid in the coming weeks, reading to her, talking with her, and attempting, as she recovered, to take her mind off the pain. She was most interested, he discovered, in the situation with Sonja, almost to the point of encouraging the relationship.

"Do you really not—disapprove—in the slightest?" he asked. His sister was obsessively duty-conscious, insisting upon performing every engagement in spite of her health. Suggestions that something be cancelled if she weren't feeling well were met with her objection that their mother had pushed on when she had been even sicker.

"No. Why should I?"

"You're always very serious about your duty—"

"Yes, but…I think perhaps it might be much harder to do one's duty in matters of the heart." She paused. "I don't think any of this is so odd, really—that Ragnhild married for love, that you're thinking of marrying for love—"

He had tried very hard not to let himself think of a marriage with Sonja Haraldsen. "I'm not thi—"

"Yes, you are," she said with certainty. "And it's odd among the Royal Houses of Europe, but I don't think it's strange at all for the three of us. Mamma and Father were a love match—an acceptable, royal love match, but a love match nonetheless. We grew up watching them and knowing that they loved each other very much. We all thought that was what marriage meant. It's perfectly natural that Ragnhild wanted that, and you want it, and—if I were ever going to marry—it's what I would want," she said softly. It was, Harald and much of the Norwegian public often thought, one of the many tragedies of Astrid's life that there was such a scarcity of available royal men her age. At nearly twenty-eight, she was beginning to be considered an old maid unlikely ever to marry. "I don't know why Father thinks you're crazy—you learned this at home."

She was, he realized with sudden certainty, absolutely right. He was unwilling to agree to a loveless marriage because he had seen something so much better in his parents, and, although he would not admit it, he thought he had a chance at an equally happy marriage with Sonja Haraldsen.

There was a knock at the door.

"Yes?" Kirstine, who was seated on one of the couches, called out.

"It's Johan!"

"Come in…the Crown Prince is here."

Johan stepped hesitantly into the bedroom, one hand behind his back. "Hello, Harald, Astrid. How are you feeling?"

She gave him a small smile. "Not much better, honestly."

He stepped closer to the bed, giving Kirstine, if not Harald and Astrid, a better view of his back.

"Oh, you brought—" she exclaimed, then broke off, clearly troubled at what she'd said. Johan froze as Harald and Astrid eyed him curiously.

"Yes," he said after an eternity, drawing a bouquet from behind his back. "For the Princess." He looked awkwardly at Astrid and then back at Kirstine, the tension palpable. Harald couldn't fathom why Johan's arrival with a bunch of flowers should cause such stress—the room was filled with the hundreds Astrid had already received from relatives across Europe and half the citizens of Oslo.

Unless, Harald realized suddenly, the flowers weren't for Astrid at all.

"Here," Kirstine said after a moment. She appeared even more flustered than she had been over Johan's first visit two weeks ago. "I'll take them and—um—find a vase." Without once making eye contact with Johan, she took the flowers and strode out of the room.

Chapter Seven

INTEREST IN SONJA DIED WHEN "ANONYMOUS SOURCES IN THE PALACE" leaked the news that she and Harald were no longer a couple, and the weeks before Christmas passed quietly. They continued to see each other discreetly, Harald and Sophie continued to correspond (although Harald had to acknowledge that her letters were both more frequent and more detailed than his), and Sonja spent the month contemplating the need to find a suitable gift for Harald. It was no easy task, she had realized with trepidation—he had the money to buy anything, and she could think of little that he could possibly still desire. She eventually settled on something she could make herself and spent weeks knitting a complex scarf pattern, working to ensure that it was absolutely perfect.

He had invited her to dinner on December 22 in his apartments at the Palace. He would also, he said, like to introduce her to his sister, who was improving but still confined to bed, provided Astrid felt well enough for visitors. Sonja was, she had to admit, more excited about seeing the inside of the building that had never been open to the public than she was about the coming holiday.

She dressed for the occasion—she knew she would likely see no one but Harald and perhaps Astrid, but it was still *dinner at the Royal Palace*, and she chose a dress she had made for a Christmas party last year. Made of red velvet with off-the-shoulder short sleeves and a sweetheart neckline, the waist flared out into a bouncy, full skirt that stopped just past her knees.

A few minutes after six, she slipped into the car Harald had sent for her and was whisked through the streets of Oslo. It had been dark for three hours already, but the city was brilliantly lit with strings of festive white lights, decorated trees, and busy store fronts, and the sidewalks teemed with crowds of last-minute shoppers.

The Palace stood quietly at the city center, floodlit and set back from the main road. There was a two-story Christmas tree overtaking the front balcony, glowing with its own set of lights. She was driven through the gates, around to the back, and straight into the entrance hall of brick, pink stone, and shiny stucco marble columns. Steps led up into the Palace on either side, and Harald was waiting on the right.

"*God Jul,*"[3] he said as he opened her car door.

"*God Jul.*" She stepped out and stood on her toes to kiss him, then passed him the shiny red package as her stomach fluttered. Should she have gotten him something at all? Was this the right choice? Could she possibly hope to please the Crown Prince, a man who surely had everything he could ever want?

"Thank you." He smiled, taking her fur coat and passing it to a waiting footman. "Come on in. My apartments are in the south wing."

He led her into a long, white, carpeted corridor with a few historical paintings and busts. The scent of pine wafted through the Palace, and all the doors were lined with greenery studded with little white lights. She tried to stare into each room as they walked past and saw very little of the first besides red walls, but the yellow room across from it had a long, official-looking table—

"That's the Council Chamber," Harald said when he saw her peering inside. "My father meets the State Council there every Friday."

He led her down the hall and into the next room, and she could not hold back an audible gasp. "Harald, it's beautiful." It was a white parlor with walls decorated in gold leaf and barely-pink panels; a ceiling painted ornately in light, feminine colors; red gilded chairs; and two chandeliers fanned out in the shape of bells. The two gold and white posts were wrapped in pine and white lights. There were double doors on the left side, one of them open, and she peeked into an even grander parlor, its walls partially upholstered in rich red fabric. There was a long mirror between its two floor-to-ceiling windows, and the chandeliers of the red room, white room, and Council Chamber were all reflected in a breathtaking line of bright crystal.

"That's the parlor of the guest suite for state visits," she heard him say, "and we use this room on state visits as well as for official meetings and presentations— but it was originally an audience chamber for the Queen in the 1840s."

"It's so beautiful," she repeated. She could hardly take in the grandeur around her and knew in some distant part of herself that she must be gawking like a complete fool, but she didn't care.

"Sonja," he said gently as she studied the chandeliers, "my apartments are this way."

---

3   Merry Christmas

"Oh, yes," she said quickly, blushing, but she saw that he was still smiling. He led her across the white parlor, into another hallway, and finally into a small sitting room. It was about half the size of the official rooms she had just seen, but its furnishings were equally fine and its chandelier, although on a more miniature scale, was still incredible. The walls were a deep shade of yellow accented with more gold leaf, and there was a beautifully decorated Christmas tree in the center. The chandelier was dimmed, and the only other light came from the candles on the tree and the many set up around the room. There was a small table with two gilded chairs next to the tree.

"I thought we'd have dinner here—it's so much more intimate than the dining room upstairs."

She nodded with a small smile. "It's wonderfully romantic."

He removed a package from under the tree and offered her a seat on one of the couches, which she moved toward hesitantly, suddenly realizing how difficult it would be for her to sit on the furniture. Her hand hovering over the gilded armrest, she stared at the red upholstery.

Harald sat and then looked at her strangely when she did not join him. "Here, sit down."

"I…" Everything in the Palace seemed to scream *Do Not Touch.*

"Sonja," he said, laughter in his voice, "this is my apartment. You're allowed to sit on the furniture."

Rather shakily—to his credit, she never heard him laugh out loud—she lowered her body onto the couch, but remained perched on the edge of it, too uncomfortable to relax.

"Good enough for now," he said, and she giggled. "But if you ever decide to make yourself comfortable, you're free to do so." Slowly, she scooted back further onto the couch, and he passed her the package. "Here, open your present first."

Reminded of her worries about his present and wishing he would just open it, she tore off the paper and opened the white box inside. It held a gold necklace with a dangling chain of three rubies surrounded by diamonds.

"Oh, Harald, it's beautiful," she gasped. She ran a reverent finger down the side of the jewels then smiled up at him, touching his hand. "Thank you." It caught the candlelight as she lifted it out of its box, the diamonds shimmering, and she stared at it, enchanted. "Would you…?" She passed him the necklace and turned away from him, lifting her hair. He fastened the chain, the familiar thrill running through her as his fingers brushed her skin, and the rubies dropped down to rest above her red velvet dress.

She kissed him, lingering. "Oh—but you haven't opened yours!" she exclaimed, pulling back as she suddenly remembered.

It was not enough, surely, she thought as he began to tear the paper, especially in light of how expensive the necklace must have been. Yet she had known all along that cost alone would be unlikely to impress the heir to the throne.

"I made it myself," she said when he opened the box.

For a long moment he said nothing, lifting the scarf and not looking at her. He did not like it, she was sure.

At last he spoke. "My mother," he said softly, "was an excellent seamstress. She sewed nearly all of my sisters' and my clothes when we were children, knitted every scarf and hat we wore in the winters, and was making things for us for most of our lives."

Had she managed to strike the perfect note? He finally looked at her, smiling broadly now, and reached out to embrace her.

They had a dinner of lamb next to his tree, talking over this year's plans and sharing stories of past Christmases as the smell of pine drifted through the room. They spoke quietly, the whole evening feeling hushed—there had been a layer of snow on the ground for weeks now, and another four inches had arrived yesterday. All of Oslo seemed quietly settled in for winter.

Sonja glanced down at the necklace more than once, noting its sparkle in the soft light. "It's beautiful," she said softly when she looked up to see him watching her.

"Mostly because you're the one wearing it." She blushed and reached across the table to take his hand.

Dessert was sweet, cold rice pudding—which she would never be able to eat without a deluge of warm childhood memories—and he mentioned as they finished that he could take her to meet his sister that evening.

"The thing about Astrid," he said, "is that she's almost *embarrassed* about being sick, or at least embarrassed that people know she's sick, or think of her as sick. Of course, the whole country knows there's something wrong—and she's very troubled about that—and everyone who knows her knows, and she hates that, too. I think she worries that people will see her as sickly first, and that will be the most memorable thing about her. So she's not exactly ecstatic that you're going to be meeting her for the first time and forming your first impression while she's recovering from having been sick."

"I don't mind waiting for another day, if she'd rather—"

"No, she decided that today was fine, because she's been wanting to meet you for months and hasn't had the chance, and she gets awfully bored because she has to lie in bed for weeks on end, even after she starts feeling better, so she wants to see someone new. But there's been a good deal of wrangling over how this was all going to occur. I couldn't take you any earlier, because it was unacceptable for you to see her lying in bed in the middle of the afternoon or evening, but she decided if we came around nine then it was slightly more logical for her to be in bed, and she looked less sick doing so then than she would at five or six, which I didn't think really made that much sense, but I'm trying to humor her.

"I've also been instructed that I'm supposed to make sure your central impression of her *isn't* that she's sick, but I wasn't given any details on how to do that, other than that I just wasn't supposed to say anything about her being sick. I guess she thinks you'll just think it's her habit to receive all her visitors in her nightgown without getting out of bed."

"Why don't you tell me something else about her?" Sonja said, laughing at the picture of their relationship that was emerging as they left Harald's apartments for Astrid's on the other end of the Palace.

"She's very sweet and very pleasant, with a tendency to be very *direct*, she thinks I'm irritating and still need looking after, she's very determined about everything in life, she's obsessed with sailing, she does quite a bit with ceramics and she's really very good, she reads constantly and she studied at Oxford despite being seriously dyslexic—which, by the way, you're not supposed to know; my father treats it like a state secret—and she's something of a romantic, but she'll be twenty-eight in February with no marriage prospects, and I've never seen her interested in anything besides friendship from a man." He thought for a minute. "I think that pretty much sums it up."

"You sound like you like her very much," she said, and he smiled. "I'm glad I can meet her, but I'll admit I'm terribly nervous." They were passing back through the white parlor, and everything around her was a reminder of who she was—or rather who Harald and his family were.

"Why? It's only my sister."

"She's royalty, Harald."

"I'm royalty. I don't make you nervous."

"That's different. I know you."

"You didn't at the beginning."

"Yes, and you had to ask me three times before I could manage to tell you my name."

"Well," he said, smiling, "Astrid already knows your name, so you won't have that hurdle."

"Princess Astrid was always my favorite, you know," she said as they walked back down the long central corridor.

"Favorite what?"

"Favorite member of the Royal Family."

He gave her a hurt look and then grinned. "I thought *I* was your favorite member of the Royal Family."

"Not when I was a little girl—you're a boy. I used to dress up and pretend to *be* Princess Astrid. My mother makes this wonderful *kringla*,[4] and when I was young my friends and I felt it needed a name." She laughed. "We agreed to name it after Astrid because we all thought she was so wonderful, and my family's called it the Princess Astrid Kringla ever since. We always have it for birthdays in my family."

She paused. "What exactly is wrong with her? That is, I know she has rheumatic fever, but I know that can be vastly different depending on the person…"

Harald sighed. "She first got sick two summers ago, and she's never been completely well since, but every once in awhile she has acute recurrences of the disease—which is what she's recovering from right now. The most serious part of it is that the heart swells, which is terribly painful at the time and can make it hard for her to breathe—and sometimes it's *very* hard, and it's frightening to watch but must be even more terrifying to experience—but the worst is that it always leaves some scarring behind on the heart, so there's permanent damage even once she's recovered." He spoke very quickly, nearly seeming to be out of breath himself. His pace matched his speech, and she felt she was half-running to keep up with his long strides as they crossed through the covered entryway and into the north side of the Palace.

"That's the most dangerous thing, but she suffers much more from the swelling in her joints when she's sick. It lasts a few hours in one place, and then it moves somewhere else. It's very dramatic, and it's horribly painful for her. It's much worse for her than for most rheumatic fever patients because she's allergic to all the pain medication that's usually given. Generally the inflammation lasts a couple weeks before it's completely gone, but she's always left in some pain afterwards." He paused and lowered his voice. "The most horrible thing is… this is all my father's fault. At least, *I* think so—I've never heard *Astrid* say that, and I've never seen the slightest resentment on her part; she's far too sweet for that, but I think it's pretty clear."

"Your father's fault?" She raised her eyebrows. "Why do you say that?"

---

4   pastry

"It started when she, as First Lady, was on his consecration tour with him—they were visiting all the coastal cities by boat. She woke up on the day they were going to Stavanger not feeling well—her fingers were swollen and stiff, and her legs were hurting. She blamed it on all the waving and handshaking and all the standing and walking in heels. She showed Father her hands and told him she felt strange, so he sent her to see the ship's doctor. The doctor took one look at her and said she was in the early stages of rheumatic fever and needed to lie down and rest for the next couple weeks. My father told him she couldn't do that—they had all sorts of engagements lined up in Stavanger, and they were in the middle of the consecration tour, and she simply had to go on. So Astrid did as he said. She got much worse from being up and about that day—she collapsed at the lunch reception, but she went on. The doctor was appalled when she got back to the ship—he went on and on about how she likely wouldn't have gotten so much worse if he'd been able to treat her right away, and now there wasn't nearly as much he could do, and so on. When she got back to Oslo, she was really very sick. The royal doctors here were horrified at the whole story. They told my father quite bluntly that all the walking around at the beginning had increased the heart damage that would result and had permanently damaged her legs, which is why she's been in so much pain since. If she'd been able to lie down right at the beginning and been given the proper medication right away, she might have recovered very quickly with no lasting effects, and she probably wouldn't have had so many, if any, relapses."

"And your father knows all this?" Sonja asked, horrified at the whole story. "He must feel terribly guilty."

"I don't know. That is, he *knows* all this, but I don't know if he feels guilty or not. I think he does. I *hope* he does." There was an awkward pause. "Anyway," he said with forced brightness, "she really is looking forward to meeting you. Do me the favor of not asking her how she's feeling or anything of the sort, or she'll think you're thinking of her as sickly, and I'll have to hear about it later."

They had come down a white corridor identical to the hall in the other side of the Palace, and a few moments ago Harald had stopped outside a pair of tall white doors edged in gold. He knocked now, and a soft voice called out, "Come in."

They stepped inside, and Sonja struggled to hold back a gasp. She did not know what she had expected a princess's bedroom to look like, but she was completely unprepared for its size alone. Her own room would have fit inside

Astrid's three or four times, and it seemed to double as a sitting room, with an array of fluffy couches and chairs covered in silk pillows and surrounding fine wood tables. Two floor-to-ceiling windows—and it was a *very* high ceiling—were draped in rich navy blue curtains, and a vast marble fireplace stood between them, a small fire crackling inside. In the center of the room hung an ornate crystal chandelier—a bit smaller than those Sonja had seen in the reception rooms for state visits, but still far bigger than anything she had seen anywhere else.

Princess Astrid herself was ensconced in a nest of pillows and half-sitting up in her bed, a four-post monstrosity with a vast silk canopy draped above the headboard. The seamstress in Sonja was dying to examine its fabric. Astrid was stroking a huge black dog—it looked more like a sheep in its size and its texture—that was curled up on the bed next to her.

"Lillebror." She looked up at Harald and Sonja's entrance and managed a small smile.

Sweet, Sonja thought, noticing that Harald did not seem to object to the address.

"Evening." Disregarding the available chair, he took a seat on the side of her bed, and Astrid closed her eyes as he laid a hand on her forehead. "Do you feel like meeting Sonja?"

"Oh, of course, of course." She looked at Sonja, who had hung back in the doorway, and struggled to sit up further, wincing at the movement, until Harald reached over to raise her himself, rolling his eyes at Sonja. "I take it you're she?"

"Yes, Your Royal Highness." Sonja curtsied and stepped closer, prompting a growl from the animal.

"Shh." Astrid patted its head. "You're the one the press worked themselves into a frenzy over last month?"

"Yes, ma'am."

"The one who has my father hanging from the ceiling?"

"I suppose so, ma'am." What was this, some sort of interrogation?

"There's no 'suppose' about it, Miss Haraldsen. He is *most* annoyed about all this." Sonja forced herself not to flinch. "Yet you've both disregarded that and continued on." She paused. "I like that—I think it shows strength of character."

Sonja blinked. Had she just been complimented? She began to relax.

"So you actually want to date my brother?"

"Yes, ma'am."

"Do you think you can fix him? He needs it."

Still nervous, she gave the first and most accommodating response that came to mind. "I'll do my best, ma'am."

Astrid laughed as Sonja felt her face grow warm, but she glanced at Harald and saw a broad smile on his own face. She realized that it was likely one of the only times his sister had laughed at all in recent weeks.

"I like her, Harald," Astrid said decidedly. "I thought I would. But don't just stand there; sit down, sit down," she said to Sonja, gesturing toward the empty chair next to her bed.

They sat and talked easily, Sonja's initial trepidation forgotten, as Astrid admired the rubies—before confessing that she herself had helped choose them—introduced the dog, and started telling stories of Harald's childhood. Sonja was struck again and again by Harald's attention to her—Astrid had only to shift uncomfortably or wrap her arms closer around her, and he was adjusting her pillows or covering her with another blanket. Despite her attempts to guard her heart, Sonja could not help but fall even further in love with his gentleness.

They did not stay more than half an hour, with Harald worried about tiring Astrid. On their way back through the hall and out of her apartments, they met a tall blond man in his early thirties with a rough, weathered appearance. Harald introduced him as Johan Ferner, the Olympic medalist who often sailed with Astrid.

He had an air of excitement about him, and his eyes danced when he spoke to Sonja. "Ah, the famous Sonja Haraldsen! And I thought the Palace had stated that you were no longer seeing His Royal Highness! Practically denied your existence! I am shocked, Harald, *shocked* to find you in this woman's company."

Harald laughed. "You know you can only believe half the official story at the most."

Johan smiled. "Isn't *that* the truth."

"What's the little box?" Harald asked. Sonja had noticed the small velvet box in Johan's hand as well; he had been nervously turning it over and over in his fingers.

"Oh, this? It's…a ring." He grinned and lowered his voice. "I'm planning to propose to my girlfriend very soon, and…I felt the ring needed a woman's approval. I thought I'd show it to Astrid and ask her what she thought. Although if Miss Haraldsen would give her opinion as well, I would certainly appreciate it. It's very simple—but I've had a few hints that that's what she likes." Johan flipped the box open to reveal a thick, shining gold band with softly rounded edges.

"It's gorgeous," Sonja said softly, studying it. "I think it's very elegant, mostly because it *is* so simple. The lady in question should like it very much."

"Excellent." Johan snapped it shut and slipped it into his coat pocket. "A *god Jul* to you both."

"Do you know who he's marrying?" Sonja asked Harald as they left.

He laughed. "Absolutely—I overheard him proposing and asking what sort of ring she'd like last summer! It's one of Astrid's ladies-in-waiting. But he wasn't going to admit it to us—for some reason it's a secret that there's anything between the two of them, and he has no idea I know anything."

She smiled. "So we're not the only ones who are secretly in love."

"Apparently not. I'm happy for Johan—he's been divorced for four or five years, and I don't think I've heard him mention a woman in all that time."

"He's divorced?" Her tone implied her shock that he was allowed to associate so closely with the Royal Family.

"Yes, and that's always made his presence at court somewhat questionable, but my father likes him, and Astrid likes him, and he's been a friend of the family since before his first marriage, so we all pretty much look the other way. He started as Astrid's sailing instructor at least ten years ago, and they still sail together—he's quite good for her, because she'll never be as capable as she was, and she hates that, but Johan manages to ignore it very well. But come on, I don't think it would kill either of us to go back for another serving of the rice pudding."

And, of course, the kisses that they both knew would follow it, she thought with a smile.

Chapter Eight

New Year's Eve found the King hosting a small dinner party to ring in 1960 with the closest friends of the Royal Family. Astrid was well enough to attend, provided she were carried upstairs and back down to her apartments again by Harald. Sonja, however, had been left off the guest list, the King responding to Harald's request with nothing more than a cold stare.

Johan Ferner arrived first and joined Olav, Harald, and Astrid for a glass of champagne in the Mirror Salon, where the party would be held. It was an ornate, sea-green, mirror-filled, and gold-leaf-covered reception room furnished and decorated by Harald's grandmother Maud. The four of them took seats on a set of silk chairs and a couch clustered next to Maud's old piano.

As Johan reached out to take the flute Harald had just filled with the sparkling bubbles, a plain gold band glinted on his third finger. An engagement ring—in Norway, it was customary for both men and women to wear left hand rings from the engagement on and switch them to the right hand during the wedding ceremony.

"Are you engaged, Johan?" Olav asked.

Johan hesitated. "I…yes. Yes, I am engaged."

"To whom?" Olav asked.

Johan paused. "My fiancée and I are trying to be discreet…for her family's sake. But I believe you know her, sir."

The King smiled. "Well, let us congratulate you."

"Thank you, sir."

"Yes, congratulations," Harald echoed.

"A toast, then," said the King, raising his glass. "To Johan and his future happiness in marriage." Olav, Harald, and Astrid took a sip of champagne, and Johan acknowledged the toast with a smile and a nod.

"And to Johan's bride, and the happiness of the couple," Harald added. He and his father drank while Astrid, he noticed, merely held her glass to her lips but did not open them, swallowing none of the liquid. She said nothing, absentmindedly fingering the chain of her necklace—Harald knew it held a locket of their mother's which Astrid always wore beneath her clothing.

"Are you all right?" Harald asked her a moment later when Olav and Johan were engaged in conversation.

"I'm fine," she murmured, setting the flute down on the small gold and glass table in front of them. "Only—I didn't think I ought to have been drinking so much so soon after having been ill."

They were interrupted shortly thereafter by the announcement of the arrivals of more of the guests. The four of them stood, and Harald moved to help his sister to the dining room.

There was something odd, he thought as she leaned against him, in her behavior during the toasts, and he was not ready to believe that it was due to the alcohol. She had, after all, not drunk very much. Had the mention of Johan's impending wedding troubled her, he wondered? She had always liked Kirstine, hadn't she? Was she worried at the thought of losing the close friendship that had developed between her and Johan and seeing less of him if he were to marry? Harald watched her carefully during dinner and observed nothing else unusual.

His curiosity faded as the party adjourned back into the Mirror Salon after the meal. It was, as always, an ideal place for a party, with its many mirrors reflecting the scene to make the room look even bigger and fuller than it already was. A small circle of female friends gathered around Astrid on one of the couches, while Harald found that his own friends were insufficient distraction to keep his mind off Sonja, who was spending the evening with her family. He would rather have been in the Haraldsen sitting room, and the rich furnishings and décor of the Palace were suddenly cheap and tawdry in comparison with the view he would have had of Sonja's eyes. Was she thinking of him now? They had promised to think of each other at midnight…

"I think your sister's tiring," he heard Johan say suddenly. He glanced over at Astrid, who was resting her head in her left hand propped up on the gold arm of the couch and who had grown unusually quiet in the midst of the girls around her.

"She is, thank you. I hadn't been watching. I'll see if she'll let me take her down."

She agreed immediately, and he scooped her up in his arms amidst a flurry of good-nights and well-wishes, painfully aware of how much weight she had lost in the last month.

"Astrid," he began as they started down the grand staircase, "I was wondering— about earlier tonight…" Ought he to even mention it? He did not wish to bring something upsetting to mind again when she was already so weak.

"Hmm?" she responded, laying her head on his shoulder.

He plunged in. "Are you upset about Johan's engagement?"

She hesitated, her voice puzzled. "Why would you think that?"

"The toast…"

"I thought I'd had too much of the champagne," she said, sounding irritated. "I told you that."

"Yes, but—I wondered if you were upset at the thought that you might not see as much of him once he marries."

She began to laugh, half hysterically, and he took it as a sign that she was more exhausted than he had thought. "No," she said at last. "No, not at all. I'm very happy about Johan's engagement—I'm sure he and his wife will be very happy together."

⌒

"I feel like a cow," Astrid said in mid-March as she and Harald settled into the back of the car that would drive them to the Norwegian embassy for the night. They had spent the evening at a party held at the Stockholm Palace by the Swedish Princess Sybilla, mother of the teenage Crown Prince and his four older sisters. Every unmarried royal between fifteen and thirty seemed to have been invited, with the intention of "letting the young people get to know one another," but it was clear to all involved that the ball had been meant as a thinly-veiled marriage market.

Harald laughed. "No, seriously," she went on. "I do feel like a cow. Just because there's music and dancing doesn't disguise the fact that we're all supposed to be looking each other over like livestock."

"You're not a cow, Astrid," he said, keeping a straight face. "You're a political bargaining chip."

"Yes, well, I feel much better about that." She smiled, and then her voice took on a bossy, older sisterly tone. "But for the record, I think you could have handled this evening better and paid a bit more attention to Sophie instead of avoiding her the whole time."

"I wasn't avoid—"

"Yes, you were. And you don't want to be—it would have made Father happy to hear you'd danced with Sophie several times tonight, and if you keep Father happy you'll have a much better chance of getting what you want."

"What I want?" He wasn't sure what that was himself.

"You know, marrying Sonja."

"I don't want to marry Sonja," he objected and was disconcerted to feel the uneasiness he otherwise associated with telling a lie.

"Really?" Astrid raised an eyebrow.

"I'm keeping an open mind about a match with Sophie." That was true, wasn't it? He tried to convince himself.

"An open mind," Astrid said, a hint of disbelief in her tone. "Right."

I don't want to marry Sonja. I'm keeping an open mind about a match with Sophie. I don't want to marry Sonja. His words to Astrid rang in his head the next day as they left Stockholm for Oslo, repeating themselves again and again when he was alone in his apartments that night. There was a sense deep within him that knew these were both lies—he knew it in every inch of his body, knew it without thought, knew it as easily and as readily as he knew when he was hungry or thirsty. And yet the thinking part of him fought to convince him of the truth of both statements, in a desperate struggle to keep his world in order. Because if he did wish to marry Sonja Haraldsen…where did that leave him?

He could not marry her. And, he attempted to remind himself, he had no wish to do so. He would go down to Greece later this year and make himself fall for Sophie. There were no other options, and he had no long-term interest in Sonja anyway…

Yes, he did. Every walk in the mountains, every evening spent with her in his arms, every conversation they had shared in the past months flooded back to him. He stood and went to the window, staring out into the darkness covering the royal gardens behind the Palace. The temperature, he knew, was below freezing, and there was a light layer of snow on the ground. Not a night on which he would usually have gone out, but perhaps the cold air would clear his mind.

The gardens were empty, and he was disturbed only by the sound of his own footsteps. He felt the cold seeping into him as he walked, leaving little room in his thoughts for anything beyond the simple fact of temperature. Yet there was a light to the left, he realized, off in the direction of the summer house, the old enclosed gazebo where he and his sisters had often played as children. Odd—why would it be lit at this hour? It wasn't usually, was it? Was that even what it was? Yes, it was partly obscured by trees, but the lit building was certainly the summer house, he realized as he walked closer.

And…was there someone inside? Surely no one else would be out here in the cold, but…squinting slightly as he walked, he glimpsed a dark figure in the center of the octagon. This part of the park was closed to the public in the winter, and the rest of the grounds closed at sunset—how would anyone have gotten in past the heavy gates? And wait…there were *two* figures, not one, standing quite close to each other.

He began to walk more quickly, curious to know who else was in the gardens so late, soon coming to the break in the path that led up to the summer house. He had a clear view here with no tree trunks, allowing him to see that one of the figures was…was it perhaps Johan Ferner? He thought so. Johan, or whoever it was, was standing with his back to Harald and blocking the other person from his sight.

Wanting to be sure, he started up the path, which curved slightly to expose the other side of the summer house and slightly more of Johan…who, Harald could now see as he crept closer, was kissing whomever he was with—a woman who was still too shadowy and obscured for her identity to be clear. But, Harald knew, it had to be Kirstine.

It all made perfect sense. Given the hour, the location, and the temperature, the couple had a virtual guarantee of privacy.

Suddenly, the woman's head moved slightly as she and Johan kissed, and the light from the old lamp in the rafters above shone on her face.

Chapter Nine

It was unmistakably *NOT* Kirstine but Astrid herself, wrapped tightly in the arms of Johan Ferner. Her own arms had entwined themselves around his neck, and there was not a centimeter of space between the two of them.

Astrid, the innocent darling of the Oslo papers. Astrid, the perfect daughter and obedient second child. Astrid, the sweet, motherly sibling who had never once crossed either of their parents. *Astrid, slipping out into the gardens at night for romantic trysts with a divorced man.* Harald moved closer to the summer house, as though expecting that a better view would reveal a different identity for the young woman in front of him. As stunned as he was to find Astrid here, and to find Johan holding her, he was most of all shocked by the fervor with which she kissed him, as though she had gone days without a drink and his lips were a source of life-giving water encountered in the midst of a desert.

Astrid, engaged to Johan Ferner. As unlikely as it seemed, the more Harald turned over the events of the last months in his mind, the more obvious it became. Her behavior during the toasts at New Year's was suddenly clear—she would not have been able to drink a toast to herself. And then there was how very solicitous Johan had been toward Astrid...and the comments she had made to Harald... How natural that Johan would want to be there when she was ill, and how little it had ever had to do with Kirstine...and how easy it was to see the "proposal" he had overheard last summer in a different light... In the space of a few seconds, everything turned over in his memory, his world flipping over only to right itself again with a different meaning for so much.

Eventually, Astrid drew back and spoke to Johan. He laughed and kissed her again, and she laid her head on his chest, an action that resulted in her looking straight in Harald's direction. He realized with a sudden panic that he was now near enough that she might be able to see him. Not daring to move and attract her attention, he stood completely still.

Astrid squinted when her eyes fell on Harald as though unsure of what or whom she was seeing. Slowly, she lifted her head and stepped out of Johan's arms. Johan followed her gaze, the couple glanced back at each other, and she dashed out the door on the other side of the gazebo, Johan behind her.

"Harald!" she called as she rushed over to him. "You mustn't tell Father," she said, her breath coming in short white puffs in the cold air. "Please, Hajan, you *know* how it *is*…"

Tell Father? He had not been entertaining anything of the sort. All he could consider at the moment were the hundreds of questions cascading over one another in his mind—how long had this been going on? How on earth did they intend to ever be able to marry? Surely they knew they would never receive permission?

"Please, Harald," she went on, apparently not sure how to take his silence. "Don't say anything. Surely you can understand…" She was shivering without her coat, and somewhere in the back of his mind he knew she ought to be inside.

"I—no, no, I won't, I wouldn't," he managed to say. "But Astrid, what… since when…"

"Oh, I don't know…it's complicated…" She looked back to Johan and smiled. "Three or four years ago—"

"Astrid," Johan interrupted, "perhaps it would be better for you to discuss everything back inside, where it's warm?"

"Yes, of course. Come back inside with us, Hajan—we have a small heater in the summer house. I told Johan once that I'm much worse in the winter and in cold temperatures, and since then he hasn't been satisfied unless I'm perspiring." She smiled at Johan, who smiled back.

"You could do with watching your step—I'm sure there's ice out here," Harald heard him tell her softly, his hand coming to rest against her back. She smiled again and paused on the step into the gazebo, using the slight increase in her height as an opportunity to kiss him again.

Once inside, the three of them took seats on the benches along the walls. The heater was not the only thing they had added—the benches now had cushions and the central table was covered with a blue cloth, all of which left Harald wondering how many evenings they had spent out here together. It was quite cozy inside the small wooden structure with the soft light from the lantern above, and it was quite warm after being in the wintry air, but Harald was too dazed to take in any details other than how close Johan and Astrid were sitting. Johan's arm had slipped around her waist and his other hand was resting on her knee.

"Anyway," Astrid continued, "I'd felt for a long time—ever since Johan got divorced—that there might be something between us at some point, and I thought he thought so, too. I think I knew in my heart for quite awhile that someday it would be the two of us, together. And then a couple years ago, everything just started to happen gradually, and now…" She shrugged.

"I've loved your sister for a long time, Harald." Johan somehow managed to draw Astrid even closer still, and she leaned against him as he continued. "I—I love her more than I ever thought possible. She's…I'm sure you understand."

He nodded, only vaguely hearing all this as he attempted to wrap his mind around the situation, as well as ignore the hand caressing his sister's leg. "And you're—you're *engaged*."

Astrid unfastened the clasp at the back of her neck, removing the chain that held their mother's locket…along with a gold band. She let the ring drop into her hand and held it out to Harald. He took it and examined it—it was the same ring he had seen in December—before passing it back.

"You've had it under your clothes all this time."

"Since Christmas—you know, since the day you and Sonja ran into Johan just before he proposed." She grinned. "And now we're hoping…we've been hoping I'll have an opportunity to receive Father's permission soon." She looked up at Johan and smiled, and for a moment they both seemed to forget Harald's presence as she kissed his cheek softly.

Permission? Surely they both knew better than to imagine that such a marriage would ever be allowed. With the added problem of Johan's divorce, their situation was as hopeless as his own. But…did she really believe she was on the verge of receiving the King's blessing?

"Do you really believe that's possible?" he asked, seeing a sudden glimmer of hope for him and Sonja in the couple sitting across from him.

There was a heavy silence, but the answer was obvious enough. "I thought—it depends—if I asked Father again…that is, I think Father…" She trailed off, and it was clear she knew she had no reason to believe her and Johan's engagement would be met with any more enthusiasm than Ragnhild and Erling's had been. "But we *are* hoping, Harald. We thought—we've decided it doesn't do us any good not to.

"I'm determined to ask Father's permission this spring," she continued. "I'm just…I'm just going to tell him I'm planning to marry Johan and see where it goes from there. I don't want—that is, we've agreed that I can't leave Norway; I'm not abandoning my responsibilities. But I thought perhaps—*perhaps* things might be different for me…since I *am* the First Lady now, and there isn't anyone else for that position."

Yes, and mightn't things be different for him, the Crown Prince? There wasn't anyone else for that position, either. He tried to force the thought out of his head. *No.* He would *not* be allowed to marry Sonja Haraldsen.

By the spring of 1960, Sonja had given up any pretenses toward guarding herself from falling too deeply in love with the Crown Prince. She knew how much she loved him, how much she loved his shyness, the sense of fun that only appeared with those he knew well, the way he made her laugh, the protectiveness in his manner whenever they were together, how easy it was for her to be with him, how readily she could relax in his presence... It was foolish for her to pretend otherwise.

She did not, however, imagine any extended future together—the idea that he might marry her, she knew, was laughable. She was not going to be Queen of Norway. Two of her friends had mentioned it once, but when the suggestion of a marriage to the future King was spoken aloud, it sounded so ridiculous that all three of them fell into a fit of giggles and could not consider it a serious possibility in the slightest.

Harald would marry royal—if the newspapers were to be believed, it would be to Princess Sophie of Greece. Sonja did not let this trouble her. She focused only on the present and the pleasure she had in his company, knowing deep down that this would have to end soon. Things would eventually become more serious between Harald and Sophie, and Sonja had no intention of becoming his mistress.

This had been her brother's concern for months now. She could recall Haakon's coming to her shortly after Christmas and asking her what she thought "Harald's intentions might be."

"Intentions?"

"Yes. Surely you don't believe he might marry you at some point?"

Sonja had laughed. "I think I'm hardly a potential bride for the Crown Prince!"

"Then why do you think he's taken such an interest?"

She shrugged—it was not something she had much bothered to wonder about. "I guess we just like each other."

"Do you think there's a possibility that he may ask something more from you at some point?"

She did not like the direction this conversation seemed to be going. "What exactly do you mean?" she demanded.

Haakon paused. "Don't take this wrong—I don't mean to imply that he *should* see you this way; I think it's incredibly degrading if he *does*—but I think it's possible that someone of the Crown Prince's background would see someone of your background—a shopkeeper's daughter, a seamstress, a girl with no significant connections—more as mistress material than as marriage material."

Her face was flushed, both at Haakon's suggestion and at the realization that she had no hard evidence that this was *not* Harald's intention.

"I don't mean to upset you," Haakon said quickly. "I only want you to be careful. I don't want you being groomed as a royal mistress."

There was nothing improper in Harald's behavior in the coming months, and she had nearly shoved her brother's comments to the back of her mind until a sudden invitation in April.

"Would you like to go out to Gamlehaugen this weekend?" Harald asked her the Tuesday after Easter. The temperature was only in the low forties, but he and Sonja were sitting outside on her porch. Easter marked the beginning of spring in Norway, and they like the rest of Oslo were determined to enjoy it, even if warm coats were still required.

"Gamlehaugen?" she said sharply.

"It's the royal residence just outside of Bergen—"

"I know where it is," she interrupted. She could not remember what it looked like—had she ever even seen a photo?—but she knew Bergen was seven hours from Oslo by train or car, so this was certainly more than a one-day visit. Her fingers tightened around the cold arm of her iron garden chair.

"We could leave early Friday afternoon, then we'd have all day Saturday— the weather's supposed to be beautiful this weekend—and we could drive back on Sunday. Wouldn't it be wonderful to have a whole weekend together?" His voice was light and airy, oblivious to any distress on her part, and she was suddenly angry that he felt so sure she would say yes.

"Harald," she began, "Harald, I—it is not my intention—it has *never* been my intention—"

"Nor is it mine," he said firmly. "I'm sorry; I should have made that clear. I meant only that I would show you the estate—I think you'll like it very much—and we could have a couple days together where we didn't have to worry about hiding. We would, of course, have separate rooms, and that would be very clear to the staff."

"Oh," she said. She was suddenly warm with embarrassment in spite of the chill.

"Sonja, I would not ask that of you." She felt her face grow even pinker at the warmth in his voice. "I do not see you," he continued, "as a plaything to be used by rich men and then cast aside when she's no longer wanted. You are worth far more than that—you are the girl I love—and I am just as concerned—perhaps even *more* concerned—about your honor, your reputation, and your name as I am about my own."

"You did understand," he began, "that is, it *is* all right with you—we'll be staying overnight for two nights, but in separate rooms?" He had picked her up at home at noon on Friday and was now walking toward his car with her. She had no visible bag or suitcase.

"Yes, of course."

"But...you don't have anything." She looked puzzled. "Clothes for this weekend. Anything else you might need. Your suitcase, Sonja."

"Oh!" Her eyes widened with the realization. "Yes—it's inside—in my room—I'll be right back." She darted back up the front walk and into the house, returning a few minutes later with a small black suitcase. "Sorry."

Who in the world attempted to leave town without a suitcase?

"You're laughing at me, aren't you?" she said, starting to giggle herself as he took it from her and set it in the backseat.

Sonja gasped as they drove through the castle gates shortly before eight. Seated on a hill overlooking the suburbs of Bergen, Gamlehaugen appeared to have leapt straight out of a fairy tale. A large white mansion with red-trimmed windows and a tower at one end, it looked more like a petite sixteenth-century French chateau than a nineteenth-century Norwegian palace. It was the most wonderfully romantic building she had ever seen.

Harald smiled. "Do you like it?"

"I think it's *beautiful*," she said, "absolutely gorgeous. I love it!" She paused, slipping into the fantasy of a young girl. "Can I sleep in the tower?"

"There aren't any bedrooms there—it's just a bunch of hard-to-heat, sparsely furnished sitting rooms that tend to be pretty drafty. Sorry to ruin that for you."

The butler ushered them inside and took their suitcases, and Harald led her through the entry hall and into the castle's main room. Intensely Norwegian in its décor, it was vastly different from the exterior. Viking dragon heads had been carved into the chairs and the walls, and the staircase was lined with carvings of scenes from Norse mythology. Everything—the floor, the partially-papered walls, the furniture, the staircase, the balcony wrapping around at the second floor level—was of dark wood, and the comfortably-padded benches and chairs looked positively medieval in their design. There was a large gray stone fireplace with a polar bear skin stretched out in front of it as a rug, and three moose heads smiled down at her from the walls. Plates and cups—designs from all over Norway, she could tell—were arranged all along the chair rail, and the upstairs walls were covered in paintings that she was dying to have a closer look at.

"I love it," she breathed. "It's so…"

"Norwegian?" he offered.

"Yes." She laughed. "That and *hygge*," she said, referring to the Scandinavian concept of perfect coziness. The whole room was an explicit invitation to curl up with a cup of hot chocolate. "Is that an old spinning wheel?" she asked, zeroing in on a spoked circle attached to a piece of wooden machinery tucked next to the stairs.

"I think so…you probably know more about it than I do—you're the seamstress."

She was already moving to examine it more closely. "1870 at least, I'd say…I'm not sure which region…can I touch it?"

"Of course." He smiled. "It's a home, Sonja. You can touch anything you like."

She was still running her fingers over it, fascinated by the antique mechanism, when the butler returned to announce that dinner was ready.

They were served reindeer in a grand, turn-of-the-century blue dining room, eating off historic china while sitting in ornately carved, throne-like chairs, the chandelier giving a warm glow to the gold curtains covering the massive windows. Afterwards he offered to show her the music parlor, where Edvard Grieg, the Norwegian composer and pianist who had written the music to *Peer Gynt*, had often played for the building's original owner, Christian Michelsen, one of Norway's prime ministers.

It was a dark green room with a beautiful grand piano—she had always wished for musical talent—as well as a small player piano. "Michelsen couldn't play at all," Harald said, sitting down at the player piano. "So he bought this for when he didn't have Grieg or other musicians around, and he recorded Grieg's playing." He turned a little knob, and delicate music filled the room as a small cylinder turned inside.

But it was the paintings in the room that held her attention, and she stared at the scenes of a Viking court, the old medieval harbor in Bergen, sun shining through a tree— "This one's remarkable," she said. "It's a very difficult technique, showing the light through the leaves like that. It's probably an Italian painting?"

She discovered that, having little interest in art himself, he knew little about the castle's paintings, but he hung on her every word as she talked on and on about what she could guess of their history.

It was nearly midnight when they climbed the staircase to their rooms. She had been looking forward to seeing hers for days, and she was not disappointed. Like the rest of Gamlehaugen, it was filled with last century's antiques, an array of fine furniture and lamps and vases and oil paintings. There was a small chandelier, a huge armoire, curtains of wonderfully rich silk…she sank down onto the bed, which could have comfortably fit at least five people. The mattress was amazingly, wonderfully soft, she discovered as she stretched out—it felt like lying on a cloud. But she did not lie there for long—a small wood door on the outside wall had caught her eye. Did she have a balcony? She got up to open it and found that she did—a covered balcony with a view over the surrounding park.

She gasped when she opened the door to the bathroom—her bedroom at home would have easily fit inside. It was complete with its own chandelier, a small sofa, a padded bench in front of an ornate gilded mirror, gold-plated faucets and handles…and the biggest, deepest bathtub she had ever seen.

Somewhat dazed, she returned to the bedroom, laughing at the sight of her own suitcase in the midst of such luxury. A shopkeeper's daughter was spending the night *here*. As she stooped to pick it up she remembered something.

The key.

To prevent the latch's tendency to spring open at an accidental touch, she had locked it when she'd finished packing last night and left the key lying on her chest when she'd walked out that afternoon. She fingered the lock for a few minutes, then picked at it with a pin she removed from her hair.

⌒

"Do you think you could break into my suitcase?" Sonja said immediately when Harald answered the knock on his door.

"Break into your suitcase?"

"It's locked, and I left the key at home."

"Where you tried to leave the suitcase itself."

She grinned. "Yes."

It was not an impossible task, but it was something of a hassle, as a small knife had to be found and worked into the keyhole correctly, all while she repeatedly apologized and he struggled not to burst out laughing. He had never met anyone quite like her.

"You think it's funny, don't you?" she demanded when he could no longer hold his smile back, starting to laugh herself.

"Relatively. There," he said as the lock gave way, "it's open. Are you going to be this much trouble every time I take you somewhere?"

"Probably," she said, kissing him good night.

The beautiful weather forecast Harald had heard aside, it rained all day Saturday—to no one's surprise, as Bergen was known for its near-constant rain. Harald and Sonja stood out on her balcony, alone in a small pocket of dryness as the rain beat down on the little roof over their heads.

The chilly air had not yet given way to spring, but Sonja was warm enough—the castle blocked most of the wind, and she was comfortably wrapped in his arms, her head resting on his chest.

He bent down to kiss her, and she stood up on her toes, her lips playing lightly against his for a moment before he straightened and she sank back down, laughing at the impossibility of a prolonged kiss while standing.

"Should I find you a stool or a box to stand on?" he said teasingly.

"I'm five-foot-three! That's not so short."

"Right." He nodded immediately, and she giggled again. They both knew, whatever her protests to the contrary, she wasn't an inch over five foot.

"Whatever you are, you're awfully cute." He bent and kissed her again.

In truth she did not mind the fifteen inches' difference in their heights, she thought as she laid her head against his chest. She rather liked the feeling of being safely enveloped in the arms of a giant, of having his hand overwhelm hers, of the restrained strength she could feel when he gently embraced her. And he had told her, too, that he found something charming in her miniature size and how delicately she fit into his arms.

Sonja took a deep breath and sighed, smelling the fresh scent of the rain in the air and feeling the soft touch of his fingers slowly running through her hair.

She spent Monday replaying the weekend. Most of her work in the store was bookkeeping and alterations, but occasionally she designed dresses exclusively for certain customers, and she spent Monday morning out shopping for new fabric. Spreading the new purchases out in her office brought Harald to mind again—nearly everything brought Harald to mind. What she had always loved about loose yards of material was the potential she could feel in it, the threads quivering with possibilities as she touched them. Their relationship was brimming with potential, too, she believed, and, although the realist in her suspected it could never last, she could not help but feel that it was leading somewhere wonderful. She toyed with unspoken and impossible dreams of marrying him just as she always imagined the hundreds of dresses that could take shape from new fabric. As she began to make the first stitches, steadily feeding the material into the machine, she felt the soft-but-insistent tug against her fingers as it pulled the fabric further along. The same sort of pull she felt in her heart.

Her involvement with Harald, however, was unnerving in a way that sewing never would be. Chief among her pleasures in the latter was the control and power it gave her to determine everything about a dress and to alter anything she chose. Love, on the other hand, could not be directed. Perhaps, she thought as she fingered the blue silk in her hands, that was what made it so thrilling.

Chapter Ten

"Sophie," Frederica instructed, "tell Harald about the plans for the ball next month."

Sophie blushed and managed a brief glance to her right at Harald. "It's for my sister's eighteenth birthday."

"You've been very involved, haven't you?" the Queen continued, with a pointed look at her daughter.

"Yes." Sophie self-consciously tucked a strand of brown hair behind her ear and smiled at Harald, then dropped her eyes again.

Harald sighed inwardly. He had arrived at Tatoi Palace in Athens on a May afternoon for a long weekend and was now dining with the Greek Royal Family—King Pavlos and Queen Frederica, Sophie, and Sophie's two younger siblings, Constantine and Irene. Sophie's shyness in his presence had led to one of the most awkward dinners he could recall ever enduring, a problem compounded by her mother's constant efforts to get her to speak.

"We're holding it at Corfu," Irene told him after it was clear that Sophie was not going to say anything further. "We'll all spend the day down by the beach and then have the coming-out ball in the evening." She paused, and a gleam came into her dark eyes. "Sophie and I will be having our dresses made sometime soon; we're just not sure about the seamstress yet. Do you know any good ones, Harald?"

The Queen laughed insincerely. "Of course Harald doesn't know anything about that sort of thing!" She raised her eyebrows at Irene in a look that clearly said *behave*. "Anyway, Harald, Sophie was just telling me the other day how much she wishes you weren't going to be in England then so that you would be able to join us for the occasion. Weren't you, Sophie?"

"Yes," Sophie answered softly, keeping her eyes lowered demurely. "But I was thinking that perhaps it's even nicer to have you here this weekend when everything isn't so busy."

The longest string of words she had uttered over the course of the whole meal, Harald thought. He took another bite of his lamb—far spicier than the dish he was used to back home. Sophie, along with her mother and sister, was a strict vegetarian and was not eating any, leaving him wondering how she would feel about the reindeer, moose, and elk that were such staples in Norwegian cuisine.

There was a silence, and Frederica opened her mouth to jump in again when King Pavlos spoke. "You have a visit planned to England next month, Harald?"

"Yes, the first state visit from Norway to Britain in years. We haven't seen that branch of the family in awhile, and we're looking forward to it."

"Philip and Lilibet are good people," Pavlos said.

"She's a sweet girl," Frederica added.

Pavlos nodded. "We haven't seen them in several years, either. Our last trip abroad was in March—the United States."

"Yes," said Frederica, seizing on another opportunity to press Sophie for conversation. "We had a lovely visit. Sophie, tell Harald about President and Mrs. Eisenhower."

The rest of the meal passed in equal awkwardness, and the family adjourned to the sitting room after a dessert of Greek walnut cake. Harald had not yet taken a seat when the Queen exclaimed, "Sophie! Weren't you wanting to ask Harald...?"

"Oh!" Sophie blushed for the hundredth time that evening. "Yes. Harald, I was wondering..." Her cheeks grew pinker, and she paused, her voice dropping to just above a whisper. "I was wondering if you would like to go out for a walk in the gardens."

It sounded like the sort of romantic situation he had been so hoping to avoid, but he very much wanted to escape her mother. "Of course."

She smiled, her blue eyes sparkling. "Oh, you would? I'll go up to my room and get a shawl; I'll just be a moment." She started out the door, only to be detained by Frederica. The two began arguing in heated whispers. Harald did not speak German, but he had learned enough basic vocabulary to determine that the source of the disagreement had something to do with Sophie's shoes.

Not envying her the argument with Frederica, he sat down on the couch next to Irene. "You're getting the best girl in royal Europe," she said, her eyes turning to black ice as she looked at Harald. "I hope you know that."

He did, after all his father's lectures. Sophie, it seemed, was the most valuable bride in any of the royal houses, thanks to the training she had received from the single-minded Frederica, her sense of decorum and duty, her grace and elegance, and the maternal character that Olav believed would lead her to raise responsible heirs.

"I think your sister's wonderful," he said, hoping she would abandon the subject.

"Do you?" She seemed to stare right through him. "Then I hope you treat her well. She's very much in love with you, you know."

In love with him? Sophie could not possibly be in love with him.

She returned shortly, a white shawl wrapped around her arms and still wearing the high heels dyed to match her light blue dress that her mother had somehow found objectionable.

"Sophie, the ground's rather uneven; you ought not to wear—" Frederica attempted.

"It's fine." She smiled at Harald. "I'm ready."

It was a beautiful evening warm with the coming summer—it was already hotter in Greece in May than it would be in Norway in July—and the gardens of Tatoi had an exotic, wild air to them that was entirely different from the Norwegian Palace's staid park. The further they walked, the more forested and overgrown the grounds became, with their snaking ivy, half-crumbling stone fountains, and towering trees. He and Sophie wandered down twisting dirt paths through a still world that carried the ancient atmosphere so pervasive in Greece. The ground was as uneven as Frederica had promised—it was immediately evident to him why she had objected to her daughter's shoes— and he stepped carefully over stones and tree roots multiple times.

"It's so wonderful to have you down here," Sophie was saying. "And we'll have all day tomorrow and all day Sunday to be together." She smiled up at him. "I don't mean to be forward, but I must admit I'm terribly excited—I've been waiting my whole life for all this."

It was no secret to him, or to anyone in royal Europe, that Sophie's mother had spent the last two decades readying Sophie for courtship and marriage to the most advantageous husband available. Yet it struck him how odd it was that someone who had dedicated twenty years to preparing to be his wife could seem so ill-suited to the role, while Sonja Haraldsen…No, he mustn't think of her now.

A weekend here would not be so awful, he told himself. He had, after all, agreed to come not only to please his father, but also because, as he had told himself repeatedly, he was at least *open* to the idea of a match with Sophie of Greece. Surely the two of them would find more to talk about and have more of a connection if they *were* married; it was just at the beginning that there was this initial awkwardness.

The next few days would be not only bearable but actually pleasant—he and Sophie had planned to go down to the coast and spend tomorrow and Sunday sailing, the one interest they both shared. It would give them a more relaxed environment in which to be together, and it would also eliminate the pressure he felt to make conversation.

Suddenly, Sophie stumbled over a fallen branch, going halfway to the ground in the split second it took him to tighten his grip on her arm to break her fall.

"Are you all right?"

"I—let me sit down for a moment," she said. He released her arm, and she sank down onto the stone path, her hand on her right ankle.

"Are you all right?" He knelt down next to her.

There was no response for a moment, and then she opened her eyes. "It's my ankle, but I think I'm all right. We—I think we can go on." She smiled weakly. "I'm okay."

Not if the look on her face at first had been any indication. "Are you sure? Let me see it." She lifted her hand, and he touched the outside of her ankle, drawing a sharp gasp of pain from her.

"Sophie…" She looked up at him. "You shouldn't be walking all over on this. We'll go back to the Palace." She nodded.

"Can you walk?" They had come quite a long way, but she nodded again. He stood then helped her up.

She managed two tentative steps, leaning on his arm, then stopped. "Harald…"

"Here, this is ridiculous; I can carry you." Sophie did not protest but slipped her arms around his neck as he lifted her. This was, he realized as he carried her back up to Tatoi in the growing twilight, a far more romantic situation than he had ever intended to find himself in on this visit, but what choice did he have in the matter? What was more, they would surely not be able to go out sailing in the morning, and he would be forced to spend the next two days sitting in the Palace, where he would be expected to talk with Sophie and where he would have to deal with Frederica's oppressive presence. If only Sophie hadn't insisted on wearing those shoes…

Once they returned to the Palace, there was a flurry of activity as they were met by Frederica and Irene (both of whom, Harald suspected, had been watching from a window), Sophie was made comfortable on the couch, ice was sent for, and the Queen pointedly reminded her daughter that she "ought not to have gone out there in those heels." Harald took a seat across the room, calculating how many hours he had left in Greece, as Sophie's mother and sister fussed over her.

"I suppose this means you and Harald won't be going out tomorrow," he heard Frederica say. She looked nearly as depressed at the recent turn of events as he felt.

"Oh," Sophie murmured, leaning back against the pillows. "I hadn't thought of that…but perhaps I'll feel better in the morning…if I could just get down to the shore I think I'd be able to do it…"

No, she wouldn't be, Harald thought with a sigh. She couldn't walk, but she thought she could help him man a sailboat?

"It's all right," he said. "We don't have to go; we can just stay here tomorrow."

Sophie blushed. "Harald, I hate for you to just have to sit inside all day…"

He hated it more than she did but doubted there was any other option. "No, I don't mind," he forced himself to say.

She lowered her eyes and smiled softly. "Thank you. It…it will be nice having you sitting here with me tomorrow."

He soon retired to his own rooms, hoping desperately for an overnight miracle but resigning himself to a weekend spent inside in awkward conversation. As he lay awake that night, he could not help but think how very different his feelings would be if it were Sonja at whose side he would be spending the day.

After breakfast Harald dragged himself back upstairs to join Sophie in her sitting room. She was stretched out on a couch, accompanied by Irene, her ankle propped up on some pillows and looking worse than it had yesterday, which killed any small grain of hope he might have had that she would have improved enough to go out.

"Good morning." He gave her the obligatory kiss on the cheek and then hesitated. He was here to see Sophie. Surely etiquette did not require him to kiss her sister as well? He did not *want* to kiss Irene—with her small dark eyes, currently narrowed suspiciously, and the general coolness of her personality in his presence, he could not help but think of a lizard. He merely nodded to her before turning back to Sophie. "How's your ankle?"

She smiled up at him. "It's a bit worse this morning, but I'm all right. Here, sit down." He moved toward a chair across the room as Irene had already taken the one nearest the couch. "Oh, you can sit here if you want to—baby, would you mind…?" Irene moved, and he was forced to take the seat next to Sophie, who gave him another shy smile.

Irene's presence, he soon learned, was a blessing in disguise, and he was left more often than not as the silent observer of conversations between the two sisters. It was a role that suited him perfectly fine, and he found himself almost thankful to Irene for keeping him from being forced to interact with Sophie.

"Baby," Sophie said suddenly to her sister, "would you go downstairs and get some more ice for me?" *Irene was going to leave him alone up here…*

"Oh, are you hurting? Yes, of course I'll get you some; I'll be right back…"

She can't be gone long, he told himself as she left. "Are you all right?" he asked Sophie.

"I'm fine." She blushed and lowered her eyes. "I just thought it would be nice to have some time alone together. Irene'll be gone at least twenty minutes. She gets distracted."

At least twenty minutes? Alone with Sophie? "Um, all right, then."

They spent an awkward half hour discussing each family's upcoming state visits—Sophie's English, it was evident, was nowhere near as good as his own, and the slight language barrier only made matters more difficult. He would have been happy enough to sit in silence, but he felt that she expected conversation from him. He also felt a certain obligation to at least attempt to talk to her if he were to keep up any pretense of having an "open mind" about a marriage. Eventually, an apologetic Irene wandered back in to rescue him. They were called for lunch shortly thereafter, and he helped Sophie downstairs, her close proximity as she leaned against him leaving him more uncomfortable than he had already been.

After lunch, Frederica drew Irene away to go over the seating charts for next month's dinner, and Harald was once again left alone with Sophie. The drawn-out silences and the pressure he felt for speech made every minute nothing less than agony. And his father wanted him to marry this woman. *He was expected to marry Sophie.* Sophie, with whom he could barely manage an afternoon of conversation. *Perhaps,* he told himself frantically, *it will be different once you're married.* Married. Married to Sophie. A wave of panic swept over him at the thought, and he felt a sudden urge to run. He did not think he could bear to sit here at her side a moment longer.

It would be different, he argued silently, *if you had gone out sailing together. It would have been fun, you would have enjoyed each other's company...* But he knew he had no reason to believe they would be any better suited for one another on a boat than they were on dry land. He could not imagine spending the next fifty years in Sophie's presence. It would not be, he realized with sudden certainty, anything like his parents' marriage. And that was what he wanted, wasn't it? The quiet, easy companionship they'd shared, the warmth in the way they looked at each other, the love their children had been so aware of... He could not imagine having any of that with Sophie, but with Sonja...

"I need to talk to you." The urgency in Harald's voice made Sonja disentangle herself from his arms and step back to look up at him. He had returned from Athens that afternoon and arrived at her house just a moment ago.

"Won't we be talking at dinner?" There was a strange intensity to his blue eyes, and she was slightly unnerved.

"No—I'd rather do it now...privately."

"My mother isn't home," she said, understanding him and leading him into the next room. Her stomach fluttered—she had known that he might have to leave her eventually for someone more suitable and had tried to protect herself by refusing to fall too deeply in love with him. Yet she had failed, and now...was tonight the night?

Harald took a seat on the couch, and Sonja delayed the conversation by crossing the room to fiddle with a lamp, though there was still plenty of light streaming through the open window. She lingered by the old stone hearth, conscious of the room's simplicity.

"Come sit down," he said after a moment. "Everything's all right.

"I was in Greece this weekend with Sophie," he went on as she took a seat. Sonja braced herself. "At one time, I thought I could marry someone I wasn't in love with. But that was before I met you. Everything's changed now, because I know exactly what my father was feeling thirty-five years ago when he met my mother. I know now what it is to love, and now that I've imagined spending the next fifty-odd years with you I can't even think of being married to anyone else." He paused. "I want the marriage my parents had, and...Sonja, you're the girl I want to marry."

"I—I—" Had he just proposed to her? She had never given marriage to him a single thought, but... She was suddenly sure, more sure than she had ever been of anything in her life. "I want to marry you, too, Harald. Very much."

He nodded. "But before you say yes—I want to be clear to you about what being my wife would mean. You would be giving up anything vaguely resembling a private life. You would be spending the rest of your life in a fishbowl—the publicity you had last winter after that article came out was nothing in comparison to how it would be—and you would be raising our children in the public eye as well. Your life would not be your own—"

"But we would be together. That's the only thing I want," she said, overwhelmed by certainty.

"It won't be right away," he said quickly. "I can't have an official engagement without the sovereign and the government's permission, and my father's very set against this—he has no idea we're even having this conversation."

She smiled. "I'm willing to wait." She was not quite twenty-three, and they had not yet been dating a full year. "I'll wait years if I have to!" She laughed, doubting it could take more than two or three before they were married. Then she paused, feeling a soft, contented happiness settle over her like a warm blanket. "Do you…really want to marry me?"

"Absolutely." His eyes sparkled as he smiled. "But I haven't asked you yet." He stood up from the couch to kneel in front of her, taking her hand in his. "Sonja," he said softly, reverently, "when the King and the Storting[5] consent to the marriage, will you do me the honor of becoming my wife?"

"Yes. But it's no honor for you, Harald," she said quietly. "I'm only a common seamstress."

"You're not 'only' anything, Sonja. You're the girl I love—the only girl I am ever going to love."

She wiped the tears from her eyes and leaned forward to kiss him.

---

5   Parliament

Chapter Eleven

WHEN HARALD TOLD ASTRID THAT HE HAD PROPOSED TO SONJA AND SHE had accepted, Astrid announced that she had finally worked up the courage to ask their father for permission to marry Johan. She would speak to him, she said, next week after the *Syttende Mai*[6] celebrations, reasoning that the national day always put him in a good mood.

Harald later wished she hadn't told him this, as it turned the day into a long, agonizing wait for his sister to break the news. It was very much a public holiday in Norway, with picnics, parties, and every school in the country organizing its own children's parade led by its marching band. The parades in Oslo began at ten and combined into one long stretch of children, all waving Norwegian flags and many wearing little *bunads*,[7] which took at least three hours to pass by the Palace. The Royal Family stood on the balcony, watching and waving the entire time, then after a brief lunch, was off to visit various celebrations in the municipalities of Oslo.

She never complained, but Harald knew it was always exhausting for Astrid, especially with all the standing required. He thus thought it was perhaps not the best time for her to broach the subject of her engagement. Yet he soon realized that perhaps it was in her best interests to approach Olav when he had spent the day watching her ignore her fatigue and her pain. The King, watching her shift her weight from leg to leg, did often suggest she take breaks during the parade, but her response was always that she felt that *Syttende Mai* was the most important time for the Royal Family to function as a symbol of Norway, and she certainly wasn't going to miss any of it. Besides, she sometimes pointed out, surely all the little girls passing by below would be disappointed to be greeted *only* by the King and Crown Prince and not by a princess.

This year, Harald suspected the paleness in her complexion had far more to do with nerves than illness or exhaustion, and Astrid spent most of the

---

6   May 17, commemoration of the signing of the Norwegian constitution

7   Norwegian national dress

day toying distractedly with the chain around her neck that held Johan's ring. When the three of them returned to the Palace late that evening, she stepped briefly away before dinner, returning, Harald noticed, with the gold band glinting on her finger.

"Father," she began as they all sat down in the dining room, "do you remember several years ago when I asked you whether it would ever be possible for me to marry Johan Ferner?"

Harald raised his eyebrows at her, surprised, but she did not acknowledge him.

The King nodded. "I was thinking of that at New Year's when he announced his engagement—I was glad we wouldn't ever have to have that argument, and from your own composure I was assured that you no longer felt anything for him, if you ever had."

"You misunderstood. Johan is engaged *to me.*" Astrid lifted her hand and held it out to her father across the table. "Since Christmas. Look."

King Olav merely stared. "Astrid, I—surely you're not—I don't—that is, Johan...this...I thought you were nothing more than good friends; I took your earlier question to be nothing more than a momentary fancy—"

"We were only friends for years, and there really was nothing between us when I asked originally, but—I thought then that there might be someday, and—now everything's changed somehow." Astrid paused but went on when neither Harald nor Olav interrupted her. "I don't know how it happened, or *when* it happened; we just fell in love, without even realizing it, and then slowly we reached a point where we couldn't stand to be apart. It's...it's the most wonderful thing that's ever happened to me. And then last December— when I was recovering—he was sitting with me one evening, and he asked me to marry him. It was such a beautifully sweet proposal, Father."

Harald could imagine that it had been, but, if his horrified expression were any indication, the King was not the least bit interested in hearing the romantic details. His Majesty said nothing for a moment, staring long and hard at his daughter.

"Astrid," Olav said slowly, "I don't think this is a very good idea."

For a moment no one spoke, as though his words could not fully crush Astrid's hopes until she responded.

"Please," she whispered. "It would make us so happy."

"You know I like Johan Ferner very much," Olav went on, "as did your mother, and I think him on the whole a decent man, but he's *divorced.* That makes this all—simply unthinkable."

"I know," she said quietly.

"You know very well the position of the Lutheran Church of Norway on the remarriage of divorcés. Surely you don't expect that as the Head of the Church I'm going to approve any such thing for my *own daughter*! And think of the public reaction. Did you happen to notice how appalled the British were several years ago when their Margaret wanted to marry a divorcé? It was always your grandfather's worst fear that you and your sister could turn into the embarrassment Margaret's always been to her family, and now you—"

"I'm nothing like Margaret! Have you seen me staying out all night and ending up with my picture in the paper stumbling out of every nightclub in London at four in the morning?"

"You're about to drag the House of Glücksburg through the same divorce scandal she dragged the Windsors through. And I must say that the issue of his divorce gives me great reason to doubt Johan's character—"

"You know very little of Johan if you can raise that objection—I've known him since I was sixteen, and I've seen nothing but infinite kindness in him! He was my best friend for years before we fell in love, and I think he even handled his divorce as best as one could in such a situation. His ex-wife has gone on and remarried; it was all a youthful mistake. Will you judge everything about him from that? Can you not take as *greater* reference to his character his treatment of *me* and how faithfully he's taken care of me for the past two years?"

"Astrid, if you're so hungry to marry—I hadn't realized you were; you've never given any indication—then perhaps we could look for someone of one of the old noble families or a prince in one of the minor German houses—"

"I don't just want to *marry*; I want to marry *Johan*. That's what you don't *understand*—Harald and I don't think of marriage as a diplomatic *game*, Father, and I would have no interest in it if that were all it was. I don't want to be the political bargaining chip that my great-grandmothers were; I want to marry a man to whom I can give not only my body but also my heart.

"And you know where I got this idea? You and Mamma. We all knew growing up that you loved each other very much, and we thought, when we were children, that all marriages were like that. Is it any surprise to you that I want to make sure mine is?"

The King sighed and tried a different tactic. "It would not be impossible to find you a *royal* love match. *And* a love match with a man who hasn't already been married.

"Even without the divorce issue, this is still a *far* worse match than your sister and Erling. Erling came from one of the old shipping families.[8] As for

***

8   Wealthy elite of Oslo

Johan—well, his family owns a store. They're merchants. Very solidly *middle class*." It was not, Harald knew, intended as a compliment.

"So he's not good enough for me," she said, the spark of a challenge coming into her eyes. "That's what you mean, isn't it? Johan's not good enough for me?"

"What I mean, Astrid, is that you're quite pretty, and your devotion to royal duty makes you an excellent catch for any Prince looking to marry," Olav demurred. "And if you *were* to marry common, then I think you perhaps...might do better than a middle class husband of questionable morals."

"Do *better*? Do better than the man I *love*? Do better than the man who's—"

Olav held up his hand for silence. "It is not that I doubt that you love him, or that I don't understand the worth of a love match. But Astrid, I simply *cannot* understand—I know he's a likable man, I know you're friends—but I cannot understand what could *possibly* have led you to develop such feelings for *Johan Ferner*, of all men! Why on earth do you *want* to marry him?"

"Well," she began after a pause, "I suppose it's first of all that I've never been so happy in my life than when I'm with him, I've never laughed so hard with anyone, I've never felt so comfortable with anyone. On top of that...I think he's the most loyal man in the world.

"Two years ago...I absolutely went through hell. And Johan went through it with me. It's horrible to be so sick so young, and it can't be much easier to be young and dating someone who's so sick. We went from racing in sailing regattas together to him helping me regain enough strength to walk five feet! It had to be terribly difficult for him to watch it all.

"Nobody would have blamed him if he'd left—we weren't engaged; he hadn't made any sort of commitment to me. So many other men would have been gone right away; they wouldn't have been able to handle it. They wouldn't have even wanted to try.

"But Johan didn't ever seem to even think of leaving me, and he's been with me the whole awful way. He's spent countless hours at my bedside, he never even blinks at spending weeks cooped up inside with me—which I know can't be easy for such an athletic man; it isn't easy for *me*—he's eternally patient with helping me up steps and carrying things for me and bringing me what I need, he's always ready to listen and he's so understanding, he never lets me feel like I'm in this alone, and—" she blushed— "he kisses me just as passionately when I haven't been able to get out of bed and shower for a week as he does when I'm made up for a state dinner."

She paused. "He says he wants to take care of me for the rest of my life, and I absolutely believe him. And I just feel so...*safe* in his arms, and so protected, like nothing's ever going to hurt again. He says I matter more to him than anything else in the world."

Harald thought he heard a slight emphasis on the word *he*, and if the irritation on the King's face were any indication, he had heard it, too.

But Astrid went on. "On top of that, it matters so much to me that he knew Mamma—long before there was anything between us beyond friendship, long before even his first marriage. She liked him very much, and he liked her, and I can talk to him about her, and it actually means something to him because he remembers her, too. I think she'd be very happy to know we were in love and very happy to see us marry. I don't think I could marry someone who hadn't known her, and who she hadn't liked." There was a distinct amount of emotion in her voice, and Harald tried to ignore her words to prevent its sweeping over him, too.

"She wouldn't be."

"She wouldn't be what?" Astrid asked.

"She wouldn't be at all happy to see you in love with him and marrying him, now that he's divorced. Your mother would be appalled."

She flinched as though he'd slapped her.

"Don't say that to her!" Harald snapped, suddenly furious.

"It's the truth, and she knows it," Olav said, his voice hard. "Not that it matters what your mother would have thought, Astrid—you yourself should be able to think well enough what it would do to the monarchy. To bring this up on *Syttende Mai*, of all days! Don't Norway and its monarchy mean anything to you?"

A new fire blazed in Astrid's piercing blue eyes. "You know very well how much it means to me!" she snapped. "I don't drag myself all over on representation duties and stand for hours on end at receptions because I think it's *good* for me—rather the opposite, in fact! And you know very well how I got so sick—the least you could do is allow me the happiness of marrying the man I love!"

There was a very heavy, very painful, and very long silence. Harald was glancing back and forth between his sister and his father, fervently wishing he were somewhere else. Astrid's gaze was fixed intently on Olav, and she barely even seemed to blink.

Olav's face was unresponsive at first, as though it took a moment for him to realize what had just been said. His face slowly began to redden, his mouth thinned to the point of almost disappearing, and there was a visible tension in his body. Then the redness drained from his face, leaving a stark and intimidating whiteness behind. Astrid did not look away.

"That issue," he said at last, in a dangerously low voice, "is completely irrelevant to this conversation."

"Please," she began again, "don't you remember what it's like to be in love?"

Olav's eyes only grew harder. "Astrid, I'm absolutely *forbidding* this marriage, and that's my final decision."

"*Pappa…*"

"*No.*"

"You don't *understand*." Her voice was thick as her tears began to spill over. "Johan looks at me like you used to look—to look at Mamma." She rose and hurried from the dining room before her father had a chance to answer her.

Chapter Twelve

FOLLOWING ASTRID'S DEPARTURE, THERE WAS AN AWKWARD SILENCE through the first half of dinner.

"Johan Ferner's a good man," Harald finally said as he pushed the last of his whale meat around on his plate. "And he certainly loves Astrid very much." He paused, but the King did not respond. He knew he ought not to press further but did it anyway. "I don't approve of divorce, and I would rather her husband had never been married before, but I think she's quite right in what she said. I think the fact that he's stayed with her so long when she's been so sick and is willing to marry her in spite of her health when he knows that he'll be taking care of her for the rest of his life…I think that says more, or at least as much, about his character as his divorce does."

Olav still did not respond, and Harald took it as his cue to say nothing further. His father did not speak until the dishes were cleared away and he gave Harald the brief, stern direction to, "Go downstairs and check on your sister."

"She's in the other room," said Johan Ferner, whom Astrid had evidently called over, as he let Harald into her apartments. "I made her lie down—this isn't at all good for her heart—but I doubt it's doing much good; she's too upset." There was a harshness in his voice that Harald had never heard before.

"He said no," she said to Johan through her tears as they both stepped into the sitting room where she was stretched out on the couch. "He said *absolutely not*, and I know he meant it." The last word was accompanied by a small sob, and Harald had the sense she had repeated this many times in the last half hour.

"After everything you've done for the Royal House," Johan muttered. "It's just ridiculous. Completely indecent. Tyrannical, I would say," he went on, raising his voice as he stormed about the room. "Does he think he has a right to forbid you to be happy? To forbid *us* to be happy?"

"I *tried*, Johan, really I did," Astrid sobbed, "but he *won't* listen. He said he won't have me turning into Margaret Windsor—"

"Margaret Windsor? The Queen of England's sister?" Johan's tone was incredulous but quickly shifted to rage. There was a sudden wildness in his whole figure that suggested he might pick up the nearest lamp and hurl it across the room in a complete transformation from the quiet, calm man Harald had always known him to be. "He compared you to *her?* The one who's out every night embarrassing herself in the papers, the one who wouldn't know responsibility if it bit her? That's an *insult*, Astrid, and I won't stand for it—you're worth fifty Princess Margarets."

She said something else, but her words were indistinguishable in her tears.

The harsh anger that had etched itself in Johan's face softened when he looked at Astrid. *"Min kjære,⁹"* he said, abandoning his pacing to come to her. Harald—who was beginning to feel ridiculously superfluous, and wondering if either of them would notice if he left—stepped back as Johan took a seat on the edge of the couch at Astrid's thin waist.

"He should be ashamed to make you this upset when you've been so sick," he said gruffly as he brushed her dark curls back, caressed her shoulder, and took her hand.

"I don't know how I'll ever accept it," she managed to say.

"Accept it?" Johan stared down at her.

"Yes—we agreed, didn't we? I can't leave Norway like my sister did; I have certain responsibilities, and we agreed we had to respect whatever my father said—"

"Well, you can forget about that conversation—I only agreed because I assumed you'd be able to get him to say yes. But I'm not taking no for an answer. I'm going to see your father right now and insist that he allow the marriage. Where is he tonight?"

"You won't really, will you?" Astrid sounded as shocked as Harald felt.

"I will, and I'm not letting go until he's agreed," he said savagely. "I'm demanding the engagement."

"He's the King..." Astrid began.

"I don't care if he's the King or a garden troll; he's not stopping us."

"You'll really do that?" Astrid's tears had slowed, and there was something near admiration overtaking the exhaustion in her eyes. In Harald's opinion, none of this was a particularly good idea—he would hesitate to demand anything from his father, and he would be much less willing to do so if he were Johan Ferner.

---

9   Norwegian term of endearment; my dear or my darling

"I don't see any other options," Johan said as he stood. "I'm certainly not going to just let you lie here and cry all night. Here, you can quit sniffling; I'm fixing this." He passed her a handkerchief drawn out of his coat pocket and turned to Harald. "Do you know where the King is?"

Harald led him to the other side of the first floor, Astrid following along, and Johan stepped into the library with His Majesty.

"Don't go," Astrid said, catching Harald's arm as he turned to leave.

"I'd rather not—" He was not much inclined to witness any more of this.

"No, I don't want to sit out here alone." She pulled him down next to her onto the hallway couch.

The conversation in the library was easily audible, Johan beginning with an impassioned, lengthy speech about Astrid—he had, in the years he had known her, come to value her spirit, her sense of fun, and her sweet nature, and he had believed himself lucky enough to count her among his best friends. He had always been struck by her sense of duty and her strength in the face of her mother's death and her own new role as First Lady.

He had fallen in love with her after his divorce, he said, and he could not say exactly when or how; he only knew that he could not imagine how he had ever lived without her, nor could he understand why he had not fallen for her at their first meeting ten years earlier. When he realized that she returned his feelings he had wanted nothing more than to shout from every rooftop in Oslo that he loved her, but her position had forced him to keep it all the strictest of secrets for years.

Then Astrid had fallen ill, and the depths of his feelings for her had become even clearer. Her sickness had only made him love her more as he came to see her strength of character as she recovered, bore all of the pain and all of the relapses, and tirelessly served her country.

Harald glanced at Astrid in the midst of this; her face was turning bright pink.

He could provide for her well, he promised—he had nothing near the wealth she was accustomed to, but he had a solid income and a steady job with the store his father owned. He would see that she was taken care of, would nurse her himself, and would be the happiest man in Oslo if he were able to have Astrid. He had been silent long enough, he said, and could hold his silence no longer. Eventually Johan requested her hand in marriage, was denied, and pressed His Majesty again. And again. And again. "I *insist*, sir. I *demand* that you approve our engagement. I refuse to accept a negative, sir, and I refuse to accept any delay in your permission—it isn't healthy for Astrid. I *insist*, Your Majesty." There were exclamations of disbelief from Olav, and declarations that it would not happen, and general gasps at Johan's boldness.

It went on for at least an hour, Harald growing more and more horrified at the situation and sure there could be no marriage now. Astrid, he realized, seemed to glow brighter with each passing minute as though she were thrilled at what she was hearing.

A hand slammed against a desk. "I'm marrying your daughter, sir! And I'm not going to Brazil to do it!"

Then they heard Johan's footsteps striding out of the room, and he burst out of the double doors, his face white with fury and his appearance disheveled. He bent and kissed Astrid firmly.

"We'll see what he does. I'll come by and see you in the morning."

In the days that followed, King Olav grumbled to himself that he ought to have seen this coming and put a stop to this misguided romance in its infancy. He ought to have noticed Johan's solicitous attentions toward Astrid. What was more, he had even been brought a few articles that had appeared in the Danish press, speculating about a relationship between the Princess and her sailing companion and suggesting it was deeper than casual friendship. How he had laughed at those articles! Astrid, in love with Johan? Astrid had no such feelings! He would know—this was the daughter who came to his rooms every night for a long chat over coffee! He had grinned about Danish ignorance for weeks.

He had been, he admitted to himself, a complete blockhead.

Olav decided he had very little choice but to allow a marriage between Astrid and Johan Ferner. Aside from his worry that Astrid might go ahead and marry Johan anyway, causing him to lose his only candidate for the role of First Lady if she followed Ragnhild into exile, he did not want to deny Astrid her heart's desire.

She had long been his favorite child, and they had grown even closer in the years since her mother had died. In fact, aside from his own father, she was the only person with whom he had ever been willing to discuss Märtha's death. He also recognized, and very much admired, Astrid's remarkable devotion to duty, and he appreciated the great success she had made of a role never intended for her. On top of that, he knew very well that, despite public appearances to the contrary, his daughter had been lonely and unhappy in recent years—most of her friends had married and grown busy with their home and their children, and she had no such future planned for herself. And

Astrid had been so ill and had worked so hard in spite of it…and it was an illness, he guiltily acknowledged only to himself, which had been made far worse by his own negligence.

In light of all that, he did not see how he could refuse her the marriage she wanted, even if he did fear the reaction of the Norwegian people.

Nor did he have any reasons to doubt that the marriage would be a successful one. It was a good match, he thought, given the easy friendship that had always existed between the two. And after Johan's brash display in the library, and his own memories of Johan's frequent presence when she was sick, he had no doubt of the man's feelings for his daughter.

Olav had many times observed Johan's attentions to Astrid, always choosing to ignore them at the time. He had so often seen him drape a shawl around her shoulders on cool evenings, silently offer her his arm to lean on when he walked next to her, gaze thoughtfully at her when she had recently been sick, or hover protectively, fetching and carrying for her on days when her pain was at its worst… He did not like to admit it, but it brought to mind Märtha and himself during the long years of his adored wife's illness.

For Olav did, in fact, remember what it was to be in love. He knew what it was to take his wife in his arms and feel that he was holding everything that would ever matter in the world, and he knew exactly what Astrid meant when she declared that Johan looked at her the way he himself had once looked at Märtha.

When he reflected on the matter, he felt he understood Johan and Astrid. He had known his Swedish cousin his whole life but had not fallen for her until he was eighteen, and thus he knew what it was for casual friendship to change slowly and irrevocably until one was hopelessly, unchangeably, deeply in love. In the context of a recently broken union with Sweden, Olav's father had preferred a bride of a different nationality, and thus he knew what it was to fight and to plead for approval for an engagement. And with Märtha struggling with a long string of illnesses for most of their marriage, he knew what it was to be forced to watch the woman one loved suffer.

In short, he knew exactly what Johan felt, and he had some idea what his love meant to Astrid.

And so His Majesty called in his Prime Minister for a meeting, sharing the news with Mr. Gerhardsen and reluctantly attempting, as best he could, to encourage the government's approval. "He's a good boy," he found himself saying of Johan, "and his first wife has remarried…and Astrid's twenty-eight; she's an adult, and she knows what she's doing."

A few days later, the government concluded that as Astrid, as a female, had no rights to the throne, this was a private matter—just as Ragnhild and Erling's engagement had been—and thus they had no constitutional objections. There were, of course, ministers who raised the concern of Johan's divorce, and those who complained about his commoner status. "A clothing manufacturer!" one exclaimed. "Marrying a princess! Doctors and lawyers may be expected to show him *deference*!" The Minister of Trade snidely commented that, "Ferner isn't much of a man, but I suppose that's first and foremost Astrid's problem," a remark that left her seething for days and muttering that she'd like to scratch Mr. Skaug's eyes out if she had the chance. An underwhelmed Johan attempted to calm her by dryly observing that whatever Mr. Skaug said about him, he was the one who had gotten a princess to marry him, an achievement that seemed beyond the Trade Minister's abilities.

Yet the Storting acknowledged that, with no legal grounds to prevent the marriage, the decision was in the King's hands. Unsure whether to be relieved or disappointed, Olav informed Astrid and Johan that the marriage would go forward in January 1961. However, the engagement would not be announced until they were two months away from the wedding, which he hoped would minimize the negative reaction.

The couple would remain in Norway after their marriage, and Astrid would continue in her royal duties as First Lady. The only change would be in her official title—she would legally be required to give up the title of Her Royal Highness and be known simply as Princess Astrid, Mrs. Ferner.

Olav had intended this last bit as a rebuke, or perhaps even an insult, but she seemed to take it in stride. He later overheard her excitedly telling Harald, "Isn't it wonderful? Father's even going to let me take Johan's last name and call myself Mrs. Ferner!"

Chapter Thirteen

"I WANTED YOU TO KNOW," HARALD SAID TO SONJA A FEW WEEKS LATER, "IN LIGHT of our discussion about marriage—it may very well take me a couple years, because I *do* need to have my father's permission, and I think that's very doable, but I don't think it will be easy. My only other option would be to give up my claim to the throne." They had been hiking in the hills outside Oslo and had stopped for lunch.

"Which leaves Norway without an heir," Sonja said, forgetting the beautiful view and giving him her full attention. She did *not* wish to be the cause of that. The British abdication crisis of a quarter century ago was fresh enough in her mind for her judgment of a King who would refuse his duty for love to be perfectly clear.

"Yes, and I thought I should be clear to you that I would never consider that. I would take you over the throne any day—I think I'd be far happier as your husband than as King—but this isn't about what I want, or what we want. I can't put anything else in front of my duty to Norway, regardless of whatever the cost to us might be."

"I would think vastly less of you if you did," she said. A child of the war, she had been brought up to believe that her country was more important than herself.

"Would you?"

"Yes." She smiled, liking the sense of honor she was seeing in his character. "I have always thought that men who abdicate or threaten to abdicate for such personal reasons were remarkably selfish."

He nodded. "I think abdication's a very serious matter, and I've seen the situations where it's appropriate and where it isn't."

She fell silent, looking down over the capital. For the first time, Harald's place in Norwegian history was clear to her. His grandfather had been King Haakon VII, the Danish Prince who had been elected the first King of an independent Norway after the 1905 dissolution of the union with Sweden, the man who had become a legend for his bravery during the war, and the King who had done so much to hold Norway together before and afterwards. Harald had been bounced on this man's knees as an infant.

Harald himself had spent the war years in Washington as the guest of President Roosevelt. Then, after a triumphant return in 1945, he had appeared with the rest of his family on the Palace balcony. Her Harald was part of a great line of Kings that would stretch on for centuries after him, and his ancestors, through the Danish Haakon and his British wife Maud, had ruled Denmark and England for nearly a thousand years. Harald's children—children, she realized with a shiver of awe, that she would carry in her own body if they did marry—would be part of this as well. Strangely, the full meaning of the fact that Harald was the Crown Prince of Norway had never before struck her in all the months they had been dating, but she was suddenly seeing him as the awe-inspiring piece of living history he was.

"Tell me about your family," she said suddenly, "during the war."

He gave her a surprised look. "Why? Don't you already know all those stories?"

"Yes, but it would be so different to hear them from you."

"I don't remember much of the beginning of the war," he admitted after a pause. "No more than anyone remembers when they're three years old, but it was all recounted to me often enough. You know, I'm sure, that when the Germans invaded Norway,[10] they didn't make it to Oslo as quickly as they'd hoped. My grandfather and my parents and sisters and I—along with most of the government—got on a train and left for Hamar and then Elverum."

About sixty miles north of Oslo, she knew. "Do you remember that?"

"I don't remember leaving home, but Astrid does—she was eight. She says she and Ragnhild were awakened early in the morning—before the sun was up—and were each given a small suitcase. They were told they were going on a long trip and to quickly pack the toys they wanted to take. She didn't have any idea why everybody was so tense or why there was such a hurry to be ready, and she was very upset at not being given time to say a proper goodbye to the dogs.

"I do have a few brief memories of the day—I thought it was all wonderfully fun, and maybe I was encouraged to feel that way to make it all easier. There were rockets fired in an attempt to destroy all the railways out of Oslo, and I took them for fireworks. Then we stopped briefly in Hamar before we were told to move further out to Elverum, and we had lunch on a farm. I know I enjoyed that very much, because I was allowed to pet the cows and the pigs and the chickens, and I had my own private zoo.

"We didn't stay very long in Elverum—at least, my mother and the girls and I didn't. We'd only missed the Germans by a few hours. We were still far too close, plus it was dangerous to be near my grandfather and so many

---

10   April 9, 1940

government ministers, whom Hitler wanted captured. That afternoon, my grandfather was meeting with some of the politicians at a nearby farm when they found themselves under attack by a small unit of German troops sent up from Oslo. The royal guards and the local men drove them off, but my father decided right then that his wife and children weren't staying. We had all just sat down for dinner, but Mamma, Astrid and Ragnhild, and I were rushed to the border of Sweden."

"Can you remember that?"

"No, I've had to rely on everyone else's recollections there." He smiled. "I'm told I had a tantrum in the car—it was all a bit much for a three-year-old. Astrid says that she was very concerned, not because she was afraid of the Germans, but because she was afraid we weren't going to have any dinner and she would be forced to go hungry. We ended up eating in the car, which she found very exciting as it generally wasn't allowed.

"My mother was born a Swedish Princess, of course, so I think she and my father had assumed that Sweden would welcome her and her children with open arms. However, we were stopped at the border and refused entry, and we only got in because our driver announced that he would drive straight through the gate if it weren't opened. Astrid remembers that—she says she won't ever forget the look on our mother's face. It was made clear once we arrived—we stayed with various relatives and moved around often—that we weren't at all wanted in Sweden and were considered a danger to their neutrality. The Swedes were making every effort to cooperate with the Nazis in order not to give Germany any reason to invade."

"I know," Sonja said, her mind filled with bitter recollections of the Swedish shops that had refused to sell to hungry Norwegians and Danes in the later years of the war.

"Quite a few of Mamma's extended family," he continued, "including her uncle the Swedish King, made no secret of the fact that they wanted us to return to Norway. The Nazis were calling for us to do so, so that I could be installed as King in my grandfather's absence and they could select a regent to rule for me. In fact, the Swedish King went so far as to send a telegram to my grandfather *suggesting* that he abdicate to make the process easier. My father and grandfather were *furious*. Father never forgave Uncle Gustaf. We children didn't have any sense of this, of course. We were having a very good time in Sweden, seeing family and playing with our Swedish grandparents, and we were looking forward to a summer there.

"My father and grandfather had been left in Elverum, and the Germans sent an envoy to meet with Bestepappa[11] the next day to demand that he approve a new Nazi government with Quisling at the head. You know what happened then." She nodded, and he continued. "Bestepappa went to the State Council members who had come to Elverum with him and told them the decision was theirs. He stressed, however, that he could never accept Quisling's government, and if the Council decided to do so, he would be forced to abdicate for himself and his descendants."

"One abdicates over things like the preservation of a free Norway," she said, drawing his conclusion for him. "And not merely because one has fallen in love." It was not said with any bitterness—she agreed with him wholeheartedly.

"Yes. Of course, the Council refused to accept the Nazi government, and Elverum was bombed. My father and grandfather hid in the woods surrounding the town. It was so surreal, my father says, how well-lit everything was in the middle of the night from all the fire. They and their government moved all over the south of Norway over the next few weeks, trying to find any areas still held by the Norwegian army. German orders were that they were to be taken dead or alive at any cost. They spent their days living in the woods, nights in whatever inns they could find. In the beginning, they often woke up to bombings and rumors of bombings and rushed into the woods again, but Bestepappa announced that he was tired of Hitler deciding when he got up, and from then on their party would be up at six, breakfast at seven, and head for the woods at eight under any circumstances. He stuck rigidly to that schedule, whether or not there were bombs during the night.

"A British ship eventually took them all up to Tromsø—the north, of course, was still not occupied at that point. By June it was clear we'd lost, and the government planned to withdraw to London. They thought they might be able to manage something of a government in exile, and they knew if they stayed in Norway, they'd only be taken prisoner. At the last council meeting, my father announced that *he* intended to stay behind in Norway. He had been considering it for days, he said, and did not feel he could leave his country at such a time. My grandfather—who I don't believe had heard anything about my father's intentions until that afternoon—refused to allow it, knowing it would cost him his life, and they all left that night for England."

"What did your mother think?"

"She didn't know—they hadn't had any contact since we'd gone to Sweden. She only had occasional messages from others about his safety."

---

11   Grandpa

Sonja shivered, imagining Crown Princess Märtha's terror at simply *not knowing* whether her husband were dead or alive at any given moment and remembering her own mother's fears for her brother, Haakon, one of the resistance fighters.

"She didn't hear from him until he was safe in London—not that they were able to speak then; it was all telegrams. Then, of course, my grandfather started his radio broadcasts on the BBC—"

"I remember those," she interrupted. She was too young to remember those made during that first summer of 1940, but she had later memories, as the war had progressed, of her family huddling around the forbidden radio in the closet to listen to the King's words.

"You do?" He seemed pleased. "What was it like to hear him?"

She thought for a moment. "Well, I mostly remember that I just couldn't really understand the whole situation—I was too young to remember peace, too young to know what it meant *not* to be occupied. But I know my family had very strong feelings about the King—I remember my mother wept once at one of his broadcasts. And I remember how often certain of his words were quoted. He had become the center of the resistance movement, really—one of the few men who could be counted on to stand firm. I can vividly remember how *H7* for Haakon VII was written everywhere, much to the Germans' irritation," she said with pride.

Harald nodded. "He used that first broadcast to talk about how many times, and from how many sources, he had been told to abdicate to appease the Germans, and he made it very clear that he had no intention of doing so. He had a duty outlined in the Constitution, and he meant to uphold it. His life had of course been in serious danger during those weeks that he and my father had been traveling across Norway, and he knew he could quite easily have ensured his own safety by the simple act of abdication."

"In light of that," she said, understanding him perfectly, "I think it would be absolutely ridiculous, and completely repugnant, for you to abdicate just so we could get married."

"Come, Miss Haraldsen, tell me how you would really feel about it." He grinned, and she grinned back.

"You left Sweden for America, didn't you?" she asked, wanting to hear more.

"My parents had become friends of the Roosevelts the year before on a tour of the United States, and the President offered us asylum. He sent the *American Legion* to northern Finland where it picked up my mother and sisters and me and a number of other refugees in the middle of August. Astrid says she and Ragnhild were terribly excited about America, because they'd seen the films of our parents' trip, and they wanted to see the country themselves. I don't remember the trip to Finland, but I'm told I played a little trumpet I'd gotten for Christmas most of the way, which Astrid thought was adorable. Ragnhild wanted to knock me in the head with it.

"As we boarded the ship, Astrid says there were sailors on the quay singing *'Ja, Vi Elsker,'*[12] and my mother raised my arm to wave to them. I've got a vague memory of crossing the Atlantic—I was enjoying myself. I had no idea how frightened I should have been, but that was a terribly dangerous trip to make in 1940 when you had no idea where the German subs might be. And we *could* have been captured at any time, of course—Astrid's said she thinks that if we had been, our mother intended to kill herself and the three of us rather than let us fall into Nazi hands.

"But two weeks later we were arriving in New York—I've heard my mother talk of what it meant to see the Statue of Liberty after such a crossing. I *do* remember arriving in America. We went to the Waldorf Astoria for the night, where the owner's wife was a Norwegian woman, Jørgine Boomer. She became a great friend of my mother's, and in the last few years she and Astrid have become very close. She had filled our rooms that night with mountains of toys. I remember having a tricycle, and my sisters had more dolls than they could count, and it was all wonderfully exciting. Especially for the girls—I was clueless, but they'd both been very upset about leaving home and had been able to feel the stress of the crossing, and Astrid says they forgot everything immediately when they saw all the things waiting for them at the hotel. It was really all so providential—that my parents had just become friends with the American President, who could offer us asylum, the year before, that we were kept safe on the crossing, and that one of New York's best hotels was owned by a man who had married a Norwegian. We stayed for awhile at Springwood, the Roosevelts' retreat out in the state of New York, and then we went to Washington where the Roosevelts welcomed us into the White House until we could find our own home. By Christmas we had moved to a house in Maryland."

"Did you see the President very often?"

"Oh, yes! He was very fond of my mother, and he was wonderful with us children—we came to call him Grandpa. Astrid had spent the first few weeks in Washington grieving over her favorite dog left behind in Oslo. She was constantly worrying if he was hungry or lonely or missing her, and the President heard about this and got her a new one. We all loved him from then

---

12   Norwegian national anthem, "Yes, We Love (This Land)"

on. I remember Grandpa Roosevelt playing games with us at Springwood, I remember racing up and down White House hallways with my sisters, and I remember him coming to tea at our home all the time. He usually brought other visitors with him—we met Winston Churchill and many of the other leaders of the early forties. All of my early memories are of the United States, since of course we didn't come back to Norway until I was eight. We had been well-prepared for it, though—my mother made certain that we spoke only Norwegian at home, that we learned Norwegian customs, and that we all knew we would return. It was never *if* we got back to Norway; it was always *when*. She must have had private doubts herself—I don't know how she could not have—but she never let us see them, and so we never had any ourselves."

"I saw you the day you came home," Sonja said softly, remembering her first sighting of the young man seated across from her. The crowds on the streets of Oslo that day in June 1945 had been twice its population as citizens welcomed the Royal Family home, and she had stood with her parents in the mass of Norwegians. "I remember watching you and your family wave from the balcony."

"The first time we saw each other, then."

"I'm quite confident you couldn't see me!" She laughed.

"The balcony's not so high up that you can't see individual faces, and I always do. Perhaps you were one of the people I looked at." He smiled.

"Perhaps." She smiled, enchanted by the idea. "Your grandfather and your whole family had meant so much during the war…I remember what it was to everyone to have the King back again."

"It all suddenly meant something to me, too. The day we came back to Norway was the first time I really understood who I was." He paused. "But what about you and your family? What do you remember from the war?"

"My family?" He had told her of his meetings with the Allied leaders and his own family's series of narrow escapes. What interest could he possibly have in her stories?

"Yes, your family. It was the Norwegian *people* who held the country together, far more than my family did."

"Well," she began, "I remember quite a bit—I think I remember more than you do. I remember the beginning of the war; I was not quite three, and I think it's my earliest memory." She looked out over Oslo again—perfectly peaceful on a summer afternoon. The calm was an unsettling contrast to her memories, as was the sparkling blue of the fjord—the fjord the Germans had sailed up. "My family left the city the night after the Germans came in." In the panic of the occupation, rumors had spread that the Allies would bomb the city the next day, and nearly all its citizens fled, or tried to. "I remember the air raid sirens blaring and being carried out to the car by my mother—we were lucky we had a car *and* enough fuel." She had seen pictures in later years of others hanging onto the sides and sitting on the roofs of overflowing buses. "My parents had some friends who lived in the countryside, in Valdres, so we went there for a week." She paused. "I found that all very frightening, because there were twenty-six other Oslovians packed into the house with us, and there was just this constant crush of strangers.

"When we got back to Oslo, I remember the Germans just being everywhere—and they would continue to be everywhere for years. That was scary, too—I didn't like seeing all the uniforms or hearing the sound of their boots. There were quite a few soldiers living in our neighborhood—the Nazi Culture Minister even lived two houses down. But the funny thing is what first gave me such distaste for the German soldiers," she said, smiling. "I was too young to understand what Norway meant, or what occupation was, or anything about war, but I saw one of the soldiers turn around and kick a dog that had been following him on the street—that alone was enough to make me hate all of them.

"My brother, Haakon, got involved with the resistance very quickly. I didn't know much about that at the time, but I do remember how frightened we all were that as a young man—he was nineteen—he would be picked up for the German army. Haakon took to sleeping in the dollhouse in my best friend's backyard, because we'd heard stories of the Germans coming looking for young men in the middle of the night. Then, of course, they arrested all the university students in Oslo. We had enough warning for him to hide, but he left for Sweden soon after. It took him weeks to get there, and he continued working for the resistance movement from abroad. I didn't understand then, of course, but my mother's said that she wasn't sure if she would ever see him again.

"But the worst of it…" She paused, unsure how much to tell him and unsure how much she herself could be certain about. "The worst of it was my sister. We think Gry was involved in the resistance movement as well, but we're not sure because she never told Mamma anything at the time, and she won't talk about the war at all now. Then one day—when I was four and she was seventeen—she went to meet a friend and didn't come home. It was days before we found out what had happened. She'd been arrested for refusing to sit next to a German soldier on the streetcar, and she spent five weeks in the horror that was Grini.[13] Soon after she was released, Gry left for Sweden, which is why we think she was involved in some sort of illegal work. She did not—she did not have an easy war, and…it has not been easy for her since. The niece and nephew I've told you so much about—they're her children, and…it has been necessary for them to spend a lot of time with my parents and me."

"Did your siblings come back as soon as the war ended?" Harald asked.

Sonja shook her head, grateful not to have to discuss her sister further. "No, it was another couple of years. They both went to the north before they returned to Oslo."

"So they were part of the rebuilding."

"Yes." As they'd retreated in 1944, the Nazis had burned to the ground nearly every Norwegian town north of the Arctic Circle,[14] and a steady stream of young southerners had gone north after the war to rebuild. A significant number of young men had been sent by the government as well to defend the Norwegian-Soviet border in light of fears of a post-war Soviet invasion. "Haakon was part of the force on the border at times, and they were both building homes and churches and town halls. It's amazing what was done in the north. They were starting from nothing but ashes, people were sleeping in tents and little dirt-floor structures, living under *boats*, even in the winters, for years…and you'd never know it to see that area today." It had been impressed on her from a young age what great effort had gone into putting Norway back together, her siblings' letters home demonstrating how much the country's future meant to them and ought to mean to her.

"Will I ever meet your brother and sister?" he asked her.

"In a couple weeks," she said with a shy smile. "There'll be a family dinner for my birthday—everyone will be there. I'd like to have you there, too."

---

13   Concentration camp outside Oslo

14   Roughly one-third of the country lies above the Arctic Circle.

Chapter Fourteen

SONJA'S BIRTHDAY ENDED UP BECOMING SOMETHING OF A FIASCO, AT LEAST for Harald. He was preparing to leave on the evening of July 4 when his father came strolling into his office, announced that Sophie and her mother had arrived for a several-day visit, and demanded that Harald go up to the reception rooms and entertain Sophie. "I didn't want to spend weeks arguing about it," he said when a shocked Harald asked why he hadn't been told sooner. Not wanting to be rude to Sophie, who wasn't at fault for any of this, Harald had briefly visited with her alone before ending up trapped in a room with his father and her mother. Frederica, who as usual exhibited the subtlety and delicacy of a charging elephant, had brought up the diamond carat weight she would find acceptable and offered Harald Sophie's ring size. Feeling that someone had to put a stop to this and panicking over being late to Sonja's, he had told the Queen that any discussion of rings was rather premature, apologized for cutting things short as he had a dinner to attend for a friend, and left for the Haraldsen home.

He had come, in the short year he had been dating Sonja, to love the place—alongside its elegance, it had retained a feeling of the traditional Norwegian. Sonja's mother might have become the wife of a successful Oslo businessman, but she had grown up in a wooden house in old Telemark, and her old-fashioned origins were evident in the embroidered tablecloth and the decorative rosemaling plates on display in the kitchen. Nor was it at all unusual for Mrs. Haraldsen to spend the day in the kitchen baking a traditional pastry from scratch, as she had done today. Sinking easily into the warmth of the family, Harald could nearly forget that he would have to spend the next few days entertaining the Greeks as he listened to stories of Sonja's childhood and savored the buttery sweetness of the Princess Astrid Kringla. However, when he returned to the Palace a few hours later, he found an offended Frederica and Sophie off to Athens and a furious Olav seething over having lost "the best bride in royal Europe."

Perhaps, Harald dared to hope, the unintended result of the evening might be to push Frederica and Sophie toward Juan Carlos, thus leaving the way open for Sonja.

~

"I want to come back here every year on our anniversary until we're married," Sonja announced two months later. She and Harald were at Akershus Castle, in one of the rooms used for last summer's graduation ball a year ago tonight. They were sharing chocolate cake and red wine and sitting on the wood floor against the stone wall, as Sonja had had scruples against using the medieval chairs and tables.

"I think most girls would prefer the Crown Prince took them to dinner at a five-star restaurant," he said, "rather than have a picnic on a dusty floor."

"I'm not most girls." She took another sip of the red wine, savoring its sweetness. Wine was an expensive drink in Scandinavia at the time, and while it was not uncommon for Harald to offer it to her, she always drank each glass as slowly as possible, unable to grow accustomed to its luxury.

"That's always been very obvious," he said, smiling.

She smiled. "Seriously, though, I like coming back here on the anniversary of the ball. This is where everything started for us." She had only to close her eyes for a moment to imagine the night. She could hear the orchestra and the swishing of girls' dresses, see the soft candlelight and the glow of the chandeliers, recall their conversation out on the fortress wall...but most of all she remembered not how it sounded or how it looked but how it felt. How it felt when her eyes met Harald's in her front hall, how it felt when he took her hand firmly in his, how it felt to be in his arms for the first time as they danced, how it felt to laugh together and talk together. It had been the first night she had been happy at all since her father's death, and although she could not have identified it at the time, she knew now that her easy happiness that evening had come from some hidden realization that this was it. *Here* was the man she was going to fall hopelessly and eternally in love with.

"You know," she said, "last summer *wasn't* the first time we met."

"It wasn't?"

"No." She had thought about her first "meeting" with Harald off and on throughout the past year. "We were both at a summer sailing camp as children, on Hankø," she said, referring to a small island south of Oslo. "I was with the girls most of the time, and I'm sure you were with the boys, but there were a whole bunch of us down by the pier one evening. I felt someone yank hard on my scarf, which annoyed me, and I turned around to see it was Prince Harald. I remember that I decided that Princes were just like other boys—irritating and mean to girls—and I told you to leave me alone."

He laughed. "I don't remember that—that is, I remember the sailing camp, but I don't remember you or your scarf."

"But do you remember everything about the ball last year?"

"Only the parts about you."

"Then you'll remember that you kissed me at the end of the evening—and for the record, I'm not the sort of girl who generally *allows* that on the first date; I just happened to really like you."

"I suspected you did. If you hadn't, I'm sure you would have told me to leave you alone." He took the opportunity to kiss her again, and she giggled. "I'm glad we had our first date here," he said, suddenly serious. "This place means something different to me now. I don't—hate it any more."

"What was wrong with it before?" she asked, setting down her wine glass. How could anyone hate Akershus? It was wonderfully romantic in its age, she thought.

"My mother—her funeral was in the chapel here," he said softly.

Sonja paused, feeling the sudden change in his manner. "We all loved your mother very much," she said at last. It was quite true—the last Crown Princess had been held in great regard and affection by most of Norway. Born a Swedish Princess, her marriage to the Norwegian Crown Prince twenty-five years after the union between Sweden and Norway had ended had been seen as a sign of reconciliation between the countries. Elegant, gracious, and motherly, her popularity had only increased from there, and she had been much admired for her strength during the war.

"Yes." Harald did not physically move, but Sonja somehow felt as though he had turned away from her or retreated a few inches farther down the wall. His expression was very, very fixed, almost stone-like, and his entire body tensed as though on guard against any outside threat.

She fell silent again, searching for a tentative way to begin removing the wall that had sprung up between them. "You know," she said finally, "when my father died—last year—I didn't want to do anything or go anywhere for months. I couldn't—I couldn't let myself be happy at all. The first time I went out was that party at Karl's where we met, and I only went because my mother insisted."

"I remember you telling me that," he said, still rather stiff.

"What was your mother like?" she asked, almost whispering.

He did not speak for a moment. "Since she died," he said slowly, "I haven't wanted to talk about her."

There was another silence, much longer than the previous ones but lacking the coldness. She took his hand, lacing her small fingers through his, and nestled closer to him, leaning her head against his arm.

After awhile, she said, "Can I talk to you about her?"

More silence. "I suppose."

She began to slowly ask him questions, and he began to answer her, hesitantly and haltingly at first, until he gradually started to tell her more and more and she fell silent to listen. Harald told her more of his childhood in Washington, telling her what his mother had meant to the family, how strong she had been during what must have been a lonely, frightening five years for her, and how insulated she had kept her children from the uncertain reality of the situation. He spoke of her warmth, the gracious calm she brought to a room, and her patience and good nature during the long years of ill health she had endured even before she had become seriously sick.

And he talked of the closeness of his own relationship with her, words which he had not spoken to anyone else in the six years since his mother's death.

As he spoke, Sonja began to speak of her father, their stories weaving together until they both fell silent, holding each other in the dim candlelight.

It was announced in November that Her Royal Highness Princess Astrid was to marry Mr. Johan Martin Ferner on January 12, 1961, and the engagement touched off a storm of controversy.

There were, of course, newspapers and magazines that attempted to take Astrid's side. With the exception of *Aftenpost*, one of Oslo's main daily papers, these were mostly women's publications whose readers were generally middle-aged and older females who had developed distinctly maternal feelings for the Princess after her mother's death. Such articles emphasized how much Astrid had done for Norway, with *Aftenpost* even going so far as to remind its readers how she had continued on the consecration tour in spite of falling ill in the midst of it. "We wish her the best," "Her Royal Highness should know that we share her joy," and "The Princess deserves to be happy," were all common phrases. The women's magazine *Norsk Dameblad* gently pointed out that Astrid "has not always had it so easy" and wished her a bright and happy future. However, even magazines and papers that put a positive slant on the issue agreed that, while Astrid had the right to do what she wished, she ought not to be marrying a divorced man.

And in quite a few newspapers, there was nothing short of an absolute uproar. "The end of the monarchy!" articles cried. "A lack of moral authority in the Royal House! King Sets Himself Against the Church!"

Vårt Land, a magazine published by the Church, wrote that the engagement had caused sorrow throughout the country and represented a "serious crack" in the relationship between the Royal Family and the Norwegian people. "We would have wished that she had had the wisdom and power to choose the path of duty as Princess Margaret did," the article stated, referencing the British Princess's decision not to marry a divorced man when she learned it would cost her her title and her status. Nevertheless, the paper noted sweetly, there was no room for any "bitter, personal condemnation."

"Yes," Harald overheard Johan snap, "it would be wonderful to have you take Margaret's view of duty. I'd actually rather have you partying recklessly till six in the morning every night than working so hard you make yourself sick." Astrid reported that Johan had seethed for days over the *Vårt Land* piece and only managed to calm himself by clipping a response article out of *Arbeiderbladet* which bluntly stated, "This sugary hypocrisy is sickening."

It also came out that the ceremony would be performed by Bishop Fjellbu of Trondheim rather than Bishop Smemo of Oslo, as would have been expected for a princess's wedding. This of course led to speculation that Bishop Smemo had been asked to officiate and refused. Smemo cleared up the confusion by snapping to a reporter that he had *not* been asked, but if he *had* been asked, he would certainly, absolutely, *most definitely* have said no. (Olav, of course, had suspected this all along, and rather than deal with the refusal had gone straight to the more liberal Fjellbu.)

Then the question was raised of whether or not Astrid and Johan could even be married in a church, or if they had to make do with only a civil ceremony. *Dagbladet* asserted that it was impossible for them to have a church wedding, suggesting instead that a nice event could be arranged at City Hall. Then the parish council at Asker, the church near Skaugum in which Ragnhild, Astrid, and Harald had grown up, refused to allow the wedding to be held in its building.

Astrid had already been pushed to her limit by the nastiness of much of the press coverage, the stress of attempting to pull the wedding together in the midst of the busy Christmas season, and the usual aggravation of her symptoms from the winter cold. The implication that she would be married in the very modern surroundings of City Hall wearing an ordinary, everyday dress with no organ music or flowers or wedding processional or any of the other traditional elements she had been expecting left her nearly hysterical.

Her father had been pushed to his limit as well—he was agitated over the negative press coverage the Royal House was facing, he was angered by the comments about his hard-working daughter's supposed disregard for duty, he was irritated that he seemed to have lost control of the whole process, and he was tired of the entire Astrid-Johan marriage issue. When he learned that the Asker parish council was denying a church wedding to no less than the First Lady, and when he found Astrid in tears over the matter, he lost his patience entirely, calling the Church Department and barking orders that he wanted the Asker council forced to allow use of their building. He then declared in the next State Council meeting that Her Royal Highness was absolutely going to be married in Asker Church.

For Harald, the most troubling part of all this was the tendency of many newspapers to use Astrid's engagement as an opportunity to speculate about his own. A few articles went so far as to state that the Crown Prince would be married in two years to Princess Sophie of Greece, with ceremonies in both Athens and Oslo. "The country looks forward to another royal wedding in the near future," one paper wrote. "Yes," Harald muttered when he read it, "go ahead and look forward to that."

To Olav, of course, the most troubling development was the drop in the royal approval ratings brought on by the engagement announcement. In a frantic effort to distance himself from his daughter, he asked Prime Minister Gerhardsen to exclude Astrid's royal allowance from the 1961 budget. She would no longer receive any state funds and would be forced to rely solely on Johan Ferner's income. Significantly reducing his sickly child's financial circumstances, Olav felt, would demonstrate that he personally did not stoop so low as to wholly approve a marriage to a divorcé.

However, with Christmas occurring a mere three weeks before the wedding, Johan was invited to attend the Royal Family's celebrations. They were also joined by Harald's mother's sister, Princess Tha of Denmark, her husband Prince Axel, and their son Count Flemming of Rosenborg's young family. Flemming had been born a minor Danish Prince but had been demoted at his 1949 marriage to the common Ruth Nielsen, with whom he now had four children. Fifteen years older, Flemming had been Harald's childhood hero. He was now a role model of a different sort—although Harald knew he did not have the option of abandoning his royal status as Flemming had done, it had occurred to him that here was a man who would be sympathetic to his situation and who could offer advice. He was counting on a private conversation with his cousin sometime over the holiday.

As was the custom in Norway, the main Christmas celebrations took place on the twenty-fourth, beginning with the family's attendance at a late afternoon church service followed by a formal dinner at the Palace. It was the usual spread of traditional Norwegian fare—*lutefisk*, lamb, pork, cod, and countless side dishes—mixed with Danish, British, and Swedish foods marking the family's heritage. Dinner ended first with English Christmas pudding, a tradition established fifty years earlier by Harald's grandmother, then with Norwegian rice pudding topped with raspberry sauce. There was always an almond hidden somewhere in the rice, and tradition held that any unmarried person who found it would marry soon—of course, it had been contrived that the nut would be placed in Astrid's slice.

After dinner—Flemming and Ruth's youngest, five-year-old Desirée, was squirming with anticipation by this point—the Christmas tree was lit, and the family circled around it to sing carols. Illuminated by the soft candlelight, Astrid's face glowed with all her hopes for the new year, leaving Johan appearing far more captivated by her than by the sparkling pine tree. Perhaps, Harald allowed himself to hope, Sonja and he would be engaged two Christmases from now, and she would be joining the family tonight as well.

The songs were followed—much to the relief of Desirée, who was now jumping up and down—by the opening of presents and the entrance of Olav, dressed in his customary red *Julenisse* suit and beard to distribute gifts to the Rosenborg children. Eventually, a wide selection of cakes and cookies and coffee was brought out, and Harald seized the opportunity to take Flemming aside.

He was encouraged to find that his cousin knew nothing of Sonja—at least not everyone in Scandinavia had heard, or remembered, last year's news story and rumors.

"So you intend to marry her?" Flemming asked with interest.

"Absolutely."

"And I'm assuming you won't do it without the King's permission, like I did."

"No, but it's a different matter entirely—I'm the Crown Prince, and I have certain responsibilities."

"And I was so far from the throne it didn't matter," Flemming finished. "I was really only giving up a title, since my succession rights were so meaningless—and the title meant nothing to me compared to Ruth. Do you have a plan as to how you're going to get your father's permission?"

"Father's obsessed with a marriage to Sophie of Greece," Harald said, articulating his thoughts aloud for the first time. "But I'm not her only suitor—Juan Carlos of Spain wants her too, and last summer I offended her mother terribly—"

"Someone offended that shrieking German harridan, rather than the other way around? Congratulations!" Flemming raised his coffee mug in a toast.

"Yes, well, I think it's caused her to lose interest in me. I'm expecting Juan Carlos and Sophie to be engaged soon, and I'm planning to just wait them out. Once Sophie's engaged, I'll have lost the opportunity to marry her, and I think that will leave my father slightly more willing to consider Sonja."

Flemming took a thoughtful sip. "You think it's going to be that easy?"

"I'm sure it will take some persuasion—especially after the negative response to Astrid's engagement—but I think the real key is waiting for Sophie to marry Juan Carlos."

Flemming nodded. "Possibly. I wish you the best with this, Harald, and I'm very much on your side here, and I don't mean to be discouraging, but... remember this isn't going to be easy. When I approached the Danish King and asked about marrying Ruth, he made it clear that I would not do so and remain a prince. And you know Frederik is far closer to the common man, and far less impressed with royalty, than your father is."

As the twelfth of January drew closer, there was vastly less time to worry about the press coverage as the family became consumed with last-minute wedding preparations. Astrid had been quite specific that she wanted a very traditional family wedding rather than a grand royal occasion, and thus the dinner afterwards would be held not in the Palace but at Skaugum, the unoccupied royal residence on the outskirts of Oslo. Merely a large estate, it was generally used for the Crown Prince's family, and Ragnhild, Astrid, and Harald had grown up there. With no large ball or banquet room in the home, the party for two hundred would be spread throughout multiple rooms, including the library.

The flowers in Asker Church—where they would, in fact, be getting married—were Johan's responsibility. Knowing Astrid loved flowers, Harald was surprised to see her passing the decisions in this area off to her fiancé and asked her why.

"Oh, but Johan's always giving me the loveliest arrangements!" she exclaimed. Harald knew what she meant—whenever she wasn't feeling well, Johan usually sent or brought over a towering bouquet of flowers. "I thought it would be romantic if he sent some over the morning of the wedding for me to use as my bouquet, and then it occurred to me that if he was going to do the bouquet, he would have to handle all the flowers so everything would match. I'm not the least bit worried about it; he knows what I like."

Johan admitted to Harald that *he* was worried about it and had enlisted the help of no fewer than fourteen different florists to ensure things came off perfectly.

In the week before the wedding, gifts poured in from all over royal Europe, the Norwegian government, and every charitable organization Astrid had ever lent her name to. Her clear favorite was a small spaniel from the Norwegian Kennel Club. The furry creature became the recipient of much affection from its new owner, the official taste tester of the menu options, and an indispensable part of the pre-wedding photo shoot.

The media, realizing that the public's desire to see and hear about the wedding was stronger than its moral indignation, quickly caught wedding fever and began furiously speculating about the dress, the maid of honor and best man's identities, and what Johan's brother's glamorous American wife would be wearing. *Norsk Dameblad* printed a three-page article analyzing every significant outfit Astrid had worn in the last year, attempting to guess the style of her wedding gown. In an effort to sound dramatic, the magazine began the conclusion of its article by stating, "She will enter Asker Church as Princess Astrid of Norway and go out again as a common housewife."

"It's wonderful, isn't it?" she said, showing Harald the article. "That's exactly what I want to be—Johan's wife."

Chapter Fifteen

THE DAY BEFORE THE WEDDING SAW A FOOT OF SNOW DUMPED ON OSLO, scrambling the travel plans of royal guests from all over Europe and resulting in a complete chaos of arrival times. Maneuvering the city was growing impossible as the day wore on, forcing the King to move the rehearsal from the church to the Palace, where much of the wedding party was already gathered. There was some question of how the wedding itself could be managed, but despite more snow in the morning, the streets were cleared and the sidewalks shoveled by late afternoon with the miraculous efficiency of a city that is well used to snow. It was still a bitter three degrees outside, yet everyone seemed willing to brave the frigid temperatures.

Harald entered Asker Church shortly before five, discovering that its interior had been transformed from a plain white building into a garden in full bloom. Johan seemed to have ordered every flower imaginable—there were roses, freesias, tulips, daisies, lilies, and others Harald couldn't name, and they were clustered in elaborate arrays throughout the church. There was a romantic arch of red roses and greenery at the entrance to the aisle, a huge cascade of flowers down the side of every pew, and massive arrangements at the altar and along the platform. Long garlands of flowers had been strung together and hung from the ceiling near the front, imitating chandeliers. It was the most beautifully decorated wedding he had ever attended, and he was sure Astrid would be pleased.

She certainly had been that morning upon receiving her bouquet, an overflowing arrangement of fragrant pink roses and freesias with a small note attached. Blushing, she had shown it to Harald: *Min hjertets prinsesse – jeg elsker deg.*[15] "He calls me that, sometimes," she said with a soft smile.

Harald took his seat on the platform and watched the opening entrances of the matron of honor, Astrid's best friend Elisabeth Bahre, and the four young children included in the wedding, Johan's nieces and Ragnhild's son and daughter. Asker Church had no central heating, and its only warmth

---

15 My heart's princess – I love you.

came from small heaters under each pew. It was nowhere near as frigid as the outside temperature, but it was distinctly cold inside, and Harald was slightly worried about the effect it would have on Astrid.

Yet any concerns disappeared when she entered with the King—Astrid was glowing with happiness, her eyes fixed on Johan.

She was stunningly beautiful. Her dark brown curls were swept back in a seamless wave, her lips were painted deep red, and a light blush had been added to her cheeks. A small crown of white beads and myrtle branches held a soft, fingertip-length veil, and the full tulle skirt and long sleeves of her dress were covered with ornate designs of point d'esprit lace. Silver threads had been sewn throughout the gown, and it shimmered in the soft light. Above her scoop neckline were her signature three-strand pearls.

Someday, Harald thought as Olav handed Astrid off to Johan, perhaps someday very soon, he and Sonja would be meeting at an altar as well, she radiant with Astrid's joy and he gazing at her with Johan's look of awe...

He could vaguely hear the opening hymns that Astrid had chosen—"The Lord Is My Shepherd" and "A Mighty Fortress Is Our God"—and the Bishop's sermon on the parable of the solid rock as he imagined the day when he might take Sonja's hand in his own, and she might be his forever. Soon he heard the Bishop announcing the marriage vows, and Astrid and Johan came to stand at the altar where the groom was addressed first.

"So I ask you, Johan Martin Ferner, before God and this assembly: Will you have Princess Astrid Maud Ingeborg, who stands beside you, as your wife?"

"Yes." His answer was loud and clear.

"Will you live with her after God's Holy Word, love her and honor her, and be faithful to her, in good days and bad, until death separates you?"

"Yes." Astrid smiled as though she had been handed the whole world at Johan's response. Any vestige of illness or pain had fallen away as though she had never been sick.

"Likewise I ask you, Princess Astrid Maud Ingeborg: Will you have Johan Martin Ferner, who stands beside you, as your husband?"

"Yes." Her voice was soft but clear, ringing with certainty.

"Will you live with him after God's Holy Word, love him and honor him, and be faithful to him, in good days and bad, until death separates you?"

"Yes."

"Then give each other your hand as a sign of your vow."

Johan took Astrid's right hand in his own, his lips moving as he whispered to her.

"In the presence of God and before these witnesses," the Bishop pronounced as he laid his hand over theirs, "you have promised each other that you will live together in matrimony and have joined your hands as a sign of this. I therefore declare that you are lawfully husband and wife."

Lawfully husband and wife. In spite of whatever objections might have been made, they were now *lawfully husband and wife*, and that could not be taken from them. Surely it could be possible for him and Sonja to hear those words soon.

In spite of all the foreign guests—Harald's table included the Crown Princess of Denmark, a Swedish Prince, the Grand Duke and Duchess of Luxembourg, and the much-talked about British Princess Margaret—the wedding dinner at Skaugum was very much a traditional Norwegian affair. Much time was spent on toasts for the bride and groom, with the accompanying cries of *"Skål!,"* the old wedding songs were sung by the Scandinavians present, and there was the occasional stomping on the floor by all the guests, drowning out the orchestra in a call for the couple to kiss.

The evening took on a magical quality around eleven when a torch parade—a centuries-old part of winter celebrations—arrived at the front of the estate. Olav, Astrid, and Johan were brought to the front door, Harald and the guests pressing close behind them or finding a spot at any available window.

There was a huge crowd of hundreds of residents of the suburb around Skaugum waiting out in the snow, all carrying brilliantly lit torches. The light of the flames caused the ground to sparkle as though it were covered in millions of tiny diamonds, the sharp scent of smoke filled the air, and the crackling of the fire made a cozy backdrop of soft noise. In short, it was everything beautiful about a northern winter.

A man in front stepped forward and delivered a short speech, congratulating the couple and saying that the community felt that Princess Astrid was very much one of its own after a childhood and youth spent in the area. After he offered his wishes for a happy future, the crowd broke into cries of "Long live the bride and groom!" "Long live Astrid!" and "Long live the King!"

A chaotic movement of people and torches ensued as most of them began to step away, organizing themselves somehow, and then the shape of a glowing heart made of torchlight emerged farther down the field. Astrid—who would later tell Harald it would always be her dearest memory of the whole day—stepped closer to Johan, his arm slipping around her waist as she laid her head on his shoulder, the two of them silhouetted against the bright light.

The wedding would have been perfect had Harald not been taken aside by his father as the party broke up. Olav informed him that Queen Frederica, who was attending along with Sophie, was quite open to the idea of Harald's taking Sophie out for lunch the next day before they were scheduled to leave for Athens. Too shocked to protest, his silence was somehow taken as agreement before he knew what was happening. He had thought last summer that the Greeks had lost interest in him, but apparently Frederica desired the match too deeply to be put off so easily. It would be much longer, he realized, before the Queen gave up on him and turned to Juan Carlos, and therefore his own wedding to Sonja was not as near as he had hoped. But perhaps, he told himself, he could somehow find a way to tactfully communicate his disinterest to Sophie tomorrow.

It was still far below freezing the next day when he and Sophie went out, a fact that caused her to cling to him on the way from the car to the café. He did not want her body pressed so close to his and was relieved when they were inside and he could step away from her to remove his coat and help her with hers. They were eating on Karljohansgate, the main street through Oslo that led up to the Palace, and the sidewalks had been far from empty at lunchtime. Aside from the glances they had attracted from the crowds of pedestrians, there had been a crush of photographers hoping for good photos to be sold once the wedding madness had ended. He regretted that he and Sophie would be the subject of many of them—he would call Sonja and explain what had happened as soon as he got home.

"Is it always this cold in the winter?" she asked him after their orders had been taken and they had each been brought a glass of wine.

"Oh, sometimes it's much colder," he said casually, "so cold your skin can freeze if you're outside for very long." It had never occurred to him before that Sophie could be put off by the idea of simply living in Norway, but it suddenly struck him that Oslo was not the sort of place that would be wildly attractive to a girl raised in the Mediterranean. "We won't see temperatures above freezing until late in March."

"It rarely even snows at home," she said.

No, Sophie, it doesn't snow much in Greece, or in Spain either, where you would be much, much happier. "There's snow on the ground nearly all winter in Oslo."

She raised her eyebrows. "Were there—did I see people sitting at tables *outside* this restaurant on our way in?"

"Probably." He had not paid much attention, but outside dining was not an unusual sight on Karljohansgate. "Eating outside is very year-round here. Even in January. Summer's too short to never go outside otherwise." Of course, there were large space heaters under every table, making the temperature quite pleasant, but he saw no need to share that information.

"Quite a few people were out on the streets," she said skeptically, as though questioning whether these northerners had the sense to come in out of the rain.

He shrugged. "There are always people out. Winter's too long here to be avoided, so the cold's generally just ignored."

Sophie looked as though she were being forced to swallow a very unpleasant drink. "Winters here *must* seem long—it was dark so soon yesterday. In Athens at this time of year it's…" She paused, and he knew she was searching for a word. He sometimes wondered if her occasional difficulties with English weren't at least a small part of their awkwardness together. "It's…there's sun until about five-thirty."

"Earlier in the winter the sun sets around three in the afternoon, and for most of December there are only six hours of daylight."

She shivered. "That sounds so…awful."

Yes, Sophie, it does, and you don't want to live here. In truth he loved Norway, and after a lifetime here was not troubled by cold, dark winters—especially with the compensation of eighteen-hour summer days. The long winters, too, had their charms in the beauty of snow-covered Oslo, the breathtaking northern lights, and the frequent opportunities to ski and watch competitions, but he certainly wasn't going to tell her any of that. *Spain, Sophie. You'd rather go to Spain.*

"Oh well, I suppose one gets used to it," Sophie said with a smile. It warmed her eyes slightly—they were the same crystal blue as his own, and they were emphasized today by the navy blue of her wool dress. He was struck suddenly by how *un*striking they were, and how very different it felt to look into Sonja's.

"Astrid's wedding was wonderful," she said as their plates were set down in front of them. They were having the open-faced sandwiches so common throughout Scandinavia. His was topped with herring, hers with merely a few vegetables. He had forgotten her aversion to meat when he'd chosen this restaurant, and it had not been easy to explain to their waiter. Not that anywhere else would have been easier. He hated to think she'd still be hungry after the meal, but what was he supposed to do with a girl who wouldn't eat most foods?

"I'm so used to the Orthodox Church," Sophie went on, "and I thought the service was beautifully simple. And of course the bride was absolutely gorgeous."

"Oh, definitely. She was very happy—she and Johan are very much in love." Sophie nodded politely, as though she knew the conversation was drifting in a direction she didn't fully comprehend. "I think it's wonderful she was able to marry the person she loves. That's why she looked so happy—so much more than so many of the royal weddings we've seen."

Sophie blushed and lowered her eyes. "I hope I'm that happy on my wedding day. I think—" she began to speak even more softly "—I think I will be."

His heart leapt into his throat. If she were willing to mention her own wedding in his presence, then surely she imagined that it would be with someone else—she would otherwise have been far too shy to initiate such a discussion. She had, in the six months when he had no contact with her, apparently fallen in love with Juan Carlos…

"Do you think your wedding day will be very soon?"

Her cheeks turned even pinker. "Perhaps," she whispered.

"I was planning on an engagement soon myself," he began.

"Oh, Harald, really?" Sophie's eyes brightened, and her face broke into sincere delight.

Her excitement at the news convinced him that she no longer had any romantic feelings for him whatsoever. She was now waiting for *him* to be married off so that her mother would let her turn her full attention to Juan Carlos of Spain, who was merely Frederica's second choice…

"I'm sure it will be just as lovely as Astrid's wedding," she told him.

"What did you have in mind for yours?" he asked, relieved to hear plans that did not involve him.

"Well, I know I would want more…what are they called? The girls who stand with the bride?"

"Bridesmaids," he offered. "But Astrid only had a matron of honor."

"Yes." Sophie nodded. "I would want more than that—I know that's the custom here, but in Greece it's common to have several girls," she said, listing a few names. "But I'm getting ahead of myself." She blushed. "Nothing's official yet. Tell me—where did Astrid go on her…is it just 'wedding trip' in English?"

"Honeymoon. They've gone to Paris, and then they'll go on to Spain and then London."

"I love Spain," she said softly. *Wonderful.*

The rest of lunch passed easily, with Harald ensconced in the relief that Sophie had fallen for Juan. She would now tell her mother that Harald was soon to be engaged himself, and she would be allowed to marry Juan Carlos, and his own wedding to Sonja could not be far off.

"I want to thank you, Harald, for doing your duty today," the King said over dinner that evening.

"You mean, with Sophie, sir?" He was not generally praised for entire weekends spent enduring Sophie, so why his father should so appreciate one lunch was beyond his understanding.

"Of course with Sophie!" Olav smiled benevolently. "All that fighting we've had, and finally you just do it!"

Perhaps that was it—he had complained so much in the past about being forced to see his Greek cousin, but he had had little opportunity to protest the lunch date in the midst of last night's reception. "I hardly felt arguing was appropriate at such a time, sir."

His Majesty laughed, his manner unusually jovial. "I should think not! But thank you, Harald. I know it may not have been what you wanted— thank you for being responsible."

Harald nodded. "Thank you, sir." All this for lunch with Sophie—perhaps his father was still exuberant over yesterday's wedding.

The spring and summer passed without event—Harald and Sonja awaited an engagement announcement from the Royal House of Greece, but none was forthcoming. Not that they were worried—certain now that their own marriage would take place eventually, they were willing to wait a year or so. Sonja was in no hurry to take on the role of Crown Princess anyway, and they spent the next few months enjoying their time together, skiing and hiking in the mountains, joining the Ferners for dinner, and taking weekend trips to London and Paris where Harald was an unknown and they could be together in public.

In August, Harald was sent down to Corfu for a weekend his father was most enthusiastic about. He was not the least bit resistant to going—the island was beautiful at this time of year, he and Sophie would be able to sail this time, and he no longer had any worries about Sophie's expectations. Perhaps, he hoped, she would be able to give him news about when she expected to be officially engaged to Juan Carlos, or perhaps they could even go to her mother together and state that they had no interest whatsoever in a match with each other, thus bringing things to a permanent halt.

He was swept into the huge entry hall of Mon Repos Palace late on Friday afternoon with what struck him as an unusually warm reception. Frederica, Sophie, and Irene all threw their arms around him, kissing him on both cheeks. He embraced them each as quickly as possible—the temperature was past ninety, and the collection of ceiling fans whirring overheard seemed to be accomplishing very little.

"Harald!" Frederica exclaimed. "What a happy occasion this *is*! Palo and I are simply *overjoyed*!"

He momentarily doubted that King Pavlos could possibly share his wife's enthusiasm about the match that he and Sophie now knew wasn't happening, but before he could fully form the thought both Pavlos and Constantine were warmly embracing him too.

"Welcome to Greece," Sophie said, taking his arm and leading him into the dining room, the smile on her face outshining the August sun.

The evening then began, much like on his last visit, with an agonizing dinner with the whole family. Frederica pumped him for information about the Norwegian royal jewels, and Irene studied him suspiciously as he thought of a small, cold-blooded salamander staring out unblinking from under a rock.

He and Sophie spent the next day sailing, and the time passed quickly. Sailing was one of his greatest passions—he hoped to make the Olympic team in a couple years—and Sophie was far more natural now than she had ever been with him. There was still a certain demure reserve to her that made her a sharp contrast to Sonja's innocent warmth and frequent laughter, but his cousin was much more at ease in his presence out here than she had been back on land. By the afternoon he found himself wishing he had planned to be here longer, under the blazing Mediterranean sun with the warm, brilliantly blue waters of the Ionian Sea that beckoned them both off the boat for a swim in the soft waves of sapphire.

They returned to the estate in the early evening, dressed for dinner, and met again in her sitting room as they waited for the meal to be prepared. It was as much of an oasis of cool as one could hope for indoors on a Greek summer afternoon, with its soft blue walls, view of the sea, and large open windows, the silk curtains blowing in the breeze.

"I was thinking," she said as they sat, "of bridesmaid dresses in blue."

Why was she telling him about her wedding?

"I thought that would look good on most of the girls—it's a particularly pretty color on Irini and Astrid—"

"Astrid?" Astrid and Sophie barely knew each other, and Sophie surely would not have any reason to include her in the wedding party...unless she envisioned herself marrying him...but surely she would not be so forward as to suggest such a thing... An uneasy feeling settled in his chest.

She gave him an odd look. "Yes, of course. Don't you want your sister in our wedding?"

Our wedding? He stared at her in horror, not hearing anything further, but he must have given some sign of agreement, as she continued on about tiaras. *Our wedding?* How could she possibly think... And *last winter* she had told him she planned to marry Juan Carlos...hadn't she? He struggled to remember January's conversation, replaying their words to each other...he recalled something about bridesmaids...something about Astrid's honeymoon...

And then he remembered his father's remarks following his lunch with Sophie—Olav had not been ecstatic because he had taken Sophie out; he had been ecstatic because...

Sophie believed herself nearly engaged to Harald himself. No...worse than that, she thought they *were* engaged. He had told her that he planned to be engaged and married soon, and she had been thrilled—" Oh, Harald, really?" rang in his ears, and he could still see the delight in her face. *She had taken the conversation as a proposal.*

This girl thought he had *proposed to her.* What on earth was he supposed to... His mind was racing with the ramifications of what had happened—how would he ever get out of this without creating an international incident?—*she thought he had proposed*—and the central question of how he had ever let this happen in the first place—*she thought he had proposed*—if only he had not been so confident about his own marriage in the wake of Astrid's...perhaps that had led him to misinterpret things, and of course the fact that they had been conversing in English, which Sophie did not speak as well as he did, had surely not helped matters... What could he possibly tell her? *She thought he had proposed.*

"Sophie...Sophie, I—"

She smiled at him. "Yes?"

Sophie, last January was a complete misunderstanding.

"Sophie? Harald? Are you ready to come down for dinner?" He looked to the door and saw that Frederica had stepped into the room.

"Yes, Mama. Harald, you wanted to say something?"

"Never mind," he said quickly. He would not embarrass her in front of her mother. The thought leapt into his mind as he followed them both out of the room how murderously angry Frederica would be when she learned the truth—Sophie had surely told her about the "proposal," and now she believed him ready to marry her daughter—not to mention how his own father might react to the news—and Sophie would be heartbroken as well as humiliated, and he had no way of letting her down easily—*she thought he had proposed*—and, as furious as his father was likely to be, he doubted he would receive permission for an engagement with Sonja for years now—he would call her tonight, he had to discuss this with someone sane—

He escaped to his rooms after the meal and made desperate phone calls both to Sonja's home in Oslo and to Flemming's estate in Denmark, where there were no answers all evening. He would be flying to a meeting in Stockholm tomorrow and would be there for several days, but when he was finally back in Norway, he would discuss this with Sonja. They would make some sort of decision about what he could do—and he would say nothing to the Greeks about the engagement yet; he would wait until he got out of here and could begin to think straight again. *What had he done?*

Chapter Sixteen

"GOOD MORNING, *LILLE JENTA MI*,[16]" DAGNY SAID SOFTLY WHEN SONJA entered the store's offices on Friday morning.

"Good morning." *Odd,* she thought as her mother kissed her. They had just seen each other less than an hour ago when Dagny had left the house, and now her mother was studying her closely.

"Are you all right, Sonja?"

"Yes. Is something wrong?"

"No, everything's fine." Her mother gave her a wide smile that did not reach her eyes.

An uneasy feeling settled in her stomach. Haakon stuck his head out of his own office.

"Sonja." He looked over at her, his eyes gentle. "You okay?"

"Yes." Why did they think she should be so upset? "Why wouldn't I be?"

Her brother gave her the same appraising look she had received from her mother. "Never mind."

"Tell me what's wrong." She felt her muscles tense as fear swept over her. What was so awful that they couldn't tell her?

"Nothing's wrong, Sonja."

His expression unreadable, he stepped back into his office, and she entered her own, trying to lose herself in the shipment records. Yet she heard the door of Haakon's office open again, and she strained to catch the quiet words he exchanged with their mother.

"—don't think she knows…must not have read the paper…not true?… of course, but Harald—" The conversation dropped to even quieter whispers, and she could no longer distinguish anything.

Harald? Was he all right? He was returning from Sweden this afternoon, and then they were going out to dinner that evening…had something happened? Her stomach twisted slightly, and she forced herself to exhale the

---

16   Affectionate Norwegian name for a daughter; literally, "my little girl"

breath she had been holding. She did not know for sure that something was wrong...yet there was clearly something in the newspaper that they thought would be terribly upsetting to her...

She had an alteration to do, but the whir of the sewing machine—usually a calming sound, when she noticed it at all—was suddenly maddening. The hours of the morning crept by as she returned to poring over the paperwork, her mind fixed firmly in Stockholm. As early as she felt she reasonably could, she announced that she was going out for lunch and rushed down to the street corner to buy a newspaper.

The headline of *Verdens Gang* screamed out at her: *ENGAGEMENT FOR CROWN PRINCE HARALD AND PRINCESS SOPHIE OF GREECE.*

No...that wasn't true... Dazed, she skimmed the article, which revealed Harald's trip to Greece last weekend—she had known, but he had assured her it was only to appease his father and that Sophie had told him she was going to marry that Spanish Prince—and asserted that after his proposal—they claimed he had first proposed *months* ago—the King had given his blessing to the match and had now entered into official negotiations with Their Majesties of Greece, and—and this was the detail that shook her most—the Greek parliament had voted to send the funds for Sophie's dowry to Norway.

It couldn't be true...Harald hadn't wanted to marry Sophie at all, he—he wanted to marry *her*—or at least he *had* wanted to marry her... She would have assumed it to be nothing more than a fabrication on the part of the press had it not been for the bit about the Greek parliament. They would only have done such a thing had the King of Greece actually told the Prime Minister his daughter was engaged, and surely the papers could accurately report on the actions of the Greek government easily enough... *which had to mean that Harald and Sophie truly were engaged.* The truth lay open in front of her, and she fought to shove it away as she folded the paper with shaking hands.

Harald wouldn't—he wouldn't—we were going to be married—I'm the only girl he said he'd ever love... Yet the article made a horrifying amount of sense. Harald *had* been in Greece last weekend, and he had, over the last few months, been far less worried about their own potential marriage. He had claimed it was because Sophie would soon be engaged and his father would permit their own engagement after that...but perhaps it was because Harald had decided to marry Sophie instead of her, and there was no longer any reason whatsoever to worry about their own marriage because he had determined it wasn't happening... Her legs were suddenly weak.

Sonja, you're the girl I want to marry.

The Greek parliament, meeting yesterday in Athens, passed a motion to transfer the necessary funds for Her Royal Highness's dowry.

Sonja, you're the girl I want to marry.

The Greek parliament, meeting yesterday in Athens, passed a motion to transfer the necessary funds for Her Royal Highness's dowry.

Sonja, you're the girl I want to marry.

And when, she thought as the first tears slid down her face, had he decided that she was no longer good enough, no longer high-born enough?

Sonja, you're the girl I want to marry.

The words played over and over again in her head as she rushed back to the store where she could fall apart in her mother's arms.

By the time she was home from work that evening and dressing to go out, her tears had dried, turning inside where they froze into an ice cold fury. She was going to dinner with Harald tonight—yes, she was most definitely still *going*. She would tear into him to the point where he'd wish he'd never heard Sophie's name.

With cool precision she arranged each strand of hair, cementing everything into place with hair spray—she had rewashed and re-curled it, intending to look devastatingly beautiful tonight. She had slipped into a fitted, bright blue dress, one that drew attention to her small waist and the curve of her hips. *How dare he,* she thought again and again, fighting to stop the angry shaking in her hands as she applied more eye make-up. Another coat of mascara and eye-liner accented her large eyes more dramatically, increasing the beauty of the feature he had always said had first caught his attention. The small blue hat she'd selected sat back on her head, casting no shadows on her face.

After a last glance in the mirror—perfect—she folded up the front page of the paper and slipped it into her purse. *ENGAGEMENT FOR CROWN PRINCE HARALD AND PRINCESS SOPHIE OF GREECE.* She felt so... used, so...*stupid*. A fresh wave of anger swept over her. She would be pulling that article out at the appropriate time to shove it in his face.

It was pouring down rain when Harald arrived on her doorstep at six that evening, his expression natural and his voice giving no hint that he intended an explanation. "Evening, Sonja." With his trips to Greece and Sweden, they had not seen each other in a week, and he reached for her immediately when she stepped outside and under his umbrella, his free arm going around her waist and his mouth finding hers. She kept her own arms at her sides and did not kiss him back. *How dare he...* She pulled away.

"Sonja, is something wrong?"

Yes, you're engaged to another woman, and you think I'm too stupid to have even read the paper this morning. "No." She turned back and kissed him more passionately. "There, is that what you wanted?" she said, acid in her voice.

"Sonja, are you all right?"

"Perfect," she snapped and started down the walk to his car in the driving rain, forcing him to follow her if he were to have any success at keeping her dry.

"How was your week?" he ventured as they drove away.

She shrugged, infuriated at his calm manner. "Fine."

"Anything new?"

"No." She could not remember ever having given anyone, much less Harald, three one-word answers in a row.

"Do you feel all right?" He gave her a concerned look, and she felt irritation boiling beneath her skin.

"No." She had not felt all right since eleven o'clock that morning.

"What's wrong? I can take you back home if you're sick; we don't have to go out tonight."

She said nothing for a moment, the sound of the windshield wipers growing maddeningly loud in the tense silence, and then the question burst from her lips. "Are you going to marry Sophie of Greece?"

"No. I want to marry you...Did you hear a rumor about something?" he asked uneasily.

"Regardless of what you want to do, Harald, are you really going to marry Sophie instead?"

"Absolutely not. I'm going to marry you. Did you hear something that made you wonder? Or have you been worrying about this since I went down to Greece? Is that why you're so tense?"

"I'm not *tense!*" she snapped.

He raised his eyebrows but did not comment. She sat in silence for awhile, waiting for him to mention the engagement, as they drove out of Oslo through the pouring rain to one of the small restaurants where Harald was often able to arrange a private room.

Even if the information were inaccurate—and she could not believe that it was—the Palace would surely have been informed of the rumor, and he would at least know the article had been printed, a conclusion which only served to confirm her suspicions. The water on the windows blurred the scene outside, and she felt as though everything in her life were disintegrating along with it.

"When were you planning on telling me you're engaged to Sophie?" she blurted out at last.

"*What?*"

"You're engaged to Sophie of Greece. When were you going to tell me?"

He gave her a disbelieving look. "Sonja, I have no idea what you've been reading, but I'm not engaged."

"Maybe not officially, but things are moving very quickly in that direction. And you haven't breathed a word of it to me—despite the fact that you seem to have mentioned the marriage to Sophie several months ago."

He paused, and then his voice took on a troubled edge. "Tell me what you're talking about."

"I'm talking about this, Harald!" she almost yelled, unable to restrain herself any longer. She snatched the folded copy of *VG* out of her purse and shoved it toward him. "The Greek parliament has voted to send the money for Sophie's dowry to Norway!"

His head snapped around and he stared at the paper, his eyes wide with horror as he read the headline. "*What?*"

Before she could react, she saw the winding road ahead turn sharply to the left as their car continued to sail forward.

Chapter Seventeen

"HARALD!" HER WARNING WAS A SECOND TOO LATE AS HE FRANTICALLY SPUN the wheel, but he was already off the road and sliding down the small hill to their right. She felt the force of the brakes as he slammed down on them, but they were moving too fast and the wet grass was too slick. Seconds later, the car came to an abrupt halt in the ditch at the bottom of the hill.

For a long moment they both sat motionless, and Sonja let out the breath she'd been holding. "Are you all right?" she heard him ask. She nodded.

"I should go look at the car."

She nodded again and watched as Harald got out in the pouring rain, struggled through the mud to the front, and surveyed the damage.

Soaking wet, he got back in the car a few minutes later.

"How bad is it?"

"It's perfectly drivable—just some minor dents—if I can get it out." He reached down, shifted into reverse, and stepped on the gas pedal. The wheels spun, grasping unsuccessfully for traction.

"Here, push on the gas while I get out and try to push the car." Harald got back out into the rain as she slid over into the driver's seat. She watched while he wedged himself into an appropriate position against the side of the ditch. *He'll be covered in mud by the time this is over,* she thought. He shoved, and she pressed down on the pedal. *Please...* The engine roared to life but the car didn't budge, even after multiple attempts.

Her heels sinking in the mud, she stepped out into what was fast becoming a torrential downpour and was instantly wet and chilled in the crisp air—though it was still summer, the rain and clouds had brought the temperature into the fifties. "Do you think it would help if we both pushed?" she offered, shivering.

He stared at her, taking in her five-foot, hundred-pound figure, and then snorted, which only served to irritate her. "No. All you're going to accomplish standing out here in the rain with me is making yourself sick. Just get back in the car."

"Fine, then," she snapped. "If that's all the effort you're willing to exert to keep us out of the morning papers. Here I am, out with an engaged man..." She gave him an affronted glare.

"I'm not *engaged,* okay? At least, I didn't know I was when I left with you earlier this evening. You're the one who knew that!"

"Well, I would have thought you would have been at least vaguely aware of what your father was doing with Sophie if you had really intended to prevent the marriage!"

"I did intend to prevent it! May I remind you that *I have been out of the country?* I have had no opportunity to speak with my father at all this week, let alone get the details on what he's arranging with the Greeks! What are you doing checking up on me in the papers anyway?"

"Apparently I have to, or you'll be married off without even noticing!" she snapped back, so hot with anger that she half-expected the raindrops to rise off of her as steam. "What did you drive off the road for anyway?"

"For some reason, you decided to show me the most shocking headline I've seen in my entire life while I'm driving through a heavy rainstorm! Perfect timing on *your* part."

"What, so this is *my* fault now? Which one of us couldn't keep his eyes on the road? And never mind about whatever your father's been arranging this week; what I really want to know is what was going on several months ago when you proposed to Sophie?"

He sighed. "I never proposed to Sophie. It was a misunderstanding—"

"A misunderstanding? So in other words, you accidentally proposed to Sophie? Do you really expect me to believe that? How on earth does someone accidentally propose?"

"I didn't *accidentally* propose; I didn't propose at all, Sophie misunderstood—"

"What about when you said you wanted to marry me, or was that a—a misunderstanding too?"

He paused. "No, *min kjære,* no. Here, get back in the car and we'll talk about this."

Min kjære. Darling. She swallowed past the lump rising in her throat as she slid back over to the passenger side of the car. He got in behind her, shut the door, and turned on the heat, encasing them in a warm cocoon out of the rain.

"When Sophie was here for Astrid's wedding in January, I had lunch with her, and she mentioned that she was planning to be engaged soon. I assumed she meant she would be engaged to Juan Carlos of Spain because I knew she had no reason to believe she would be engaged to me. I told her I was hoping to be married soon myself—meaning married to *you,* because I *was* hoping—I *am* hoping—we can be married soon. And Sophie—I didn't realize it at the time—but she thought I meant I was hoping to be married to *her,* and I realized last weekend when I was in Greece that she took it as a proposal. I was horrified, but I was going to figure out how to clear everything up when I got back from Sweden. I tried to call you several times, but I couldn't reach you. I didn't have any idea there would be an official engagement announced without my father having spoken to me. I haven't got any idea what happened—I can't imagine how horrible it must have been for you to find this in the paper. But the engagement's going to be cancelled immediately. I would *never* agree to marry Sophie—you know I couldn't ever love anyone but you."

There were a few minutes of silence as she stared straight ahead, not reacting at all to his words and unsure of what she felt. She wanted to believe him, desperately, but after the last seven hours her response was slow in coming, and she was hesitant to let herself slip back into his love.

After a moment he said quietly, "I'm going to go up to the road and see if I can get a passing car to stop so we can get a ride to somewhere we can use a phone." She nodded, and he left her alone.

She realized slowly that everything he had told her was reasonable—it was not unbelievable that perhaps Princess Sophie, who had been raised for an arranged marriage and thus did not expect a great deal of affection to be attached to her engagement, had misunderstood Harald to be offering her marriage. It was also possible for Harald, who had been overconfident about his own understanding of the situation, to miss any further signals from her. And it seemed not only possible but likely that the King, who knew how resistant Harald was to marrying Sophie, would have begun the official arrangements without the knowledge of his son, who had, after all, been out of the country.

Which meant that Harald was not engaged to Sophie of Greece...or at least wouldn't be as soon as he got back to the Palace. And he had certainly not proposed to her at any point.

The sensation of warmth slowly filled her in spite of her wet clothes, replacing any doubt she had had of his love.

Her realization of his innocence in the matter left her mortified over her own behavior, and she got out of the car again, flushed with embarrassment as she hurried up the hill to Harald, who was leaning in through the passenger window of a stopped car.

"Harald?"

He turned to look at her, and she could see the man in the shadowy interior of the car do the same.

"Harald, I'm so sorry; I should have let you—"

"It's fine," he said quickly, cutting her off. "I understand." He turned back to the driver. "Would you mind giving us a ride?"

The man nodded. "Absolutely, sire. You're more than welcome—I would be honored." Harald opened the door, and they both climbed into the backseat.

"Marius Lund," the driver said in introduction, offering his hand to Harald and then to Sonja.

"I'm Sonja Haraldsen," she said in return and received a horrified look from Harald. *Stupid,* she thought. She had now revealed her identity to someone who could call the papers.

⌇

By the time the car had been retrieved, they had eaten dinner, and he had driven Sonja home, it was after nine when Harald entered the King's sitting room in the Palace.

"Harald—what on earth happened to you?" his father exclaimed, taking one look at Harald's muddy figure.

"I've been engaged without my consent, that's what's happened to me," he snapped.

The King nodded knowingly. "I wouldn't say it was entirely without your consent; you indicated to Sophie at your sister's wedding that you were interested in marrying her. But what have you been—"

"I never indicated anything of the *sort* to Sophie; she took everything I said entirely the wrong way, and if you had bothered to mention this to me I would have told you so before it showed up in the papers. Do you have any idea what it was *like* for Sonja to read about my engagement this morning and *believe it*? Have you given any thought to her feelings *at all*?"

"*Her* feelings? Don't you think I've got more important things on my mind than a shopkeeper's daughter's *feelings*? Harald, I've arranged a match for you with the most desirable Princess in Europe, and all you can think about is the reaction of—"

"Of course I'm thinking about Sonja's reaction; I love her, and that's why I'm refusing the engagement—"

"We need you engaged to Sophie of Greece, and it isn't as though you had no idea this would ever happen."

"The marriage isn't going to happen, Father."

"Sophie's coming up to Norway next week for an official announcement from the Palace, and we're holding the wedding next spring. Do cooperate and make this easy for everyone. I would advise you to put that shopkeeper's daughter out of your head immediately—"

"It's not my head you should be worried about things being put out of; it's the Greek Royal Family's and the population of Oslo's."

"The Norwegian people have forgotten about the shopkeeper's daughter, and Frederica believes you're no longer involved with her—"

"That all depends on what's in tomorrow's newspaper."

There was a heavy pause. "And just what might that be?" the King asked slowly.

"Sonja and I were out tonight, and we had an accident—"

"What?"

"—so it doesn't really matter whether or not you agree to cancel the engagement tonight. If my accident with Sonja comes out, I think we can expect the Greeks to call things off."

"You've ruined your entire future!" Olav stood and made no effort to hold his voice down. "You very nearly had *Sophie of Greece,* and you've wrecked your chances with any Princess on the continent now—how do you imagine this will look to the other royal houses?"

"How do you imagine the engagement looked to Sonja this morning?"

"That is not your concern! Your only concern is the future of the House of Glücksburg!"

"The House of Glücksburg, the House of Glücksburg—is that all you care about?"

"What I care about, Harald, is finding you a suitable consort, while all you seem to care about is how in love you are with this seamstress!"

"Yes!" he shouted back as he stormed out of the room. "You're right—all I care about is marrying Sonja!"

～

"Sophie, this is Harald." He would rather have had red hot needles forced under his fingernails than talk to his Greek cousin right now, but he felt that some sort of phone call was necessary. The story had appeared in the morning papers, and Olav had received a terse telegram from Frederica that afternoon cancelling the engagement.

"Hello," she said after a pause.

"I saw your mother's telegram," he began, unsure how to continue. He had never wanted to break her heart, had always been trying to extract himself from the situation without hurting her, had desperately wished she would fall in love with

Juan Carlos and move on, and now… He had no idea what he could possibly say to her, and there was dead silence on her end of the line as well.

"I'm sorry," he finally managed, wishing that could somehow cover everything. "I had no idea we were officially engaged last night when I was out with Sonja Haraldsen. This isn't—this isn't how I would have chosen for things to end. I never intended to hurt you, and I would not have let things go on so long had I thought you believed…I completely misunderstood last winter…I thought you meant something else entirely when we spoke after the wedding. I never imagined that you thought we had—had an *understanding*…and then when you mentioned all that about the bridesmaids last weekend, I…I'm terribly sorry that I've hurt you; it was the last thing I wanted to do." A hollow-sounding apology given what had happened, but he had nothing else he could possibly say.

"You never wanted to marry me." It was not an accusation—her voice had more regret in it that anything else. "I ought to have realized it."

"No, I'm completely to blame." *Along with my father and your mother,* he added silently. "You're beautiful and charming and born to be Queen, and you've done nothing wrong here."

"Harald?"

"Yes?"

"I don't want it to be awkward between us from now on. Promise me you won't be uncomfortable with me every time I see you at a family event."

"Of course not." He paused. "I hope everything works out for the best for you." And he did sincerely hope so. "You deserve to be Queen, but you also deserve far more than I would have ever been able to give you—you deserve to be loved."

"Thank you." She paused, then suddenly asked, "Do you love that girl?"

"Yes. Yes, very much," he said, taken aback at the question.

"I am glad for her, then." It was said sadly, but without a trace of bitterness.

"Sophie, I…" What else could he say? "I'm very sorry about all of this," he said again.

"Thank you."

He managed a delicate goodbye and hung up, relief sweeping over him.

"Miss Haraldsen!"

"Sonja!"

"*Sonja!*"

She quickened her pace on her way home from work but did not look up, refusing to acknowledge the photographers who had become a constant nuisance over the past few days. Eventually, she hoped, she might grow used to it, but she was nowhere near such a feeling yet and found herself self-consciously touching her hair and worrying over her appearance in the photos she knew would be printed up and down the country.

Not that she was out much—with the exception of her necessary trips to and from work, she had made every effort to stay home in the three days since the story had broken. She detested being pursued by paparazzi and hated the unashamed stares she was now attracting everywhere. *Is that her?* she could almost hear the other passengers on the streetcar thinking. *That girl the Crown Prince was with? The one the engagement broke up over?* She kept her eyes to the ground, willing herself to disappear.

There were, naturally, articles speculating about the nature of the relationship, many of which had leapt to the conclusion—*the correct conclusion,* she thought wryly—that the Crown Prince was planning to marry this girl, a possibility that was viewed as a monarchy-ending crisis. But it was the reaction on the editorial page by the middle of the next week that she was so wholly unprepared for. Most focused on the damage a common bride would do to the monarchy and called upon Harald to think of his duty.

The thought that she, a young shopkeeper's daughter of no particular social standing, might be the downfall of the Norwegian branch of the centuries-old Royal House of Glücksburg would have been laughable had it not seemed so very serious. "Such a match would finish the monarchy," she read over breakfast Wednesday morning. "If he chooses a common wife, the Crown Prince would have no further choice but to refuse the throne."

Then there was, "Miss Haraldsen is an unattractive, selfish young woman who is far more interested in her own advancement than she is in the future of this country. This entire affair is an unspeakably poor decision on His Royal Highness's part."

Affair? Her cheeks burned at the implications of the word. How dare they... She dumped the rest of her bowl of cereal into the sink, too nauseous at everything she'd read to eat any more. Would her marriage to Harald—if it ever happened—actually result in the ruin of the Norwegian monarchy?

No, she tried to tell herself, *they're all just overreacting, it's only the press being alarmist...* She forced herself to go in to work and go through with the rest of her day, ignoring her doubts and fighting to put on a natural expression in front of her mother and Haakon. They had no doubt read the morning paper, she decided, as they both welcomed her with unusual warmth when she arrived and kept giving her sympathetic looks throughout the day.

She was not sure she was capable of surviving months and months of this sort of thing, but she was determined to try and told herself that it would get better with time. Of course, despite Harald's predictions to the contrary, it did not get any better—the press's fascination with the topic did not wane, and Sonja did not grow any more accustomed to it. In the space of a few weeks, she made the decision to return to dressmaking school in France for a semester. She would be left alone there, and a few months without her in the country would give the story time enough to die.

Chapter Eighteen

"SO YOU WILL NOT BE HERE ALL YEAR?"

Her roommate's French was far more standard than the Swiss accents Sonja had grown accustomed to hearing in Lausanne a couple years earlier, and she was struggling to train her ear to comprehend it.

"I'm not sure," she replied, hoping her own accent was not too thick. It depended on how much the press had calmed itself by December and how homesick she was for Harald. "I'm most likely leaving at Christmas."

"Well, I'm sure we'll all enjoy the semester together." Léa smiled. "Which beds do both of you want?"

She would be rooming with two young women from Lyon, Léa Morel and Isabelle Simon. They were not, she discovered as she unpacked, overly friendly, but she told herself she should be grateful for an opportunity for solitude—there was precious little of that in Oslo, where she was constantly looking over her shoulder for a photographer. Still, she was unpleasantly reminded of her first time away at school in Lausanne at age seventeen—she had arrived to find her French was far less fluent than she had imagined and had rented a room from a Swiss widow obsessed with saving electricity. The building had thus been left so dark and cold that she was forced to sleep in a winter coat and gloves. Ten hours a day had been spent in class, and with her poor grasp of the language she had been far too self-conscious to put herself forward to make any friends. Thus, she had spent the first semester holed up in her frigid bedroom in the evenings, trying to soothe her loneliness with box after box of Swiss chocolates—it hadn't helped, and she had only ended up forty pounds heavier. She shoved the memories of those dark few months to the back of her mind, telling herself that this semester would be closer to her second than her first in Switzerland, after she had found better housing, improved her French, and finally met other international students.

The first hint that this would not be anything like that pleasant Swiss spring came a few nights later in the dining hall. She heard her name suddenly spoken a few tables away and turned toward the speaker—she recognized her as Emma Woods, a British girl she'd had a class with. She strained to catch the rest of the conversation. "Really?...That's what I heard...Has anyone asked her?" She froze. Did these girls know who she was? Surely not, surely she had not appeared in the press anywhere outside of Scandinavia. It was an overreaction to imagine they knew about her and Harald when any number of harmless rumors could have sprung up about her in a week's time. She tried to concentrate over the next few days on her work and her sketches, reminding herself how glad she should be to be here for the semester. This was the part of sewing she loved, far more than the daily alterations she did in the store. It was the making of something out of nothing, the conscious shaping and designing of a dress, the creation of a tangible piece of clothing out of a mere thought conceived in her imagination, that had always so attracted her, and she tried to remember that it was what she would be doing all semester. Yet she could not shake the feeling that her classmates' eyes lingered on her longer than was natural and that conversations were suddenly hushed when she walked by.

You are paranoid, she was rebuking herself when she returned to her room one evening. *No one here knows or cares who the Crown Prince of Norway is, much less who he's dating.*

Isabelle and Léa looked up from their desks as she stepped inside. "Sonja," Isabelle began, "is it true—we have heard—and there is a photo—" She looked to Léa, who held up an open magazine.

"There's a photo of you in *Point de Vue.*"

Her mouth too dry to speak, Sonja took the French celebrity magazine from her and looked down to see a small photo of herself next to an article claiming Harald was very near to refusing the throne for the sake of his fiancée, "Sonia" Haraldsen.

"Are you really going to marry your Crown Prince, Sonja?" Léa asked with interest.

She did not respond, still absorbed in the photograph. Had the whole school seen this? The magazine, or at least the story, had probably made the rounds very quickly in the last few days. She had had no idea she was known outside of Norway... the semester would certainly not be the escape she had hoped it would...perhaps it would be worse than Oslo, as she had no friends here, no family, and no Harald...

"Sonja?" Isabelle said gently. "Is it true? Is that really you?"

What good did it do her to deny it? "I...yes, I mean, it's me. But the article...isn't entirely truthful."

"But you are dating the Crown Prince?" Léa asked.

She gave a noncommittal shrug, her guard suddenly up. "You could say that."

"We won't repeat any of this," Léa said quietly. "I know it must be difficult for you, having to hide all this and not having anyone here you can talk to."

It was, and it would be—now that she knew they all knew, the sense of isolation she had felt over the previous days would only grow worse. Both girls smiled, and her resolve crumbled. In that moment, it would have been a physical impossibility for her *not* to trust them, and suddenly it was all pouring out of her.

—◠⌒—

Three weeks later, when she realized that the whispers and stares had taken a dramatic increase, she asked Isabelle and Léa if there had been anything more printed about her, and they denied having seen anything. Yet their eyes did not meet hers when they spoke. She was soon making her way through the streets of the small town searching for a magazine shop, where she flipped through everything she could get her hands on.

She was in *Point de Vue* again, she discovered, only this time it was not a photo; it was a brief article stating where she was studying, summarizing the history of her relationship with Harald, and—worst of all—detailing her most intimate feelings about her situation. "'She's terrified that nothing's ever going to change and they'll never be allowed to marry,' a fellow student said. 'She's imagining herself alone for the rest of her life, because the Crown Prince is surely going to take a royal bride eventually, but she can't believe she'll ever be able to love anyone else.'" Not exactly what she'd said—she didn't think Harald would "surely" marry royal; that comment made it appear that she was pathetically hanging onto a Prince who saw her as perfectly disposable—but the substance of everything she'd told Léa and Isabelle was there. And yes, she *knew* it was either Léa or Isabelle because she had never spoken to any of the other girls about Harald, and surely none of the others could have provided such accurate information about her first meeting with the Crown Prince or the night of the graduation ball. She burned with embarrassment and indignation.

She did not want to finish the article but forced herself to read on, hoping for some sign that she was mistaken. She immediately wished she had stopped—"another student," a phrase that by extension now implicated both her roommates, had spoken about Harald's feelings for her. Yet it was not Sonja's words on the subject but Harald's own that were being repeated: "'My dearest Sonja, the lingering warmth of summer in Oslo mocks me, as your absence makes the whole world seem covered in ice...' 'I was in Bergen yesterday and I could think only of our time at Gamlehaugen. The dark wood inside reminded me of the depth of your brown eyes and I was gazing into them again as we sat by the fire, the winding road sweeping up to the castle whispered of your soft curls and I was running my hands through them once more as we looked down at the river, the high ceilings replayed your laughter ringing off them…' 'My dearest Sonja, can I begin to tell you what you have meant, what you have done in my life? For years after my mother's passing, I thought I might never feel true happiness again, and then…'"

For a moment she could not think or even move. The contents of her love letters, translated into French and printed for the whole world to read? It was sickening, and she was momentarily thankful that Harald did not speak French and thus would never read this article. She did not rebuke herself for not hiding her letters better or for leaving them in plain sight, for she had never realized there was any reason they should be hidden. Léa and Isabelle knew whenever she received one, and they knew she stored them in her desk drawer. It had never occurred to her that any of this ought to be a secret, and she would have been shocked enough to find her roommates had so much as attempted to translate one, much less repeated their favorite parts to a reporter. She was too stunned to feel anything beyond a creeping nausea.

The painful truth swept over her: she had no friends here and could not make any. She would be spending the remainder of the semester alone, and she could trust no one. She returned to school, confronted her speechless roommates, and demanded to be moved to a single room.

Sonja soon discovered that the most damaging part of the article was the opening line she had breezed past—the sentence that revealed the name and location of her school. The French press now knew exactly where they could find her, and there were photographers popping up all over the small campus. They were far subtler here than in Oslo—as they were technically trespassing—but it was somehow even more disconcerting to have men crouching in bushes near her than to hear her name shouted on the streets. She was left dashing to and from her classes and the dorms, attempting to conceal her identity with scarves, low-brimmed hats, and sunglasses, and she rarely ventured into town. Then there were the other students—she could not bring herself to go near anyone since the day she had found a flier tacked to one of the bulletin boards, offering cash to anyone who could provide good photos of her. And to think she had come to France to get away from all this…

She was naïve enough in the beginning to believe that the French press would lose interest in a week or so but quickly realized they would be a permanent fixture for the whole semester. Her prayers soon shifted from pleas that she might be left alone to requests that December come very, very quickly.

It was only a few days after the article that she discovered how much more aggressive the foreign press could be. She was seated in class when the office secretary stepped in and handed a note to the teacher, who read it and glanced up at her. "Mademoiselle Haraldsen? You're needed in the main office."

Without an ounce of suspicion and expecting nothing more than a scheduling issue, she followed the secretary next door to find two men waiting with the headmistress in the office lobby. The one on the left held a large camera in his hands, and she felt her muscles tense. But surely she would not have been called out of class to meet a reporter…

"Sonja!" Madame Bouleau exclaimed warmly as soon as she stepped inside. "These men are journalists from *Le Monde*, and they're doing a piece on foreign students in France. They heard we had a young Norwegian woman here—they even knew your name—and wanted a few photos. I knew you'd be happy to chat for a few minutes." The headmistress gave her a soft smile of innocent ignorance. *Does this woman never read the papers?* Sonja wondered.

"Mademoiselle," the first man began, "do you have a moment?"

No. No, she did not have a moment. Her whole body stiffened, and she felt sweat gathering in her hands. Did they want an interview? She could not bring herself to open her mouth.

"Are you enjoying your time in France?" he asked.

"I—yes," she lied. "Yes, I'm enjoying it." Should she just walk out? Surely that would look worse… She would *not* discuss Harald.

"Is this your first time abroad?"

"Yes," she lied again, taking a perverse pleasure in feeding him false information for his article.

"You are studying…?"

"Dressmaking."

He nodded, and she felt a small sense of triumph as she read his hunger for longer answers. He was unwilling to mention Harald, she realized, and reveal his true interest in her.

"Tell us what you've enjoyed most about France, about the beginning of your semester here? What do you miss most about Norway?" His last sentence was said blandly enough, but she was suddenly hot with anger at the knowing look in his eye.

"I—I have—I—" she stammered. She did not wish to discuss anything further with these men. "I am sorry," she said, thickening her accent. "My French—I do not—it is not very good yet." Madame Bouleau, who knew her to be perfectly fluent, shot her a strange look.

"A few photos, then, mademoiselle," the reporter said, his disappointment evident in his voice.

The photographer stepped forward, and she knew suddenly exactly what an animal feels when a hunter steps from behind a tree.

"Please—I—" she began wildly, wishing for an escape. Then there were five quick flashes—the best pictures any photographer would have of her, shot at such close range as she looked right at the camera—and it was done.

"Merci, mademoiselle." He smiled.

She struggled with herself, fighting an urge to rip the camera out of his hands and tear the film to shreds. She clenched her fists, waiting for it to pass—nothing good could come of *that* sort of behavior in front of the press. After an eternal few seconds, she managed a curt nod and darted out of the office and into a nearby empty classroom where she sank down onto the floor, trying to quell the uncontrollable shaking in her body.

The next week an "exclusive interview" with "Crown Prince Harald's secret love" was published, most of it made up and accompanied by the photos shot in the office.

Not having Harald was the worst of it, she thought over and over again in the coming months. She could have endured anything with him at her side, she thought, and some nights she was nearly ill with wishing for him. She wanted to feel his strong arms go around her, protecting her from this *mess*, she wanted to laugh with him again, she wanted to merely sit and *talk* to him…but for now, pouring her heart out in her letters and receiving his in return would have to suffice. Not that she could keep his, no matter how much she treasured every stroke of his pen—she did not trust herself to find a suitable hiding place, so she would read each new letter repeatedly, memorizing the words she loved most, and then burn it in the common room fireplace or dissolve it in the bathroom sink.

December, she reminded herself daily, *you can go home in December.*

Chapter Nineteen

As Harald stepped through the front door of the Haraldsen home on Friday evening, December 15, Sonja was running down the steps, her brown eyes sparkling and her face flushed with excitement.

But he had barely had a glimpse of her before she jumped into his arms, burying her face in his neck as he lifted her. He savored the feeling of her skin against his and then set her down to look at her at last.

She could only have grown more beautiful, he thought, as he studied the shape of her face, the roundness of her nose, her soft pink lips, and those *eyes*, the eyes he had thought of for months—surely they had not been so big, so bright, so deep when she had left, because surely he would have remembered that. He looked down at the rest of her figure—she seemed even more perfectly formed than he had remembered. He wanted, desperately, to take her in his arms again, for *months* he had been longing to kiss her, but he could not bring himself to stop gazing at her...

"Oh, go on and kiss her, Harald," he heard her mother say with a laugh, and then he could wait no longer. He bent and kissed her, softly at first, and then again and again—how *had* he survived three months without this?— before he stepped back, reminding himself that they were not alone.

"You look beautiful," he said, gazing at her again.

"Do you like it? I made it in France."

This comment seemed so off the mark from his—he had been thinking of *her*, not her hairstyle or her dress or her make-up—that it took him a moment to realize she was referring to her clothes. She was wearing a dusky pink satin dress covered in elaborate designs of beads and sequins.

He smiled. "Yes, it's nice, but I didn't mean your dress."

He helped her with her coat, they walked out into the cold night air together...and *now* they were alone. "Wait, stay up there," he said as he stepped down off her front step, and she giggled—it was not the first time they had made use of a step to decrease their height difference. Their arms slipped around each other, and he kissed her again, hungrily this time. It was a far different kiss than the ones they had shared in front of her mother. He no longer needed air, or food, or water, or anything else in life—he only wanted *her*, and he did not know how he would ever let her go. He felt her press closer to him, her arms entwining themselves more tightly around his neck, and he pressed closer to her, his hands running up and down her back as he remembered how it felt to hold her.

When at last they broke apart, he picked her up off the step before she could move to walk down on her own, setting her next to him. He felt her tug on the lapel of his coat—her signal for him to bend down so they could kiss again. Had her lips always been so soft, her waist such a perfect fit for his hand, her hair so smooth as he ran his fingers through it?

"Here," she said, laughing and pulling away after far too little time to suit him, "it's cold out; let's go—we have all evening together!"

We have much longer than that together, he thought. Tonight he would be giving her the news…

They were soon on their way to Skaugum, where they would make dinner together and then set up the Christmas tree she'd wanted in the home that would be theirs at marriage, and then he would have her in his arms for the rest of the evening…

She leaned against him as he drove, and he struggled to keep his mind on the road as he breathed in the scent of her hair. "It is so wonderful to be near you again," he heard her whisper, and he laid a hand on her knee in response—he did not trust himself to turn to look at her, or she'd have him veering off into another ditch.

She was eager to decorate the tree first, and he was ecstatic merely to be with her as they did so. She seemed to find the dinner preparations hysterically funny—and he admitted he was inexcusably inept in the kitchen.

"Harald," she said as he fumbled with a fork in an unsuccessful attempt to turn the reindeer steak over, "you are nothing more than horribly, horribly in my way. Just…" The rest of her words were lost as she collapsed with laughter and he joined her, so relieved to be together again that everything was funny.

"I don't think I've laughed that hard in months," she said as they sat down to eat. "Actually, I don't think I've laughed at all in months."

"Were you miserable in France?" he asked, covering her hand with his own. Her letters home had been quite cagey, but he had had the sense that the semester had not been the relaxing escape she had had in mind.

She seemed to be on the verge of saying something, but then shook her head. "Let's not talk about France tonight."

After they had finished dinner, Harald slipped off into the kitchen to retrieve the rice pudding, and Sonja curled up on the couch in the grand salon known as the Crown Princess's Drawing Room. It occurred to her for the hundredth time how strange it was that a young seamstress should have grown so comfortable plopping down onto such rich furnishings, surrounded by ornate splendor, a priceless chandelier hanging over her head. It was at such moments that it was incomprehensible to imagine herself living here...as mistress of the Skaugum estate.

What was equally incomprehensible to her was how comfortable she, of all people, had grown in the Crown Prince's presence. Something of a perfectionist, it was only with the closest of friends and family—and certainly not with anyone she had ever dated—that she was able to truly let herself relax, cease weighing her every word and movement, and enjoy herself. Yet she had felt it with Harald almost from the beginning, and he had once told her that what he loved most about her was not her perfection but her flaws, her spaciness, and her ability to make him laugh.

"Sonja," he had once said, laughter in his eyes, "the night of my graduation ball—you had me falling for you before you'd even looked at me. I can see you now, standing at the top of your steps in a dress you'd made with far too much fabric to walk down the stairs, and I don't think it had occurred to you that you had a problem until that very second. I kept thinking about the first time I'd seen you, when you'd been laughing over that wine stain, and...you had me completely."

It had been an eye-opening conversation for someone like her.

She had been thinking about this evening for months, she thought as she spread the warm, heavy reindeer skin on the back of the couch over her legs. There was a fire blazing in the marble fireplace, the candles around the room and on the tree glowed, their soft flames wavering slightly, and a hint of spices drifted in the air. She had so often dreamed of the coziness of Norwegian winter nights.

Harald returned shortly with the rice pudding, and she was immediately drowning in their conversation again with no desire to come up for air. This was heaven, she thought, as the cool, creamy sweetness of the pudding slipped down her throat and the rich tones of his speech filled her ears.

She was raising her spoon to her mouth when she glimpsed a light brown oval amidst the white liquid and rice. She'd been the one who'd made the pudding, and she hadn't bothered to include an almond, which had to mean…

Harald was watching her intently.

"Surely I'm not going to be married very soon!" she said, trying to make light of it but feeling her heart climb into her throat at the thought that this might be a prelude to a real proposal.

"I beg to differ, Miss Haraldsen. Sophie and Juan Carlos's engagement was announced last Tuesday."

"They're engaged?" It was what they had both been hoping for—now the King knew he had lost the Greek Princess to Spain, and it would be so easy for Harald to convince him to allow an engagement for the two of them.

"They are. My father's not pleased in the slightest, but once he's had some time to calm down—"

"We'll be getting married," she whispered, kissing his cheek. It was easy, in such a moment, to forget that public opinion remained so adamant against them and to believe that their own engagement would come just as easily as Astrid's had. Indeed, in the flickering light of the candles and the fire, only ten days away from Christmas, and on the joyful night of her return home, it was impossible to feel anything but the peace of absolute trust that such fervent hopes would come true. He pulled her closer into a long kiss, the sweetness of the rice paling in comparison.

"She does seem like a very nice girl, Harald," Countess Ruth of Rosenborg, Flemming's wife, said to him over Christmas dinner. "And she's certainly made you happier than I've seen in years."

Having taken seats at the opposite end of the table from Olav, the Rosenborgs were free to quietly discuss their introduction to Sonja with Harald. It was an even larger group than the year before, including not only the Rosenborg family, Flemming's parents, and the Ferners, but also Flemming's brother and his wife and Harald's Swedish uncle Carl and his daughter.

"I have half a mind," Ruth continued impetuously, "to go to your father myself and tell him what I think of her and suggest that he quit digging his heels into the mud and agree to meet her. Eat your *lutefisk*," she said to six-year-old Desirée, who was making ghastly faces while poking the shaky white fish on her plate.

"It's *slimy*," the little girl murmured, but she shoved a piece in her mouth anyway, an expression of surprised pleasure registering on her face.

"Somehow I doubt that would much help Harald's case," Flemming said dryly.

"You heard, of course, that Sophie of Greece and Juan Carlos of Spain are engaged?" Harald said. "The wedding's in May, and after that I don't think we'll have to wait much longer."

Flemming raised his eyebrows. "Perhaps."

"Don't be so pessimistic, Flemming," his wife said with a laugh. "We're sitting here after twelve years of marriage and four children!"

"At a price which meant nothing to me but which Harald, for his country's sake, cannot afford to pay."

"I don't think I'll have to. My father's choice bride is engaged to someone else." He ignored his cousin's implied discouragement—it was far too ill of a fit with the happy atmosphere, the bright decorations, the excited Rosenborg children, and the sweetness of the sugary *lefse* flatbread.

As usual, Christmas dinner ended with English pudding and rice pudding—the almond landing this time in a delighted Desirée's plate—and the family circled around the tree to sing. As they made room for the larger number of guests, Astrid blurted out, "There will be one more of us next year!"

The chattering ceased as everyone turned to look at her. She was beaming, her smile made softer in the candlelight. "There's going to be a baby," she said, laughing.

"When?" someone called out as congratulations began to pour forth.

"August," she said, her hand slipping into Johan's as they smiled at each other.

⌒

"Astrid's expecting? How wonderful." Sonja smiled as she poured a bottle of champagne into the glasses on the counter. Standing in her kitchen with Harald on New Year's Eve, it was easy enough to forget all the difficulties of the past months. 1962 promised an engagement following Princess Sophie's marriage in May—next Christmas, their own wedding plans would be set. News of Astrid's pregnancy only brightened her evening more. "She's well enough to bear children, then?"

"Most likely." Harald paused, and she read the trepidation in his hesitancy. "Most rheumatic women can—it only causes further heart damage in a small percentage of them. But it's a *small* percentage, really."

"Do you think she'll have more children if everything goes all right?" Sonja asked.

"Oh, absolutely. She wants at least three, maybe four or five."

With her siblings so much older—and out of the house for most of her childhood—she had often felt like an only child and had always been in awe of larger families. "I'd like that," she said softly.

"What?"

"A large family. Five or six babies." In a couple years, she thought with a smile, she would likely be holding her first.

"I'd like that, too." He smiled back, their hands lingering to prolong their touch as he passed her another glass to fill.

Would her children suffer from the press attention as she did? Of course not—Harald hadn't. They would have the protection of being royal. She had only been home for two weeks, and the photographers had been just as bad, if not worse, as they had been in the summer.

She sighed and filled the champagne glass.

"Something wrong?" Harald asked.

"No," she said automatically, not wanting to ruin the moment or the evening. "That is, yes—I was thinking of the press—but never mind."

"Are you all right?"

She hesitated. "Yes," she decided. "I think it's only because I've just gotten back—I wasn't around to have my picture taken all fall. I think it'll get better."

~

Of course, it did not get better. It was not as hard as in France as she did not have the isolation and loneliness to contend with, but Sonja still could not keep herself from glancing at the covers of tabloids, reading the letters to the editor in the morning paper, and listening to the radio. In addition to being an unattractive snob who imagined herself superior to the rest of the country, she was "an unspeakably poor choice," "the indication of everything wrong with the monarchy today," and "indisputable evidence that the Crown Prince does not, will not, and cannot understand his responsibility—does he really imagine that a *seamstress* makes an acceptable candidate for Queen?" The occasional letter of support did little to calm her.

"I feel like a zoo animal," she confided in Harald over dinner. "It's the way people *look* at me that I hate the most. I'm just constantly *stared* at, *everywhere*." It was the same whether she was walking down the street, riding the streetcar, standing in line in a shop…her skin crawled as she felt unknown eyes focusing on her. The increasing number of spectators in the Haraldsen family store had come to mean that she confined herself only to the back room. "And the *photographers*…They're all over, even when I'm just going in to work."

"What if I bought you a car?" he said suddenly. "And I'll pay for the gas, the maintenance, everything."

"A car?" Her parents had always had one when she was a child, and her mother still owned one, but it was not driven very often. She had never had her own.

"Yes," he said. "You won't be nearly as exposed that way—you won't spend nearly as much time in crowds—it'll be much harder to get good photos of you—wouldn't it be easier?"

"Well, yes, I—thank you," she said, still trying to wrap her mind around the offer. Of course Harald had the money, but she had never been given anywhere near such a large gift before. "Thank you. That would be really wonderful of you." It wouldn't solve everything, but it would make things easier.

He smiled. "It's the least I can do—I'm the reason you're dealing with all this anyway."

She did not know quite what she had expected—of course he wasn't getting her an old clunker that barely ran—but when he handed her the keys to a new BMW later that week, she almost fainted.

There were fewer photos once she started driving, and she had far more peace than before, but there was still no getting rid of the photographers when she *wasn't* in the car. The photos that *were* taken were still splashed across magazines up and down the country. And of course nothing could be done to improve what was written about her.

The few photos continued the process which had begun in August of making Sonja into even more of a perfectionist than she had ever been. She was unwilling to go anywhere without make-up more suitable for an evening in Hollywood than a trip to the dry cleaners, and she obsessed about her hair, spending hours blow drying and curling and brushing and beginning again if she weren't completely satisfied. Worse were the little things she could not fix about her appearance, the little things she had barely noticed in the past but which had become glaring flaws now that they had been sneeringly pointed out. Her nose, for one—*Could the Crown Prince not at least choose an unacceptable bride with a smaller nose?* rang in her head. She had never before considered it the least bit large, but now it was a horrific monstrosity. And of course there was nothing she could do about any of it, in spite of all the time she now spent staring into mirrors and berating herself. Her only "comfort" was the articles that criticized her looks only for being far *too* perfect, accused her of wearing enough make-up to find a position in a circus, and questioned exactly how natural her face was. Once—in some distant past where she had laughed at everything—it might have all been funny. It wasn't now.

"I hate this," she said bluntly to Harald one evening as they sat on the sofa at Skaugum. "I know we can be engaged this summer and then married, and I know it'll be much better at that point, but for now..."

"I know," he said regretfully. "I know they write horrible things about you—"

"And about my family."

He nodded. "But—and I wish I had a better solution—it won't be like this after the engagement. You'll be the Crown Prince's fiancée. It will be very, very different press coverage."

"Yes." The fact that, at the end of this, she would not only be treated more fairly by the press but would be *able to marry Harald* was what kept her going. "Marriage is...the light at the end of all this. And it's worth it to me, but right now...it's just so awful. It's...hard to read in the newspaper every day that half the country hates you."

"Half the country doesn't hate you, *min kjære*. It's a very loud, very small minority."

"I know that, but it seems that way from what I'm reading. This morning it was, 'Sonja Haraldsen is nowhere near the beauty one would expect the Crown Prince to marry.' Being involved with a common seamstress is 'the height of shabbiness' on your part. Of course, that's nowhere near the worst of it. Sometimes I lie awake at night worrying about what I'm going to find in the morning, but today's actually been a rather tame day."

"Sonja, there's nothing I can do to fix this."

She stiffened, stung by the irritation in his voice. She had never wanted to whine about the press and had made a conscious effort not to, nor had she wanted to turn every evening spent together into a long complaining session. She had thought she'd been successful. "I don't mean to complain," she said softly.

"It's not that you're complaining—I wouldn't mind if you were. It's that you keep asking me to fix it, and I *want* to fix it, and I can't, and it's frustrating."

"I've never asked you to fix it! I know you can't do anything," she said, suddenly both defensive and annoyed.

"You've been asking me to fix it tonight. And all the other times you've mentioned the press coverage."

"I don't ask you to fix it! I'm only talking about it—I just want to talk to you about it. I need to talk to you. It *helps* to talk to you. I don't need you to fix it; I just need you to listen to me."

"Oh." He paused. "I didn't think—I'm sorry. It's just—I want to fix it for you, and I can't...I didn't mean to hurt you."

She smiled. "Typical man. A woman tells you something's wrong, and you need to fix it. Which is sweet of you, really." She kissed his cheek. "But no. Just listen to me."

"All right," he said, quite seriously, "I'm listening." She laughed softly.

"I think," she began slowly, "that it's almost *worse* for me than it would be for some girls...not that anyone would like it. It's...I always want to make things perfect, I want to come across perfectly, I want everything to be *right*. It's just how I am; I can't help it, and it's stressful in normal situations—I feel like I'm *performing* sometimes. And with this...they're picking at everything they think is wrong with me, they're analyzing all my flaws, they're announcing why and how I would fail as Crown Princess...I don't *like* it when they tell outright lies about me, but it's the stuff that I think might be true that bothers me much, much more. I'm so much more stressed about myself, and everything I do, and everything I wear, just *everything*, because I feel like I have to perform for the whole country, because they're all watching all the time, and I feel like I'm getting it horribly, horribly wrong. I can't get it *right*—it's...about as impossible as threading a needle with no eye."

"You don't have to put on a performance for any of these people."

"I know...but I feel like I am anyway. I nearly always feel that way."

"You certainly don't have to do it for me."

She smiled slightly. "I don't do it for you. I don't feel that way when I'm with you. I've never felt that way with you. It's...rare for me."

He smiled. "Maybe you realized you couldn't possibly pull off a perfect impression when the first time I saw you, you had wine all over your dress, and you gave up." She laughed. "But seriously, Sonja," he went on, "I don't love you because you're perfect."

"I know." She slipped her hand into his, comforted by the way it completely enveloped her own. "And that's wonderful." She sighed. "But it isn't that way with the press. It's a perfectionist's nightmare, and...it's completely out of control. I...like to feel like I have some control over things."

"And of course, you can't control the press at all. But you're trying to."

"Yes."

He caressed the back of her hand with his thumb, and she shifted closer to him to lay her head against his arm, calmed by the silence and by his presence.

"I keep praying it'll just *stop*," she said after a moment. "Or that I'll just get used to it! But neither of those seem very likely."

"I pray for you, too, Sonja," he said softly.

"Thank you." She paused. "The worst thing is that sometimes I wonder if any of it's *true*."

"It isn't," he said immediately. "It's all a bunch of lies."

"I think there might be some truth in how I'll fail as Crown Princess—"

"There isn't. You'll be a wonderful success. Norway will love you—once it has a chance to know you. It'll all be very different this summer, once we're engaged and the public knows more about you than just all the nonsense the press is printing right now."

"This summer…" She paused, hopeful again. She only had to make it past Princess Sophie's wedding in May, then she and Harald could soon be officially engaged, and all of this would change.

"Can you make it till then?"

"Yes. Absolutely. It isn't so very long." She could make it until summer.

Chapter Twenty

"DO YOU THINK SHE'LL LIKE ME?" SONJA WHISPERED, FIDDLING WITH HER pearls. She and Harald were following the butler through a mostly-white room filled with moose and deer heads at Fredensborg Palace, the fall and spring residence of the Danish Royal Family. They had been over this before, but now that they were minutes away from meeting Crown Princess Margrethe, she wanted to run through it once more.

Harald had an afternoon event at the embassy in Copenhagen and had suggested Sonja come down to Denmark with him and make a day of it. They had flown in early in the morning—making an elaborate show of *not* noticing the other's presence in the Oslo airport—and then driven out to Fredensborg, where they would have lunch with Harald's cousin, the Danish Crown Princess, whom he said he thought Sonja would like very much. In the afternoon they would return to Copenhagen, and he would attend the event while Sonja toured one of the city's art museums.

Harald sighed. "You know I think she'll like you. I'm only introducing you to her because I think you'll like each other."

"And you don't think I'll mess up? Or embarrass you?"

"You'd never embarrass me, and you can't possibly mess up—you're only meeting my cousin. And she's three years younger than you. Don't be intimidated by a twenty-two-year-old."

She had tried to remind herself of all that, but she could not manage to see Her Royal Highness The Crown Princess of Denmark as "only Harald's cousin," despite the equality of their ranks. In truth, she was dreading the meeting, sure that Her Royal Highness would not approve of her or her relationship with Harald and would instantly mark her as unsuitable.

"Regardless, Daisy will love you—she nearly always likes people, and I think the two of you will get along very well together."

"Daisy?"

"The family calls her that sometimes instead of Margrethe—it's such a long name."

It was, but it was very pretty, she thought, as she rolled the three syllables over in her head—*mar-GRAY-dah*.

"Do you think I'm wearing the right thing? Am I overdressed or underdressed?" Unsure how one dressed to meet a foreign crown princess, she had changed her plans for her clothes multiple times over the past few days, settling on a houndstooth wool suit—it was April, but it was still quite cold—with a small white hat, gloves, and heels. It seemed the conservative, fashionable, proper thing to be wearing, but now she was debating whether it was too much or too little.

"How should I know? You look beautiful."

Sonja sighed. She was thankful that the furnishings and décor here were not nearly as grand as at the Palace in Oslo. This was quite clearly Harald's Danish cousins' country residence, and the lesser amounts of gold leaf and crystal made her slightly less uncomfortable.

"Your Royal Highness?" the butler said as he opened the doors to the next room. Suddenly sickeningly nervous, Sonja hung back behind Harald and made no effort to glimpse inside. "The Crown Prince of Norway and Miss Haraldsen to see you, ma'am." He nodded and left them.

Harald stepped in alone, Sonja following no further than the threshold. It was a sizable sitting room, she could see, with silk wall hangings, a painting of angels on the ceiling, and a purple couch and chairs. There was a tall young woman standing inside, her light brown hair pulled up into an elegant chignon with a small, feathery maroon fascinator attached. She was wearing a dress covered in maroon and gold flowers with a slightly flared skirt, a matching jacket, and a single strand of pearls. It was slightly fancier than Sonja's outfit, but within a similar range, and she felt a sense of mild relief.

Margrethe and Harald kissed each other. The most striking thing, Sonja thought, was that she was nearly Harald's height and thus had to be at least six feet. Sonja felt even shorter than usual.

"So this is her, then," Margrethe said after they had greeted each other, glancing at Sonja with a smile. She spoke in Danish, the two languages being close enough for easy understanding.

"Yes," Harald said. "Daisy, this is Sonja Haraldsen."

Sonja curtsied elegantly from the door, her eyes downcast, then forced herself to swallow her nerves and make eye contact.

She could see at once that the Crown Princess was not beautiful. She had a rather plain face, she had been unsuccessful in her attempts to cover the many imperfections in her complexion with make-up, and her left eye was not only slightly smaller than her right, but also not focusing in quite the same direction. Yet she had a certain graceful elegance about her, and there was something wonderfully warm and kind in the smile she offered.

"It's lovely to meet you. Don't stand back there in the doorway; I generally don't bite guests." She laughed softly. Her voice was certainly very pretty, with the softness of velvet and the smoothness of silk, and there was something quite calming in its slow cadence.

"Your Royal Highness," Sonja said, beginning to sweep into a second, flawless curtsy as she joined them in the center of the room. But somehow—and she wasn't quite sure how, after practicing it a million times—she managed to step backwards awkwardly with her right foot, and suddenly her legs were giving out beneath her and she was tumbling. In her moment of panic, she frantically reached out for the nearest solid object to break her fall. Her right hand hit the crystal lamp on the table next to her and knocked it crashing to the floor. Before she could join it, she managed to catch her balance on the table, falling against it.

The lamp, she thought immediately, still leaning on the table and closing her eyes. *Don't be broken, please don't be broken…*

Harald was at her side in an instant, pulling her back to her feet. "Are you all right?" she heard him ask.

She ignored the question, forcing herself to glance at the carpet. The lamp had shattered. She hadn't been at Fredensborg half an hour and had already managed to break something. Maybe she should just hang a sign around her neck with "Unsuitable Consort" written across it.

"I'm so *sorry*—your lamp—I'll pay for it—really," she gasped, wishing the carpet would swallow her whole.

Margrethe waved the offer away. "Are you all right, dear?"

"Yes." *How humiliating…it was a* curtsy, *for heaven's sake; it hadn't been that difficult.*

"Well, that's all that matters, then," Her Royal Highness said with a shrug.

"But your lamp…" Sonja looked down at the splinters of crystal. The thing was probably worth more than her whole family made in a year.

"Forget the lamp; we've got a room full of them. I can't begin to tell you how many my sisters and I have broken ourselves." Margrethe laughed. "I'm sorry—I'm not laughing at you—but that was the most entertaining curtsy I've seen in my entire life. Which," she added thoughtfully, "is probably saying something."

Harald grinned. "Not a bad introduction, Sonja. You've certainly made an impression."

Obviously. They would be telling this story for years in royal circles. She attempted a weak smile.

"Shall we pick this up and go in to lunch then?" Margrethe asked, turning to Harald. Sonja stood rooted to her spot, watching in mortified silence as the heirs to the Danish and Norwegian thrones knelt and cleaned up after her.

"Really, Miss Haraldsen, it was actually rather charming," Margrethe said, smiling warmly as she stood. "I do get a bit bored, you know, with the endless perfect curtsies."

Sonja managed a smile in response. "Thank you. But really," she added, "I could pay—"

"Nonsense." Margrethe shook her head. "I don't want to hear another word about it—I'll send someone in to vacuum up the rest later. But now," she said, taking Sonja's arm, "we have a lunch ready for both of you."

Harald followed behind as Margrethe led Sonja off through the grandest room yet—the Garden Room, she would later learn—a gold-leaf-encrusted hall with groups of gold chairs and scenes of a crumbling Rome painted directly on its walls. Yet she had little time to concentrate on her surroundings as Margrethe was chattering on about how "Harald's told me you've spent some time in France and you've got to tell me all about that; I'll be studying in Paris at the Sorbonne all next year..."

There was something charmingly awkward-yet-natural in her mannerisms and her speech with its hesitant pauses, as though she were only a bit more sure of herself than Sonja, and she seemed to stammer slightly at times in search of the best phrase. Her Royal Highness was wonderfully open over lunch in the smaller and homier red dining room, telling them of the year of school she was about to finish at Århus University on the Danish mainland—she was home this week for Easter break. She drew Sonja into conversation about the time she had spent abroad, appearing decidedly interested in everything she had to say. Sonja, rather flattered by the attention she was paying her, was just beginning to let herself relax when Margrethe said, "And then after you came home from England, you met Harald."

Sonja shot a nervous glance at Harald. This was the area in which her own inferiority was so evident, and she was certain that she would catch a hint of disapproval in the Crown Princess's face or tone, even if Margrethe were too polite to say it directly.

"I—yes, I did," she said, hesitant to say any more than was necessary. She nervously fingered the swirly F and I, their backs to each other in a mirror image, on the back of her fork, King Frederik and Queen Ingrid's monogram.

"You were at a party, weren't you? And Harald spilled wine on your dress?"

Sonja nodded, surprised at the level of detail Margrethe remembered from what Harald had apparently told her.

"And then he took you to his graduation ball. But that was all I could get from him—men do a horrible job with such stories." She laughed. "Will you tell me more, Miss Haraldsen?"

Tell her more? Sonja could not believe that the Danish Crown Princess desired to hear any more of the origins of what was quickly becoming the scandal of the century for the Norwegian monarchy, but her expression seemed to be one of genuine interest. Unwilling to divulge much of her own feelings to a near-stranger, she gave her a guarded version of events that nonetheless left Margrethe hanging on her every word, her eyes widened in enchantment.

"That's wonderful, just *wonderful*—I think it's just so beautiful that you two have stayed together through all this and that you're so willing to fight for your love, and I'm sure you'll be married eventually; I don't have any doubts. And the way you met is just lovely, and I can't imagine anything more romantic for your first date than a *ball*..."

It was a vastly different reaction than the sniff of disapproval Sonja had been expecting, and she smiled cautiously. "Thank you."

"You must tell me what you wore."

What she wore? The Crown Princess of Denmark, the contents of whose closet were probably worth more than Sonja's entire house, cared what she had worn to a ball? "I designed this pink floral evening gown—"

"Oh, do you design your own clothing? Did you make that suit? It's pretty."

"Thank you, but I bought this. I do sometimes design things myself—that's what I was going to school for in Switzerland, dressmaking. I'd like to go into fashion design at some point."

"Really? I love that sort of thing, and I'm always drawing up sketches for dresses—I'd like to make one of them sometime; I do know how to sew—but I don't really feel that I know what I'm doing, so I've never actually done it. Would you mind having a look at some of my drawings?"

Harald glanced at his watch. "We'll have to be getting back to Copenhagen soon—"

"Oh." Sonja had not noticed the passage of time, but she looked at her own watch and saw that he was right. "I would love to see them, though," she said, disappointed. "Do you think there's time if I look quickly?"

Harald hesitated. "If it's only a few minutes."

"You can stay here this afternoon, Miss Haraldsen, if you would like; I don't mind. Harald can go to the ambassador's reception and then come back and get you—would that be all right with your flight time this evening?"

Harald nodded. "If you want to stay, Sonja—"

"We can sit and talk about clothes all afternoon while he stands in the receiving line," Margrethe said with a soft laugh. "Unless you had your heart set on doing something in the city."

"Oh, no! I'd love to stay," Sonja said. She liked Margrethe and was relieved to find herself so readily accepted.

Harald left for Copenhagen, and Sonja and Margrethe returned to the sitting room with the purple furniture, Margrethe retrieving a stack of drawings. "I left most of my better sketches back in Århus, but I can show you some of my older stuff," she said, passing them to Sonja.

She was impressed, she noted to herself as she looked through the stack, especially if Margrethe didn't even consider any of this her best work. It was apparent that Her Royal Highness was quite a capable artist. "Some of these are exceptionally good, ma'am...did you study this somewhere?"

Margrethe shook her head. "No, that is, other than looking at all the designs that have been drawn up for my sisters and me over the years." The two girls spent the next hour poring over sketches and discussing fabrics. The conversation soon turned to art in general, they discovered a mutual interest in painting, and Sonja mentioned her own love of art history—had she gone to university, it was absolutely what she would have studied.

"Oh, well then you simply must see some of the paintings we've got here at Fredensborg! I could show you everything in all the rooms—I've grown up hearing about all of it. Are you interested?"

A private tour of all the art in one of the Danish Royal Family's residences? With someone who knew it as well as Margrethe surely did? She nodded enthusiastically, nearly salivating at the suggestion.

"Harald ought to have suggested this to me; I'm glad it's come up. Are there any periods you're particularly interested in? We have nearly everything here; it's a pity you're flying out tonight, we could have spent all day tomorrow running all over Copenhagen, and I could have shown you even more..."

The rest of the afternoon was spent traipsing about the Palace, Margrethe chattering excitedly about everything as Sonja gazed in awe at the centuries-old works, struggling to soak everything in. She lost all remnant of nerves or shyness in the first twenty minutes and was soon jumping in with questions and observations of her own.

Several short hours later, Harald returned for her—they would have dinner together in the capital before flying back. "Perhaps," Margrethe said before Sonja left with him, "if you aren't too busy this summer, Miss Haraldsen, I was thinking it might be nice to have you down to Denmark a couple times—I'll bring all my sketches home from Århus, and I was wondering if perhaps you could help me make something—"

Margrethe wanted to see her again? That was certainly how it sounded, because surely someone far more qualified than she could be found to help the Crown Princess with her sewing.

"If you've got time for it, that is," Margrethe said quickly. "And of course I would show you all the best art in Copenhagen—"

"Oh, of course, ma'am, of course! I would love to." She was flattered at the invitation.

"Good." Margrethe smiled. "I thought—I thought it might be rather fun to have you here."

Chapter Twenty-One

HER ROYAL HIGHNESS PRINCESS SOPHIE OF GREECE MARRIED HIS ROYAL Highness Prince Juan Carlos of Spain in Athens on May 14, 1962, in the presence of hundreds of government officials, members of the nobility and aristocracy, and representatives of all the European royal houses. She married him twice, in fact, and having to attend both the Catholic and Orthodox ceremonies in one morning did nothing to improve King Olav's temperament. He spoke very little to Harald, who accompanied him and who was aware of the blackness of his father's mood. Harald was not at all displeased at this, as it marked for him the King's full realization and acceptance that Sophie was lost for good…leaving the way open for Sonja.

The Catholic wedding was remarkable for its grandeur, with the golden carriage the bride and her father arrived in, the vast floral arrangements erupting all over, and the expensive gold-fringed cushions provided for Sophie and Juan Carlos to kneel on during the ceremony. It was nothing short of what Harald would have expected Frederica to produce for her favorite child, although he did think she had outdone herself with the thrones set off to the side at the front of the church for her and King Pavlos.

As the guests stood at the bride's entrance, Olav sighed audibly and gave Harald an irritated look. Sophie *was* beautiful, Harald admitted to himself, watching his cousin process down the aisle in a lace-covered gown of silver lamé. Her veil—five yards of handmade lace—was held in place by a diamond tiara, and a twenty-foot train trailed behind her. Yet her face lacked the radiance that had so transfigured Astrid on her own wedding day—there was only a small smile playing across Sophie's lips, and her eyes seemed empty of any emotion.

In the oddest behavior Harald had ever seen for a groom, Juan Carlos still had his back turned as she approached, not having yet looked at his bride. Harald felt as though he were watching a bad play. When Sophie reached the altar and exchanged her father's arm for the groom's, Juan gave her nothing more than a cursory glance before turning again to the front of the church.

Juan's manner was the detached cool of a businessman, while Sophie seemed so deadened that Harald was almost relieved to see her weeping halfway through the ceremony, although he did not for a moment mistake them for tears of joy. Juan did not react until Irene, who was standing behind him, stepped forward and passed him a handkerchief that he handed to Sophie without looking at her.

Harald felt for her as she wiped her eyes, took her vows, and knelt at the altar—she was sweet and kind and, yes, very beautiful, and while he did not love her and was certain now that Juan Carlos did not love her either, he knew she was far from unlovable. Had she been born anyone else, had she been nothing more than a young Greek girl in one of the country's many tiny villages, she would surely have met a young man who would have fallen in love with her, and her wedding would have been the celebration Astrid's was. He was struck by a sudden grief for the life, the home, the happiness his cousin might have had.

But Sophia Margaret Victoria Frederica had been born a Princess of Greece, eldest daughter of Their Majesties, and her mother had been determined to make her a Queen. There had been only two men in Europe who could give her a throne, himself and Juan Carlos. The fact that neither of those men loved Sophie was irrelevant.

After the Catholic ceremony ended, all the guests moved to the Metropolitan Cathedral where the Greek Orthodox wedding would be held. The interior of the building looked to Harald like one vast mural, the walls and ceiling covered in centuries-old icons. The setting, he knew, would have been a deeply meaningful one for Sophie, and he was struck by the contrast of her empty, meaningless marriage.

The ceremony was a haze of rituals and rites drawing upon that ancient atmosphere that seemed to seep from the Greek soil itself. There were no vows exchanged in the Orthodox church, and the emphasis on ceremony, so different from his own background, served to make it all seem that much more of a performance. One of the many priests—a bearded old man in jeweled gold robes and headdress whose finery rivaled those Harald had seen worn at coronations—opened the service with the burning of incense, a stiflingly sweet smell in the heated building. His chanting and the clanging of the censer's bells replaced the loud buzz of conversation, and then the blessing of rings was performed. *A blessing for* what? Harald could not help but think as the priest lifted Sophie and Juan's rings before them. Their marriage would never be any more than a façade. He looped the rings through the air in the sign of the cross and then placed them on the couple's fingers, switching them back and forth between them three times. Once he had read from the gold-plated Bible in his hands, the priest held it before the bride and groom, who each kissed it and then drank from a cup of wine.

King Pavlos stepped up behind Juan and Sophie to lift two jewel-encrusted gold crowns over their heads in a symbol of the glory of God. The crowns, too, were moved back and forth three times before Constantine came forward to take Sophie's from their father. Slowly, the priest led the couple in three processionals around the altar as Constantine and Pavlos, still holding the crowns in the air, and the bridesmaids, managing the massive train, followed. In addition to those tossed by Frederica and Juan Carlos's mother, rose petals showered down from the ceiling as they walked.

How strange it was, Harald thought, that two weddings of such pageantry, meant to display the splendor of the Greek court and to showcase the amount of money Frederica could afford to lavish on her daughter, and held in the two Christian churches most known for elaborate spectacle—how strange that these ceremonies should seem nothing more than cheap imitations after he had witnessed Astrid's simple service last year.

After the second wedding a reception was held at the Greek palace. The room itself was something of a joke—the Greek Royal Family did not have the wealth of many of the others, and the smaller scale of its palaces reflected that. The room and its furnishings were a mere shadow of Oslo's palace, and if the occasional cracks in the columns lining the edge of the ballroom were any indication, money for upkeep was in short supply. Yet Frederica had once again outdone herself with what she could buy—she had brought out the most expensive dishes, the finest silver, the most exquisite rugs, and Harald expected she had spent half the household budget on flower arrangements. It was an elaborate show of a pretense of money. Harald watched as the towering wedding cake, topped with a crown, was wheeled out into the banquet room and Juan and Sophie awkwardly cut into the bottom layer with a sword. He suspected, as at many royal weddings, that it was the only layer of actual cake—the other pieces were merely decorative. There were infinitely less expensive sheet cakes in the back that would be cut and served to the guests.

The crowds at the tables dwindled after the cake was eaten and the dance floor was opened. Constantine was with Princess Anne-Marie of Denmark, whom he had been hovering over throughout the banquet and during all the pre-wedding festivities of the last few days. At fifteen, Margrethe's beautiful baby sister had the air of a butterfly and the innocence of a newborn kitten.

It was apparent in her giggles and her starry eyes that she was flattered by the Greek Crown Prince's attentions, yet Harald doubted the twenty-two-year-old young man could have much sincere interest in a schoolgirl. Then he caught a glimpse of Frederica smiling approvingly at the couple. So that was it. Constantine hoped to please his mother, who rumor had it was not the least bit amused by gossip of her son's alleged relationship with a Greek actress. He felt a stab of pity for pretty little Anne-Marie, merely a pawn in this nonsensical game and too naïve to recognize it for what it was.

"Well, you've just seen the best bride in royal Europe married off to Spain," King Olav said sourly, breaking into Harald's thoughts. "You've managed to lose Sophie for good while you were running about with that shopkeeper's daughter."

"Yes." Harald glanced around—with the orchestra playing and most guests out on the dance floor, it appeared that they had at least a few moments for a relatively private conversation. "We *have* lost Sophie, Father. I was thinking that perhaps now might be the time—now that we have no hope of a match with Sophie of Greece—to consider going ahead with an engagement with Sonja Haraldsen."

The King laughed in response.

"I'm serious, sir."

"And crazy, apparently," Olav said dismissively.

"Sir, I think perhaps you might consider this situation in the same way you considered Astrid's, especially now that Sophie is no longer an option. You allowed Astrid to marry because she was the only woman available to fulfill the role of First Lady, and I'm the only man available to inherit the throne one day."

His Majesty laughed again, but there was no humor in his laughter this time. "Do you really believe that the reason I allowed Astrid and Johan to marry was that I was afraid to lose her as First Lady? Are you really so deluded as to believe that I'm that easily blackmailed? I was concerned about that issue, yes, but there were issues in play for Astrid that do not apply to you. Astrid is never going to be anything more than the King's daughter or the King's sister; you will be the sovereign. Her spouse will never be of any consequence to the monarchy, whereas yours will be Queen and the mother of the future King. Tell me you haven't been operating all along under the theory that, once Sophie married Juan Carlos, I would allow you to do what Astrid did because you imagined your situations identical."

It was exactly the theory Harald had been operating under, and the King's eyes bulged in anger at his silence.

"You—you—of all the most *irrational* ideas, Harald—some of the most harebrained logic I've heard out of you yet—if I'd known you were thinking this, if I'd only known—rest assured you would have been set straight *months* ago—and here we've lost *Sophie* over this, *Sophie*! Which is not to imply, Harald," he continued, his eyes narrowing, "that we have run out of royal brides for you, as you seem to have assumed. We may have lost the best to the Spaniards, but there are princesses all over this blasted continent that you can marry, and *I will see you marry one of them before the decade is out* if it kills us both. Among the other Scandinavian houses alone you could have Désirée or Christina of Sweden or Benedikte or Anne-Marie of Denmark…"

A horrific line of royal brides seemed to stretch on before him as his father continued to rattle off names: "…to say nothing of Juan Carlos's two sisters in Spain, or one of the Dutch princesses! You are *not* finished, Harald—you have a meeting with Princess Margriet of the Netherlands at the end of the summer—"

This had to be stopped now. "I'm not marrying Margriet or Benedikte or any of the others, and it's a waste of my time and theirs to pretend it's a possibility. I have every intention of marrying Sonja Haraldsen, and an engagement ought to be announced sooner rather than later because she's falling apart under the press attention."

"Harald," the King said in a tone that suggested he was fighting to hold his voice down, "I have explained this before. That shopkeeper's daughter's feelings, your feelings, and everybody else's feelings are *absolutely irrelevant* here. *This is about the future of the monarchy.* I can't think of anything that could possibly matter any less than how some shopkeeper's daughter feels about this."

"I can't think of anything that matters more!"

The King paused and gave their surroundings a quick glance. Apparently satisfied that they had not been overheard but not wanting to risk it any further, he turned back to his son. "Princess Alexandra of Kent is alone. Go dance with her."

There would be no marriage within the year, then, as he had assured Sonja on so many occasions. He did not doubt, however, and would certainly tell her, that there would be one eventually because he was determined to bring it about. *And how?* he asked himself. *How are you going to do that?*

"I spoke to my father about our engagement when we were in Athens," Harald said as he and Sonja sat down on the couch in her living room. It was the evening of May 17, *Syttende Mai*, and Harald had come after the day's celebrations to enjoy the rest of her mother's homemade ice cream. The national day had been relatively warm this year with temperatures in the sixties, but as twilight had fallen around ten the air had grown chillier and they had moved inside from their seats in her backyard.

"And?" Her eyes sparkling, she reached for his hand. She had not raised the subject herself and had been hoping all evening that he would give her the news she had been waiting for.

"Sonja, it's not going to work the way we've been hoping. He—he said no."

She tightened her grip on his hand, understanding in her body what her mind could not yet comprehend. "But you—your sister and her husband—didn't the King…"

"He says Astrid's situation was vastly different."

No, that couldn't be the case…Harald had said again and again that once Sophie was married, the way would be clear for them…

"And he told you we're not getting married?" she asked, her voice shaking slightly. She had hung everything on a summer engagement for the better part of a year, and she felt the hope slipping through her fingertips, as insubstantial as a silk thread.

"He refused to approve the engagement right now—"

"Which means we're not getting married," she said slowly, no longer able to look at Harald. She tried to withdraw her hand, pulling into herself as the news sank in.

He held on. "*No.* It means we're not getting married now, but we *will* be married eventually, I promise—"

"Nothing's going to change." With no heart for false hope, she pulled her hand away and stood up. The afternoon's parades and parties suddenly seemed very, very far away, and the celebratory mood of the day felt horribly wrong. "There's no reason we'll ever be allowed to marry."

"Sonja, listen to me. It may take awhile longer, *but I will make my father see reason. We will be married.*"

Waves of desperation were sweeping over her, and she wondered as she paced if this sense of disorientation and panic was what it was like to drown. "You can't make it happen, Harald, you just can't, there's probably a whole string of princesses your father has for you after Sophie, and there's no reason the King will ever agree." She heard the pitch of her voice beginning to climb, and she paused, fighting to control it.

Harald's next words seem to come from a great distance, and she was only half-aware of them. "It's only the first time I've directly requested an engagement, and it may take a few attempts. This will just take a bit more time—"

"No, it won't *ever* happen, it *won't*, we'll never get there, we'll still be waiting twenty years from now…"

"No, we won't. We won't, Sonja, I promise you I won't let that happen," Harald whispered, coming to her and taking her in his arms. She let him hold her for a moment in silence.

"There's nothing you can do; we're just not ever getting married," she said softly, finally pulling away. "There's nothing either of us can do." The illusion that she and Harald had had some sort of control over the situation by simply waiting out Sophie had been torn apart, and she was painfully realizing that they had absolutely no power to change anything.

"Sonja, I'm going to keep working on this." He reached out for her again.

She wanted his embrace but at the same time could not bear it, and she stepped away and sank down onto the couch. She knew that, in a more rational state, she might accept his assurance and agree that there could very well be some progress made in another six months. But tonight, when she had been expecting for so very long to be engaged in a few weeks…

"Sonja—"

"Please, Harald," she whispered, "I need you to go." She wanted to be alone with her tears, alone to calm herself, alone to convince herself the conversation had not happened.

"No, I'll stay—I don't want to leave you alone."

"Just go! *Just go!*"

He hesitated for a moment then bent and kissed her. "I love you. I'll call you tomorrow."

She heard his footsteps as he crossed the room, then the front door opened and shut behind him, and she was alone.

Chapter Twenty-Two

IN THE WEEKS THAT FOLLOWED THE GREEK-SPANISH WEDDING, SONJA could not bear to be at home, she could not bear to be in the store offices, she could not bear to be with Harald—everything in Oslo was a stifling, oppressive presence, and she was nearly collapsing under the strain. *We are not getting married, we are not getting married, we are not getting married…* the thought repeated itself to her thousands of times each day.

The fact that it was summer felt nothing short of ridiculous. Oslo was a festive city in June, with eighteen hours of sunlight, ice cream for sale on every corner, and a fountain in every square turned on full blast. Early March would have felt more natural, she sometimes thought, when the days were still dark and it seemed as though nothing would ever thaw. In her own world, it would *never* be summer.

She desperately wanted some sort of escape, but she was not at all sure what that could be—even time spent in Harald's arms, far from Oslo at Gamlehaugen, could not soothe her. It was only a reminder of what she could not and would not have.

"Sonja, you have a letter from the Danish palace!" she heard her mother call one afternoon. The Danish palace? She had all but forgotten Crown Princess Margrethe's invitation to visit over the summer and had nearly convinced herself that Margrethe herself would surely not remember. But perhaps…

She hurried into the kitchen and took the envelope from Dagny, opening it carefully so as not to damage the address on the back: *Amalienborg Slot, Amaliegade 18, 1015 København K, Danmark.* Inside was a thin sheet of fine paper with the words *H.K.H. Kronprinsesse Margrethe* printed at the top beneath a small monogram of two M's swirled together beneath a crown. *Miss Haraldsen,* the handwritten note read, *I've been very much hoping that you're still able to come down to Denmark this summer as we discussed at Easter. I'll be returning from Århus on Friday, June 29, and should be available most days with the exception of the third week of July.* It was signed simply, "Margrethe."

Sonja slowly ran her fingers over the lines of text. *Thank you.*

Upon her arrival the next Wednesday at the Danish Royal Family's summer palace in the countryside, Gråsten, she was brought to Margrethe's apartments and let in to a sitting room where the Crown Princess was waiting for her. Sonja was in a hat and gloves again, but Margrethe was merely wearing a light cotton summer dress with a slightly full skirt and a blue floral pattern, and Sonja was glad she had packed more casual dresses.

"Your Royal Highness," she said, attempting to sink into a shaky curtsy while still holding her suitcase.

Margrethe raised her eyebrows. "You had better not try that while you're holding that. Here." She stood up and came over to her, her eyes twinkling. "Let me take it, or we may be losing another lamp."

Rather surprised, Sonja passed it to her and dropped into a perfect curtsy which Margrethe, who was already leading her out of the room and still carrying the suitcase, seemed disinterested in. "I've got your room back here, and then I thought perhaps we could sit out on the terrace and have a drink; it's such a beautiful afternoon…"

Margrethe stepped into her kitchen on their way outside, offering Sonja a glass of wine to take with her. Expecting to be given nothing more than lemon soda or a cup of tea, she was momentarily stunned but accepted. Margrethe's wealth aside, it was something of a surprise to be considered worthy of the expense.

Once outside, Sonja was asked, naturally, about Harald, and she told Margrethe briefly of their failed hopes about Sophie and Juan Carlos's wedding. They had taken seats on the terrace in the back of the Palace, overlooking a large yard that led up to the blue water of the Flensborg Fjord, which separated the country from West Germany. The whole area was completely and utterly still except for a light breeze and the occasional bird, and it was quite easy to feel she could say absolutely anything here.

"So now," she said, hearing herself give voice to the fear she had not mentioned to anyone but Harald, "I'm not sure—I'm not sure it can ever happen. The King's sending Harald off to Amsterdam soon to see a Dutch Princess."

"Whatever does that have to do with it? I'm quite sure Harald will make it clear to her that he isn't interested."

"It's not just the Dutch Princess, ma'am, it's the endless string of princesses that I'm sure are lined up behind her."

Margrethe shrugged. "But I don't think Olav is willing to play this game forever. He knows he's got to marry Harald off, and if Harald's firm enough about this, he won't have any choice but to give in. That is, my parents did."

"Are you getting married?" she asked excitedly. Harald had not mentioned anything about an engagement for Margrethe, but perhaps it was very recent news.

"No." Margrethe blushed. "Not at all. It's only that I don't want to be forced into an arranged marriage, so to speak—I've always been terrified of arranged marriage, because I simply can't imagine getting married without being *madly* in love—so I've told my parents not to go looking for a match for me. My father didn't care, but I don't think my mother was the least bit pleased, but she did agree, and I think Olav will, too."

It sounded far too simple in Sonja's opinion, but it was worth a great deal to her that Margrethe did seem to honestly believe their marriage would happen. It was more than she could say for herself, or, she had long suspected, for her family, and some days she was not sure whether Harald himself could believe as strongly as he claimed to.

"The whole country's against it, not just the King," Sonja said, annoyed with herself for arguing and hoping there was no evidence of a whine in her voice.

"The whole country? Miss Haraldsen, I would imagine that the majority of the country thinks very little about your marriage, very little at all."

Perhaps, she thought now that she was hearing it from a second source, there was some merit in Harald's oft-repeated comments that it was merely a vocal minority. "That's not how it seems in the papers, ma'am."

Margrethe set her glass down, her eyes warm with sympathy. "Well, I think you're remarkably strong, though, for holding up under all this, considering you didn't grow up in this world."

Strong? She did not feel strong in the slightest.

"But isn't the press horrid sometimes?" Margrethe went on.

It occurred to Sonja suddenly that she was in the presence of another young woman whose situation, at least as far as the incessant press coverage, was somewhat similar to her own. "I hate it," she said with feeling. "Even if they aren't writing about me, it's just the being *followed* everywhere, and then the stuff they *do* write…"

"You should quit reading the papers, although I'm the last person who should ever give you that advice, because I can't ever seem to keep from reading things about myself."

"I don't always read everything," Sonja said. "Sometimes it's just… something of a shock to find certain things—whether they're true or not—and I…everyone thinks…they think they *know* me, and they *don't*, but…I'm not sure I would want them to anyway."

Margrethe nodded. "I know what you mean. Everyone in Denmark thinks they're *intimately* familiar with me. The things that get written can be laughably ridiculous." She paused. "But sometimes," she said, the bitter edge in her voice at odds with the warmth of her manner and the lazy summer day surrounding them, "I think journalists must get paid more by the word if their editor thinks they've come up with something particularly cutting. The things they'll write about a girl's looks…" She laughed humorlessly, and Sonja felt a stab of pity for the Crown Princess, along with the realization that there were ways in which her press coverage could be worse. Despite whatever snippy comments might have been made, she knew deep down that she was, in actuality, an attractive young woman, and there was little that could be convincingly said. Margrethe, on the other hand, surely did not feel herself to be all that pretty, and, although she was very popular in Denmark, comments about her appearance were surely made on occasion in the press.

The rest of the afternoon passed easily as they went inside to look over the sketches Margrethe had brought home from Århus and set about drawing patterns and ordering fabric for one of them. It was warmer here than Sonja was used to in Norway, and somehow the slight heat of southern Denmark was relaxing as well, as exposure to it absorbed the energy she would have spent worrying about her and Harald.

They found themselves sitting up far later than they had planned that night, talking over cups of hot chocolate in the cool of the evening and laughing over everything and nothing. There was something soothing about long, lazy summer days in the Danish countryside spent doing what she loved best—designing and making a dress rather than merely altering one—with breaks from the indoor summer stuffiness that consisted of strolls through the vast gardens or a trip down to the nearby beach to swim in the cool fjord. And it was wonderful to have a couple hundred miles between her and Oslo, to be so far away from the whole mess, and to be secluded here in Gråsten where there were no photographers or Norwegian newspapers or reminders of the impossibility of her position.

When she left the palace on Sunday evening for an overnight ferry, it was with Margrethe's request that she return again that summer—"I'm sure I'll need more of your help on that dress, of course"—and Sonja had readily agreed.

Over a summer's worth of phone calls and visits to Gråsten, they would grow increasingly easy with each other, and trips to Denmark would become welcome respites for Sonja, the only days on which she was not required to worry about the press or the King or the marriage.

On the morning of July 23, the news spread through Oslo that Princess Astrid, Mrs. Ferner had prematurely given birth the night before to Cathrine—coincidentally on her husband's birthday. Both mother and baby were doing well, Astrid having suffered no further heart damage and Cathrine having suffered no worse effects from her early birth than a low weight. Sonja, of course, began sewing little pink outfits.

"Do you want to hold her?" Astrid asked her a week later.

"Of course," Sonja said, smiling as she sat down next to Harald's sister and held her arms out for the little girl. She loved babies and had been eagerly anticipating this visit to the Ferner home for months.

Astrid passed her the infant, and Sonja felt the warm weight on her arms as she held her against her chest. "She's beautiful," she murmured, glancing at the small bit of blonde fuzz on Cathrine's head, the tiny bump that made up her nose, and the bright blue eyes that gazed back up at her. She brushed her finger against the baby's hand and felt the tiny fingers curl around it. "Does she look like anyone in your family?"

Astrid smiled. "Johan thinks she looks like me."

"Yes, she's a beauty like her mother," Johan said, and Astrid blushed.

"Actually, they're both just glad the thing doesn't look like me," Harald said with a grin.

"He was the world's ugliest baby," his sister said. "After he was born, I just thought all babies looked that awful. Then I got a little older and started seeing pictures of other ones and I realized there had just been something dreadfully wrong with my little brother."

"Oh, I don't believe that; he's so wonderfully handsome now," Sonja said absently, preoccupied with Cathrine's little movements and noises and the softness of her skin. She lifted her up to kiss her plump cheek.

"You've never shown her pictures, Harald?" Astrid gave him a wicked smile.

"Oh, you must show me some!" Sonja interjected.

"I don't know," Astrid said. "It's probably a good idea to keep those hidden, *lillebror*; she may not want to marry you any more if she realizes there's a chance of her own babies getting that face you had."

Her own babies. She heard Harald's laughter only distantly as the phrase overwhelmed her. Would she ever have a child of her own in her arms? She could not bring herself to fully believe that she would.

Had it not been for the King's objections, she and Harald would have been married over a year ago and this baby might have been hers. Hers. Hers and Harald's. Theirs. The familiar, painful longing filled her body again, this time with an entirely new dimension.

She raised her eyes to see him looking intently at her, and she knew he was thinking the same thoughts. The idea that *she* might someday have a child who had the potential to have *Harald's* features, that she might someday hold a child that was both hers *and* Harald's, that they might someday have a child *together*… It was nearly impossible to contemplate.

And impossible not to.

Chapter Twenty-Three

"WHAT'S WRONG?" HARALD ASKED AS SOON AS SONJA OPENED THE FRONT door. She had called him half an hour ago in tears, saying she had to see him and, in response to his questions, had managed to tell him only that, "it's horrible, just *horrible*."

"It's—it's the newspaper," she whispered as he stepped inside to embrace her.

What had they said about her *now*? He had had an early meeting that morning and had not had time do anything more than skim the front pages, but he could not imagine anything much worse than what had already been written over the past months. Could they not just have the decency to leave the girl *alone*?

"Here," she said, stepping away, "come look at it." He followed her into the living room, where a copy of *Dagbladet* had been folded up on the coffee table, and took a seat on the couch. She sat down next to him, and he slipped his left arm around her as he reached for the paper and skimmed over the small print in search of her name. All he could find was a short letter to the editor:

"Given the constitutional impossibility of such a match, it would seem clear enough that the Crown Prince has no business involving himself with Sonja Haraldsen. Courting a mere shopkeeper's daughter amounts to an incredible lowering of standards in the royal house. Does His Royal Highness recall anything of his duty to his country? The flagrant disregard for propriety is shocking."

He had been prepared to be infuriated by an outlandishly cruel article or letter, but the most he could work up over what he had just read was a sense of mild annoyance. It was nothing that had not been said in various forms hundreds of times, and it was nothing that would not be repeated again and again in the future. He did not find it particularly offensive, and, in comparison to the lies that had been told about Sonja's background, the ridiculous declarations that she would bring down the monarchy, and the spiteful remarks made about her appearance, it was almost complimentary. Had Sonja truly been in tears all morning over *this*? Surely not, he thought, and he flipped through the rest of the paper in an unsuccessful search for something more.

"Sonja," he asked gently, "is there anything else, or is it only this letter?"

"It's *horrible*."

No, it wasn't. "What makes it so different than all the other articles?"

"It's—it's not any different."

"Then what's made you so upset?"

"Because—because—I've just had *enough*! I can't stand it any longer—I thought this would all be over this summer, and now it doesn't seem like it's ever going to end. It's just all *horrible*, Harald, all of it," she said, beginning to cry harder. "The photos, and-and the stuff about how unsuitable I am, and the-the way I *look*, and my family. I hate it, and I hate this-this endless *waiting* and not knowing if anything will ever change."

"I know," he said. He brushed a strand of her hair back and studied her face. This was not, he understood, about the letter. She had simply snapped after months of stress, and it had not come without warning—in their conversations about the press lately, she had been steadily growing more and more emotional.

She was, he slowly realized, an absolute wreck. Thanks to him.

He pulled her into a tighter embrace, and she buried her face in his chest. Yet her body did not melt against his as it so often did when he took her in his arms—she was shaking, and the tension he could feel in every muscle gave her the feeling of a statue. His own hands were shaking with anger at how she had been treated and with frustration at his own inability to *do something* to fix it—the protocol that demanded he never respond to the press forced him to stand idly by and passively observe as abuse was heaped on Sonja. He had so many times wanted to call a newspaper office and demand a retraction, or get his hands on certain reporters and shake them until their teeth rattled, but he could not imagine that such behavior would help his case with his father.

Her tears were soaking through his shirt, burning his skin like acid. He had been a complete failure at protecting her, a complete failure at dealing with her suffering, and had only managed to make her miserable. He ought to just get out of her life and leave her in peace.

"I'm all right," she said softly as she finally sat up. "It wasn't really that letter, it was only…everything was on top of me, suddenly."

Yes, everything—everything that had happened because of him. It was not fair to ask all this of her. Not when he knew deep down that there could be no wedding. He should never have gone anywhere near her—all he would ever manage to do would be to ruin her life. The most decent thing he could do for her would be to leave.

She gave him a shaky smile, and he knew he could not do it today. Instead, he wiped away her remaining tears, kissed her, and suggested they go outside. They spent a warm afternoon together in her backyard as he tried to forget his intentions.

"Sonja," he said, seated in her living room later that week, "I have wanted—all along—to protect you." He paused. "And I haven't ever been able to do it."

"None of this is your fault," she said immediately. She was dressed for a summer evening in a little blue floral dress, and they had plans to drive out to the Skaugum estate. "I told you last winter—I don't need you to fix it. I don't expect you to fix it. And there's nothing you could have done to stop it."

"Yes, there is." He paused again, unsure he could make himself go on. "What I wanted to say is…" He forced the rest of the words out. "I think—I think I ought to leave and let you be happy."

She laughed. "Harald, don't be silly—that would never work!"

He covered her hand with his own. "I'm serious, Sonja."

She stared at him for a moment, shock and horror in her eyes. "I don't want that! I won't be happy without *you*!"

"But can you keep going like this?"

She looked away. "I know I—I can't stand this any more. This—this *knowing* we can't go anywhere, this constant treading water, this watching everyone pry into our lives and having my name dragged through the mud and seeing my heart laid bare in the papers, this wishing and self-delusion, this—this impossible *wanting*—" She shrugged, her words trailing off.

"Sonja, I—I'm going to do what I should have done months ago—leave and let you go." He saw her tense, but she did not respond, and he went on. "You've been a mess—you can't live like this. I don't *want* you to live like this. You should be free to be happy, free to marry and have children, free to have your own life away from me and all this."

"No," she whispered. "No, Harald, don't."

"Sonja, I—"

She looked up sharply, desperation in her eyes. "Please, it won't make anything any better for me!"

"Yes, it will! You'll be left alone by the press if I'm gone, and you can go off and fall in love with someone who will actually be able to marry you—"

"You're the only one I'm ever going to be in love with." Her voice dropped to a whisper. "I'll never change."

He gazed into the deep brown eyes that had first caught his attention three years ago. But no, *he could not stay*. She deserved far better than he could give her, and he could not allow her to suffer any further on his account.

"Don't go, Harald," she pleaded. "I won't be able to stand it, please don't go…" He said nothing, forcing himself not to reach out for her.

After a long silence he stood, and she stood as well. "Kiss me first," she said, her voice sharp.

He knew as soon as he did that it had been a mistake. It was suddenly painful to feel her lips moving against his, but it would have been far more excruciating to separate from her, and he wondered how they would ever stop, knowing the kiss would be their last. He pressed her body close to his, memorizing the feel of her in his arms and breathing in her scent. At long last he gave her one final kiss.

"I'm leaving, and I want you to move on with your life," he whispered, letting her go. She nodded, her eyes closed.

He wanted to kiss her again but did not let himself do it. As he shut her front door behind him, he heard her burst into sobs.

He stood on her porch for quite some time.

Chapter Twenty-Four

SONJA WANTED TO DO NOTHING BUT WEEP, TO LIE DOWN ALONE AND CRY for days, for weeks even, until all feeling left her, until she no longer felt as though her heart had been sliced open. She longed for the relief of sleep but it came rarely and with difficulty. She barely spoke and ate very little, food turning to ash in her mouth. The stress she had felt over the last year seemed laughably insignificant in comparison.

It was not the sort of thing she could hide from her family with any success, and she was aware that Haakon and her mother were worried, that they gave each other long, troubled glances and whispered to one another, that they spoke to her in hushed, calming tones accompanied by forced smiles. Their behavior was unnerving, and she tried to appear somewhat recovered for them. She could see that her mother especially was not fooled, and forcing all her wounds inward made her wonder if she might go entirely mad while she slowly bled to death inside.

Please, Lord, let this get easier, she prayed. *Let me have peace about this, let me move on…I can't go on like this forever…*

She had planned to return to Denmark in early September, and she could not think of anything she wanted to do less. Visits to Margrethe had been wonderful breaks from the press and from all reminders of her situation, but she knew that this trip would only serve as a source of memories of Harald. Surely the Crown Princess would ask about him, and she did not think she could bear the conversation.

She was driven to Copenhagen's Amalienborg Palace, Denmark's main royal residence. Amalienborg was a complex of four separate Palaces surrounding a large, very public cobblestone square. Originally aristocratic homes, the buildings were nearly identical, four-story baroque mansions of off-white stone. At their back was a picturesque view of the city's main canal—an area busy with boats and picnickers on a warm summer day.

Margrethe's family only lived in one of the Palaces, and then only part of the year. They would not ordinarily have been here in September at all and usually went straight from the summer at Gråsten to their fall residence at Fredensborg. However, Margrethe and her sisters had all needed to return to the capital to pick up some things for their coming semesters at school in France, England, and Switzerland, and the Crown Princess had offered to meet Sonja there to show her the city's art.

Sonja had begun to grow used to wandering around in royal residences, but she was still aware of the gold leaf and the marble and the chandeliers as she was led through the Palace and up to Margrethe's bedroom on the third floor. It was a surprisingly small blue room with a high, ornate stucco ceiling, Grecian-looking white posts along the walls, and a massive chandelier.

"Oh, you're here already!" Margrethe exclaimed. She was lying across her bed, piles of clothes on both sides of her and a lengthy list in her hands. She smiled with sincere delight. "I'm sorry; I'm trying to figure out what I'm taking; I'm leaving for Paris on Wednesday, and I still don't know..."

"Can I help you?" Sonja offered, wondering if perhaps this might serve as a distraction from any questions about Harald.

"Oh, would you? It would be so wonderful to have you tell me what you think I ought to take..."

Margrethe took her to the other side of the third floor where there was a hallway with four doors, labeled "HM The Queen," "HRH The Crown Princess," "HRH Princess Benedikte," and "HM The King, HM The Queen, HRH Princess Anne-Marie."

"My father doesn't have nearly enough clothing to warrant his own room, and my mother's accumulated so much over her life that she's spilling out of hers. My little sister Anne-Marie—she's only sixteen—has far less clothing than my mother and Benedikte and I, as she's too young to have many official functions to attend, and thus she's the daughter who ends up sharing space with our parents. And yes, we've had quite a bit of whining about this recently."

Stepping inside Margrethe's clothing room, with its rows and rows of designer dresses and suits and evening gowns, overflowing racks of expensive shoes, and boxes and boxes of hats, should have been an awe-inspiring experience, especially for someone with a fashion background. Sonja wanted to be excited, and she tried to think of nothing but her immediate surroundings, but...

"Are you all right, Miss Haraldsen?" she heard Margrethe ask her suddenly.

"What?" She had meant for Margrethe to see nothing unusual about her, frightened of how the Crown Princess might react to the break-up—she would likely have no further interest in her; surely all the gestures of friendship had been possible only because she believed Sonja would likely be royalty someday herself.

"Are you all right? You just seem rather..." Margrethe shrugged.

"I'm fine, ma'am."

Yet conversation continued to be a strain for her throughout the afternoon as they finished with Margrethe's list for Paris and Margrethe showed her around the Palace. With most official functions occurring at other palaces and castles in Denmark, Amalienborg seemed much more of a home than Oslo's Royal Palace, albeit a very grand one. The ceilings of even the simplest rooms were at least a story and a half, there was gold everywhere and multiple tapestries, and each room held at least one elaborate chandelier. Large, gold-plated mirrors on all the walls made the already-sizable rooms seem even bigger, yet most of the rooms were filled with soft, inviting couches.

As they worked on the nearly-finished evening gown, Sonja was surrounded by thoughts of Harald evoked by the mannerisms his cousin shared with him, the rich fabric that reminded her of the dress she herself had once worn to his graduation ball, the royal monogram on the cup of tea Margrethe had brought her, and the continual realization that last time she had seen the Danish Crown Princess, she had still had Harald. She did manage to successfully brush off questions about him—when Margrethe asked how he was, she responded vaguely and changed the subject.

The next day offered plenty of distractions as she and Margrethe raced all over Copenhagen. Wandering the city with the Crown Princess was a surprisingly normal experience—they rode bikes to the National Art Gallery, sat down in a nearby park for a picnic lunch, rode the bus halfway across the city to the Glyptotek for sculptures, and then strolled down Strøget, the walking street of shops that ended at the harbor. Margrethe was acknowledged, and the crowd parted in front of them as they walked, but they were not mobbed or excessively stared at. Sonja noticed that she herself was the subject of an occasional glance or smile, and she realized that the Danes must know her, too, but she seemed to be regarded more as a curiosity than as a threat to the monarchy.

The festive atmosphere of Copenhagen in the very last days of summer far outdid Oslo, and that was saying something. The parks were packed at lunchtime, with sunbathers stretched out all over, Strøget was brimming with street musicians, and nearly everyone they passed seemed to be licking an ice cream cone. Sonja and Margrethe were on their third each as they returned to the Palace that evening.

"Summer's almost over, and you're here—I think that justifies more ice cream than usual," the Crown Princess said brightly.

Sonja found herself sitting up late with Margrethe in her bedroom, where they talked for hours, sipping hot chocolate in the cool night breeze blowing in through the open window. It was like being thirteen years old again at a sleepover, and addressing each other as "Miss Haraldsen" and "Your Royal Highness" seemed ridiculous now. They slipped easily into "Sonja" and "Margrethe."

"I never did understand," Sonja said, "why you were calling me 'Miss Haraldsen' in the first place. I'm only three years older than you, not thirty."

"Yes, but you were addressing me by a title, and I felt rude just calling you Sonja!" Somehow, the fatigue brought on by the late hour made this seem hysterically funny, and Sonja found herself laughing for the first time in weeks.

They spent the second day on Margrethe's private tours of every painting hanging in any of the four palaces in the Amalienborg complex, and of all the art and tapestries in Christiansborg, a former royal residence now used only for government functions and special occasions. Sonja enjoyed it as much as she could under the circumstances, trying to forget Harald and focus on the paintings and monuments in front of her.

The visit steadily became more a source of comfort than of further misery, and as a result she unwittingly began to lower her façade of happiness. By the third day she was aware that Margrethe, with her kind smiles and curious glances, knew there was something wrong with her but was not forward enough to ask.

"Sonja," she finally said during a silence one evening as they sipped glasses of red wine, "is something wrong? Have there been...more articles or something of that sort?"

"No, that's been lots better in the last few weeks." And it had, as the news had been leaked—probably by Harald himself—that they were no longer dating. She was suddenly overwhelmed by the urge that had been building for days to tell Margrethe the truth, and she blurted out, "Especially since we've broken up."

For a long moment the words seemed to hang in the air between them, and in a sudden sense of panic Sonja wished she could reach out and grab them back.

Yet when Margrethe spoke, her words were quite warm, with none of the sudden coldness Sonja had feared. "Oh, I'm so sorry; I didn't know...may I ask what happened?"

What exactly had happened? It seemed to have been an eternity ago, and her thoughts had been so consumed by memories of his last few words and his last kisses and her wishes that it had turned out differently that she had to think for a moment to reconstruct why he had left.

"You haven't got to tell me if you don't want," Margrethe said quickly.

"No, I don't mind. I think he wanted to spare me the press attention, and all the horrible hiding and waiting and uncertainty that went along with being his girlfriend. He wanted—he said he wanted to protect me. He said I should be free to be happy."

"And are you happy?"

"No."

"I didn't think so. But can you be at some point? How long ago was this?"

"It was last month. But I don't think—I'm not sure I'll ever be happy again," she said, giving voice to what she had felt for weeks. "It's not getting any better. I think about it all the time, I can't imagine the rest of my life without him, I—it's like looking at the whole world through a black veil. It wasn't easy when we were together; it wasn't ever easy, but…this is so much worse. I just want—I just want to be near him again…"

"Does Harald know this?"

"No, I haven't seen him."

Margrethe paused. "You ought to go see him."

"What?"

"You ought to go see him. You're completely miserable, and I don't doubt that he's pretty miserable himself, and you ought to go and tell him you do want to be with him, and that's more important to you than anything else. It is, isn't it?"

"Oh, absolutely. But I—I'm not sure I can do that." The thought of seeing Harald again, when he might very well push her away a second time, when he might have moved on with his life and no longer have any need of her, was painful even to contemplate.

"May I tell you something, Sonja?" Margrethe's eyes were suddenly both serious and warm, and Sonja looked up to meet them. "I think what you and Harald have is remarkable, and—as someone who's never been in love and who isn't sure if she ever will be—I think it's very rare and something that's worth fighting for."

"I'm not sure I've got the strength to see him," Sonja said quietly, imagining how much it would require to do such a thing.

"You do. I don't have any doubt after what you've done so far, surviving the way you were treated in the press and lasting so long with Harald when you both knew how uncertain the future was. And you're willing to go through all that again so you can have him. That must make you stronger than average, yes?"

Sonja shrugged. She did not feel strong in the slightest, given that she had often felt as though she might collapse at any moment over the last months. How she could manage to go through it all again—or, alternatively, continue on without Harald—she could not imagine.

"Sonja?" Harald stopped midway through the door to his office, staring at Sonja, who was sitting across from his desk. It had been over a month since he had last seen her, but thoughts of her had so filled his mind that, had she not turned to speak to him, he would not have been sure she was real.

"Your sister met me here and let me in. I had to see you." Her face was oddly expressionless, but that did not stop him from studying it. He already knew every last eyelash, but he found himself examining her nose, her cheekbones, her lips—trying not to think of their softness—and *her eyes*—those beautiful *eyes* that he had seen every time he had closed his own...

Everything in him begged to run to her and take her in his arms again, but he stood rooted to the spot, his hand gripping the door frame, so that he would leave a safe twenty feet between them. If he touched her, he would be lost entirely...he could imagine the feel of her skin under his fingers...

There was a long silence as they gazed at each other, he with longing and she with a strange intensity. He allowed himself to caress her with his eyes, running over her chestnut brown hair, the round softness of her face, the depth of her beautiful, doe-like eyes, her partly-bare shoulders at the top of her purple sleeveless dress, the curves of her hips and her waist and her legs, her miniature hands...

"Are you all right?" he asked at last.

She nervously uncrossed her legs, recrossing them at the ankle. How he wished she wouldn't do that. It was so much harder when she *moved*.

"I haven't gotten over you, Harald," she said. "And I don't think I'm ever *going* to get over you."

He wasn't going to get over her, either. Silently, he went to sit behind his desk, every muscle in his body screaming for him to reach out for her. He was nearly dizzy with her scent, and he was so very hungry for her—hungry to touch her, to hold her, to kiss her, but also to talk with her and to laugh with her and to bend down to hear her whisper in his ear.

"It's been six weeks," she went on when he didn't respond. She was holding her face as she often did when she spoke—with her chin tucked as though to nod or look down and her eyes turned upward at him. It was a mannerism that seemed to enlarge her eyes and drew even more of his attention to them. He forced himself to look down at his hands.

"If you thought I was a mess then," she continued, "you should see me now! I think of you all the time because everything brings you to mind. I feel your hand in mine and then I realize I'm alone, or sometimes I feel your arms slip around me—all I want is to feel you holding me again—but of course you aren't really there. When I think of the future—and I can hardly bear to think of the future—all I see is emptiness now. I—I can't go on without you, Harald."

No, if he left her alone she might be able to go on...

She brushed her hair back, and he quickly looked away again. Each word was like the thrust of a knife, but there was no emotion in her voice, and he was thankful for that much—he still had a chance at hiding his own feelings. "Give it some more time," he began but broke off, knowing how feeble that sounded in the face of everything she'd said.

There was a long pause while she studied his face. *Sonja, Sonja, min kjære, Sonja, my life...* Then she spoke. "Oh," she whispered. "You *have* gotten over it. You don't still think of me. I'm the only one still missing the other."

No, not an hour goes by that I don't think of you, long for you, dream of having you close, wonder if you're all right... But he said nothing.

"Well, then." She smiled bravely. "I suppose I'll be going. I'm sorry—I've only managed to embarrass us both." She stood, scooped her purse up from the floor, and headed for the door.

He knew that if he let her walk out the door she would not return, and so he did not watch her go, afraid that to take a last look would be to rush after her. No, he would only end up hurting her...he had to let her go...

He could hear her laughter ringing in his ears, feel the silk of her hair between his fingers, see every happy weekend spent at Gamlehaugen...visions of everything she'd ever done to make him laugh were dancing before him, she was giggling over the wine stain again, they were holding each other on the couch at Skaugum, her small body against his...

No, he could not—from the sound of her footsteps, she had nearly crossed the threshold, he had nearly made it...

"*Sonja!*" he burst out, suddenly breaking and instantly thankful that he had. Immediately he was at her side, gently turning her to look at her face and wrapping his arms around her. "*Sonja.*" He touched her delicately, reverently at first, half afraid that he had dreamed it all and she would suddenly disappear. Then he felt her melt against him and he held her tighter, running his fingers through her soft curls, drinking in the sensation of having her so near once again. "I do want you, I feel the same way you do—I've thought of you constantly—I *need* you—but I meant to protect you—"

"I don't want to leave, Harald." She looked up from where she had buried her face in the middle of his chest, and he thought again of the difference in their heights he had always loved. "Not having you is worse than any of the rest of it—it hurts far more than anything they can throw at me. I want you, and I'll put up with whatever I have to in order to be yours. Do you—do you still want me?"

"Do I want you? Are you out of your mind? More than anything!"

She made a sound that was half a sob and half the laugh he had been longing to hear. "See? I told you I'm a mess!"

<hr />

A weekend at Gamlehaugen seemed in order after having been separated for so long, and they went out to Bergen at the beginning of October. Harald had arranged for the royal yacht to meet them there, and after one night at the castle they boarded the boat for a trip up the coast and into the fjords.

Western Norway was beautiful in the fall, with its tourists gone and its brilliant autumn foliage erupting all over. Of course, the fjord region was breathtaking at any time of year. Towering cliffs soared on each side of a deep blue waterway, with waterfalls appearing every few hundred feet, and it was possible to go for miles and see no signs of life beyond a single farmhouse clinging to the rocks. Rays of sun bathed the occasional valleys, turning them into baskets of golden light.

They stood out on deck for much of the trip, determined to enjoy the dramatic view in spite of the cold temperatures exacerbated by the wind from the boat's speed. Their conversation was nearly constant all day, and there seemed to be so much to tell each other that it was unbelievable to them that they had only been apart for a few weeks.

Harald had not fully realized what Sonja meant to him until he had forced himself to do without her. A shy man who had never relished his public role, he had found himself slowly changing in the three years he and Sonja had been together. Having her to talk matters over with, with her apparent admiration and confidence in him, had so much altered him that he had wondered, in the weeks they had been separated, whether he could manage to be King without her at his side.

"You know," Sonja said when they had at last fallen silent, "the fjords are one of the few places where I always feel exactly the same way I felt when I was a child here. That is, *almost* exactly the same way—I'm not terrified of trolls any more."

"And how do you feel?"

"Small. Very small." He nodded, understanding her perfectly as they sailed along in a huge yacht that was a mere pebble in comparison to the surrounding mountains. "And in awe."

He nodded again. "In awe of what?"

She paused. "Norway. Just the country itself. Everything feels so ancient here, and it's like I can read every line of Norway's history in the cliffs. I can imagine life here centuries ago, and I think of all the traditions that still survive, and I feel like a very small, insignificant part of it. And it's humbling to think that if I do marry you, then someday..." It was as though she could not quite bring herself to form the words.

"You'll be Queen of Norway," he finished for her.

"Yes," she whispered. "And of course...I'm in awe of God, in a way I sometimes forget to be at home in Oslo. It's always so instantly clear out here how powerful He is, and I was only thinking that surely the God who made these mountains can handle something as simple as our marriage!" She laughed softly. "I forget that, sometimes."

They returned to Gamlehaugen late that evening, shared a dinner of eel, and took seats on the couch in the main room by the fire, the old polar bear skin on the floor at their feet and cups of gløgg in their hands, the Nordic drink of warm mulled wine and cinnamon. "I'm glad we're together again," she said, slipping her hand into his as they sat in companionable silence.

When the gløgg was finished they moved into each other's arms, drawing nearer in the flickering firelight. Slowly, their kisses lengthened and deepened, becoming nearly frantic as they pressed their bodies closer. He felt the light weight of her arms wrapped around his neck, he had one hand in her hair, the other against her waist as he pulled her nearer...he was drinking in the feel of her in his arms...the curve of her hip beneath his hand...the warm touch of her skin to his...he thought he might go wonderfully, blissfully mad as she kissed him...he could think of nothing but *her*...

And then she was slowly leaning back to lie nearly flat against the couch's pillows...and he was following, lying half on top of her...wanting her, desperately...

She shifted slightly, and somehow the movement of her body against his awakened him.

"Sonja," he said suddenly, forcing himself to go no further.

"Yes." Her voice was immediately sharp and serious as well.

"This—this isn't…We can't." He sat up.

"I know," she said softly. "It's wrong. It's…intended for marriage."

She was still lying back against the pillows, and he took her hand. "I love you," he said, after a moment of struggling with himself.

"Yes, but it doesn't make any difference; it's still—"

"It does make a difference," he said firmly. "It makes all the difference in the world. The morality of it aside, I might be more willing to do it if I didn't love you…it's because I *do* love you that I'm not going to disgrace you in front of the whole country or leave you in even more of a mess than all this already is." He meant it, but he found it the hardest thing he'd ever had to say.

Chapter Twenty-Five

Just after Christmas, Sonja joined Margrethe at Amalienborg Palace in Copenhagen to finish the Crown Princess's dress before New Year's Eve. "Do bring something of your own to wear," Margrethe's letter had said, "because you're quite welcome to attend the party with me."

Margrethe met her in the entrance hall and brought her into one of the huge first floor sitting rooms. It was a large hall with three arched window alcoves, spaces large enough for couches, armchairs, and small tables. There were three elaborate chandeliers whose crystals looked like giant bead necklaces strung around the lights, and two faded old tapestries hung on the walls at both ends.

This room was as filled with wall mirrors as many of the others at Amalienborg, and they gave a perfect view of every angle of the room. Sonja could see Margrethe's teenage sister, Princess Anne-Marie, lounging on a couch with its back to them. Barefoot and in a simple blouse and skirt, she had curled up with a plate of leftover Christmas cookies and, in spite of the maturity of her face and figure, looked rather childlike. She was twirling something small and sparkly on the coffee table in front of her and watching it spin.

Margrethe followed Sonja's gaze. "Anne-Marie," she said sharply, "that's that ring, isn't it?"

Anne-Marie caught the little object in her hand and closed her fist around it. "No."

"Yes, it is. Mother told you not to play with it—you're going to lose it. It's not a toy. Either wear it or put it back in the box."

"Stop giving orders, Daisy," Anne-Marie said sullenly, but she replaced the ring on her finger.

"She's halfway through the second year of finishing school," Margrethe said softly to Sonja with a smile.

"Already? I thought—isn't she only sixteen?" Sonja had thought finishing school was usually undertaken only after a high school education was completed.

"My parents realized awhile ago that going any further with her regular schooling was...perhaps not quite within Anni's abilities, so to speak," Margrethe said delicately.

Sonja nodded. "And how was Paris?"

She had barely finished the sentence before Margrethe began to answer. "Wonderful, wonderful—Paris was beautiful as always! I spent whole weekends in the Louvre and days sketching on the banks of the Seine, and of course it wasn't only Paris, but I went out into the Loire Valley—if you haven't seen any of that, you simply must—and I was all over the south of France as well as the Norman coast. The south is so wonderfully tropical, and it's another world entirely from Scandinavia; it feels like it's always a summer afternoon, and I think if I weren't going to be Queen I should like to spend the rest of my life there amidst the vineyards and the mountains and the warmth—"

"Is there a Frenchman living out this fantasy with you?" Sonja said, giggling.

"Absolutely. We have a centuries-old medieval chateau that we've fixed up ourselves in the middle of an ancient winery, and I sit outside and paint and then take walks with him through our vineyards while we discuss art and philosophy and don't worry about the succession or memorizing ambassadors' names or court protocol." She laughed and launched back into a description of everything else she'd seen and done, naming individual paintings in the Louvre and analyzing them with Sonja and discussing her studies at the Sorbonne, which she had somehow managed to fit in amidst everything else. Her enthusiasm for all of it was such that Sonja found herself struggling to believe it was not Margrethe's first time in France. She seemed to greet the whole world with the wide-eyed interest of someone who had first opened her eyes the day before. It was, Sonja realized, only a slightly more exaggerated version of Margrethe's excitement a few months earlier while touring her own city and family home.

The last days of 1962 were spent putting the finishing touches on the dress, and it was soon New Year's Eve. Made of silk with an elaborate bustle spilling down the back, Margrethe's gown was a pale, icy blue. "It matches your eyes," Sonja had said when they'd chosen the fabric, noting the pretty brilliance of their light color. The comment had resulted in a moment's awkward silence, as the Crown Princess immediately suggested something else and Sonja realized why she would be hesitant about a fabric that brought out her eyes. "No," Sonja had insisted, "it's perfect; I think we should use it." She was glad now that they had. Silver beadwork had been stitched in swirls along the skirt, and it slid so perfectly along every curve in Margrethe's figure that it appeared to have been sewn on. Margrethe was delighted with the results of their work, which slightly calmed Sonja, who was nearly in knots about the evening ahead of her. She herself had slipped on a full-skirted, strapless, evergreen taffeta ball gown with a ruched bodice, as well as a diamond necklace borrowed from Margrethe.

"I'm going to be spending the first hour of the party stuck in the receiving line with my parents," Margrethe told her as they walked down the central staircase, "but my sisters won't be, and they've both said they'd be happy to take you under their wing at the beginning. I'll come find you later."

Sonja nodded, distracted and nearly dizzy with nerves. She adjusted the diamonds around her neck for the tenth time.

"And do stop touching those," Margrethe murmured as they reached the bottom of the steps outside the banquet hall where the ball would be held. "It makes you look like you're not used to wearing them."

"You mean," Sonja said, a slight giggle escaping the tension in her body, "it looks like I borrowed them from someone?"

"Yes, precisely." Margrethe laughed softly. "Here; you go on in—my whole family and I have to enter together, but then Benedikte and Anni will come find you."

Sonja breathed a sigh of relief when the two young Princesses appeared ten minutes later—their company would distract her from her nerves, and surely they would both be as kind as their older sister. She had yet to have a long conversation with either of them, despite spending so much time in the apartment Benedikte shared with Margrethe, but they had both always seemed pleasant.

The seamstress in her took in their dresses as they approached—both girls were in satin, Anne-Marie in a deep red and Benedikte in bluish-green. Anne-Marie's gown had a wonderful excess of material in its skirt, which flared out dramatically at the waist; the neckline was traced in small diamonds; and there were thin, off-the-shoulder sleeves. Benedikte's dress was far plainer, drawing its elegance from its straight simplicity, and it seemed designed to showcase a perfect figure.

"Miss Haraldsen!" Princess Anne-Marie exclaimed, taking her hand and pressing it in both her own. "Your dress is absolutely *gorgeous*, and I just love the one you've helped Daisy with—everyone loves it. Could you make something for me?"

"Anni, you've got plenty of dresses," her sister said, giving Sonja an apologetic smile. It was the most striking of her features—while Anne-Marie was the prettiest of the Danish Princesses, Benedikte had a fragile beauty to her willowy figure, and her smile was the dazzling sort that could turn a room full of heads.

"I'm going to need more, you know," Anne-Marie responded, her tone heavy with hidden significance.

"Hush," Benedikte hissed. A *you-know-better* look crossed her face. "You *do* look lovely this evening, Miss Haraldsen," the Princess went on, flashing another perfect smile that somehow lacked the warmth of Margrethe's. "Especially with all of those diamonds—it really is the jewels that make an outfit." Her eyes lingered on the stones at Sonja's neck. "Although I must say... this necklace is quite like one my sister has." She closed the gap between them and reached out for it. Sonja drew back instinctively, and Benedikte raised her eyebrows slightly in a challenge as she lifted the necklace and brushed her thumb against the diamonds. Sonja forced herself not to pull away at the icy touch of her fingers.

Benedikte dropped the jewelry and stepped back, still smiling. "You must have *very* similar tastes. In fact, all of your jewelry looks *quite* familiar..."

Sonja heard the message clearly: *You are a shopkeeper's daughter who cannot even slip into a court ball for an evening without borrowed jewels.* The sting of the insult was quickly replaced by outrage, and she held Benedikte's cold gaze.

"Shall we all get a glass of champagne?" Anne-Marie said after a pause. "I'm allowed this year."

There were nods of assent—particularly enthusiastically from Sonja, who was grateful for the change of subject.

She could not shake the sense, though, that she would be quite unequal to any partner that asked her to dance. She knew the most common of the Scandinavian dances and a few of the waltzes but was at a loss to name half of what she was watching.

She directed a few questions to Anne-Marie, who launched into a lengthy explanation of the most complex ones until her sister interrupted.

"Surely you were exposed to all these dances in finishing school, Miss Haraldsen?" Benedikte said with an innocent smile that did not quite reach her eyes. She took a casual sip of her drink.

"I didn't go to finishing school," Sonja said, almost defiantly. She had been well exposed to finishing schools and their students during the time she had spent studying at a Swiss dressmaking school, and the divide between her own classmates and the finishing school girls could not have been clearer. She and her classmates had been preparing to work; the others had been preparing to marry aristocrats.

"Oh, you didn't?" The cold smile faded, Benedikte's lips closing into a smirk. "Well, it's no matter. At least you can *sew*."

And what good is it doing you, ma'am, to go off to Switzerland every semester and pour tea and dance and walk around with a book on your head? she wanted to snap. Yet she knew that finishing school, as silly as she might find it, was a nonnegotiable prerequisite for moving in these circles.

Anne-Marie was regarding them both with a rather lost look. "Don't all girls go to finishing school?" she asked in a tone of sincere confusion.

"No, dear, they don't," her sister said sweetly.

"Oh," said Anne-Marie, still looking as bewildered as though Benedikte were discussing something as far removed from their own lives as the customs of an isolated rainforest tribe. Sonja was struck by how very small their world must be.

To her relief, Benedikte accepted a request for a dance, leaving her with Anne-Marie.

"Do you want to know a secret?" Anne-Marie said immediately, suddenly even more beautiful in her excitement. "I'm engaged!"

Engaged? No, she wasn't—the girl was sixteen and acted twelve. "Are you really?" she said, humoring her.

"Yes," Anne-Marie responded with a giggle. "To Crown Prince Constantine of Greece. He's *amazing*—he's charming and funny and strong and *so* handsome."

"Is he your age, ma'am?"

"Oh, no!" Anne-Marie laughed. "He's Daisy's age—twenty-two."

Then surely there was no real engagement. Perhaps there had been talk of an arranged marriage at some point, and that was all Anne-Marie meant.

"But you mustn't tell anyone," the Princess went on, her eyes widening as though she had just realized the scope of her indiscretion. "It's supposed to be a complete secret—we're not announcing the engagement until the twenty-fourth, and I'm not even allowed to wear my ring in public until then. But sometimes it's so wonderful that I just can't help telling people."

Suddenly, Sonja recalled the conversation from several days ago—"that's that ring, isn't it?" *She really is engaged,* she thought incredulously. "Since when?" she managed to squeak. "How long have you—"

"Since early last summer," Anne-Marie said gaily. "I'd met Tino a couple times before—and I could tell at his sister's wedding in May that he really liked me—and in June he wrote to me and said that he was going to Norway and wanted me to meet him there—only he wanted me to keep it a secret, so I didn't tell my parents or anyone else. I just arranged a little trip with my governess up to Oslo, and then Tino and I both acted as though we were completely shocked to run into each other. I spent quite a bit of time with him over the next few days, and then finally he asked me if I would like to come and stay with him in Greece—as his wife. So of course I said yes—who *wouldn't?*—but I told him we couldn't tell my parents right away because I *knew* they'd have a fit; they *don't* trust me to make my own decisions, and they *never* let me do what I want. I broke it to them after my sixteenth birthday in August, and they certainly weren't thrilled, especially Mamma—I can't *tell* you how many lectures I've had to listen to about being too young for marriage; she thinks I'm eight years old—but they finally agreed to it. I mean, I had already rather obligated myself to him, after all. Isn't it all just terribly exciting?"

"Terribly," Sonja echoed. "Congratulations, Your Royal Highness." Yet she was most of all struck by the distinct *sliminess* of the entire operation on Constantine's part—what sort of man would, at age twenty-two, set up a secret meeting with a fifteen-year-old and propose marriage to her? On top of that, she was in perfect agreement with Queen Ingrid's attitude. Anne-Marie was barely mature enough to date, much less to be married.

By the time midnight arrived, Margrethe had rescued Sonja and found her an evening's worth of dance partners, and she rang in 1963 with hope for a better year mixed with a deadened feeling that another twelve months would change very little for her and Harald.

And very little *did* change. They stood paralyzed, unwilling to move backward by separating and unable to step forward into an engagement while life went on around them. Sonja did not grow any more comfortable with the press coverage, the constant photographs, and the frequent mentions of her own inadequacy, but she slowly found that she was growing used or perhaps numb to it, and it faded in and out in frequency. Yet as she became less focused on the press—the newspapers' opinions really mattered very little, she realized—she became more focused on the King, whose thoughts were very important, indeed. She knew intellectually that His Majesty's attitude had little to do with *her*—they had never even met—and everything to do with her common status and his concern for the monarchy. Harald perpetually insisted that she was correct in this assessment. Yet she could not help but feel as though it were all somehow very, very personal. It was exactly the same problem she had with the media—she knew the reaction would be the same toward any commoner dating the Crown Prince, but she was frequently convinced that both the King and the country hated her, Sonja Haraldsen, personally.

Chapter Twenty-Six

Sonja visited Margrethe in Paris in April, the two of them becoming what Margrethe referred to as "art museum rats" who spent most of their time buried in the Louvre, L'Orangerie, or the Cluny, surfacing on occasion to stroll down the boulevards, consume French pastries and desserts, and shop. The Crown Princess was the only one who purchased anything in the high-end stores they visited, but Sonja found a mysterious package of two of the dresses she'd been eyeing waiting for her when she returned home. She went to Denmark often in the coming months, and one afternoon at Fredensborg, Margrethe would invite her to scratch her name into the glass of one of the windows. It was a tradition that had been shared with visiting royal relatives, heads of state, and other honored guests for the past hundred years, and Sonja understood the invitation as a declaration of Margrethe's faith that she would someday join the family.

Just after New Year's, it had been suggested by a never-married aunt that Sonja ought to go to university. "If you aren't going to marry," her aunt had said, "you ought to have an education. I think every woman should, but especially those who aren't going to be married. There won't be anyone else to support you."

"I am going to marry," Sonja said sharply.

"Are you?"

She had not responded, not wishing to acknowledge how likely a future alone sometimes seemed. However, she was forced to admit that a university degree was not such a bad idea. The only reason she did not have one was because her parents—assuming she would someday be married—had agreed that her education did not matter terribly much. Had she wanted one, it would have been given to her, but there had been no objection when she, at seventeen, had wished to go to dressmaking school instead of finishing her final year of secondary schooling and going on to college. She would never make much money as a seamstress, but she would likely be living at home until her marriage, and then it would make no difference at all. "I wouldn't allow this if you were a boy," her father had said, "but, of course, you're not."

Now the question of having to support herself for the rest of her life was beginning to appear more likely, and it would perhaps do her good to have an education even if she did marry Harald—her English could use a great deal of improvement if she was going to spend her life conversing with foreign diplomats and heads of state, and surely the role would be far more interesting if she knew more of the world. She thus did the work required for a secondary school diploma and then enrolled in English language and literature courses in Cambridge for the summer term, intending to apply the credits to a degree that she would put together in her spare time over a number of years.

In August, the Norwegian government faltered, losing a no confidence vote but reestablishing power a mere three weeks later. The Socialists had been in power since the war, with Einar Gerhardsen—a resistance hero regarded as *Landsfaderen*, the Father of the Nation, for his work in rebuilding Norway—at its helm. The thought that there might be a change in government in the next election was as incomprehensible as it was likely, and Harald and Sonja spent many hours wondering what, if anything, this all might mean for the King's willingness to ask the Storting's approval for their engagement.

But with September came Sonja's return to Oslo and the welcome distraction of Astrid and Johan's second daughter, and in October Margrethe left for a seventy-two-day diplomatic tour of Asia, from which she sent Sonja letters brimming with tales of ancient temples, elephant herds, mist-covered Himalayas, and spice-filled foreign marketplaces with camels and goats for sale. It was all, of course, approached with Margrethe's typical breathless enthusiasm, and Sonja could easily imagine that she was a handful for the royal handlers who had been assigned the unpleasant task of moving the Crown Princess from place to place when she was bursting with questions about the people and the customs and the history. Sonja was looking forward to going through the hundreds of pictures Margrethe must surely have taken on the little camera she'd stashed in her handbag.

Shortly after nine on a Friday evening in late November, Harald and Sonja arrived at Gamlehaugen and were met in the front hall by the butler, his expression even more solemn than usual.

"Your Royal Highness," he said, "His Majesty wishes to speak with you immediately."

"I'll call him as soon as we're settled—"

"I beg your pardon, sir, but he was adamant that you were to call him as soon as you arrived."

Harald glanced at Sonja, who shrugged. There was likely a foreign princess on her way to Norway this evening, and Harald was expected to be in Oslo to meet her tomorrow. "Go call him and say you can't see whoever she is this weekend."

Harald laughed. "I'll tell him precisely that."

She climbed the main staircase alone, set her suitcase down in her bedroom, slipped off her heels, removed her hat, and touched up her make-up in the antique mirror before heading back down to the great room. The evening had the warm, cozy feel of the fur lining the collar of her suit, she thought as she absentmindedly fingered it. A cup of hot chocolate would do nicely for them both. She would have Harald ring for some...

He met her at the foot of the steps, an expression of shock on his face and one hand on the banister as though it were some sort of anchor.

"I have to go back to Oslo first thing tomorrow," he said abruptly. "The President of the United States has been shot."

"What?" She stared at him, not comprehending.

"The American President was shot a couple hours ago in Texas. My father wants me back in Oslo by noon so we can decide who's flying to Washington and when."

"President Kennedy..." she began, still trying to process the news.

"Is dead," he finished for her.

A slight nausea slowly replaced her shock as she thought of the vibrant young man she had seen in news broadcasts and papers. "That can't be true," she said at last. She felt the strange sense that her body was not fully her own as she made her way down the last few steps. *"How?"*

Wordlessly Harald crossed the room to turn on the small television. She turned on the radio.

They sat motionless for hours, her hand tightly clutched in his, watching and listening to the news coverage of the assassination mixed in with old footage and recordings of John Kennedy. Distantly, she heard it announced on the radio that the King or Crown Prince would likely attend the funeral. The *Ich bin ein Berliner* speech was played again, delivered a mere six months ago in Berlin...six months that were now an eternity ago, she thought. There was footage of his inauguration, then a few brief shots of Kennedy smiling and shaking hands as his wife accepted a small rose bouquet in the background.

"She's so young," Sonja murmured. *And everything she had three hours ago is gone.* Everything Jackie Kennedy had envisioned for the future had changed, all her dreams for the coming years shattered in an instant. History, Sonja knew, would remember this as a national tragedy mourned on the world stage, yet she was struck by the intimately personal tragedy of the smiling woman on the screen, a mere eight years older than herself. Yesterday Jackie had surely thought she had decades left with her husband. Now she was contemplating raising her two small children alone.

They did not have forever. Sonja was struck by a sudden sense of urgency in their own situation—she and Harald had waited years for a marriage and were prepared to go on waiting indefinitely. Yet everything could vanish in a second. There were no guarantees that they had endless years to spend together.

"Harald," she said softly, "I want us to be married as soon as possible."

Understanding in his eyes, he squeezed her hand.

Of course, they could not be married as soon as possible, and in the coming months as their situation seemed increasingly hopeless there were tears and sleepless nights and days filled with worry and frustration. There were happy moments, too—afternoons spent playing with Astrid's girls, time wandering in the mountains together in the spring, and days where they forced themselves to forget and let themselves laugh and talk of nothing and enjoy each other as they had in the beginning.

Yet the waiting was agonizing, and it weighed on them both. It was all the worse because they were not sure what, exactly, they were waiting for—the King's permission, of course, but what event might precipitate it they could not imagine.

"This is impossible," she told him bluntly one evening just after Christmas. "I think I always knew it might be, but when I was young..." she thought back to her ready assurance the night he had proposed three and a half years earlier... "I thought the impossible would be nothing more than a small obstacle to *us*, but..."

"You are young, Sonja. You're twenty-six."

She shook her head. "We were young when we met five years ago. We've aged decades since then." And they had, she thought—she believed she had felt more disappointment and anxiety and longing than she might have in a lifetime. "Sometimes I think—we don't have any assurance we're getting married, do we? We're always going on as though we've got some absolute assurance we're destined to spend our lives together, but...do you really believe God intends for us to marry?" The thought had pressed on her heart for some time.

"Yes," he said slowly. "Yes, I do."

"Then why have there been so many setbacks?" she said, hating herself for bringing this up. "Why has it been prevented for so long, and why does it look to any rational person that it won't ever happen?"

"If we *aren't* meant to marry, why have we been brought so far and allowed to love so much?" Harald answered immediately.

They both fell silent. "Harald…" she began eventually, not sure what she was going to say.

"This is not a question we can answer, Sonja. There is no reason in God's eyes that it would be *wrong* for us to marry, no reason that we *shouldn't* marry, but His intentions…we can't know."

"Do you think…" She paused. "Do you think…we ought to separate…for a time…and see what happens from there…if we're brought back together… if we're not…" She trailed off, unsure how exactly to put it.

"No, I don't think so," he said, quickly and directly. "I don't want to… Is it what you want?"

"I—I don't know. I don't want to. But part of me feels—it might be best—for a time. I…" She shrugged miserably. "I don't know what to do."

They agreed soon afterwards to break it off, half entertaining the vain hope that they might each be able to go on with life. Harald threw himself into his royal duties; Sonja returned to school in Cambridge for the spring semester. She intended to think of nothing beyond twentieth-century British literature and English grammar, hoping it would distract her from Harald long enough to move on.

It did not—Forster, Kipling, and discussions of relative clause verb tenses proved to be poor substitutes for love. But she was determined to make it until summer without contacting Harald, telling herself that she would be "over it" by then. She was reminding herself of this goal one morning in April as she headed down the front walk of her residence hall.

"Sonja!" She stopped dead at the sound of Harald's voice, wanting to believe in its reality but suspecting it to be nothing more than the fanciful leftover of a dream from last night.

Then she heard it again. "Sonja!" Slowly, she turned around to see Harald, calmly sitting on a bench. "You walked right past me," he said, smiling as he stood to pick up the books she'd dropped. "You dropped these," he said when she didn't take them from him.

"Oh!" She hadn't noticed. "Are you real?" she asked, then laughed at the foolish sound of the question, giddy at his presence. "How did you…oh, but you're here!" She laughed again, then stopped at the sudden realization that she didn't want Harald here at all. She wanted them both to move on—didn't she?

"Harald," she said quietly, wanting the world to stop spinning and everything to be rational again, "what are you doing here?"

"I'm here to see you."

"Yes, but we agreed—we're not—we said—"

"I know. But I can't stand it. I came down here to tell you that I believe—that I *know*—we have a future. I'm sure of it. I'm determined that we do and we will. I need you, I love you, and I am going to fight for us. I'm determined, Sonja, because I can't stand to be without you."

"I can't stand it either," she heard herself saying. She knew instantly she was making the right decision—four months of longing had been evidence enough that a separation was not a realistic option. "I've called you—did you know I've called you?" He shook his head. "I didn't think so; I've called you more than once and hung up when you answered; I didn't intend to talk to you, I didn't think I ought to talk to you, but I wanted to hear your voice—to know that you were there—"

"I keep thinking about your eyes," he interrupted. "Every day. The way they look when you tilt your face down and then look up at me—you're doing it now. I've been half crazy just remembering that!" He laughed. "There's nothing like your eyes, anywhere."

"You came all the way to England to tell me you miss my eyes? Wouldn't a phone call do?" She was kidding, but he shook his head quite seriously.

"No," he said. "A phone call wouldn't do. I had to come. There's no one like *you*, anywhere, no one who laughs like you or whose face is like yours—sometimes I don't hear a word you say because I'm so busy watching your expressions. There's no one else who can be both complete perfection and a complete mess in the space of an hour. And there's no feeling in the world like having your hand in mine." She was laughing, too, now, both at his description of her and with happiness at being together again.

"Sonja." He brushed his fingers across her cheek, and she felt a shiver run through her at their first touch since December. "I need you. In Oslo. In my arms."

She nodded quickly and stepped forward to kiss him, thankful that no one in Cambridge would give them a second glance. "I'll finish the semester first," she said when they broke apart. "But I'll be home in June."

"Of course." He nodded. "But I'll stay all weekend—I have a table tonight at The Ivy, and rooms at Claridge's for tonight and Saturday. There's a train to London in an hour, if you can be ready then."

Harald had become everything to her, she realized that weekend, and very little else seemed to matter. Life with him was all she wanted, and every moment she spent with no guarantee that she could have it was a painful ordeal. Her desire to be his wife was all-consuming and almost frightening in its intensity.

For his part, Harald never failed to be awed that he could love her so deeply. It was not something he had ever fully expected to feel, having been prepared for a match with someone he merely *liked*. That such strong feelings and such delirious happiness could exist seemed a miracle to him; that he should feel all this and not be able to act on it seemed pure cruelty. As he promised, he spent the spring and summer pushing his father hard.

He was still enduring meeting after meeting with a variety of suitable princesses, all of whom merged into a nondescript blur. Queen Ingrid of Denmark, who had been a close friend of his mother's, had taken over much of the logistics, stating that matchmaking was a woman's job. There was a slight reprieve for him in the weeks before her daughter Anne-Marie's September wedding to the new King Constantine of Greece, but it was all back in full swing afterwards. However, he had come to see these meetings as opportunities to argue his case with his father—each time he returned home demanding an engagement with Sonja, Olav grew more and more agitated.

In October, Harald represented Norway as a member of the 1964 Olympic sailing team in Tokyo. He returned home without a medal, but, far more significantly, he returned home to find a King stretched to the limit of his patience…

Chapter Twenty-Seven

"If we're really going to have a seven-layer cake, can't we have seven different flavors?" Sonja said, laughing. She had been laughing constantly over the last few days it seemed, ever since Harald had given her the news. After countless arguments and countless declarations on Harald's part that he had no interest in a royal bride, the King and his advisers had determined that the simplest course of action might be to approach the government about the possibility of an engagement. On Friday, His Majesty intended to use his weekly meeting with Prime Minister Gerhardsen and the State Council to raise the subject. Then, with the blessing of the highest men in the country, the engagement would be put to a vote in the Storting for parliamentary approval, after which it would be announced to the public and a wedding date would be set. It was, Harald and Sonja had agreed—and a depressed Olav himself seemed to believe—highly unlikely that the government would oppose a marriage the King had already approved. They had therefore spent hours planning the wedding and their life afterwards—it was all now a reality that they had not allowed themselves to fully envision before. Sonja had often marveled as they talked at the quiet intimacy of the subject even in the face of a state wedding.

"Seven flavors would be odd," he said, laughing with her. "But if it makes you happy, we can certainly do it."

What made her happy was the thought of the simple gold monogram they had decided would be prominent on the side of each layer—an S tucked inside an H—and imagining his hand covering hers as they cut into it.

"Tell me more about the ball," she said. Unfamiliar with the grandeur of a royal wedding, she was relying on his descriptions of how everything would be. As he began to speak of the waltzes—and the music that would be composed for the occasion—she was nearly dizzy with happiness as she imagined the two of them opening the ball, she in his arms in her wedding gown…

She had already made sketches of various designs, intending to make her dress herself. Too secretive to share them with Harald, she had pored over them with her mother and her friends and Haakon's wife, and she had sent carbon copies to Margrethe. She had barely been able to still the excited trembling in her fingers at the thought of what she was drawing.

"Where do you want me to take you for the honeymoon?" Harald whispered in her ear one evening. "Paris? Rome? Or would you rather I took you somewhere you hadn't seen—the Caribbean? Egypt?" He kissed her softly.

She smiled, reminded that they would soon be able to celebrate the wedding night they had longed for. A year from now, she would be his in every way.

"No, Harald," she said. "I don't care about going to any of those places on our honeymoon." She kissed him, her lips only lightly brushing his at first until she slowly deepened the kiss, savoring the moment. "I had something much simpler in mind," she said when she drew back. "I want you to find us a little cabin in the mountains here in Norway. A place with no distractions, where we can be together and think of nothing else. All I'm going to want is you."

"I think I can live with that," he said with a small smile before kissing her again.

The coming days were filled with thoughts of the ceremony and ball— she dreamed of colors and flowers and music and dinner courses—and of the marriage that would follow. She and Harald would move into Skaugum together, and she would have him near her always, their lives merging into one. There would be no more waiting or worrying or fear that she might never be his; instead there would be a home and babies and decades spent at each other's side.

Every thought brought her back to her dream of the moment when they would meet at the altar and speak the sacred words that would at last make her his and him hers for the rest of their lives. He would place his ring on her finger, and she would never take it off, secure in the knowledge that they would never have to leave each other...

At long last Friday arrived, and she was driven to the Palace, the King having suggested to Harald that it might be simplest if they were both available to greet the Council upon its adjournment. Sonja met Harald in the entrance hall, and he led her to a side room, the deep red color of the walls making the space seem small, happy, and cozy, and the heavy blue curtains reminiscent of the elegance of the nineteenth century when the Palace had first opened.

Everything seemed to be moving so quickly and easily toward a wedding, reminding her of the needle of a sewing machine running smoothly over soft silk. She had made a new dress for the occasion, a dark blue velvet with bunches of fabric in the full skirt and in the three-quarter length sleeves. She was leaning against Harald, absorbed in the softness of the moment and the dress as they sat waiting on a silk couch. His lips brushed against her forehead, and she settled closer into his arms, both of them laughing as he attempted to avoid being hit in the face with her feather fascinator. They did not speak as nearly an hour passed, the afternoon seeming too profound for words, and merely held each other in the silence. *Engaged*, she thought. *And married next year.*

Sonja looked down at their laced fingers and then up at Harald, smiling. He smiled back, lightly pressing her hand. Surely they would be summoned soon, or a page would at least bring them word of the results of the meeting.

But the hands of the grandfather clock in the corner slowly slipped past the hour mark, and then another ten minutes had passed, and then another fifteen, and then another twenty, and no one came.

"Should it be taking this long?" she asked, a slight trepidation creeping over her despite her attempts to ignore the sensation.

He hesitated. "Most weekly Council meetings would be over by now, but you never can tell. There's no reason to worry." But he *was* worried, and she could tell, could feel the change in his body, and she was worried, too. Perhaps the King had been slow to raise the question, she told herself, perhaps there had been other business to attend to. Perhaps some earlier issues had taken more time than expected...because surely there was no problem with their engagement, surely not...

The old clock went on ticking as her heart climbed into her throat. She pressed closer to him, and their grip on each other's hand tightened. Surely any minute now. Harald had been so sure the Council would easily agree, he had said the King had been so sure, and the King's advisers had apparently been so sure... There couldn't possibly be a problem, there couldn't be... They were going to be engaged today, weren't they? *Engaged and married next year. Engaged and married next year. Engaged and married next year.* The words tumbled over each other, racing through her mind as though their frantic repetition would somehow assure her of their truth.

Tick, tick, tick. She would go mad from the noise, a reminder of time's passage that seemed to grow louder and more insistent with each second. The blood red walls seemed to be closing in, forcing them into a tighter, suffocating space, and the curtains suddenly seemed more an oppressive addition to hide sunlight than an example of old world elegance.

"It'll be all right," she heard Harald say softly as she closed her eyes. Yes. Yes, it would be. It had to be. Panic seized her, squeezing her ribcage until she could hardly breathe. *Please...please...please...* She could not shape a prayer into anything more coherent than this.

"Surely it won't be long now," he said a few minutes later in a tone of desperate hope.

"Surely not," she said, trying to play along with his charade that nothing was wrong. She failed utterly at this, her terror returning as she pulled away to look at him. "What's taking them so long? What is it? What are they doing in there?"

He was silent for a moment. "It may not have anything to do with us— there might have been a longer agenda than usual this morning."

She wondered, as she settled back into his arms, if he were not trying to convince himself as well. *No*, she told herself. *They'll vote yes.*

At long last, the white doors opened, and an older man stepped into the room. Her breath caught in her throat as she examined his face. Completely expressionless.

"Your Royal Highness, the King wishes to see you." With a final squeeze of her hand Harald left, and she sat alone, half terrified, half hopeful. Shouldn't they have both been summoned if the results were favorable? She smoothed her hands over the velvet of her skirt as though trying to calm herself with its softness. Surely there was no reason the engagement could not go forward; it was the King's permission they had truly needed, and the Council and the Storting were mere formalities.

It seemed an eternity, but according to the clock no more than five full minutes passed before Harald returned, his face stark white with every bit of color drained from his cheeks.

She could read the truth in his eyes, but she would not believe it. She slowly stood, closing the gap between them, walking as though the rich carpet were quicksand.

"Yes?" she whispered as she took his hands, hope and panic swelling up inside her.

"The government…says it is not possible."

⌒

"Sonja," Dagny said, "perhaps they'll change their minds—or perhaps there'll be a change in government in the near future and the next party will be sympathetic—"

Sonja cut her off. "It doesn't matter. The King won't ever go to the State Council about our engagement again—he was hesitant in the first place, and now he's seen they can easily tell him no." She had come home, given her mother the news, and sunk into a chair in the front room.

"*Lille jenta mi*,[17] I think this is going to happen eventually. I don't think you should tell yourself it's hopeless."

She barely had the strength to tell herself anything at all.

"If the King approved the marriage, I think he'll find a way to get the government to agree," Dagny went on.

She could not bear these meaningless reassurances. "Mamma, please stop. I...just don't say anything else."

"Do you want me to let you be alone?" Dagny said gently.

"No. No, stay with me." With effort, she forced herself to move from the chair to sit on the couch with her mother, laying her head on her shoulder but too numb from the shock of the day's events to cry.

After awhile the doorbell rang, and she moved to allow Dagny to stand and answer it.

"Mrs. Haraldsen?" she heard Harald's voice say a moment later. "Is Sonja at home?"

Harald. Harald had come back. He had brought her home after the vote and offered to come in with her, but she had shrugged it off and gone in alone. She should be glad he was here, she knew, but she felt a strange lack of emotion—she could hardly feel anything at all.

She heard her mother answer him, and then their footsteps left the front hall to join her in the sitting room.

"Sonja." She forced herself to look up and meet his eyes. Hers, she was sure, were dull pools of despair, but his were alive with a steely determination. "May I see you for a moment?"

She nodded slowly, only vaguely aware of the hand slipping around hers as he sat down on the couch and her mother stepped out again.

"We *will* be married someday. I'll find a way to make it happen. I've given you my word, and I want you to know I'm not taking no for an answer." She could manage only a vague nod, and he gently took her chin in his hand, forcing her to look up at him.

"I am marrying you someday, and I don't want you to have any doubt about it. I want you to know that I'm not going to have anyone else, and I'm not going to stop fighting. Do you understand?"

She nodded miserably.

"I went and got something for us after I dropped you off earlier." He

---

17   Affectionate Norwegian name for a daughter; literally, "my little girl"

reached into the pocket of his jacket and withdrew two small black velvet boxes, then opened one of them and removed a simple gold ring.

"Harald…" she whispered. "I…it's beautiful." She could see engraved letters inside. "What does it…" He shifted it so that she could read the two words: *Your Harald.*

"I will love you and honor you, and be faithful to you, for better, for worse, until death do us part," he whispered as he slipped it onto her finger. She shivered slightly at the weight of his words.

"Is there one for you?" she whispered. He handed her the other box, and she removed a second gold band, slipping it onto his hand as she repeated his words back to him, her voice trembling.

In the silence that followed she gazed down at her ring, moved by the love that had inspired its purchase but struck suddenly by its meaning—it was an empty placeholder, a sad mockery of what they could never have, the symbol of a love that would never be satisfied.

Chapter Twenty-Eight

"Sonja hasn't been out of bed all day," Mrs. Haraldsen said quietly when she let Harald in the next afternoon.

"Is she sick?" She had not seemed to be, yesterday.

Dagny paused. "Not physically. But she's...very upset about what happened."

So upset she'd lacked the energy to get out of bed? His stomach flip-flopped at the realization that there was something very wrong. He was very upset as well, but he'd gotten up that morning. "Can I see her?"

"Of course. I think it would do her good," she said with false brightness. "But first—why don't you sit down for a moment?"

Nervous, he followed her into the front room and took a seat on the couch.

"Harald," Dagny said bluntly, "we have a family history of...some would say...depressive tendencies. It comes from my late husband's family—although there was never anything in my husband himself, and he thought—and I thought—that perhaps his branch of the family had been spared, as some had."

She paused. "But then—well, the war started. And my older children both became involved with the resistance movement. My eldest daughter Gry was arrested—she was seventeen at the time—and sent to Grini. She was eventually released and fled to Sweden, but when she came home after the war she...she was never the same. She hasn't been...*well* for the past twenty years." She took a deep breath. Harald realized he was holding his own, terrified of where this speech was going. "Sonja does not know this history because we've always sought to protect her. We never even discussed very much about Gry's... struggles in front of her. As she got older I saw signs of—this—in her at times— that first semester she was in Switzerland when she was seventeen, and I think it was apparent the spring her father passed away. She would hardly go anywhere for months; I doubt I saw her smile once...until she met you."

He was half stunned at the information, half hating himself for not suspecting it before. He had known how dark Sonja's mood had been at times over the last few years; he ought to have worried that there was something more there. He ought to have *dealt with it* somehow.

"And so when everything became so—stressful—for her in your relationship, I was naturally very worried, and there were times when I thought—but it never seemed too serious—but now…" Dagny had ceased to make eye contact with Harald and was absently fingering the wool of her skirt. He looked away, suddenly horribly ashamed to be sitting in her home. "I told you she hasn't been out of bed all day. She hasn't eaten—she won't speak to me; she looks at me when I talk to her but it's as though…I can't reach her."

There was a heavy silence. Harald felt as though the floor had dropped out from beneath them, leaving him nothing solid to lean on. The guilt weighed so heavily he could barely breathe—guilt at what he'd done to Sonja simply by being in her life, guilt at what he hadn't been able to protect her from, guilt at what he hadn't even been attentive enough to see coming. "I'm so sorry," he said at last, feeling that any feeble apology could never be enough. "I'm so very sorry—I never wanted her to be hurt in all of this—"

Dagny shook her head. "It's not your fault. But…does this…make you feel any differently? About Sonja?" She glanced up at him, fear in her eyes.

The question would have been laughable in any other situation—it would never have occurred to him that he could possibly feel differently about Sonja. "I still have every intention of marrying her and every reason to still want to be with her, if that's what you're asking me."

She laid a hand on his knee. "Thank you, Harald."

He was suddenly afraid as Dagny led him up the stairs toward Sonja's room—unaccountably nervous about seeing her, afraid of what he would find, afraid to see her face, afraid of how real it would all be. Her mother left him at the threshold, and he paused to say a silent prayer for his own strength and for a way to comfort her.

"Sonja?" he whispered, still standing in her doorway. "Sonja?" After a moment she rolled over to look at him. It was like making eye contact with a ghost. Her eyes were open, but their brown pools held no life at all, possessing instead a dim, haunted stare. She did not, he thought, look at all like Sonja.

"I'm here," he said, stepping into her room and over to the side of her bed where he laid a hand on her arm.

"Harald." Her voice was merely a thin breath of air that stabbed him with its emptiness.

Slowly, he took a seat in the chair next to the bed—likely the one her mother had occupied all day—and reached his hand out to her. She slipped hers into it, but her cold, still fingers did not curl around his. "I love you," he said as he rubbed her hand, instinctively trying to bring some life back into it.

She did not respond.

He returned daily to find her improving only slightly, to the point where she would speak to him but still seemed wholly incapable of getting up, and he did not push her to do so. He was utterly useless to ease the tortured look in her eyes, unable to do anything to help, and he hated his complete impotence in the face of her suffering.

⟊

"I have been trying to think what to say to you," her mother said a few days later. She had been sitting with Sonja for hours in silence, and Sonja looked up at the sound of her voice.

"There isn't anything," Sonja said dully. "We'll never be married."

"I think it is still possible that you will be, but I know I have no business trying to assure you of that. The only thing I think I can say—and I'm afraid it won't sound comforting at all—is that this is all in God's hands."

Sonja had grown up admiring her mother's strong faith, and these kinds of conversations were not unusual between them, but... "I know. And...that *isn't* comforting." She knew in her heart that she would rather control it herself.

Dagny nodded. "I can imagine that it isn't. I know how you like to have control of things." She smiled, and Sonja tried—and failed—to return it.

"I try to have faith," Sonja said. "But in the midst of this...it is *so hard*."

"I know, *lille jenta mi*. And I can understand something of your feelings...I was not, in any real sense, a religious woman at all until after your brother died." Sonja knew that her parents had had another son, a boy who had died at age seven in a boating accident the year before she herself had been born, but it had never been a subject often discussed.

"I remember being told at the time that God was in control, and it would just make me want to *scream*, because if He was in control, then He clearly had no desire to do what was good in my life. The idea of a sovereign God being in control wasn't a comforting one at all, not if that God had taken my child."

Her mother reached out to stroke her hair, and Sonja felt the slight trembling in her hand. "Over the next few months, I sought comfort in His word and in prayer—I couldn't find it anywhere else—and God drew me nearer to Him. I began to see that the promise that our Lord works in all things for the good of those who love Him isn't at all an empty promise. Our Lord sent His Son to die in our place—there can be no clearer evidence that He cares for us deeply and wants only the best for us. It's a very comforting thought that God holds everything in His hands, when you think of what He's already done."

"I have never thought of it that way," Sonja said after a moment.

"Think of Grundtvig's hymn,"[18] Dagny said. She hummed softly. *"In God's fatherly hand all rests, / Works the Spirit His behests; / Our reward and lot secure / With God's only Son endure."*

Sonja closed her eyes, knowing the truth of her mother's words but struggling to believe it all in her heart. "But it is still—the thought that we may not marry is still so very hard," she said at last.

"Of course it is. Acknowledging that there was a good and loving God in control didn't make your brother's death any less painful. This doesn't mean that our lives will be insulated from pain; it means that we can be secure in the knowledge that God will do what's best for us. Even if we don't understand why in this life."

"Our hope is not in this world," Sonja whispered. It was an easily forgotten truth that she had always been conscious of.

"No, it isn't."

Sonja reached her hand out for her mother's. "I would like...to give this over to God," she said softly. "Pray...pray that I can."

"So you haven't been out of this room in a week," Margrethe said, looking down at her. The Danish Crown Princess had arrived in Oslo that morning, intending to help with the early stages of wedding planning and finding a wholly different situation.

"I can't make myself get up," Sonja whispered. Her mother's prayers aside, she was not sure she would *ever* be able to get up. "We thought we were so close," she whispered. "We were picking out cake fillings, for heaven's sake!" She gave a hollow laugh.

"This doesn't mean it won't ever happen," Margrethe said. Sonja had come to find the softness and perpetual calm of Margrethe's voice very soothing over the past couple years, but it did not reach her now.

"It does."

"No, there will be a change in government soon, and perhaps then—"

"That's *only* a 'perhaps,' and I can't take any more of this!"

"Sonja, you—"

"I can't, I can't. I can't last any longer!"

---

18   N.F.S. Grundtvig, a nineteenth-century Danish pastor, hymn writer, and author who was heavily influential in Scandinavian culture.

Margrethe sighed and fell silent. "Sonja," she ventured at last, "do you think—do you think you might be able to get up if I—or if Harald—if one of us helped you?"

"I can't," she whispered. "I just *can't*."

Margrethe studied her, her eyes soft and warm. "Then I'll lie down next to you so you don't have to lie there alone." She pulled back the covers and slipped in next to Sonja, who was instantly comforted by the warmth of the embrace, and they lay there together, the shopkeeper's daughter and the daughter of one thousand years of Danish Kings.

⌒⌒

"Do you think you would be able to get up today before Harald gets here this evening?" Margrethe offered the next afternoon.

"No, I can't." She had prayed for strength, she had prayed for courage, she had prayed for faith, and yet...

"You don't think you would be able to get up *for him*?" Margrethe emphasized the last two words.

"I..." She suddenly wanted to do it for Harald's sake, to ease the worry she had seen in his eyes.

Margrethe pushed on. "He gave you a wedding ring, Sonja. That means something."

She nodded.

"It means he's going to fight for this. Do you think—in light of that—you could get up and go downstairs for the day?"

"I..." It was a daunting prospect, and she... "I just can't." She leaned back against the pillows. "I...I'm not strong enough..."

"I don't believe that, Sonja." There was warmth in Margrethe's eyes, but also a firm determination, and they were fixed intensely on Sonja's. "You can't lie in this room forever. Come on; I'll be right here with you. Think how happy you'll make Harald when he sees you tonight."

Sonja nodded slowly, pushed the covers back, and stepped onto the hardwood floor.

It was a decided first step at returning to life, a life which she was not sure had any further direction and whose future seemed so inexpressibly barren. Her legs shook slightly, and she was suddenly ready to crumble, but she found she was able to do it if she did not think past the moment, if she poured all of her strength into each individual step. Once she had reached the front room, she perched nervously on the edge of the couch, where Margrethe insisted on bringing her some of the alterations that her mother had brought home from the store. She had no feeling for it at first, but she slowly became grateful for the suggestion as she discovered that it gave her something to focus on, something to pour herself into, some purpose in the moment that did not require her to think about Harald or the State Council or the future.

Harald was nearly giddy when he found her seated on the couch, and seeing him in such high spirits lifted her own. This, in addition to her mother's relief when she had returned home earlier that day, gave her incentive to get up again the next morning, and she slowly began to recover.

She often took refuge in her sewing—there was something immensely comforting about the whir of the machine, the steady feeding of fabric into it, and the familiarity of something she'd been doing since childhood. Simpler tasks were soothingly mind-numbing; more difficult parts barred any other thoughts. Most calming—although she would not have admitted it to herself—was the fact that, when she sewed, everything could be made to come out perfectly.

Chapter Twenty-Nine

"I HARDLY EVEN KNOW HOW TO PRAY," SONJA ADMITTED TO HER MOTHER one evening. She was on the verge of collapsing again; she had said nothing but knew Dagny could sense it. "I *try*, but…I don't even know what I would pray for." Further requests that there would be a marriage had come to seem hopelessly empty.

"I suggest you ask for strength."

"I feel so horribly weak," Sonja said, her words pouring out in a rush. "So unequal to this whole situation; I don't think I can stand it, I don't know how I'll keep going…"

"Do you not trust that God can give you the strength that you need? Hasn't He so far?"

"It has not always felt like I've been given strength. It certainly didn't that week last month," she confessed.

"God did not abandon you even then. Your *feelings* about it matter very little. You were not abandoned, and you will not be."

Sonja looked away.

"I don't mean to be harsh," her mother said gently.

"No, you're completely right," Sonja whispered. "But I…I'm so ashamed of this, in front of you. All that's happening is I can't get engaged and married—that's all! And I think back to how strong you were during the war—I can't comprehend how hard it must have been, but…I never saw anything in you, other than peace and calm, and strength. And here *I* am, a *wreck*." She had thought often of her mother during the early years of her own life—the war had begun not so long after the death of Sonja's brother, and then Dagny's two older children had fled to Sweden with no guarantee that she would ever see them again.

"It was not my own strength that got me through," Dagny said. Sonja nodded, and after a moment her mother reached out to brush her hair back. *"Lille jenta mi,"* she said softly, "you will get through this."

"God has not always seemed to be very near," Sonja admitted. "I know He *is*; I know He has not left me, but sometimes I feel…" She shrugged. "It has been hard even to pray sometimes, this last month."

"I consider it a privilege to pray for you. No doubt Harald prays for you as well."

"He does. He prays for us, and for me." She paused. "I suppose I just wish—I don't know—on darker days, that I had some sort of sign, *evidence* that I haven't been abandoned."

"You do have evidence," Dagny said immediately. "Our God put on flesh. He left heaven to walk among us for thirty years. He's intimately aware of human frailty, and He was willing to die for you…could there possibly be any more evidence that God knows every centimeter of your heart and cares for you far too much to ever leave you?"

"Yes—yes, of course, I realize that," she stammered.

"But think what it means, Sonja. Think what the incarnation itself means."

"It means that God understands us, completely," she said, repeating what she had always believed. "He knows grief, and pain, and temptation, and weakness."

"And He is not some shadowy, far-off being who has no idea what you feel. He has not given up on you, and He is not going to."

In the middle of January she went to Copenhagen to see Margrethe, arriving on a freezing cold day that was spent returning to favorite places and pieces of art from Sonja's last visit to the city two years ago. Back in Margrethe and Benedikte's apartment that evening (with Benedikte thankfully away at finishing school in Switzerland), they curled up in comfortable chairs next to one of the marble fireplaces to begin thawing out, steaming bowls of soup in their hands for dinner.

"What do you think will happen?" Sonja asked suddenly.

"If and when Norway has a new Prime Minister, I think the King will eventually ask him about the engagement," Margrethe said, understanding Sonja's question without any need for clarification. "And a few years from now, I think the government will be a lot more willing to approve it. They'll start worrying that Harald won't marry anyone and won't produce any heirs."

"I'm not sure I can last a few more years," Sonja said.

"Of course you can. Consider how far you've come. I think most girls would have run screaming in the other direction, quite awhile ago." Sonja laughed softly, and Margrethe went on. "I have no doubt you will last a few more years until your engagement is approved, and I think the strength you've shown in the last five and half means that you'll handle the role of Crown Princess and its pressures far better than many."

"Oh, but—I don't think it *will* happen in a few years; I don't think it can ever happen!" Sonja was almost surprised to hear the words burst out of her with such force.

For a moment the only sound was the crackling of the fire. "Sonja," Margrethe said soothingly, "is there anything I can do?"

Sonja shook her head.

Margrethe paused. "You know, you aren't the only one who's unhappy."

"What?" Surely Margrethe didn't mean herself.

"I'm not saying this to make you feel guilty for reacting the way you do, nor am I saying it to make you feel sorry for me—I'm only saying it because I think it might do you good to remember how lucky you are, so to speak, to have Harald in the first place. I think—I think sometimes you forget to be grateful that you're in love and that Harald is going to do everything he can to marry you someday. Because...I don't think I'll ever marry."

"Why, of course you will," Sonja said, somewhat surprised. "You may not have met him yet, but that doesn't mean you'll never marry. You're three years younger than me; you've got time."

"No." A strained quality came into Margrethe's voice that was at odds with her usual manner. "I don't think I *will* marry—I'm afraid I'm going to be alone and terribly unhappy for the rest of my life. Sometimes I wonder what's to become of me, because I just can't imagine...I don't imagine anyone ever wanting to marry me." She slowly twirled a strand of brown hair that had escaped from her chignon.

"Why do you think that?"

Her words spilled forth in a rush as her fingers toyed with a loose thread on the quilt. "First off, I'm going to be Queen, and very few men are willing to marry Queens—it's a horribly difficult position for a man, to spend the rest of his life walking three steps behind his wife, that is, and to never be able to do much of any significance. And being a future Queen means there are very few men that I could—that I myself would be willing to marry, because I cannot imagine anyone in whose power I would want to place myself once I've ascended the throne.

"I think I'm oddly picky about men—I've never had more than a passing interest in anyone. I'm not like my little sister; I'm not the sort of girl who falls in love at a glance and a smile and whom men fall for even quicker. I think

I'm a little too…intellectual. I'd want someone who's prepared to debate world affairs until four in the morning or analyze art and pick apart literature over breakfast, and I don't think there are that many men out there like that. I think it's intimidating."

Sonja laughed at the description—it did seem to be such a perfect fit for Margrethe. In a confession that had left them both giggling, the Crown Princess had once admitted that her most reckless youthful indiscretion had been digging up some fifteenth-century clay pipes in London's Hyde Park with her cousin Count George and smuggling them back to Copenhagen for further examination. That Margrethe's idea of a good time with a man was more along the lines of theft of antiquities than a fine dinner with good wine perhaps limited her options somewhat, but… "That doesn't mean you'll *never* find someone," Sonja said.

Margrethe shook her head. "Even without all those issues…I can't imagine anyone at all falling in love with me because…I'm not beautiful in the slightest." It was not said as a complaint, nor was there any regret in her voice—it was simply a statement of fact, and the plain way she said it only made her admission starker.

"And that's why I'll never marry. I—there might be some men in the German houses who are willing to marry me, simply because they want the boost in their status that marrying the Queen of Denmark would give them, and perhaps they might be exceptional, intellectual enough men, but they certainly wouldn't be marrying me because they were in love with me.

"And I couldn't ever marry unless we were both madly in love; I just can't *imagine* a wedding under any other circumstances, and I desperately *want* someone to fall that much in love with me, but I—I don't think that will ever happen."

"Margrethe…" Sonja began.

"I know you've noticed I'm not very attractive; I don't see how you could not have. You haven't got to pretend otherwise."

Intellectually, Sonja knew that she had not, upon first meeting Margrethe, found her pretty in the slightest. She could readily recall her first impressions of the Crown Princess's appearance and remembered easily that her thoughts had not been favorable. Yet three years later, after countless moments of shared laughter, after all the warm smiles Margrethe had offered her, after so many soft words had been spoken at exactly the right moments…her earlier opinions of the other girl's looks had come to seem ridiculously incorrect.

"I think you're very pretty," she said softly. "More than pretty—beautiful. You're beautiful, Margrethe."

"You don't have to say that."

"I'm not lying. I—I'll admit I didn't see it at first, but now...now that I know you...I see it every time I look at you. It's...your warmth, your kindness, your excitement...it fills your face, it fills you entirely. Once someone knows you...they can't help but find you beautiful."

"There might be an argument to be made there if I were merely plain. But I'm...Sonja, you must have noticed that my eyes..." Margrethe blushed and looked away.

Yes, she had also noticed that Margrethe's eyes were not the same size, that her left did not always look in quite the same direction, and that this was what contributed to the initial impression that she was unattractive. "I have noticed." *But not for quite some time,* she added silently.

"I was in a car accident when I was a child and my left eye was injured." She shrugged. "It's a muscle issue—that's why it's not always like that; I can control it sometimes, but not always."

"I'm sorry," Sonja said quietly. "But I don't—Margrethe, I don't *see* that when I look at you now; it's not what I'm thinking about when I look at your eyes. I notice how bright they are when you're excited, I see how warm they are, and I think of how much love was in them when you came to see me in November. When I look at your face, I see the kindness you extended to a shopkeeper's daughter who arrived in your apartments three years ago, I see your passion for your art and for nearly everything else in life, I see your intelligence, your talent...all that's what I see. And I believe it's exactly what some man is going to see someday, and he won't be able to see you as anything *less* than beautiful."

Chapter Thirty

THERE WAS TO BE AN ELECTION IN 1965—RUMOR HAD IT THAT IT WOULD BE in the fall—and Harald was optimistic that the expected change in government might provide them with another chance for an engagement. Sonja was not so sure. The darkness of last fall was still with her at times, and she was beginning to feel that she had lost any power for hope.

"I'm going away for the summer," she told Harald in May. "I've found work as an *au pair* in Sorèze—it's a small town south of Toulouse. I think—I think—it might be best if we tried…to separate again…after I leave."

"We'll have a new government soon—we'll have another chance with them," he said.

"I know. But there's no guarantee. There's no reason it should be any different. We always have a plan, an event that's going to change everything. Sophie's going to get married. Your father's going to get tired of waiting. The State Council is going to vote. The government is going to change. This could go on forever, Harald, and at some point it has to stop. I think…I think I'm done." She waited, not moving, desperately wanting him to convince her otherwise.

"I think you may be right," he said slowly, not meeting her eyes. "We haven't got any guarantees—and I can't ask you to keep waiting, to keep having your hopes crushed like this. If you need to stop…"

"Maybe just for the summer?" She was hedging now. "And then see how we feel about things?"

He had laid his hand on her knee at the beginning of the conversation, and his grip tightened. He still did not look at her. "Whatever you need to do," he said finally, stiffly.

"I need…to be away from all this. Just for a few months. I just…need a break," she said miserably. "And maybe we'll find…that we can manage without each other."

They did not, of course. For Harald, it was the longest, darkest, coldest summer he could remember; for Sonja, the four Garnier children, the excitement of a new language and culture, and the beauty and warmth of summer in southern France made for a refreshing three months, but she missed Harald more each day. Nothing in Sorèze could remind her of Norway, and she plunged into French life headfirst, yet she could not shake her memories of Harald. She spent most of the summer entertaining a guilty hope that, when she returned to Oslo after the children started school in the fall, she would find Harald on her doorstep. Thus it was no great surprise when he did, in fact, knock on her door the day after her return.

"Sonja?" he said hesitantly.

She nodded immediately and stepped into his arms.

As anticipated, Prime Minister Gerhardsen's government fell at the October 1965 election, marking the end of the Socialists' twenty-year rule. In its place would be a center-right coalition headed by Per Borten.

Borten was a vastly different man than Gerhardsen, and Harald believed he might be more inclined to look favorably on the engagement. Gerhardsen was a dignified, old-fashioned traditionalist interested in preserving the old Norway; Borten was a down-to-earth farmer with a reputation for lacking certain social graces, a contrarian sort who had once welcomed a reporter and photographer to his farm while wearing nothing more than a hat and a pair of shorts. If any Prime Minister would approve a royal-common marriage, it would be he.

As soon as the election results had been announced, Harald had intended to ask his father to return to the State Council—an entirely different group of men now—and request approval for the engagement again.

"Is there any possibility of raising the subject of an engagement to Sonja with Borten's government?" Harald asked over dinner one evening.

The King did not even glance up from the fish he was cutting. "Absolutely not. Out of the question."

"Why not? It's a new government—"

"And I'm not eager to start off by embarrassing myself in front of it as I did last year."

Harald's teeth clenched at the implication that the worst part of the incident for his father had simply been *embarrassment*. "These are different men, Father, and it's entirely possible that they might be in favor of the marriage."

Olav raised his eyebrows. "On the contrary, Harald, I think it's highly improbable. The Norwegian people do not want it. And if anyone was going to approve of a shopkeeper's daughter as our next Crown Princess, it was the

Socialists—the party of the common man. These new men are centrists and conservatives who are much less likely to accept the thought of a seamstress sharing your throne."

"But the Socialists were far more worried about stepping incorrectly because they knew they were losing control of the government, plus public opinion was worse a year ago; now there are a number of people who just want to see their Crown Prince married, and they don't care to whom. I think that Borten would have far less problem with the idea than Gerhardsen did." He paused. "Sonja and I would like to be engaged as soon as we can, for her sake especially—the strain is too much for her. If there's even the remotest possibility that the current government might approve it, then I want you to pursue it—"

"You forget the central issue here." The King set his fork down and looked squarely at his son. "I do not *want*—and I believe most of Norway does not want—you engaged to a shopkeeper's daughter. I was briefly persuaded to test the waters with Gerhardsen's men because of your resistance to every royal woman I put in front of you. I will not be so persuaded again."

Had his mother been gone so long that his father had forgotten what it was to love a woman? "Father—"

"The subject is closed, Harald."

Another hour of Harald's arguments fell on deaf ears.

Weeks passed after the installation of the Borten government, and it appeared that Olav was no more likely to approach the Council about the engagement than he was to name Ragnhild his heir. There was, however, feverish speculation in the press about the issue, constant news coverage that perpetually reinforced that the marriage could not happen, and Harald knew it was doing nothing for Sonja.

Mrs. Haraldsen called him one evening in early December, trepidation in her voice, to tell him she'd found her daughter counting out a large quantity of sleeping pills.

"What was she doing with them?" he asked.

"Just—counting them. She poured them out, counted through them, then put them away."

"Did you ask her why? Where did she get them?"

"No, I didn't ask. They're hers—she hasn't been sleeping well for awhile. Ever since what happened last year. That's why she has them."

Sonja had not told him that, but he did not find it at all hard to believe.

This was not abnormal behavior, Harald tried to tell himself. Plenty of people might count out medication for any number of innocent reasons. Yet he could not shake the fear her words had created.

"I'm frightened," Dagny admitted. "I—I told you about our family history—about my worries about Sonja. And I can't help but think…"

"But you don't have any reason to believe she intended…" he began, trying to calm both of them.

"No, no, not at all," she said quickly. "No reason. We didn't talk about it, she hasn't said anything that would indicate that's on her mind at all, she didn't spend very much time *looking* at them… It's only—maybe I'm overreacting, but it didn't feel *right* to me."

Perhaps she *was* overreacting. The family history Dagny had shared with him, as well as the problems she had alluded to with Sonja's sister, clearly troubled her, as had Sonja's behavior last November. In such a context, it would not be unusual for a mother who had already lost one child—Sonja had told him about the brother who had drowned a year before her own birth—to leap to such a conclusion.

But he was unwilling to disregard a mother's instinct, especially given what Dagny had already told him and what he'd seen in Sonja last year. He would be half-mad with worry in the coming weeks.

⌇

"You have noticed, I am sure," his father said just after New Year's, "that the media is in an absolute frenzy about the possibility of your marriage to this common girl—and the possibility of your subsequent abdication—"

"I'm not abdicating—"

Olav ignored him. "—and it is my opinion that something must be done."

"I agree, sir. Sonja's a nervous wreck."

"Absolutely. The public needs to hear—what did you say?"

He hid a smile, having known full well that it was not what the King had wanted to hear. "I agreed something had to be done about the press coverage because Sonja's a nervous wreck."

Olav stared at him for a moment. "This hasn't got anything to do with *her*. We need to announce to the Norwegian people—who are quite in a ferment over this issue—that you have no intention of marrying a commoner."

"This has everything to do with Sonja, and I have every intention of marrying a commoner," Harald said. His determination only grew stronger as he witnessed her crumbling, and he had sworn to himself that *he would not allow the marriage not to happen.*

"It remains legally impossible for you to do so, and I think it would be wise for the Palace to issue a statement denying such intentions. This isn't about your feelings, Harald."

"No, it's about Sonja's feelings. She's already been eaten alive by the press for years, and she wakes up every morning to read that the man she loves won't ever be able to marry her. How do you think it will be for her if she reads in the paper that I've dropped her like a rock? I'm not going to throw away the girl I love because of her birth, and I'm not approving any such statement."

"Harald—"

"I'm not going to do it. I'm just not, under any circumstances whatsoever."

The King had said nothing more, and so Harald had assumed that the idea had been dropped on account of his refusal. On the contrary, he opened the morning paper in his office a week later to read the headline, "Palace Declares Crown Prince Will Not Marry Commoner."

Surely this wasn't...horrified, he scanned the article and discovered it detailed the exact statement his father had mentioned as though he had never voiced any opposition whatsoever.

And what on earth would Sonja think?

Chapter Thirty-One

ACROSS TOWN, SONJA WAS STARING NUMBLY INTO A MUG OF BLACK COFFEE, the morning *Aftenpost* folded next to her. She should have left for work half an hour ago, but all sense of time had left her.

The article began, "Palace officials announced that Crown Prince Harald has stated that he has no intentions of marrying a commoner. 'His Royal Highness understands his duty to his country and his people,' a spokesman for the Crown Prince said in an official statement released yesterday. 'He intends to wed a young woman of royal or noble birth.' This announcement certainly raises questions about the Crown Prince's relationship with Miss Sonja Haraldsen, the common-born seamstress to whom he has been romantically linked off and on for the past six years. The Palace has refused to comment on the matter, although one official was willing to speak on condition of anonymity. 'I don't believe His Royal Highness was ever particularly serious about Miss Haraldsen,' he stated. 'He never appeared to have any plans to marry her, and he clearly will not do so now.'"

The room, it seemed to her, was still spinning from her first read of the article, and every time she glanced at it she felt dizzy all over again. *How dare he...* She did not for a moment take the statement as truth, but she could fully imagine Harald agreeing to it in the hope that it might appease his father. It was the sort of thing he always did—see the princess, ignore the press, never do anything more than tentatively raise the subject of their engagement...and someday, his theory seemed to be, this would all lead to the King approving a marriage.

Rationally, she knew there was truly very little that Harald could do—the Council had spoken, he was prevented from responding to the papers, and they had both agreed abdication was out of the question. But to have announced to the whole country that he had never had any interest in her, after everything he knew she'd gone through...

She read on to discover that a government spokesman had, in response to questions, declared that "the matter of a common marriage has certainly never been discussed in the government." A blatant lie, but it did not irritate her nearly as Harald's had. It was one thing to be denied by faceless ministers, quite another by the man she loved.

The doorbell interrupted her thoughts, and she rose to answer it, finding Harald on her front step.

"Yes?"

"May I come in?"

She nodded curtly and stepped back.

"I'm so sorry you had to find that," he said as he stepped inside. "I told my father I did not want that statement to be issued."

"So you knew about it," she said, cold steel in her voice.

"I knew my father wanted to do it, but I tried—"

He had allowed the statement to be released, had told all of Norway that he didn't care for her in the slightest, and was now attempting to worm his way through an apology. "You *tried*?" she said, suddenly snapping. "Is that *all* you can say? Do you really think that *means* anything to me? You know how this is for me, you know what I've put up with, and you can't even stand up to your own *father*? Is that really asking so much?"

"Sonja, let me explain—"

"No, let me explain something to *you*. The last six and a half years have been one long history of you backing down. You *never* fight for me, and you *never* stand up for me. All you ever do is say you'll keep fighting, you'll keep trying, you'll talk to your father, you'll figure it out—but nothing ever comes of it. The King tells you to go to Greece and see Sophie? You do it. Protocol demands you never respond to the press, even when they're ripping me to shreds? You don't. Your father refuses to allow the engagement? You shrug your shoulders, say nothing can be done, and don't bring it up in front of him for another three months.

"And what did you do when you discovered that Sophie thought you were engaged? Nothing—*nothing!* You were afraid to tell her because you thought you might hurt her feelings. Never mind about *my* feelings—I was the one left to find your engagement announcement in the paper! And of course you can't stand up to your *father*! Have you ever *demanded* our engagement? Told him you would take no more refusals? All you ever do is *ask* him, isn't it? Has it ever occurred to you to stand up for me? Would it *ever* occur to you? I don't think it would! I shouldn't be at all surprised that the King suggested this statement and you went right along with it!"

"That's *not* how it happened! My father suggested it, I told him I would never approve it, and nothing more was said—I assumed he wasn't going to do it without my approval—"

"You assumed he wouldn't do it without your approval?" She burst into humorless laughter. "Tell me you're not that naïve!"

"Sonja, I cannot control my father—there was nothing I could do about this—"

"Nothing you could do about this? *Nothing you could do about this?*" she shouted. "Harald, you may not be able to keep the papers from lying about me and calling me names, and you may not be able to make the Council approve our engagement, but I think you could very well have stopped your father from doing *this*! You 'told him you would never approve it'—and I'm sure that's just what you did! That's all you ever do—tell him things! Would it have ever occurred to you to make a scene over it? To actually *fight*? To make sure he knew he'd better not *dare* to release that statement, and if he did he'd be answering for it?"

"I am *trying*, Sonja. I don't know what else it is you expect from me—I didn't have any idea this was going to happen, I've told you there was nothing I could do, I've apologized anyway—I don't know *why* you're still so upset, you know nothing in that statement was *true*—"

"You don't know why I'm so upset?!" she shrieked. "You've let it look like I've been unceremoniously dumped in front of the whole city!"

"You haven't been dumped; you're overreacting—"

"Overreacting? That's right; I'm an insane, hysterical woman, and I'm overreacting. Never mind that if you ever listened to a word I said you would understand that reading that was the worst thing that could have happened to me—I have to live with feeling like the King hates me, like the press hates me, like half of Norway hates me, *then* I find an article announcing that the man who keeps telling me he loves me has no particular interest in me! And may I remind you that this is only the most recent event in a long string of your failures to protect me? I'm absolutely falling apart, Harald, and you *know* it!"

"Sonja, I—"

"I don't want to hear anything else, Harald—I just want you to go!"

"Sonja—"

"Just *go*!"

His other attempts to contact her over the next few days were met with similarly hostile responses as fury froze over her. Hardened toward him, she felt nothing else at his phone calls and further appearances on her doorstep. The ice surrounding her heart did not begin to thaw for days, when it was slowly replaced by hurt and the sharp sting of his negligence. Did he expect her, she wondered, as the common shopkeeper's daughter, to put up with anything? To merely be grateful he liked her at all? Did he see her as someone not *worth* standing up for?

She told herself she did not care if she ever saw him again.

She lost herself in her work and her studies—she had taken courses off and on at the University of Oslo, but it was not easy to concentrate in Norway amidst the perpetual distractions of her memories and Harald's attempts at contact. When the Garniers, the family she had worked for the previous summer, invited her to France, she accepted the offer immediately and enrolled in art history courses at a school near Sorèze. She would return home and enroll in Oslo once the term ended at Easter, hoping her mind would be clearer by then.

In early April Sonja met Margrethe in Switzerland to ski and told her everything, attempting to disguise her hurt behind her bitterness. She was sure from the sympathy in Margrethe's eyes that she was not fooled, but the Crown Princess did profess to be appalled and indignant on Sonja's behalf. To have someone else royal on her side was comforting, and she was grateful for the solidarity in place of an outward show of compassion that might have caused the shell she had built around herself to break.

But—and Sonja was glad for the distraction—Margrethe did confess some news of her own. After their excited shrieks of greeting in the Zurich airport, they had gone off in search of lunch, and, as soon as they had placed their orders, Margrethe leaned closer across the table, her eyes bright.

"I'm seeing someone."

"You mean…"

"Yes. His name's Henri, Henri de Monpezat—he's a Frenchman—and I think he's *wonderful*. Everything I ever imagined, only I don't think I ever came up with anyone quite so perfect in my dreams. He's tall and handsome and wonderfully sweet and absolutely brilliant—he's fascinating; he's lived all over and he speaks *Chinese*, of all things—and he's always *so* romantic. I've never been so absolutely *captivated* by anyone."

They had met in September at a dinner party in London, where Margrethe was studying for the year and where Henri was working at the French Embassy. Discovering they had some mutual friends, they started seeing more of each other, although Margrethe had thought very little about him at all, beyond finding him very likable and intelligent.

A couple of weeks ago, however, she had attended a wedding in Scotland— coincidentally, for a friend who had met her husband at the same dinner party— and found Henri there as well. They were both among the guests who stayed at the family estate for a few days after the wedding, "And Henri and I spent most of it walking together around the lochs—the countryside is so romantic in Britain—and I just…completely fell in love with him. We ended up in the same car on the way to the airport, and then next to each other on the flight back to London, and suddenly he was wanting to take me to lunch. He picked me up in an open green sports car—England's been having a wonderfully warm spring—and I don't think I'll ever forget any detail of the whole evening. Then we went out to dinner, and then dancing, and everything started happening very quickly. I wanted to call you, but I knew I'd be seeing you soon, and I thought it would be so much more fun to discuss it in person. It was all…it was like the sky just exploded. At first I wasn't sure if I was falling in love or losing my mind; it was all so new and so strange and so wonderful!"

He was a commoner, she said in answer to Sonja's question—there was some documentation of an attempt to grant his family a title centuries ago, but it didn't seem to have fully happened, so he was very much a common Frenchman. Yet Margrethe was assured that it would not matter much in Denmark.

"I can't wait to get back to London and see him again. I don't know how I ever lived without being in love…" She chattered on happily, and Sonja joined in with enthusiasm, finding the news a welcome distraction. And she was so glad for Margrethe's sake…provided the relationship really *would* be allowed. She did not want Margrethe to suffer as she did. *Please,* she found herself praying, *let Margrethe and her Henri be happier and luckier than we have been.*

⌐⌐

For Harald, the worst of it was that he soon realized that Sonja was right. No, he had not imagined his father would go ahead with the statement, but perhaps Olav would not have had Harald objected more vehemently, or perhaps he would have known not to even consider it had Harald not established a reputation with the King as a man who did nothing.

There was an uncomfortable amount of truth in Sonja's claim that he never stood up for her. Yes, every one of his excuses had felt credible at the time—they would have more luck if he didn't make the King too angry, Sophie didn't deserve to be harshly rejected, protocol dictated that he not respond to the press and doing so would irritate Olav further, he had no power to force his father to return to the government…yet it all blended together into *nothing* on his part. He had a history of doing nothing, a history of backing down.

And he was morbidly ashamed of it. Sonja Haraldsen was worth the whole world to him—why hadn't he fought harder for her? He suspected now that part of why Olav had allowed the Ferner marriage had been Johan's display in the library—there could be no doubt how highly he thought of Astrid if he were willing to take on his sovereign.

He ought to have done as Johan had done, stood up to his father and demanded an engagement. Yet Johan had had some hope of getting an engagement with Astrid—her marriage didn't matter nearly as much as Harald's did. He himself had *no* hope of succeeding, regardless of how much he insisted or how hard he fought.

That made no difference, he told himself. It was only an excellent excuse to avoid the fight. They would perhaps still not be married if he had adopted such tactics, but she would still be his and would know she could count on him to fight for her. He wanted to crawl under a rock every time he thought about how much she had suffered for him and how little he had done for her.

He tried repeatedly to call her, he went to her house, he wrote her letters, and she refused to see or hear him. There was, he realized after several weeks, simply nothing left for him to do. His guilt reminded him daily that he did not deserve her anyway.

Yet he was determined this time not to take this lying down from his father. There was vastly more yelling at the Palace in the coming weeks than it had seen in years, and, once it was clear that there was no hope of getting in touch with Sonja, he left the country. He would not continue playing the game of the perfect Crown Prince—let Olav figure out what to tell the press about his absence.

Chapter Thirty-Two

HARALD RETURNED TO NORWAY IN MID-MAY TO PARTICIPATE IN THE *Syttende Mai* celebrations, feeling he ought not to miss the national day. He received a phone call that evening from Queen Ingrid of Denmark, which he expected would be a prelude to another meeting with yet another suitable princess. He would absolutely refuse this time.

Ingrid quickly stated that she was thrilled he was back on the continent, and, if it weren't too much trouble, would he be able to invent a reason to go to Greece for an evening?

Greece? Did she want to match him up with Irene, Sophie's still unmarried sister? Surely the Greeks had no further interest in him—

It wasn't Irene, he discovered. It was Anne-Marie. Ingrid had a distinct sense—despite her daughter's protests to the contrary—that she was unhappy, and Ingrid had grown increasingly worried. "She won't talk about it with her sisters or the King or me, and she pretends she's perfectly happy, especially after I suggested there was something wrong," the Queen explained. "I want to know what it is, and I have a feeling if someone outside her immediate family, an older cousin, perhaps, whom she trusted, went down to see her, she might confide in him, or at least let her guard down. I was hoping that might be you—you were her hero growing up, you know. For all I know she's just homesick, or stressed after living with that—that—*German hag*; any sane person would be, but if there's something wrong with her…I want to know."

He smiled at Ingrid's contempt for Frederica—the Danish Queen's personality was equally strong, yet her sophisticated dignity was about as far from Frederica's grasping pushiness as it could be. Harald knew the two Queens had likely battled multiple times over the Greek-Danish wedding two summers ago—the story had been gleefully passed around royal Europe that Ingrid had said to Frederica, "My dear, you tend to forget that I am a queen, too."

He had no doubt of the truth of Ingrid's assessment of Anne-Marie—he had sensed the insincerity of Constantine's affections four years ago, and it was no surprise that Constantine's wife had finally noticed it herself. Adored for her sweetness, her angelic ways as a child, and the simple fact that she was among the youngest, Anne-Marie was a great favorite among her older cousins, and Harald was no exception. How exactly was she being treated in Greece? Determined to find out, he invented an engagement in Rome and arranged to spend an evening at the Greek Royal Family's summer residence on Corfu while he was in the south.

"How are you doing here—really?" Harald asked. He was sitting on the terrace of Mon Repos Palace with Anne-Marie—who was nowhere near the giggling sprite he remembered—sharing an after-dinner glass of wine. Dinner had been an awkward affair, with Frederica taking the head of the table opposite Constantine and behaving as though she were still mistress of the estate, rather than the widow of the former King, and Irene refusing to speak to or make eye contact with Harald, except for unpleasant glares.

"I'm fine. A bit homesick, but fine." Anne-Marie sighed, staring down at her lap. "I miss everyone terribly."

He was listening intently now. "I'm sure you do."

"I suppose Thursday's St. John's Eve back home," she said, mentioning the Scandinavian summer solstice holiday.

"Yes." A holiday celebrated with bonfires was the last thing he wanted to think about tonight—it was uncomfortably warm outside, but it was an improvement over the stuffy indoors. He only wished for a bit of shade—the palm trees surrounding the terrace were not quite enough.

"Anyway…" She thoughtfully swirled the wine in her glass, seeming to search for another subject of conversation. "Oh, do thank your girlfriend for all those little outfits she sends."

"Little outfits?"

"Yes, she makes little dresses for Alexia and mails them to me. I write her a letter every time, but thank her in person for me, will you?"

He had not known, but the news did not surprise him, given Sonja's penchant for sewing clothes for Astrid's babies. "How is your daughter?" he asked, avoiding the necessity of a response.

"Oh, wonderful, wonderful!" Anne-Marie's face lit up at the question. "You'll have to see Alexia before you leave. She's gotten so big, and she's just *beautiful*."

"You certainly gave her a pretty name," he said, searching for something to say about a baby he had only seen photos of.

"I didn't give it to her," Anne-Marie said quietly.

"You mean, Constantine named her?"

"No, Frederica did. I wanted to name her Ingrid—after my mother—but…" She shrugged. "I was told to name it Alexia if it was a girl, Pavlos if it was a boy…But she *is* beautiful, all the same."

Frederica was naming Anne-Marie's children for her? It was not surprising, but Harald fought the urge to roll his eyes. A good deal of whatever Anne-Marie's problem was, he suspected, came from living in the same household as her domineering mother-in-law.

"I want to apologize for how dinner was with Irene," Anne-Marie went on.

"It was all right." He had ignored her rudeness, knowing it had everything to do with Sophie.

"It's just that that's not how Irene is at all—she's been very kind to me these past two years. You mustn't take it personally; I think she's only upset with Juan Carlos, and you were a convenient person to take it out on."

"Juan Carlos?"

There was an uncomfortable silence as his cousin seemed to weigh her words. A seagull squawked in the distance, and the sound seemed to push her into speech. "Well—and please don't repeat this; I don't think Sophie would want many people to know, I probably ought not to even tell you—but it's been very difficult for her in Spain. Partly because she's very lonely, but the worst of it is that her husband—" she glanced around to make sure they were alone and then lowered her voice "—is far too busy with some Italian woman to pay any attention to her."

He said nothing in response but felt a fierce anger sweep through him—anger at Juan Carlos, yes, but also at Sophie's mother for pushing her into the marriage and at the entire structure of the royal marriage market that not only allowed but likely encouraged such outcomes.

"Irene keeps getting these tearful phone calls from her, and she hates the whole situation. It isn't your treatment of Sophie five years ago that makes her angry, at least not in comparison to Juan Carlos's treatment of her now, but you're here and available, and of course Irene *was* very upset about your—incident—with Sophie, so I'm sure it's very easy for her to remember all that now."

"I do still feel terrible about that—"

"You did the absolute right thing, Harald," Anne-Marie interrupted sharply, and he was taken aback at the conviction in her declaration. "You behaved far more decently to her than most royal men would have.

"Your situation isn't uncommon at all, you know. Plenty of princes and kings fall for unacceptable women and are then presented with a royal bride. They nearly always do what's expected of them—marry the royal girl—but then they take the other woman as a mistress. It's gone on for centuries, and it's exactly what happened to Juan Carlos. But you're different, Harald. You're doing the honorable thing—you're going to marry the girl you've fallen in love with, and you're not going to pretend differently to any of the princesses you're offered. I know the press is going on about how you've forgotten your duty and you'll collapse the Norwegian monarchy and your behavior is completely inappropriate in the heir to the throne. It's odd, really, since I think what you're doing makes you one of the more honorable men our family has seen in ages."

There was a shift in her tone. "It happens so often that a Crown Prince takes a young royal girl and makes her believe he loves her, a girl who's far too naïve to suspect otherwise, and soon she's leaping at the chance to leave her home and her family and everything she knows to go off and marry him, ecstatic in the thought of being his bride. And then, of course, once they're married and there's no going back for her, she realizes it's all been nothing more than a game to him and he's gone most nights, off with some actress or in some socialite's flat, and she herself is of no use to him except to bear him heirs."

He was certain that she was not speaking of Sophie or of centuries of royal brides in general, and he was now equally certain that Frederica's behavior was not the root cause of the unhappiness Ingrid had observed. "Anni..." he said slowly.

He heard the door to the back of the palace open, followed by a cry of, "Mama!" Anne-Marie's eleven-month-old daughter had arrived on the terrace in the arms of her nurse.

"Hello, sweetheart," she cooed in English as the nurse passed her the little girl.

Babbling happily, Crown Princess Alexia twirled a strand of her mother's hair between her small fingers. She giggled as Anne-Marie covered her with kisses.

"Would you excuse me, Harald? I'm going to put her to bed..."

"Of course." The light he remembered had returned to his cousin's eyes.

She stepped back inside, carrying Alexia and talking quietly to her in English, and he was left to contemplate her words.

Off with some actress or in some socialite's flat. Harald did not know who the socialite was, but he recalled the rumors long before Anni and Constantine's engagement of his relationship with a Greek actress. According to the stories, a disapproving Frederica had cut the romance short and guided her son in the direction of one of the Danish princesses.

Yet the affair had *not* stopped, if Anne-Marie's words were any indication. Lacking the backbone necessary to stand up to his mother and marry the woman he wanted, Constantine had married an acceptable girl and carried on with his mistresses.

When Anne-Marie returned, he saw her agitation immediately, her hands fidgeting nervously and a look of panic in her eyes. "Harald," she said, "when we were speaking earlier, I believe I may have implied—that is, I think what I said could have been taken to imply—I didn't mean to say…I misspoke, and I don't want you to misunderstand—"

He cut off the tortured monologue. "I know," he said, standing and looking her in the eye. "It's all right, Anni. I know."

She stared at him for a moment, her uncertainty visible in the dim moonlight. "Oh, Harald, please don't tell anyone," she gasped. "I couldn't bear it if people knew, please Harald, it's so humiliating. Please, I don't want—"

"Your mother…" he began, unsure where he was going with the sentence.

"Oh, especially not her; I don't want my *parents* to know, after they kept telling me I was too young—I don't want to admit I can't handle it—"

"It isn't you, Anni. It isn't anything you're doing wrong."

"I know," she whispered. "But…I feel like it is."

He saw tears come into her eyes and reached out for her, but she shook her head. "There's nothing that can be done about it," she said. "I can't leave; I wouldn't be able to keep Alexia because she's the heir, and she's the only good thing in all of this. I don't have any choice but to stay. But I beg you, don't tell anyone, even my family."

"I won't," he said softly. "I won't say a word if you don't want me to."

When he returned home the next day, he would call Queen Ingrid and tell her he thought Anne-Marie was merely homesick.

Chapter Thirty-Three

SONJA HAD JUST LAIN DOWN ON THE NIGHT OF JUNE 23 AFTER THE ST. JOHN'S Eve bonfires when she heard the phone ring. Who on earth at this hour... She pushed the covers back and hurried downstairs to answer it in the sitting room, more curious than irritated.

"Hello?"

"Sonja? I hope I'm not calling too late; I figured you had been out celebrating yourself, and I have the most exciting news."

It was Margrethe, nearly breathless with excitement and clearly hardly able to bear waiting for permission to go forward.

"No, go ahead—"

"I'm *engaged*! Henri's just proposed, just this evening!"

Engaged? She sat down on the sofa, shocked at the news—they had been dating less than three months. "You're engaged? I hadn't expected—it's so soon—but that's wonderful, Margrethe, wonderful—"

"Oh, but we just *couldn't* have waited any longer; now that the school year's over I'm back in Denmark and wouldn't have had much reason to be in London very often, so Henri said he thought he'd better get me now, because if he let me go it'd be the dumbest thing he'd ever done. And we're both just absolutely *sure* it's right, surer than we've ever been about anything, and we're so very much in love. It's like I've been telling you, this is so much more wonderful than I ever imagined it could be.

"Congratulations! I was only surprised that it's happened so quickly..."

"Well," she said happily, "it really all started a few weeks ago before I came home. We were walking along the South Bank of the Thames late one evening, and he told me—" she paused, and Sonja could imagine a glow coming into her face— "he told me he thought I was beautiful. And I could tell—I could tell he was completely sincere. Then he told me that he loved me and *had* been head over heels in love with me from the moment he'd first laid eyes on me last fall. I was *thrilled*, but I told him I would much prefer if he would make up his mind, so to speak, and let me know whether he wanted to marry me or not—"

"Margrethe!" she exclaimed, too overtaken with laughter to say anything further. She could so easily imagine her friend being so forward and taking such immediate control of things without once wondering if it were at all improper.

"Well, I wasn't going to just carry on with this man forever if something serious wasn't going to come of it someday! So anyway, I had just been back in Copenhagen a few weeks—and we had been writing to each other every day; I've got the most *beautiful* letters from him, and he writes poetry, so sometimes he would send me the most *romantic* French love poems that he'd written for me..." Sonja could envision the blush in Margrethe's face that she had seen in April when they had first discussed Henri, and she smiled.

"But anyway," Margrethe went on, "Countess Armfeldt's sister and her husband live over at Rosenfelt Castle—it's a family estate a couple hours from Copenhagen—and they were having a party tonight, and, in addition to all of the Danish guests, they'd invited three of my friends from London to come for a long weekend, and one of them was Henri. So the sun had just set, and everyone was outside with the bonfire, and he asked me if I would come back inside with him for a moment, which I did—Rosenfelt's the loveliest, rambling old castle. He brought me into a small side room where he'd scattered daisies all over the floor, and it was lit only by the fire out the window, which made the whole room with all its shadows so pretty. I knew right away what was happening, and suddenly he was down on one knee and reaching into his pocket for the ring, and he—oh, Sonja, it was just... wonderful."

"I'm so happy for you," Sonja said softly. "I'm sure you must be ecstatic."

"Oh, I am, I am!"

"And what does the ring look like?"

"Gorgeous, just gorgeous. It's two round diamonds next to each other on a thin gold band—two *large* diamonds, I was surprised at the size, I wouldn't have thought that he could... It's *so* pretty, but of course I can't wear it in public until the official announcement. Henri put it on my hand when he proposed, but then it had to be taken off again when we went back outside, and I just took it back to my room with me later."

"But I'm sure you have it on now."

"Yes." Margrethe laughed. "I'm sitting on my bed, admiring it alone while I'm talking to you."

"And when is the official announcement?"

"I don't know; I'll discuss it with my parents."

"You haven't called them?"

"No, but I'm sure I'll tell them first thing when I get back to Copenhagen on Sunday evening. I'll simply explode otherwise."

"But—what will they think?"

"My mother will be absolutely spitting nails," Margrethe said pleasantly, "and my father will be overjoyed and fully prepared to trust my decision."

"So he'll give you his permission?"

"And his blessing."

"And your parliament?"

"Oh, the Folketing doesn't much care who I marry, within reason."

"Do you think the Danish people will approve?" Sonja continued, finding the succession of non-existent obstacles slightly incredible in the face of the past seven years of her own life.

"The Danes will be thrilled; they're always going on in the papers about how I'll never marry." She paused. "Sonja, it isn't like in Norway. People are very different here; they won't care whether Henri's royal or not."

Yes, it was different in Denmark, which lacked the nationalist fervor of Norway. As a smaller nation with its people concentrated in its main cities rather than scattered in distant villages extending north of the Arctic circle, Denmark was also a more open country, a more relaxed country, and a more equal country. Its royal family had the stability that came from tracing their own House back a thousand years, as opposed to Norway, where Harald's line extended no further than his grandfather, a Danish Prince who had been offered the throne a mere sixty years ago when Norway had ended its long union with Sweden.

"I'm glad you'll be allowed to do it," she said, meaning it. She did not want Margrethe to suffer as she did, and it would not have brought her any closer to marrying Harald had the Danish Crown Princess been denied an engagement as well. "Do you have any idea when the wedding will be?"

"Well, it all depends on the royal calendar, which I'll have to discuss with my father this week, but if it were up to me…I'd like to marry in May, right when the days are first getting warm, which of course means we'd need to start making plans right away, because eleven months isn't very long in the world of royal weddings, so I don't know. I'll call you as soon as I'm sure… oh, and Sonja?"

"Yes?"

"Would you be one of my bridesmaids?"

"I…" Margrethe, who had royal cousins spread across the continent, a younger sister who was Queen of Greece, and surely countless friends among the daughters of the nobility to fill her wedding party, was asking *her* to be a bridesmaid? Would King Frederik and the Danish court truly give such recognition to the girl who had caused the royal scandal of the century in Norway? Did Margrethe really think that highly of her? "I…" she began again, still stunned.

"Oh, please say yes, Sonja, I would so want to have you in my wedding!"

"Yes, of course, I'm happy to do it, it's an honor—I'm just surprised you asked me, of all people."

"Of course I would ask you; you're one of my best friends."

"Thank you," she said softly. "I'm honored."

The engagement, Sonja learned the next week, had been wholeheartedly embraced by the King and would be announced at the beginning of October, at which point photos would be taken and released and there would be press conferences and a balcony appearance and a celebration at Fredensborg Palace. She was invited to Denmark for the occasion—"And don't worry about having to run into Harald; he isn't able to come, his father's coming instead," Margrethe assured her—and eagerly accepted, relieved that she would not have to go to great pains to avoid him at the party. She had not spoken to him since January and did not intend to begin now.

When she arrived in Copenhagen on October 4, there was already an air of excitement in the city, as the news of the Crown Princess's engagement had been leaked a few weeks earlier, and King Frederik had announced that he intended to ask Parliament for their formal consent on the fifth. Sonja was driven the hour from the airport to Fredensborg Palace, where Margrethe met her at the top of the entry steps, embracing her warmly.

"You look so pretty!" Sonja exclaimed after they had greeted each other. And she truly did.

"Thanks—you don't think this is too garish, do you?" Margrethe was wearing a green dress with bright pink flowers.

Sonja hadn't meant the outfit. "No, I think it's rather nice," she lied.

"Yes, well, we're just about to take the official engagement photos, and I thought some sort of pattern would be best for the black-and-white. But you must come and meet Henri; I can't wait to introduce him to you…Oh, and my ring, I have to show you my ring!" She extended her hand, which Sonja imagined must have required quite an effort to move given the size of the diamonds. "Two stones, see? For the two of us…" Her words continued to bubble over one another as they headed down the hall. Sonja had the strong impression that Margrethe had not been this excited since she'd been five years old on Christmas morning.

She led Sonja into Fredensborg's Garden Room, the gold-covered hall with the Roman scenes on its walls. A tall, dark man with the dramatically handsome face of a Hollywood actor was seated on one of the antique couches, watching the photographers set up lights and cameras and tripods, but he turned when they entered the room.

"Marguerite," he said softly, standing. There was something quintessentially French in his manner, and his smile left even Sonja slightly weakened.

She looked to Margrethe to see a faint blush giving way to a smile far broader than the one she had displayed in the entry hall, if possible. It filled her whole face, lit her eyes, left her whole figure absolutely glowing with happiness, and in that moment Sonja wondered how she could have ever considered her anything less than stunningly beautiful.

"Henri," Margrethe said after an eternal second, *"voici Sonja Haraldsen, l'amie norvégienne dont je t'ai parlée."*[19]

"Enchanté." He held his hand out to Sonja, and she slipped hers into it, expecting a shake and receiving a kiss and a slight bow instead.

"Enchantée," she repeated. *Charmed.* And she was. Absolutely. There were a few more minutes of French conversation before Henri and Margrethe were called over for the photos.

That he had fallen hard for Margrethe was obvious, she thought, observing the way he gazed at her, the way he touched her, the way he spoke to her—everything in him communicated absolute awe, to the point of incredulity, that she was his.

She heard Margrethe laugh as the photographer's assistant moved them into the first pose, and for a second it was almost a shocking sound. It was the laughter that came not from humor but from sheer pleasure, from complete happiness in the present. It was a laugh she herself had given in the past, but not for so long, not since the early days of her time with Harald, before everything had been made such a mess of. She felt a sudden ache for him and an ache for more innocent times, when she had been capable of so much more hope.

---

19   This is Sonja Haraldsen, the Norwegian friend I've been telling you about.

She was happy for Margrethe, truly happy, as she recalled their late-night conversations, the regretful way she had seen her friend glance at her own reflection, the pain in her voice when they had spoken of the subject. And yet, as she watched the whispers and hand-holding and brief stolen kisses between photos, she wished desperately for Harald.

But no, she told herself firmly as Margrethe slipped out of the room to change into another dress, that marriage had never been going to happen.

"Sonja?" she heard Margrethe call. "Would you come and tell me which necklace you think I ought to wear?"

She plastered her happy smile back across her face.

Sonja declined Margrethe's invitation to accompany the royal family, Henri, and the Monpezats to Copenhagen the next morning, assuming she would only be in the way. Margrethe, Henri, and the King and Queen would attend a brief session of Parliament and receive the government's formal approval, then His Majesty would personally drive the young couple through the streets of the capital to Amalienborg Palace, where Margrethe, Henri, and both sets of parents would appear on the balcony before returning to Fredensborg for an afternoon press conference in the Garden Room. Sonja watched the events in Copenhagen on television with Anne-Marie, marveling at the thousands lining the streets and packed into the Palace square, unable to move an inch and cheering as though this were the wedding itself. Benedikte had gone into the capital, but the bride-to-be's youngest sister, who had arrived from Greece yesterday for tonight's party, had declined to tag along, saying she wasn't feeling well. And she did look quite drawn, Sonja observed, deciding she must be coming down with something—Anne-Marie was nowhere near the bubbly, giggling teenager she had encountered on previous visits.

Sonja went down and watched the press conference in person, smiling at Margrethe and Henri as they struggled to keep their minds on the hundreds of reporters and their hands off each other—an impulse that seemed beyond Henri's control as he drew his fiancée closer and kissed her cheek for the tenth time.

Was King Olav here yet? she wondered as Margrethe and Henri disentangled their entwined fingers in order to show off her engagement ring. He would recognize her at the party, surely, after all the newspaper photos. What if he looked in her direction? Or what if she were ignored completely, as though he had never seen her before? She was not sure which was worse.

Sonja dressed alone that evening, slipping into a slinky, sleeveless, midnight blue silk evening gown, with a scoop neck and a small band of pearls and silver crystals defining a high waist. She then started on her hair, piling it up on top of her head and pulling a few curls loose. Her earrings she kept as the simple pearls she had been wearing all day, and she wore no other jewelry, preferring not to stand out at all. She smiled slightly as she brushed on her mascara—in spite of the dull grief she still felt over Harald, it was, she admitted, exciting to attend the engagement party of the Crown Princess of Denmark, and as no less than a future bridesmaid.

The festivities were held in Fredensborg's banquet hall, and Sonja felt as though she were walking into a dream the moment she stepped inside. The room was at least three stories in height, its white domed ceiling with red and blue designs and little windows soaring high overhead, and its doors, chair rail, and fireplaces were of fine marble. She had not seen anything, even the ball held at Akershus so many years ago, that compared to the grandeur surrounding her in the dresses and jewels of the royal and noble women and the government ministers' wives and the architecture of the eighteenth-century baroque palace.

Margrethe was wearing a perfectly lurid, one-shouldered gown with no waistline and a bizarre ruffly appendage attached to her left hip. The fabric consisted of a strangely-shaped, blue floral pattern over a purplish-burgundy background, and it looked as though she had merely wrapped herself in horrid living room curtains. The entire ensemble was a textbook example of artistic sensibility overtaking good sense, and Sonja had tried desperately to talk her out of it. Yet the glow of happiness in her eyes made her dress completely insignificant.

In the few minutes before they had gone in, Margrethe had taken a moment to pull Sonja aside to meet another bridesmaid, Birgitta Hillingsø, a friend she had known since childhood. An hour later they were still chatting easily as they examined a table full of small, ornate chocolate creations. "Do you think anyone would mind—or notice—if I took a fourth?" Birgitta sighed.

"I've had four, too." Sonja smiled.

"Yes, but it doesn't show on you," the Danish girl said with a soft laugh, eyeing the silk dress that accentuated Sonja's small figure.

"Excuse me," Sonja heard a familiar male voice say as its owner bumped into her. She whirled around to see Harald strolling past, accompanied by Margrethe, who was talking enthusiastically.

"Harald." The name escaped her involuntarily, and, although it had been nothing more than a soft whisper, he turned immediately, the shock in his eyes matching her own. For an eternal second they stared at one another, until Sonja tore her gaze away to glance at Margrethe, who, she realized with a sudden irritation, did not look the least bit surprised by her Norwegian cousin's presence. It occurred to her with an immediate and absolute certainty that Margrethe had *known* he was coming and had purposefully *arranged* this meeting between the two of them.

"Sonja," she heard Harald say, having evidently recovered his voice, "what on earth are you doing here? I didn't know…Daisy said you hadn't…"

She ignored him, looking only at Margrethe. The Danish Crown Princess said nothing, a look of passive disinterest on her face.

"*Tu savais!*" Sonja hissed in French, the language she shared with Margrethe that Harald had never studied. You knew!

"*Je savais quoi?*" Knew what?

"*Tu savais qu'il venait!*" You knew he was coming!

"*Oui, bien sur. Pourquoi Harald ne viendrait-il pas?*" Of course. Why wouldn't Harald come?

"*Tu m'as dit qu'il ne serait pas ici!*" she snapped, infuriated at Margrethe's pretense of ignorance. "*Tu savais que je ne voulais pas le voir!*" You told me he wouldn't be here! You knew I didn't want to see him!

"*J'ai dit ça?*" Margrethe blinked. Did I say that?

"*Oui! Plusieurs fois!*" Yes! Multiple times!

"*Je ne m'en souviens pas.*" I don't remember that.

"*Si! Tu l'as fait exprès!*" Sonja responded, struggling not to raise her voice. You do! You did it intentionally! Had she known Harald would be here, she would have certainly still come, but she would have been *prepared* for it and would certainly have paid careful attention to the other guests nearest her to ensure against the chance meeting that had just occurred.

Margrethe shrugged and switched back to Danish. "Well, never mind. We're all here now, at any rate." She paused at this point, as though expecting a response, but Harald was still too speechless with shock and Sonja too speechless with anger for either of them to say anything. Unperturbed, Margrethe went on. "But I must be going—why don't you two go out for a walk in the gardens together?"

This was such a blatant attempt at pushing them back together that they both just stared at her.

Margrethe responded with an unembarrassed smile. "We'll talk more later, Harald. Thank you for coming." She kissed him on the cheek and waltzed off, taking Birgitta's arm and leading her away from the couple.

There was a moment of awkward silence, and Sonja took in the starburst design on the black-and-white tiled floor, the tiaras of the royal women nearest her, and the string quartet to avoid looking at Harald. Of all the places to meet, she couldn't imagine any that could be more awful that someone else's *engagement* party. She would be having words with Margrethe later.

"You look beautiful," Harald said at last.

"Thank you." Another silence. Then she added, "Margrethe looks very pretty." And she did, in spite of her clothing.

"Yes. She and Henri seem very happy."

"Of course they seem happy. They *are* happy," she said tartly.

"Sonja," he said after a heavy pause, "I still feel awful—"

"So do I," she snapped.

"I know, and that's why I feel horrible. I wanted to say—"

She was very conscious that a significant number of eyes had begun to turn in their direction and was almost able to hear the whispers of their owners: "That's Harald of Norway, and that's that girl, isn't it? The seamstress? The one there's been all the trouble over?"

"Maybe we should talk outside," she interrupted.

"What? Oh, yes, yes, of course we can't discuss it here." He blushed, and she was reminded of his sweet shyness when they had first met. *No,* she thought firmly, *don't think about that right now.*

"I suppose we might as well go out in the gardens like Margrethe suggested," he continued, offering her his arm.

She froze. How like Harald. Always the gentleman. Didn't he realize what would happen if they touched? She would melt entirely, and they would end up in each other's arms before the evening was out, hopelessly entangled once again.

"Sonja? Are you all right?"

She took a deep breath. "Fine." But she ignored his arm, and he awkwardly dropped it. Silently, they made their way out of the hall and back into the Garden Room, where they left through one of the doors opening out onto the gardens behind the Palace. She didn't dare speak for fear that something would burst inside of her, letting her feelings pour out in a torrent that would wash away her resolve and drown her completely.

She stepped outside ahead of him, and the October chill swept over her, calming her and cooling her emotions. For a moment she let herself take in the quiet stillness of the grassy, flower-sprinkled plain and the towering shadows of trees in the distance. She started off along one of the four gravel paths branching out ahead of them, assuming he would follow her.

He fell into place next to her as they drew away from the Palace and its light, becoming more and more dependent on the three-quarters full moon. "You must be awfully cold," he said suddenly as they walked, his voice startling her. He was looking down at her bare arms. "Here, you ought to wear my coat." He slipped it off and held it out to her.

She couldn't. As soon as she put that on, she would be surrounded by his scent, she would imagine his arms around her, and she would be utterly lost. *No!* she wanted to scream. *Don't you* know *what will* happen? "No," she said, walking more quickly. "If I take it, you'll be cold."

"I'll be fine; I've got on long sleeves. Look, you're shivering."

She was, and she couldn't deny it. She sighed. "Thanks." Annoyed with herself, she reached out and took it, hurriedly putting it on before he could move to help her. It hung down past her knees, and the sleeves ended far past her fingertips, but its size was somehow comforting. She was instantly warmer and thought of the moment several years ago when they had stood out on a cold night and he had held her as they shared the kiss that had led to that first photo in the papers... She slammed the door to her memory shut.

She stopped just before the path entered a dark corridor of trees, turning to look at him. They stared at each other for a long moment. She drew a shaky breath of cold air as she traced his features in the moonlight. *Please,* she thought, unsure what she was pleading for.

"Sonja," he said slowly. Something halfway between a sob and a gasp for breath escaped her body, and suddenly he took her in his arms. He leaned down and kissed her, and, trembling, she returned it with a hunger that had lain dormant inside of her for ten months. She thought at first that they might never stop, and she would have been eager to go on all evening long, basking in the relief of having found her way back into his arms. Slowly, they sank down onto a nearby bench together to compensate for the fifteen-inch difference in their heights.

When they broke apart at last, still breathing hard, he laid his hands on her shoulders. "Listen," he said, and she nodded. "I think you were absolutely right in January."

Her decision to push him away felt like stitches run through a machine far too quickly, resulting only in a tangle of fabric and thread that would have to be undone. She was suddenly finding herself ready to yank them out and begin again.

"Harald," she began hesitantly, regretting the lecture and having long felt that she had been too harsh, but still feeling the general truth of her words, "I didn't—"

"No," he said. "You were *absolutely right.* I *haven't* fought for you; I *haven't* stood up for you. I'm ashamed of it, and I'm sorry. You deserved better."

"I'm nobody, Harald," she said quietly.

"*No.* You are the girl I love. You deserve better—you deserve for me to fight harder than I've ever fought in my life, for me to press my father to his limit, for me to lay everything on the line as though my life depends on it—and if I won't do that, I don't deserve to have you. You are *worth* my life, Sonja, you are worth *everything* to me, and I haven't acted like it. I'm sorry."

She nodded, not trusting herself to speak.

"But that's going to change—if you're willing to give me another chance. I'll demand an engagement, I'll insist, and I'll push him daily. I may not win, but that doesn't matter. I'm going to fight with everything in me, and I'm going to refuse to accept anything but a yes." There was a fire in his eyes she had never seen before, a new firmness in his manner, and a determination that she could feel in the hands still placed squarely on her shoulders.

"Thank you," she whispered after a moment.

"I love you." A gentle edge crept into the steel in his voice.

She nodded again and moved closer for another kiss. His hands slipped down to rest on her hips as he pulled her toward him, and suddenly there was more hunger this time than the first. She paused only to remove the pins holding up her hair and then felt his hands running through it and up and down her back as she pressed as near to him as she could. She wanted him, desperately, and she was half-mad with desire as he whispered her name and left a soft trail of kisses along her cheek and down her neck.

At long last she sighed, and they both pulled away. She settled into his arms, unaware of the evening chill.

Chapter Thirty-Four

"ABSOLUTELY *NOT*! THIS—HARALD, THIS IS INSANE. THE ANSWER WAS NO seven years ago, the answer is no now, and the answer will always *be* no. That you are even bringing this up again—when I thought you were no longer seeing the shopkeeper's daughter—"

"I insist, Father. I demand you return to the State Council and press the issue." Harald had returned from Copenhagen and gone straight to the King's office, where he had spent the last two hours demanding an engagement. "Sonja and I are sick of waiting, sick of watching everyone else get engaged, sick of you sitting here twiddling your thumbs!"

"I have done what I can, Harald, but the Norwegian people remain set against your marriage—"

"You haven't got any idea what the people think; you're the one who's stuck on Sonja's bloodline! We want to be married next year, and I insist that you let us do it!" he shouted.

"It is not your place to insist on anything—"

"It is my place to do what's necessary to make this marriage happen! Seven years of refusals is unreasonable!"

"All you are thinking of is this marriage! You've completely lost sight of the monarchy as a whole—"

"And you've completely lost sight of what it means that I love this woman!"

"It means very little in this situation, Harald—"

"Did you love my mother, sir?"

There was a moment of deathly quiet. *"Excuse me?"* Olav looked as though he'd been slapped.

"Did you love my mother?"

Another pause. "You know I did, Harald," he said quietly.

"Did you love her because she was royal?" he pressed, smelling the King's discomfort.

"No—"

"Would you have loved her any less had she been a common-born shopkeeper's daughter?"

"Of course not, but I would not have found myself in such a situation with a shopkeeper's daughter; I would not have allowed myself to fall in love with—"

"No, you only allowed yourself to fall in love with a Swedish princess twenty years after the union between Sweden and Norway had been dissolved." A very heavy silence fell as Harald made the argument he had hesitated to bring up for years.

"Anything Swedish was unpopular in Norway in the 1920s, wasn't it?" he went on. "And your father didn't think the marriage was a good idea, did he? He told you the Norwegian people wouldn't accept a Swede for Crown Princess, told you he couldn't allow it, told you it was terrible for the monarchy, didn't he?" Olav was silent. "Didn't he?" Harald pressed.

"Yes."

"And you fought with him. Pushed him for months on end. Insisted he let you marry her. Because *you loved her.*" He stood and leaned over the King's desk. "You loved her in spite of her birth, in spite of what she might have represented. You didn't care if she was Swedish, and you wouldn't have cared if she'd been a seamstress. You didn't see her as that; you saw her as the woman you loved. Your father gave in and you married her—which *pleased* the public, I might add; they saw it as a healing between the two nations. You were happy, very happy, for the twenty-five years you had with her, and when she died—" his voice cracked— "you were a broken man because *she was the world to you.* How can you deny us an engagement?"

His Majesty's face was red with fury, and it was a moment before he responded. "Your mother was *royal.* The shopkeeper's daughter is not."

"My mother was *Swedish* royalty. And you loved her."

The engagement was demanded again and again in the coming months, never with any results, and, as willing as Harald was to go on fighting, he was beginning to feel that they had reached a stalemate. He could continue to insist and continue to push, and he felt he did Sonja justice in his efforts, but, he realized uneasily, he was at the mercy of Olav's whims.

—

"I'll be thirty this year, Harald," Sonja said softly. They were standing in Karl Stenersen's kitchen on New Year's Eve 1966, having stepped away from the party for a moment. There had, in the last couple months, been very little discussion of their situation—he was doing everything he could, and she knew it, and there was simply nothing to be said.

He recognized immediately that she was not remarking on her age for conversation's sake. "I know, Sonja. I know."

She said nothing else for a moment, fingering the glass of champagne she was holding with one hand and absently twisting the satin of her short red evening dress with the other. The clock on the wall seemed unusually loud in the silence.

"We were both standing here, almost eight years ago. The night we met." She did not say it happily, and when she looked up at him again, there was something near panic in her eyes. "If we wait another eight years, I will be thirty-eight. I cannot promise to give you an heir when I am forty! You are endlessly fertile; I am not!"

"Sonja…" He had no idea what he could possibly say. "It won't be another eight years." *And what gave him the right to promise her that?* "I'll find a way with my father—"

"Harald," she said suddenly, setting the glass down on the counter and reaching up to touch his face. "Tell me you're as scared as I am. Tell me I'm not the only one going crazy, the only one terrified that it's never happening."

He said nothing—he was frightened, too, scared to death at the thought that he might truly end up living without Sonja, but he never told her so, thinking it his role to reassure her.

"Please, Harald," she went on desperately, "it doesn't help when you just tell me it'll all work out. I want to know I'm not alone in this."

"You're not," he said softly, taking her hand. "You're not."

1967 arrived as scheduled at midnight—they marked it with a bittersweet kiss—and the hours and days and weeks continued to slip by, silent thieves of youth and children and the years of married life they might have had.

The next few months somehow seemed the most painful yet. Worst was the acute feeling that they were running out of time, or at least running out of youth, and that they were rapidly losing time together. "We'll wait another year or so," had been said flippantly and easily at twenty-two; at twenty-nine it was a different matter entirely.

There was also a growing realization that everyone else around them was engaged or married, settling down for the rest of their lives. Their own lives were going nowhere, and their future was a terrifying blank.

Sonja was halfway to a degree at the University of Oslo and knew the stress was showing in her grades. She toyed with the idea of another semester abroad but doubted it would help—being alone, she assumed, would only make matters worse.

She made numerous trips to Denmark in the spring, helping with plans for the wedding, looking at and discussing the sketches Margrethe and her mother had drawn for the reception tent and its chandeliers, and, of course, trying on the bridesmaid's dress being made by one of Copenhagen's designers. It was a floor-length, azure silk gown, gathered in slightly at the waist with a short, long-sleeved jacket of the same material—simple and elegant, to match the style of the bride's dress, and Sonja had fallen in love with it.

And yet she could not help but remember, each time she visited, that Margrethe and Henri knew exactly where they would be in twenty years—married, living together in one of the Danish palaces, accompanied by their teenage children. Where would she and Harald be? It was horribly frightening to be no closer to an engagement than they had ever been, at an age when she had always expected to be a married mother of at least two, perhaps three.

As Harald struggled with Olav and they both struggled to survive the endless waiting and hoping, they felt themselves struggling more and more with their own desire for each other. It had happened more than once over the years that one of them had whispered, *"Would it be so wrong?,"* knowing even before the words had been said that the answer was unalterably *yes.* Yet it seemed that their feelings had only grown more intense with time and their refusal to give in more painful. They had ceased spending occasional weekends together at Gamlehaugen, believing that the temptation might be nearly too strong.

"We would be married if it were up to us," Sonja said bitterly to her mother one evening.

"But you are not married, Sonja."

She sighed. "It seems so unfair to both of us. Sometimes I…it isn't that I doubt that this is God's desire or the right thing to do, but…I find it hard—and I think Harald finds it hard—not to question whether this is really the best thing for our lives. We know, intellectually, that it is, but we struggle—in our hearts—not to second-guess that."

Her mother was silent for a moment. "It is not unnatural, and it is not wrong, that you desire intimacy with Harald, or that he desires it with you. It's meant to be a beautiful thing, a wonderful thing, something to be enjoyed—within the context of marriage. There are reasons that you are to wait for marriage, and it is for your benefit that the Lord requires you to do so. Your purity is meant to glorify God, but it is also meant to serve your own best interests."

"I know," Sonja said quietly. "I know. It is only—it is hard to believe all of that at times…"

"I don't doubt that it is. But at some point you'll be able to see the truth of it all far more clearly than you can now."

"When?" she asked, hoping for sooner rather than later.

Her mother paused. "Sometimes I think you—very understandably—believe that you and Harald will go on as you are indefinitely, that you might still be dating this man when you're my age. I doubt very much that that will be the case. At some point, *lille jenta mi*, this is all going to end. Either you'll be allowed to marry, or you'll both be forced to recognize that you'll never be married, and you'll move on." Sonja said nothing, hearing the truth of her words but not wanting to agree.

"And when either of those things happens, you will be thankful you both behaved as you did. If you do marry, having waited for marriage will make intimacy vastly more meaningful. If, on the other hand, you end up separating, having given each other your bodies will make that separation vastly more painful. Given all that, you ought to look at what's required of you not as a burden or a loss to your relationship, but as a blessing."

Sonja nodded as her mother squeezed her hand. "Thank you."

Chapter Thirty-Five

THE DAYS LEADING UP TO THE DANISH ROYAL WEDDING ON JUNE 10, 1967, were filled with official receptions, visits to the theatre, and a lengthy string of other pre-wedding events. The best of these by far, in Sonja's opinion, was the party held the night before the ceremony.

After an exquisite dinner in an Italian restaurant, Margrethe and Henri returned to Fredensborg Palace, but her sister Benedikte (who had become somewhat more pleasant since her own recent engagement to a German prince) had organized a trip to Tivoli Gardens for the younger guests.

Tivoli was the idyllic amusement park that had stood in the heart of Copenhagen since 1843, and, although it closed at eleven, the royal party was allowed in after-hours. Sonja had not been since childhood, but she could remember the magical atmosphere the park acquired at night and had been looking forward to an opportunity to enjoy it semi-privately with Harald for months.

She was not disappointed. Stepping inside the gates was like entering a fairy garden—the management had always seemed just as concerned with planting flowers as it was with building rides, and the result was a neatly-manicured floral wonderland. Small lights were strewn among the flowers and the trees, and the whole place seemed to have changed little from its original nineteenth-century innocence. On the right was a brilliantly lit Arabian palace; on the left, a series of fountains. Sonja was wearing a dress that Harald had bought her earlier that spring on a weekend trip to Paris, and its frilly fullness seemed an exact fit for the enchanted surroundings, even if she, like the other guests, was rather overdressed for an amusement park. Sleeveless with a square neckline that dropped into a v in the back, it was made of a gold layer of pleated silk chiffon over a full tulle skirt.

She scanned the crowd for him—they had not been seated together at dinner, and they had not walked the block between the restaurant and the park together due to the photographers crawling all over the street. There would be photographers inside Tivoli as well, she knew, but only the very few who had been given passes by the royal court, and they would be far more interested in the newly-engaged Benedikte and Richard than in Harald and Sonja.

She felt a hand come to rest against her back, and she spun around to face Harald.

"You look lost, Miss Haraldsen."

"I was looking for you!" She laughed, taking his hand. "I think this is going to be a wonderful evening." It was a bold statement—there had been very few of those in recent months, overcome as they were by the despairing sense that it was simply too late for them.

"Of course it will be," he said as they followed the group off to the Rutschebanen, a fifty-year-old wooden roller coaster built as a mountain train. She recognized in his voice an immediate agreement to play along with her fantasy that everything was perfect.

And it almost seemed to be. It was a relief to be with Harald, having spent several stressful days attempting a performance as a perfect bridesmaid in front of scads of foreign royals, nobles, and government ministers. And it would have been difficult *not* to have fun at Tivoli, even with the evening's light drizzle of warm summer rain. As she clung to Harald's arm on the drops and through the dark tunnels of the Rutschebanen, she felt like a sixteen-year-old skipping class for a day at a carnival with a secret love. This was followed by a ride on the Galejen, a series of Viking ships that spun around a bumpy, circular track mimicking rough waves—it somehow seemed a perfect moment to them both to steal a kiss—and a ride on the old carousel, its organ music suggesting an easier, carefree era. He bought her one of Tivoli's most popular desserts, and she was eating it as they strolled. It was a flat circle of popcorn coated in dark chocolate and stuck, lollipop-like, on a wooden stick, and its rich crunchiness returned her to a childlike feeling of complete contentment.

Sonja watched Benedikte and her fiancé curiously as the group wandered through the park, slowly dispersing. Margrethe had told her about the engagement: "I don't think they're at all in love," she'd said. "They like each other, but they make no pretense of *loving* each other. They're both just marrying a title. It's depressing—Richard's a decent man, and he'll be kind to her, but it won't be anything like what we're both going to have. My sister's going to be satisfied in her marriage; nothing more. Never ecstatically *happy*."

It was clear to Sonja as she watched their interactions that they were, indeed, a couple who liked each other well enough, and a couple who were certainly quite attracted to each other, but she could not shake the feeling that they were not engaged but merely on an awkward third date. There seemed to be no great connection in the way they looked—or didn't look—at each other, and even the many affectionate touches and caresses from Richard were all somehow lacking. It was not the way Harald touched her.

I'm glad I'm not her, she thought, and it was a sentiment she was surprised to hear from herself in regards to a soon-to-be-married woman. *I'd rather be in* this *situation than marrying a man who doesn't love me.*

She drew closer to Harald, and they were soon leaving the others, abandoning the rides and games for a walk alone around Tivoli's small lake. She had long known that the park was like a scene from a fairy tale—she half-expected little magical creatures to come popping out of the bushes—but what she had not recognized as a little girl was that it was also a world built for lovers. They kept their voices low as they wandered through the flowers along the water, the atmosphere somehow forbidding much noise beyond the swishing of the chiffon skirt.

Their fingers laced together, she talked of tomorrow's wedding, how happy she was for Margrethe, how excited she was for the ceremony and ball, how pleased she was to be a bridesmaid…

"You will be wonderful with everything tomorrow," he told her. "Don't be worrying about it all night."

She smiled, realizing that, as usual, he had sensed her nerves. "Thanks."

They wandered in silence for awhile, she asking him at one point if he had come to Tivoli often as a child.

He had, and he began to tell her stories of summer visits to Denmark and his early relationship with tomorrow's bride, who had been, as he put it, "an absolutely rotten little girl."

After awhile they stepped into a small gazebo by the lake. It was not raining hard, but it was a relief to have a few moments of dryness.

"You're really wonderfully beautiful," he said suddenly.

She laughed. "And it's really wonderfully dark out." She knew she was still pretty but was also perfectly aware that eight years of worry had aged her slightly from the fresh young girl he had met in Karl Stenersen's kitchen.

"No, I'm very serious, and you're very pretty." Her hair would be redone tomorrow afternoon, but, not wanting to be a damp, frizzy mess by the end of the night, she had covered it in a scarf upon leaving the restaurant.

He reached out and tenderly tucked a loose, wet strand back into the scarf. *"Min kjære."*

She stepped into his arms for a kiss.

Margrethe was married the next day in Holmens Kirke, a three-hundred-year-old Navy chapel in the heart of Copenhagen. Some had thought it an unusual choice, considering the national cathedral would have been at hand, but it was not so odd, Sonja thought, for the daughter of a sailor.

She, Birgitta, and the four noble young flower girls had lined up beneath the canopy erected outside the church, awaiting Margrethe and King Frederik's arrival in their horse-drawn carriage.

The bells were chiming, and Sonja soon heard the distant clopping of the horses whose riders formed an honor guard before His Majesty and Her Royal Highness. Then the cheering of the vast crowds grew more and more audible, sweeping down the street, and...

Her breath caught in her chest as the carriage came into sight. Sonja, Birgitta, and the girls dipped into curtsies as it rolled to a stop in front of them. A footman leapt down from the back to open the door and King Frederik IX—dressed in full military uniform, his chest covered in orders and an old-fashioned, feathered hat on his head—climbed down, nodding to Sonja and Birgitta as they came forward to assist with Margrethe's gown.

Sonja had helped her dress earlier that afternoon at Fredensborg and had taken the opportunity then to have a long, unhurried look at the bride. Margrethe was a perfect vision in white, a statuesque beauty in a simple, long-sleeved Swiss silk gown with a panel of lace down the front. The fifteen-foot train attached to her shoulders, spilling out dramatically behind her, and she was wearing her late grandmother's delicate, swirly tiara, a 1905 wedding present from the Khedive of Egypt. It held a long, sixty-year-old veil in place, made of the lightest, softest lace and already worn by her grandmother, her mother, and Anne-Marie at their own weddings.

As Margrethe passed yard after yard of white silk out to Sonja and Birgitta, there seemed to be vastly more to the train than there had been earlier that afternoon, but they managed to gather it all up to allow her to step out of the carriage and forward to take her father's arm. A military band struck up a march as the bridesmaids straightened the fabric and Margrethe arranged the veil.

Then she and the King were off, walking down the red carpet between a naval regiment standing at attention. The bridesmaids followed, adjusting the train as they went. Once inside the vestibule, Sonja and Birgitta moved to the front of the line and began their slow procession down the aisle.

Sonja had noted its incredible wideness—perhaps ten feet—at the rehearsal, but it was different now, and she felt suddenly very isolated, vulnerable, and alone as she walked. The pews and balconies were nearly overflowing with the nine hundred wedding guests, the women's dresses and tiaras a menagerie of fine fabrics and bright colors and massive sparkling jewels. There were flowers everywhere, and then there was the fine carpet spread down the aisle as a runner, and the rich Persian rug lying across the platform before the altar…and the incredible, ornate woodwork of the altar itself, and the pulpit…it was absolutely overwhelming, and Sonja's head swam as she tried to take it all in.

As she drew near to the front she spotted Harald in the rows of relatives seated on the platform to the left of the altar. He was looking straight at her, and they both smiled.

Sonja slipped into the front pew next to Birgitta as she heard the choir intoning the first ethereal notes of *Sicut Cervus*, the old Latin arrangement of Psalm 41 that Margrethe had chosen for her entrance. The other guests got to their feet as well, and a wave of curtsies and bows swept through the church as His Majesty and Her Royal Highness passed each aisle. The King's expression was the soul of solemn dignity, but his eyes, Sonja could see as the couple drew near, were growing moist and bright with pride in his eldest daughter. And Margrethe herself…

Sonja nearly forgot to breathe when she looked at her, so much more beautiful had she become in the few seconds since she had laid eyes on Henri.

Chapter Thirty-Six

HARALD COULD NOT KEEP FROM STARING AT SONJA AS SHE PROCESSED DOWN the aisle. She was stunningly beautiful, the brilliant blue of her dress contrasting with her big brown eyes, white gloves covering her small hands, and the silk of her hair piled up elaborately. She was, unlike the rest of the women in attendance, wearing no jewelry but two little pearl earrings, yet it somehow made her seem fresh and genuine rather than out of place. She was smiling nervously and sweetly, and there was a soft pinkness to her cheeks, likely a combination of nerves, excitement, and the warmth of the church. As she drew closer her eyes finally locked with his, and her whole figure brightened considerably, her smile erupting to show teeth for the first time.

Her participation in a royal wedding made her seem such an easy fit into his world, yet he could see his father seated two rows ahead of him, in front of the Duchess of Kent, his entire figure stiff as iron during Sonja's entrance. King Olav did not turn his head to take so much as a brief glance at the bridesmaids, and Harald remembered his dark muttering when he had learned that Sonja had been chosen to be among them.

But then the blast of trumpets signaled the arrival of the bride, and Harald stood with the rest of the guests.

She was radiant. He was vaguely conscious of the elegance of Margrethe's upswept hair and her flowing gown, but her glowing face outshone the rest of her appearance and that of every other jewel-covered royal lady in the church.

He had never seen anyone look so happy or, indeed, so beautiful.

Margrethe's eyes were fixed immovably on Henri as though she were unaware that anyone else was present. Henri was gazing back at his bride, the love in his eyes so intense that Harald had to look away, feeling that he had intruded on something deeply private.

As she and the King approached the altar, Henri stepped forward immediately, pulling her into his arms for a kiss, his lips lingering against the edge of her cheek near her ear. It was *not* the custom in Scandinavia to kiss during weddings, and Harald knew he ought to disapprove—Olav's posture suggested that *he* certainly did—but he could not help but rejoice at the groom's excitement.

There was surprise in Margrethe's eyes when Henri drew back, as though she were not quite sure what to think of his behavior, and then her face broke into its most dazzling smile yet. Harald thought uncontrollably of Sonja. She deserved the happiness of a young bride, and he had wanted with all his heart to give it to her, had always *intended* to give it to her.

Henri and Margrethe pledged each other their lives and exchanged rings—the groom, in his nervousness, needing several attempts to place the gold band on his wife's finger. His difficulty drew a warm laugh from Margrethe that rang across the front of the church. Then they knelt and received the Bishop's blessing, his hands resting over their heads, before taking seats on the two gold chairs placed before the altar.

Last year Harald had seen, in the stark light of his own grief over what he had thought was lost forever, his abysmal failures in defending Sonja. He had done what he could to change that, refusing to cooperate with his father and making repeated demands for an engagement. Yet it hadn't been enough.

He would previously have been inclined to lay the blame for all this elsewhere—if only he had been born someone else, if only his father had acted in mercy, if only the Council had been able to feel some compassion for them… But suddenly, he wanted to reserve all the blame for himself and his own inaction—perhaps if he had only begun making stronger demands years sooner, it might have been he and Sonja standing in Margrethe and Henri's places. They would have given voice to those sacred vows, he would have slipped a real wedding ring onto her finger, and she would have been the girl beaming with joy and he the young man bursting with pride and love for her. Instead, he sat alone—surrounded by royal relatives, yes, but more alone than he had ever felt—while Sonja watched from a pew a mere thirty feet away, thirty feet that might as well have been a million.

No, that was ridiculous. He had never had any hope of succeeding, regardless of how much he insisted or how hard he fought. His hands were tied. Except…his father could not force him to marry, so…

Harald gazed steadily at the couple sitting before him, their hands clasped as they had been throughout the service. "Love," he heard the Bishop say, as if from a great distance, "is as a flower, delicate and fragile, and yet of an almost invincible robustness…" The love he shared with Sonja had certainly proven itself invincible again and again, but he felt instinctively that it could not last forever in this uncertain in-between world. *Their* love had been a flower that had been forced to endure eight years of winter, eight years of snow-covered, frozen solid ground, and there was no promise that spring would ever arrive.

He was suddenly angry at the Bishop for his metaphor, at Margrethe and Henri for their happiness, at his father and his government for what he and Sonja had been denied, and he made an immediate decision to confront the King with the only threat in his power.

After the wedding Harald went to Fredensborg Palace, along with the half of the wedding guests who had also been invited to the banquet that would begin in a couple hours. There was a family group photo to be taken first, however, and having arrived an hour before Margrethe, Henri, and their respective parents— the six of them having to make a balcony appearance at Amalienborg, following the bride and groom's lengthy carriage ride through the streets of Copenhagen— Harald and the other royals were forced to mill about in the Garden Room. Thoughts were tumbling through his mind in mad confusion.

"All in all, a beautiful wedding," he heard Olav say and looked to see that his father had joined him. "I will say that Ingrid did make the most of it."

His anger bubbled up again at the words. Olav had made no secret in recent months that he disapproved of Margrethe's match and thought that the King of Denmark would have done well to refuse her, and it was equally no secret that Queen Ingrid had not wholeheartedly endorsed her daughter's choice, preferring a son-in-law of royal blood. And yet...

"Have you seen how Ingrid's been smiling all day? She doesn't see fit to sacrifice Daisy's happiness over her fiancé's bloodline," he said pointedly, not caring to conceal the fury in his voice.

King Olav glanced around. "Harald, we can't discuss your marriage right now..."

"I can't think of any better time to discuss it than after what you've just seen! The heir to the Danish throne wed to a commoner, and unless I'm very much mistaken all those thousands of cheers we could hear on the streets were not the sound of the monarchy being overthrown—"

There was suddenly a great deal of noise as the parents of the bride and groom arrived and were deposited at the foot of the front steps outside. A round of applause went up amidst the assembled royals as the four climbed toward the open doors into the hall.

"How you can continue in your refusal after today—" he began as the Queen attempted to quiet the crowd, thanking them for their attendance and announcing that Margrethe and Henri had stayed at Amalienborg for a few photos but would be arriving shortly.

"Harald, now is simply *not the time*, and may I remind you that the Council said *no*, so my consent—which I'm not willing to give—is wholly irrelevant—" Staff members were pouring into the room, armed with lists of who was to stand where and attempting to group the rows together.

"You have a new government now which might very well approve the engagement if they knew you had given your approval, especially in light of Margrethe's marriage." *And,* he added silently, *especially in light of what I'm about to tell you.*

Olav was guided to stand near the door with Ingrid's father, King Gustaf VI Adolf of Sweden, and Queen Juliana of the Netherlands. The three of them, along with the bridal couple and their parents, would make up the front row. Harald was brought into a bigger cluster of royals behind them who would stand in the second row. Upon the bride and groom's arrival, they would all be brought outside to line up along the front steps. The world's press was already assembled at the bottom.

"Harald, we cannot discuss this here—"

"Have you any idea what it was like to sit through that ceremony?" he hissed.

But Margrethe and Henri were pulling up outside, and Olav ignored him. They were embraced by their parents, and then King Gustaf Adolf stepped outside, opening his arms to his newly married granddaughter.

"Look," said Harald, attempting a light tone and failing, "there's someone else who's on record as strongly disapproving of unequal marriages. Doesn't Uncle Gustaf look *unhappy?*" The Swedish King was grinning ear-to-ear as Margrethe kissed him, looking as though he might burst with pride. "Daisy's one of his favorite grandchildren, you know—you'd think he'd want her marrying better," Harald continued sarcastically. "It's almost like—he's just happy to see her happy. Odd, isn't it?" He paused, and Olav said nothing. *"Can you possibly continue to refuse us?"*

"Yes, Harald, I can." Olav glanced nervously around them, but no one appeared to be eavesdropping.

The staff was calling for the first row.

"Father—"

"I'm not approving a marriage between you and a shopkeeper's daughter just because our Danish cousins have lost their minds. This is insanity, Harald, absolute insanity." He attempted to follow Queen Juliana out the door.

Harald caught him by the arm to force him to turn back. "I *demand* an engagement with Sonja Haraldsen. I absolutely *insist* that you give us your blessing and bring the matter to the Council and the Storting." He spoke very quietly and very evenly, but left no room in his tone to doubt his seriousness.

He had nothing near Olav's full attention. "Harald, we cannot discuss this now—" The King was eyeing the pages lining up the others, clearly nervous about losing his place.

"If you don't allow the engagement, I'll never marry at all."

"What?" His father had begun to edge outside again, but now his eyes snapped back to Harald.

"I'll never marry another woman. I would swear it on the throne itself—if I can't have Sonja, I won't have anyone." It was the only threat he had, and he felt the truth of the words as he spoke them—indeed, he had known their truth for quite some time. "You can prevent me from marrying the girl I love. You can't make me marry one I don't. And I *won't* ever love anyone else—I can't love another girl the way I love her."

"Harald, I-I-that is, I don't understand," the King sputtered. "You-you will have no heirs…"

"Olav!" Ingrid called, looking behind her. "Olav, are you coming?"

"I—yes, I'm coming!"

No sooner had the last picture been taken and the crowd dispersed than a frantic King Olav was at his side and grabbing his arm. He had seen his father angry, exasperated, and all possible variations therein over his involvement with Sonja, but he had never seen him truly shaken.

"This has been my concern all along," His Majesty said, his words tumbling over each other as they stepped back into the hall. "You don't grasp the seriousness of the situation; you never *have* grasped the seriousness— where do you imagine this leaves the Norwegian monarchy fifty years from now when you're eighty and childless?"

"I don't know; ask your precious government. It's for you and them to answer—I'm suddenly finding that there are a *great deal* of questions for you and the government to answer. What if I start responding to the press and ignore all this idiotic protocol? What if I march into the parliament chambers myself and demand they all approve an engagement? And what if I do die without an heir?"

"You—Harald, you have a *duty* to produce heirs—" There was panic in the King's eyes, and Harald enjoyed the sight immensely.

"I refuse to produce an heir with any woman other than Sonja Haraldsen. I'm not going to take a wife and treat her as Sophie and Anne-Marie and centuries of other royal brides have been treated." He was already trembling with anger, but his feelings only grew harder as he recalled last year's visit to Greece with its stark display of the results of Constantine's weakness. "I have a far greater moral duty not to marry a girl I don't love."

"Harald, I can't—you can't—this just can't—you *must* have a bride—"

"Then give us our engagement!"

Sonja and Birgitta were hanging back at the edge of the Garden Room, watching as the royal relatives streamed back through and commenting on each dress and tiara.

Suddenly, Sonja was aware of raised voices—voices she recognized. She strained to pick up the Norwegian in the mess of languages.

"…give us our engagement!" she heard Harald say, finally spotting him as he and King Olav drew closer.

"There will be no engagement! Not now, not ever! Not to *a shopkeeper's daughter*!"

"I am serious, Father, quite serious about that threat—"

"Then you are selfish and irresponsible, but that does not mean I am going to allow such a disastrous marriage—"

"You do as you like. But if you *don't* allow this marriage, the monarchy ends with me!" Harald turned from his father, plunging back into the crowd without a second glance.

"We ought to be heading up to meet Margrethe," said an oblivious Birgitta. Grasping the back of a nearby chair for support, Sonja heard her only distantly. *The monarchy ends with me.* Was Harald truly about to give up his right to the throne…over her? Had she truly brought down her country's monarchy? She closed her eyes against the spinning of the room.

"Sonja? Are you all right?"

She swallowed. "Yes," she said weakly, forcing a smile onto her face. She could not think about this now. "Let's go up."

Chapter Thirty-Seven

ALTHOUGH THERE HAD ALREADY BEEN A BRIEF ROUND OF PHOTOS TAKEN AT Amalienborg, there was to be another bunch shot upstairs at Fredensborg, a few of which featured Sonja but all of which seemed to require her help in managing the train, arranging the folds of the gown, touching up Margrethe's make-up, and so on. It was all done in a hurry so that the bride and groom, their immediate families, and the bridesmaids could have a moment to relax before the banquet began at eight-thirty, and Sonja was grateful for the hectic pace.

The tent on the grounds was like walking into a fairy queen's court. Everything was decorated in tones of yellow and gold, the antique chairs looked to be of solid gold, there were thousands of twinkling candles and twenty glittering chandeliers, and ivy and other greenery was wrapped around everything. The tent was positively overflowing with cascades of a total of thirty thousand flowers, and each of the long tables had a lush flower bed running down the center of it, brimming with roses in multiple shades of red, yellow carnations, and, of course, white daisies.

Sonja had been with Margrethe the day they had first begun drawing up the plans, and seeing it all brought to life was like a dream. She caught sight of Harald at a far-away table—no, she could not think about that right now or she would collapse completely.

Margrethe and Henri, she thought quickly, trying to force herself to concentrate on happiness for her friend as she watched the King toast his daughter and son-in-law, his pleasure in the day's events quite clear. Then the newly-created Prince Henrik, as he was now known, stood to deliver his wedding speech, thanking his own family, the King and Queen, the Danish government, and finally Margrethe. His Danish was still poor and unpolished, and he struggled for the correct pronunciations, yet his rugged attempts still managed to form one of the loveliest speeches Sonja thought she had ever heard. The two of them bathed in the soft glow of the candles, he spoke of the flowering beauty of Denmark, and his wife reached up to take his hand, pulling it close to her. He paused in his speech, gazing at her as their entwined hands rested against her neck. "And this girl," he said with a smile, "is the most beautiful flower in it."

Once dinner had been finished and the seven-layer cake wheeled out, cut, and eaten, the party moved back into the Palace for the ball, which was to be opened with the traditional Danish wedding waltz. The hundreds of guests began to form a circle around the ballroom, leaving an open place in the middle, and Sonja was guided near the front by one of the various pages arranging the guests. She knew Margrethe had been dreaming about this moment for a quarter of a century, and she had heard many descriptions of the *Brudevals* in recent months. The bride and groom would come to the center of the dance floor, she had been told, their guests clapping in time to the music and slowly moving forward as the song neared its end, making the circle smaller and smaller until the couple had no room to dance at all. The ritual ended with a kiss and had to be completed before midnight.

Soon, King Frederik, Queen Ingrid, and the de Monpezats entered the room through a gap in the circle and took positions in the front row. To much applause, Margrethe then entered on Henri's arm and the couple made their way to the center as the first notes of the waltz began, he drawing her close into his arms as they twirled. Laughing, she buried her face against his neck, and then they were dancing with their cheeks together. Sonja's eyes fell on Harald across the circle, and she felt as though her chest might burst. This could be theirs now, if he were going to abdicate…but she *could not* allow it. She knew in her heart that she would have to refuse him.

At some signal in the music heard by the Danes among the guests, the crowd slowly moved forward, closer and closer, forcing the waltz into a tighter and tighter area…Margrethe was laughing, Henri was beaming, and they were soon surrounded by rejoicing friends and family…and all Sonja could think of was Harald. Dizzying images of a life together danced through her mind. She could see her mother pinning her veil in the moments before the ceremony, Harald carrying her over the threshold of their new home, the two of them gazing at their newborn baby, celebrating Christmas with their young family, sharing dinner on their twenty-fifth wedding anniversary…perhaps… *no. It would not be right.*

As the music ended, she saw an exultant Henri kiss his bride to the cheers of the hundreds assembled. Her own heart was dragging on the ballroom floor.

The crowd slowly began to back away, and another song began. Couples formed themselves around her, beginning to dance despite the limited space. She was drowning in the crush of people—she could not bear to watch any more of this celebration—she needed to *breathe*—to think—

It was as though all her emotions had gone numb as she made her way to the edge of the dance floor, taking the same pathway into the darkened gardens that she and Harald had taken in October. Yet it was far darker tonight—there was no moon this time, she realized as she walked briskly away from the Palace, no moon at all, and the light spilling out of the building did not reach very far. She was in pitch darkness as she sank onto the same bench she had shared with Harald.

The monarchy ends with me. Harald's intention to abdicate was perfectly clear. And it would be entirely her fault if he did.

I pushed him. I told him I wanted him to fight for us, to stand up for me, to push his father harder—and now it's led to this! This had not been *at all* what she'd meant. Remembering his story and her own history lessons, she thought of King Haakon and then-Crown Prince Olav traveling hastily across a newly-occupied Norway, desperately hoping to find their way into safe territory before being captured. A simple abdication would have assured their lives, but they had not even considered the option.

And now their son and grandson was about to refuse the throne over *her*!

She knew instinctively that she was not worth the collapse of the monarchy. She thought of her brother risking his life along with so many countless, nameless others—men who had sabotaged rail lines and taken up arms and hidden out in the mountains for years and died in the short-lived battles of April 1940. Men who had sacrificed all for Norway.

She could not tear down one of the country's central institutions. Especially not the institution that had symbolized so much during those dark days. She thought of her mother's tears as they listened to King Haakon's voice on the forbidden radio, and of the scribbled *H7*'s all over Oslo.

She had to leave Scandinavia, go somewhere where Harald would not have access to her, get *away* from him for the next few months. She would take a train to the south of France tonight, she decided—she had friends in Annonay—and she would send Harald a letter, telling him she did not wish to marry him if the price were his abdication.

Her stomach rolled, and for a minute she fought to hold back the reception dinner. She would be alone for the rest of her life...alone without *Harald*... childless...no grandchildren in her old age...a life spent wasting away in the store offices, looking in at everyone else's happy life...everyone else's *families*... while she was left alone. She wanted to marry Harald, had waited eight years to marry Harald. She was not asking, she thought, so very much—she only wanted to marry the man she loved. Such a simple thing.

And for a moment she believed that she needed Harald far more than Norway did.

Yet she knew—as much as it all meant to her—that the desires of one young seamstress would not matter a hundred years from now. The Norwegian monarchy would. In comparison, her own private happiness was worth very little.

She would be on a train to France in a few hours.

Chapter Thirty-Eight

HOW LONG HAD SHE BEEN OUT HERE? SHE WONDERED WHEN SHE HAD DRIED her tears. The waltz had been just before midnight, and she had left shortly thereafter, only to lose all sense of time.

Margrethe, she thought distantly. She was supposed to be in her room at two, helping her get dressed to leave. And before then she had to somehow force a smile onto her face—she didn't want Margrethe to know about any of this tonight. She wiped her eyes, leaving a streak of mascara across the back of her hand. Surely her emotions were evident in her make-up, and it needed to be fixed before she went up to Margrethe.

She forced herself to walk back to the Palace. She had half an hour, she realized when she drew close enough to be able to read her watch.

Couples were twirling together in the center of the ballroom, the light of the chandelier catching the ladies' jewels and the men's orders; a dizzying combination of music and languages filled the air; and the black and white floor tiles seemed to spin beneath her feet. Leaning against the wall, she squeezed her eyes shut and drew two deep breaths of air, then plunged into the crowd, fighting her way to the restroom on the other side.

She opened the door into a sizable foyer, gold-framed mirrors stretching along all four walls and groups of lavishly upholstered chairs and cushions arranged in front of them. Women stood in clusters along the mirror, the least crowded area a set of seats occupied only by Harald's cousin's wife, Countess Ruth of Rosenborg, who was rolling on another coat of lipstick.

With a brief nod to Ruth, she took the seat farthest from her, then opened the evening purse she had slung over her wrist. She realized with sudden dismay that she had no more than she usually carried—eye-liner, mascara, lipstick… no foundation or powder to replace that which had been washed away or to conceal the red splotches she was sure had appeared on her face. She had not bothered to bring anything extra because she had known there would be royal make-up artists to touch up her face during the photo session before the dinner. Hesitantly, she removed the eye make-up and lipstick, setting all three items on the counter in front of her as her mind raced, searching for a solution.

"Sonja," she heard Ruth say softly, "I have more make-up than you do, if you think you could use it."

"I'm all right—"

"No, you're not; you're a mess. Start with washing some of that mascara off." When Sonja did not move immediately, Ruth reached for one of the hand towels folded next to the sink, wet it, and moved to a closer chair to begin wiping the smudged, streaked eye make-up away herself. When she had finished, she passed Sonja two small bottles drawn from her sequined evening bag, and Sonja quickly applied their contents, despite the trembling in her fingers, then reached for the thin tube of mascara lying in front of her.

"Let me do that," Ruth said, taking it from her. "Your hands are shaking so that you'll end up with this on your nose."

"It's Harald," she said as Ruth worked, feeling she owed her some sort of explanation and hungry to tell *someone*. "He—he's going to do what your husband did. Give up his right to the throne to marry me."

"You're serious? There must be some mistake—Harald couldn't—"

"No, I heard him tell his father. I'm quite sure," she whispered.

Ruth said nothing for a moment, screwing the lid back onto the mascara. "What are you going to do?"

"I'm going to refuse to marry him under that condition. I—I'm leaving tonight, and I'm not going back to Norway for awhile. I can't let the monarchy collapse because of *me*."

Ruth softly touched her arm. "I'm sorry."

A dry sob escaped.

"Oh, don't get that started again, not when we've just fixed you up," Ruth said, not unkindly. With the warmth of a mother, she reached out and tucked a loose strand of hair behind Sonja's ear.

"Wasn't it all *wonderful*?" Margrethe sighed as Birgitta unzipped the back of the dress. "Wasn't the service just *beautiful*?"

Sonja heard the other girl murmuring an enthusiastic assent as she herself attempted to fold the detached train. Handling Margrethe's gown was the closest she would ever come to wearing one herself, she thought, as she fought the urge to bury her face in the soft silk and weep, smearing tears and make-up onto its perfect whiteness.

"And the *Brudevals*—it was *everything* I'd always dreamed of—and then dancing the *lanciers* as well…" She trailed off, catching sight of Sonja's face as both women helped her out of the dress. "Oh, what's wrong?"

"Nothing." She forced a smile. "I'm perfectly fine. I thought the whole evening was absolutely marvelous. I thought…" She paused, searching for inspiration. "It was lovely when he kissed you at the altar. You looked so surprised, and of course he wasn't supposed to do it, but all of that's what made it so sweet," she babbled. In her effort to perform as a carefree, happy bridesmaid, her tone was an octave higher than usual, but Margrethe, who had been easily swept away by the wedding again, did not seem to notice.

Sonja half-listened to her go on about the banquet and the toasts and the music and the crowd and the carriage ride. Very little response was required of her or Birgitta as they laid the gown out on the bed to be packed away later, boxed up just like her own marriage plans… Her hands were trembling again, and she fought to control them, hanging back as Birgitta fastened the simple white dress Margrethe would leave for her honeymoon in. As a result, she was left to pin the hat as the bride sat down at her vanity to apply more make-up.

"Your hands are shaking, Sonja," said Margrethe softly, catching one in her own as Sonja inserted the last hatpin.

"It's…I'm excited for you, that's all," she lied. "I've been excited all day." She looked down at Margrethe's hair, pretending to adjust an imaginary strand to avoid meeting her friend's eyes.

"You're sweet." Margrethe squeezed her hand and then released it. "I almost can't believe it's really happened," she whispered, gazing at her reflection. "I'm *married*. There was actually someone…"

"I never thought otherwise, Daisy." The affectionate nickname she had heard Harald and other relatives use slipped out without a thought, and she froze after she said it. Had she spoken too presumptuously? The night had been a sharp reminder that she was, after all, nobody.

Margrethe appeared not to notice. "And you were right." She laughed softly. "I'm half-afraid to fall asleep tonight and wake up in the morning with all of it a dream."

"I can tell he loves you very much," Sonja said, nearly choking on each word. When she and the Danish Crown Princess had first met, Sonja had believed herself very near to a wedding of her own, and Margrethe had still despaired of ever being in love. How strangely ironic, she thought, that it should be at Margrethe's wedding that she should learn she would spend the rest of her life alone.

Margrethe stood and embraced her and Birgitta, Sonja parroting the congratulations and well-wishes pouring from Birgitta's lips. They followed the new bride down to the Garden Room where the guests had assembled. In a rush of cheers and applause, she and Henri were out the front door and into the car—decorated with the obligatory cans and signs—that would drive them to the harbor where they would embark on the royal yacht.

Sonja slipped back to her small bedroom. She would change out of her bridesmaid's dress, pack her suitcase, and get a ride to Copenhagen's train station.

In the crush of wedding guests that had cheered Margrethe and Henri's departure, Harald had been trapped in the center with very little hope of extracting himself anytime soon.

He was hoping, desperately hoping, that his threat would force the King and the Storting's hands, but he was fully aware that it might very well not. And he had been entirely sincere—he could not imagine ever loving anyone but Sonja.

He had been desperate to speak with her all evening and tell her everything, but he couldn't see her anywhere in the crowd—but if he *had* to wait, they would be on the same flight back to Oslo tomorrow.

Suddenly, his left arm was tightly seized. "Harald!"

His nerves in no state to be startled, he whirled around to see a breathless, agitated King Olav.

"Harald—what you said earlier—there *must* be an heir—"

His father wanted to argue about this here, *now*? "I'm not marrying anyone besides Sonja," he asserted again.

"I understand you—I understand you perfectly—I do not *doubt* you. But you *cannot* remain unmarried—it would be a *disaster*—a far greater disaster, if possible, than your marriage to the shopkeeper's daughter—and thus I—I—" His Majesty struggled with himself for a moment, and everything around Harald suddenly seemed to be moving at one-fourth its natural speed.

"I will do everything possible—everything within my power—whatever it takes—to see that you marry Sonja Haraldsen—"

Harald had barely processed this news before Ruth of Rosenborg, who had appeared out of nowhere, was pulling him away from the distracted King, whom her husband Flemming was drawing into conversation.

"Harald, I've been looking all *over* for you," she said. "You're not—you're not really giving up your rights to the throne, are you? You can't, Harald, you just can't, I think it's horrible—"

"What? What are you talking about?" The strangeness of this conversation, followed by his father's last statement, had him beginning to wonder if he were dreaming.

"I just spoke to Sonja Haraldsen—she's terribly upset; she says she heard you talking to your father, and you told him you would abdicate if he didn't allow the marriage—"

"I never said that!" What on earth had Sonja thought she overheard? "That isn't true *at all*—"

Ruth nodded. "I didn't think it could be, but Sonja was awfully certain. She was absolutely horrified, I think, at the whole idea, and she wasn't going to marry you under that condition. But you've got to find her—tonight—because she's planning to leave the country so that you won't be able to get to her, and she didn't say where she was going—"

He could imagine that she *was* horribly upset. He knew enough of her character to realize she would never consent to a marriage at the price of the Norwegian throne. What could she have possibly heard? His final words came back to him: *The monarchy ends with me.* Her conclusion was easy enough, if she had missed the earlier part of the conversation…

He did not hear any more of what Ruth said—he was already pushing past her, *forcing* his way through the hundreds around him, back into the empty ballroom, in hopes that one of the cleaning staff might be able to direct him to Sonja's room. He prayed he would find her there, still packing—the thought that she might already be gone, might have slipped through his fingers *now*, was too awful to contemplate.

He had to find her. *They were getting married.*

What time was it? He glanced at his watch—2:40. Margrethe and Henri hadn't been gone any more than ten minutes. Surely Sonja, who had helped dress the bride, would not have had time to leave the Palace yet.

The ballroom was the mess he had expected after a party for four hundred, and there were staff scattered all over it—few of whom, he realized with growing panic, would be likely to have a list of room assignments in their back pocket.

"Excuse me," he began, pulling the nearest man aside. "Would you happen to know—would you be able to direct me to the room assigned to a certain guest?"

"I'm sorry, sir, I haven't the foggiest idea about any of the rooms." This was followed by the man's shouted inquiries to others nearby, an effort that proved fruitless. He was then given the name of the head of staff, as well as the woman who oversaw the wing where the majority of guests had been housed, and a few of the members of the wedding committee, although, as the young man added, "you'll have a job finding them right now."

He managed a halfhearted thanks and turned back to the Garden Room, entertaining the desperate hope that Queen Ingrid would be easily accessible and would know where the bridesmaids were staying.

The hall was a maze of hundreds of evening gowns and tuxedos and military uniforms pouring in multiple directions—upstairs, outside, through various side doors—with an accompanying cacophony of languages. He plunged in but was soon forced to acknowledge that the mother of the bride was nowhere to be found. He checked his watch, his heart climbing into his throat. 2:55. Would Sonja even still be here if he ever located her room? Wildly, he searched for a plan. Ought he to begin scouring the hallways, knocking on each door and calling her name? He was long past any fear of embarrassment, but he knew such a process would take hours.

He fought his way back to the ballroom, intent on grabbing another staff member and insisting they find someone who knew the room assignments.

By some miracle, no such insistence was necessary. "That lady over there, sir," he was told immediately. "Johanna Sønder. She planned all the guest rooms—I'm sure she'd be able to help you right away."

"Sonja?" He knocked on the door again, trying to ignore a sinking feeling that he was too late—it was now 3:10, and Sonja had likely already left Fredensborg.

"Sonja!" There was no response to his voice or the pounding of his fist. She was not gone, she *could not* be gone…how would he find her? Surely she would at some point call her mother and tell her where she had gone, and he could get the information from Dagny. At the thought of the older woman, their conversation three years earlier after the State Council had voted rose unbidden to his mind. Worse, he remembered the more recent incident when Dagny had found Sonja counting out the sleeping pills.

Had Sonja's intention been to leave the country, or had it been something much darker?

His heart racing, he struggled to convince himself he had no basis for such thoughts, and there was no reason to believe she had not merely left for a week abroad, yet getting to her immediately was suddenly vastly more imperative.

Perhaps, he lied to himself, *she's merely asleep.* It was unlikely, he knew, given the racket he had been making outside her door, yet he tried the knob anyway, found it unlocked, and stepped into an empty room. The bed had been turned down, but it had manifestly not been slept in. Were any of her things still here? He scanned the room and saw no suitcase, opened the large wardrobe and found no clothing hanging inside.

She had left, then. And she would not have gone to the trouble to pack had she not truly meant to travel somewhere. It was her intentions once she reached that location that worried him now—or, even if she had no such intentions, he had no idea what might develop in the coming weeks.

He forced himself to think clearly. Sonja had likely been driven away by one of the chauffeurs who would be working until sunrise ferrying wedding guests back to Copenhagen, to various train stations, harbors, and airports, and to other cities in Denmark. His panic growing, he left for the garage.

Chapter Thirty-Nine

"Shall I wait a few minutes, ma'am, in case you aren't able to leave tonight and want to return to Fredensborg?"

"No, thank you. I'm quite sure I won't be going back."

"I'll stay twenty minutes regardless, ma'am."

Sonja nodded. "Thank you." She could imagine the chauffeur did find it odd to drop her off at Copenhagen Central Station at three-thirty in the morning when she had acknowledged that she had no particular train in mind. She shut the car door behind her and took a deep breath to empty her mind—it had been racing with memories of the recent months, the words she had overheard from Harald, and her vague plans.

The sky was pitch black with no moon and sunrise an hour away, and the train station had the frightening exterior of a dark, forbidden castle. There was not, in the middle of the night, anything charming about its old, last-century turrets and towers or anything attractive in its black roof and reddish-brown bricks. The three porters working at this hour were gathered in the shadows under the covered walkway, and she felt their eyes raking uncomfortably over her.

Clutching her suitcase tightly, she drew her light coat closer around her against the chill of the night air and hurried inside.

Perhaps it was her imagination, but it did not seem any warmer. She stepped into the small foreign ticket office—a hallway of dark wood with several ticket windows—and inquired after the next train to the south of France.

There was a 5:05 to Lyon. She bought a ticket and walked slowly out into the main hall. At this hour, it was nearly deserted, and the click of her heels on the tile echoed loudly.

With its soaring rafters and Gothic-style windows, it felt almost like an abandoned cathedral—abandoned not only by man but by God as well, as the dark interior seemed to squelch any prayer before she could form it.

"I'm sorry, sir, there isn't any way to tell where Miss Haraldsen was driven." The answer should not have been a surprise to Harald—the garage was a mess of post-wedding chaos. Of course the harried man who was attempting to direct things had no idea where a single guest had gone.

He could not reach Sonja tonight. The truth was hitting him with a sledgehammer, but he refused to acknowledge it. He would find her, regardless. He was determined not to fail her in this.

"However, we *were* trying to keep a list of who left in what vehicle with which chauffeur," the man went on. Harald let out the breath he'd been holding, feeling a slight jump in his chest at the news. "Christian!" the man called out. "Have you got any record of a Sonja Haraldsen?"

He was informed that she had left around three in number seven. *Three o'clock.* The time was like being punched in the stomach, and all the air left him just as quickly. He had arrived in her room only shortly after that—she had still been at Fredensborg while he had been searching the ballroom and the front hall for someone who could give him directions. If only everything had happened just a bit sooner.

Should he just choose either the airport or the train station and go? No, that was foolish—they were both too large to lose time combing the wrong one. He would be far better served to wait here for her chauffeur, who he prayed might even know her intended destination.

If the driver didn't know and could tell him nothing more than Kastrup Airport or Copenhagen Central Station... He realized with growing terror that he had no plan. He could search either one of them, but given their sizes it would be no simple task, and there was nothing to prevent her leaving the city in the interim. There were countless places she might be going to—she had lived in Cambridge, Lausanne, and Paris; she had friends in those locations, in London, in many small towns in Britain and France and Switzerland; she might have gone somewhere she knew no one and had never been before, Spain, New York, Italy...the possibilities were limitless.

And would she be all right when she got there? Was she about to collapse as she had three years earlier after the Council had refused the engagement? What would that be like with no one to look after her—would she even eat if there were no one to insist on it? Would she be able to force herself to call home and give her family some indication of her whereabouts? And did she have—other intentions—in mind?

His insides were turning to ice at the possibilities his frightened mind was suggesting. By the time car number seven returned at twenty after four, he believed he could have run the thirty miles back to Copenhagen faster than he could have been driven.

"Miss Haraldsen only asked for Copenhagen Central Station, sir," the chauffeur said again in response to Harald's repeated inquiries as they drove.

"But she must have—surely there was *some* indication as to where she was going?" This man had been his last hope, and his efforts to maintain a blank demeanor were quickly crumbling in favor of the near-hysteria underneath. "She *must* have said something!"

"I'm not sure she knew herself, sir—said she was going to buy her ticket when she got there, and she wasn't entirely certain which train she'd be taking."

"She didn't mention—"

"She was quite distracted, sir. I didn't press her."

Distracted? He did not like the word's implications. What had her thoughts been? The knowledge that she had been seated in this very same car a mere hour ago, watching this very same scenery pass by in the dark that he was now passing in the early light of dawn, tormented him.

"Could you drive a bit faster?" he asked. But what difference did it make? What did he think he was going to do when he got to the station? He had no idea which platform she'd be leaving from, no way of knowing if she'd already left, no guidance as to where to begin his search.

Had anything she'd ever said suggested where she might run in this situation? Sonja went to Denmark when she was upset, he knew—yet this time she was leaving Denmark. The only other place she had ever run to was a semester of dressmaking school in France in the fall of 1961—a semester, he remembered, that had been a disaster. She would surely not have gone back there. She had admitted so herself the night she had returned to Oslo.

"You can count on my never escaping *there* again," she had said with soft laughter. "I ought to have just gone to stay with friends for several weeks. Somewhere peaceful—Annonay, maybe. Cécile lives there—we were at school in Lausanne together. *That* would have been a better refuge."

Annonay. It was by no means a guarantee, but it was a far better guess than anywhere else.

He arrived at the train station shortly before five and leapt out of the car, desperately hoping she was still there waiting on a platform for a train to a destination that would be obvious as southern France. He doubted she had a train to Annonay itself—he had never heard of it and expected it to be far too small to merit direct service from Copenhagen.

There was a 5:05 to Lyon, according to the signs in the main terminal. It would be pulling away in less than ten minutes from a platform on the other end.

He did not entertain the thought that he would miss her as he sprinted through the hall. She would be on that train, clearly visible from a window, and it would still be waiting patiently when he reached it. He would tell her what the King had said, they would return to Norway together, and *they would be married.*

He arrived at 5:02 by the clock on the platform and began to scan the windows and the passengers boarding at the last minute. A brunette was facing away from him in a car farther down…she turned her face, and it was clear that she was not Sonja.

His panic grew as his eyes settled on each window at a time. She was not there…she was not there…she was not there… He was calling her name, half-crazed, but knew his voice was drowned out in the bustle of other passengers and the last calls blaring over the loud speakers. His heart pounding in his ears, he was conscious of the passage of each second, realizing his time was dwindling…and then the train was pulling away.

Was she on it, leaving now for Lyon? There had been a 7:45 for Paris, but surely this one would have made more sense. Should he fly to Lyon and meet her at the station when her train arrived early the next morning? Assuming that had been her train… Or shouldn't he search the rest of Copenhagen Central first?

Had she changed her mind about taking a train somewhere, left the station and… He could not let himself consider other possibilities.

Was she all right? He turned away from the empty track, planning to scour the rest of the platforms before making any further decisions. There were a few other people on this one and those nearby, ready to leave on later trains, he assumed. He passed by an older couple as he walked, a businessman reading Copenhagen's daily newspaper, two German women in quiet conversation…

Suddenly, his eyes fell on a young woman asleep on a bench, her coat draped over her and her head resting on a suitcase.

Sonja.

Something was brushing against her hair, and she was lying on a hard surface, her face against rough fabric…

"Sonja…Sonja…"

Someone was calling her name…

"Sonja!" A hand was gently shaking her arm…

She opened her eyes to see Harald bending over her.

"Oh, Harald, you came after me," she murmured sleepily, slowly sitting up.

"Yes, *min kjære*, and it wasn't easy." She heard overwhelming warmth in his voice.

"I have to catch the train to Lyon—"

"Miss Haraldsen, I believe you've missed your train." He laughed softly and kissed her forehead.

"I heard you after the photo was taken," she said suddenly as she awakened enough to clearly remember the events of the preceding hours. "You told your father—you told him—"

"What is it?" He sat down next to her, pulling her into his arms.

"You told him the monarchy ends with you. You said you'd abdicate if he didn't allow the marriage."

"That's not at all what I meant. I demanded that he approve our engagement; I absolutely *insisted*. I threatened to go to parliament myself, to start responding to the press, to do whatever I had to do to get his attention, because I'm through with all this nonsense. But what really got him was *not* that I threatened to abdicate; it was that I said if he didn't give us our engagement, I'd never marry at all. Then there won't be any heirs—*the monarchy ends with me*. I swore I'd never marry anyone but you because I can't ever love another girl the way I love you."

She paused for a moment, letting his words sink in. "Thank you," she said softly.

"Don't you want to know what he said?"

"I know what he said—I overheard part of this, remember? He sputtered on about how you had to have an heir, but you certainly weren't marrying a shopkeeper's daughter." Nothing had changed, she realized, and she was suddenly very, very tired.

Harald's eyes sparkled. "But you weren't there when he spoke with me at the end of the evening. He'd been in a panic all night, and he found me just after Margrethe and Henri left…and he said he's going to see to it that you become my wife."

"I—what?" She sat up and stared at him. She had heard Harald's words, and recognized the excitement and joy in his voice, and saw the ecstatic happiness on his face, but it did not all come together immediately in her head.

"We're getting married, Sonja."

She let his statement sink in, replaying the images of their life together that she had conceived during the wedding waltz.

"Sonja?" he said softly after a moment. "What are you thinking?"

"I'm thinking," she said slowly, "that I feel like the most wonderful man in the world has just spilled wine on my dress...and I love it."

He took her hand. "Would you like to dance, Miss Haraldsen?"

She laughed—the laughter of complete happiness, of sheer joy, of overwhelming satisfaction that she had heard from Margrethe last fall, the laughter she thought she would never feel again—and she kissed him.

Chapter Forty

"This veil," said Margrethe, "is absolutely the thing. It's *perfect* for you, Sonja." She and Sonja's maid of honor, Ilmi, a girl who had been her closest friend since childhood, were spreading it out on the white cloth on the floor behind Sonja. It was August 29, 1968, and Sonja was dressing in the apartments she had been given at the Palace for the days before the wedding.

"It is, isn't it?" said her mother as she inserted the small tiara-like flower arrangement that held the veil in place. "I thought she'd rather outdone herself when I saw how much lace she was ordering, but now that I see it I wouldn't have it any other way."

It was a long cathedral-style veil that descended all the way to the floor and then continued on for several more feet, and it had required massive amounts of lace. Its vastness was not confined to its length; the veil was also substantial in its width, height, and layers, an ethereal white cloud spilling out behind and around her. She had worried at first that it might have the effect of swallowing her up, yet it instead had made such a striking frame for her whole appearance that it was nearly impossible to see anything but her. Every inch of the veil seemed to scream, "*Here* is a bride."

Sonja was nervous and happy and excited, but nothing about the day seemed quite real to her yet. She had spent so many years wondering if this day would ever come and doubting that it would that, now that it had, she was somewhat dazed.

"We're getting married," she said quietly to herself, half forgetting that there were others present until she heard them laugh.

"I'm horribly, horribly nervous," she admitted suddenly, turning away from the mirror to address the other women in the room: her mother, Margrethe, Ilmi, and Astrid. "About the ceremony—about being *watched*—"

"Naturally," said her mother softly, touching her hand.

"You won't notice the people or the TV cameras or any of it, once you're up there with Harald," Margrethe offered. "My wedding was the only time in my life that I was at any significant event and forgot how many people were looking at me."

"And the ceremony won't last for very long anyway," Astrid said. "You're not nervous about the banquet and the ball, are you?"

Sonja shook her head no.

"You look beautiful," her soon-to-be-sister-in-law went on. "Stand up and show us the dress with the veil?" Astrid herself was wearing a silver gown that was mostly covered by an elegant, floor-length, midnight blue jacket. The empire waist and loose cut hid the small bump that was beginning to show— she was expecting her fourth child, but there would be no announcement until after the wedding. She had already asked Sonja to be godmother.

Sonja stood carefully, sweeping her veil and train—like Margrethe's, it attached at the shoulders—off the back of the chair, her mother arranging it behind her as she stepped to the center of the room.

"I know I've been saying this all afternoon," Ilmi said, "but you look simply *incredible*."

And she did. Sonja was wearing a simple dress with a bell-shaped skirt, the edges of its three-quarter length sleeves and its high collar embroidered with pearls and diamonds. There was a small train in the back of the skirt in addition to the vast one that spilled from her shoulders, and the fabric was a heavy, rich silk that had felt like soft, cool cream in her hands as she'd sewed, amazed at how much hope and happiness she could stitch into the gown. Her mother had suggested she wear ivory, perhaps a better complement for her fair skin, but she had been determined to have something absolutely white. The dress was thus a pure, blazing white that nearly glowed.

"May I," she said softly, "have a moment alone with my mother?"

"Mamma," she said, taking Dagny's hand when the others had left.

"Are you happy, Sonja?" Her mother smiled.

"Yes. Yes, I'm very happy." She laughed. "I'm so nervous I think I might faint, but I'm very happy."

"I'm very happy, too—nothing could bring me any greater happiness than seeing you have your heart's desire. I'm happy to see you marry Harald—not because of who he is as the Crown Prince, but because of the kind of man he is. The sort of man your father and I always wanted to give our daughter to." Sonja felt her throat constrict at the thought of her father, who was not there to walk her down the aisle.

Dagny paused, then laid a hand on Sonja's cheek. "I'm very proud of you, *lille jenta mi*. I'm proud of how you've handled the last nine years, I'm proud of how dignified you've been, and I'm proud of the standard you've held yourself to." She paused again. "I'm proud of everything you are, of the woman you've grown up to be."

Her mother kissed her, and Sonja embraced her tightly. "I will miss being at home with you," Sonja said, half laughing as she stepped back.

"Nonsense. You'll be twenty minutes away; we'll still see a great deal of each other." Dagny glanced at her crystal watch. "I ought to be down in the front hall, ready to leave."

Sonja looked back at the detailed schedule lying on the dressing table, a copy provided for everyone with any role to play in the wedding day. She saw where her mother's departure from the Palace was mentioned, but her eyes shifted further down to the end of the ceremony. Up to that point, she had been referred to as "Miss Haraldsen:" "10:00 – His Royal Highness the Crown Prince and Miss Haraldsen arrive at Fornebu airport to welcome wedding guests," "12:45 – Miss Haraldsen returns to her apartments to dress," "4:45 – His Majesty the King and Miss Haraldsen depart the Royal Palace for Oslo Domkirke," "5:00 – His Majesty and Miss Haraldsen arrive at Domkirke," then suddenly, out of nowhere, "His Royal Highness the Crown Prince and Her Royal Highness the Crown Princess depart Domkirke."

Her Royal Highness the Crown Princess. It was almost frightening in its simplicity—less than two hours from now, a few words from the Bishop would make her Norwegian royalty. She, a shopkeeper's daughter, a seamstress, would be Crown Princess of Norway. She was thrilled to be marrying Harald, but the thought of her new position was terrifying. It had felt many times in the past few months as though she were jumping off a cliff.

She kissed her mother goodbye, thankful for solitude to collect her thoughts. Suddenly nauseous with nerves and the weight of the occasion, she took a seat again and began to pray.

Half an hour later, Sonja was standing in the foyer of the Oslo Domkirke on the arm of His Majesty the King, waiting for the swell of organ music that would signal the entrance of the bride. Then the heavy oak doors in front of them would open, and King Olav would escort her down the aisle of the national cathedral and up to the altar, where Harald would be waiting for her. It had always been the Haraldsen family's intention for Haakon to give Sonja away, but His Majesty, wanting to demonstrate his acceptance of the soon-to-be Crown Princess and to present a united front, had offered to do it instead, and he could not be refused.

Sonja was consumed by nerves and concentrated on stilling the trembling in her hands. Soon the doors were opening, she was stepping inside with the King, and…

It was absolutely overwhelming. This was what they had waited nine endless years for, what they had often feared would never happen, what they had spent an eternity hoping for…an hour from now, she and Harald would be *married*… Her thoughts were tumbling over one another as she made her way down the aisle, past pews brimming with hundreds of royals and aristocrats and government ministers, all standing in deference to the King…and to the bride.

She was almost too nervous to breathe. She tried to smile, but only managed to hold it in place briefly…then suddenly she was fighting back tears, overcome by both happiness and the immensity of the occasion. She swallowed them, wishing desperately that it were Haakon leading her instead of King Olav.

And then she drew close enough to see Harald, finally locking eyes with him. He was looking at her so softly, caressing her so gently with his eyes, that she felt herself relax slightly and smile naturally.

She wanted nothing more than to get to him.

When Sonja and the King stepped up onto the platform, he did not hand her off to Harald, but there was a long moment where they stood, a few feet apart, and gazed at each other. It was all so very near now…

Then they took their seats, Sonja on the left side of the altar next to her mother and Harald on the right side with the King.

It was strangely surreal now that she could see all the most honored guests gathered on the platform with them. Her mother was at her side, and they had smiled at each other as they had taken their seats, Dagny mouthing *I love you*. Two rows back were Henri and Margrethe, Margrethe smiling almost as broadly as she had at her own wedding last summer. Two rows behind the Danish couple were Sonja's siblings and their spouses.

Across from Sonja, behind Harald and King Olav, she could see Margrethe's parents the King and Queen of Denmark, the King of Sweden, the people who had been introduced to her at last night's Akershus banquet as the King of Belgium and the Grand Duke and Duchess of Luxembourg…then there were Flemming and Ruth of Rosenborg, and Harald's sisters and their husbands.

Sonja's family…and Harald's family…and the crowned heads of Europe…all mixed together here…as the choir sang the first hymn of *her and Harald's wedding*…as she looked around the celestial, colorful interior of the Domkirke…covered in twenty-five hundred flowers…in her *wedding dress*…nine years to the day after that ball…after nearly a decade's worth of waiting and wishing, separating and finding each other again, false hopes and dark, lonely nights…they were at last very nearly *married*…this was their *wedding day*…it did not seem to be quite real, and she would not have been at all surprised to wake up and find it all a dream.

The soloist began to sing, and the peaceful strains of *"Alt Står i Guds Faderhånd"* calmed her whirling thoughts. It was an old Danish hymn that she had always loved. She closed her eyes at the words that had become so comforting in recent years: *In God's fatherly hand all rests, / Works the Spirit His behests; / Our reward and lot secure / With God's only Son endure…*

Sonja heard Bishop Birkeli's sermon only distantly, knowing it would be followed by the vows. Then they would be married, and there would be no more separations, no more time apart, no more longing to see each other again, no more *waiting*. They would be joined by God, and no one would be able to separate them. She had awakened alone this morning; tomorrow she would wake up in his arms, and every morning after that. Fifty years from now she would still be spending her days at his side.

Soon they were asked to come to the altar, and the Bishop was addressing Harald. "I ask you, Crown Prince Harald, before God and this assembly: Will you have Sonja Haraldsen, who stands beside you, as your wife?"

"Yes."

"Will you live with her after God's Holy Word, love her and honor her, and be faithful to her, in good days and bad, until death separates you?"

"Yes." It was a syllable she had heard Harald pronounce countless times over the years, but it was suddenly the most beautiful sound she had ever heard.

"And I ask you, Sonja Haraldsen, before God and this assembly: Will you have Crown Prince Harald, who stands beside you, as your husband?"

"Yes."

"Will you live with him after God's Holy Word, love him and honor him, and be faithful to him, in good days and bad, until death separates you?"

"Yes." Her yeses had both been shy and soft, but they had been perfectly clear, and the weight of the past nine years slipped away as she spoke them.

"Then give each other your hand as a sign of your vow."

They turned to each other and smiled, and he took her hand, gently rubbing the back of it with his thumb. There was somehow more love in his gesture than in ten long kisses, and its tenderness filled her with a sense of overwhelming calm and happiness.

The Bishop laid his hand over theirs, said a prayer, and then…they were pronounced husband and wife.

The closing readings and hymns passed in a blissful daze, and soon Harald—*Harald, her Harald, her husband*—was leading her back up the aisle. Her only worry now was that she might burst from joy, and she felt a smile erupting across her lips. There was a slight tremor in her hands again—from happiness and excitement now, not nerves—but Harald stilled it with a squeeze from his own.

They stepped out of the sanctuary and into the vestibule, pausing before a pair of three-hundred-year-old bronze doors. On the other side was a crowd of thousands of Oslovians whose cheers she could already hear. Harald motioned to the pages to wait a moment before opening them.

Then he turned to look at her, and their eyes locked for a long gaze that somehow seemed outside time.

"Are you ready?" he whispered.

She pressed his hand. "Yes." And she was—ready for a lifetime at his side. She had always been ready.

Outside the church, there was a lady-in-waiting to assist with her veil and train as she and Harald took their seats in the back of an open car to be driven through the cheering streets of Oslo. They were off to make their balcony appearance, off to attend the banquet and magnificent ball at the Palace, off to spend a quiet honeymoon alone in the Norwegian mountains, followed by Hawaii and Mexico.

Off to make a home together at Skaugum, off to have babies and raise children, off to spend their days and months and years together, off to succeed to the throne, off to watch their grandchildren grow up, off to the rest of their lives…together.

Epilogue

SONJA WAS QUICKLY ACCEPTED AS A MEMBER OF THE ROYAL FAMILY BY THE Norwegian people, with even King Olav later remarking that his earlier resistance had been the most foolish mistake he had ever made. As Crown Princess, she spent much of her time working to improve the plight of refugees around the world, eventually serving as Vice President of the Norwegian Red Cross. In 1982, Sonja was the recipient of the Nansen Refugee Award, one of the highest honors given by the United Nations. She donated the prize money to the building of schools in Tanzania. As Queen, she has been particularly concerned with the situation of immigrant women in Norway. Sonja has also been extensively involved with artistic and cultural organizations.

Sonja received her degree in English, French, and art history from the University of Oslo in 1971. She and Harald became the parents of two children, Märtha Louise and Haakon, and the grandparents of six. Both children grew up to marry commoners despite public controversy.

After his father's death in 1991, Harald ascended the throne as King Harald V. While he devotes much of his time to official audiences, State Council meetings, and visits to various institutions, he is especially interested in environmental issues and the welfare of children. He has also remained an avid sailor.

Margrethe and Henrik had two sons, Frederik and Joachim, who later married commoners as well. Margrethe became Queen of Denmark following her father's death in 1972, eventually becoming one of Europe's most popular monarchs. She is known for her artistic abilities, illustrating multiple books and designing costumes for various films and ballets in Denmark. She and Sonja have remained close friends.

Johan and Astrid Ferner had a total of five children. Although her representation duties lightened after Sonja became First Lady in 1968, Astrid continued to serve on official occasions. She has also worked extensively with organizations that assist children with dyslexia, as well as with Dissimilis, an organization that provides artistic opportunities to the developmentally disabled. Her health improved in the late 1990s, and the government awarded her an honorary pension in 2002 in recognition of her service to Norway.

Author's Note

A Shopkeeper's Daughter is a work of fiction, but it has been based on a true story. Where it has been necessary for the plot, I have altered or deleted events and invented others. The characters in these pages truly existed—several are current monarchs—and in most cases, I have tried to be faithful to them. However, their thoughts, feelings, reactions, and conversations are all my own inventions, as are certain of their actions. While space does not permit a full list of the novel's factual and fictional elements, a few general highlights are listed below.

Crown Prince Harald did meet Sonja Haraldsen, the daughter of an Oslo store-owner, at a party in June 1959. Captivated by her brown eyes, he invited her to attend the Military Academy's graduation ball at Akershus Castle. The couple fell in love and hoped to marry, but King Olav—and much of the country—were set against a common marriage for the Crown Prince. The King hoped for a royal bride for his son, with Princess Sophie of Greece the first of many candidates.

Harald and Sonja separated several times over the years, but, as Sonja has said, "we always found our way back to each other." On multiple occasions, one or both of them left Norway in an attempt to stay apart.

In the fall of 1967, King Olav, worn down by years of arguments and especially troubled by Harald's recent threat that he would not marry at all, approached Prime Minister Per Borten about a marriage. Borten was delighted, and a disgruntled King allowed an engagement to be announced in March 1968. The wedding followed that August.

While the specific visits between Sonja and Crown Princess Margrethe of Denmark are my own inventions, the two women did become friends, and Margrethe was very supportive of Harald and Sonja's relationship. The details of her own romance and marriage with Henri de Monpezat are largely historic.

The portrayal of Harald's sister Princess Astrid and Johan Ferner's romance is mostly factual as well, as is much of the information about Astrid's health. I have also tried to be accurate regarding the physical details of specific settings, and the information Harald and Sonja share with each other regarding their families during World War II is historic.

I have also tried to be as accurate as possible, and invent as little as possible, regarding the characters' religious beliefs. On several occasions since her marriage, Sonja has spoken openly about the importance of her own faith, as has her mother, and I have tried to represent their beliefs accurately.

CPSIA information can be obtained at www.ICGtesting.com
Printed in the USA
LVOW08s1931200514

386563LV00002B/3/P